Science Fiction Stories

The
Random House Book
of
Science
Fiction
Stories

Edited by
Mike Ashley

Illustrated by
Paul Finn

Random House 🏠 New York

Library of Congress Catalog Card Number: 96-70318

ISBN: 0-679-88527-7

http://www.randomhouse.com/

Printed and bound in the EC

1 3 5 7 9 10 8 6 4 2

Contents

Contents

Foreword:
Journeys into Space

MIKE ASHLEY

This book will take you to the stars, and back again. Have you ever wondered what it's like out there in space? Well, these stories will show you.

Just imagine, for a moment, that you couldn't see the stars at night. That you are far beneath a surface long built over. That's what you'll find in "To See the Stars" by Lawrence Schimel and Mark A. Garland, which opens up our imagination to the wonder of space and sets us on our journey.

In this book you'll travel the shortest journey, to our moon, in "The Long Night" by John Christopher, and you'll travel to the farthest stars and discover new worlds as yet unheard of. You'll even find a few stories set on Earth, even though they're still space-travel stories. Try "The Chosen" just as one example. I won't spoil the others.

I've arranged the stories so that we work our way through our solar system and beyond, though I've left a few surprises on the way. You'll soon figure out on what planet "City of Ancient Skulls" takes place, but are you so sure about "The Hunters"? Once we reach "A Walk in the Dark" we're way beyond our solar system, out there in the deepest reaches of the universe. Here you'll get some ideas about just what might be awaiting humankind once we travel far into space.

And these stories will not only tell you something about outer space, but about the nature of human beings. What do you think we might do when we venture to the stars? See what you think when you've read "The Cage," "Status Extinct," "Intelligent Life Elsewhere," and "Thoughts That Kill." You may hope that humans don't conquer the stars until we're ready to.

You'll find some of the best writers of space stories here. Douglas Hill has written many adventure novels including the Huntsman trilogy—*The Huntsman*, *Warriors of the Wasteland,* and *Alien Citadel*—and the Last Legionary series, which began with *Galactic Warlord*. Douglas Hill has not only provided a story for the anthology but has kindly written an introduction.

John Christopher wrote the Tripods trilogy about the invasion of Earth—*The White Mountains, The City of Gold and Lead,* and *The Pool of Fire*—as well as the connected novel *When the Tripods Came.* Here he provides us with a scientific puzzle set on the moon.

Arthur C. Clarke must be the best known science fiction writer in the world. Have you ever seen the film *2001: A Space Odyssey*? That was based on a story by Clarke. He's written lots of excellent space travel stories, such as the one included here, which considers the perils facing you on a walk in the dark on an alien world.

Nicholas Fisk is probably best known for his Starstormers series, which runs *Starstormers, Sunburst, Catfang, Evil Eye,* and *Volcano*, but he's written a lot more besides—try and find his bumper volume *Extraterrestrial Tales.*

I'm sure many of you will know the books by Piers Anthony, especially his Xanth series of fantasy novels.

If you haven't read these yet, you've a long way to go, as there's at least fourteen books in the series and still counting. His short stories are less well known, but I've found a rare early story that brings us into contact with one of the strangest and most alien of life forms I've ever known.

There are two stories about the adventures of the crew of the starship *Falcon* by Stephen Baxter, whose recent novels, *The Time Ships* and *Flux*, have made him one of our most exciting new writers.

Voyaging into space is similar to the time five hundred years ago when Columbus set sail for Cathay and found the New World, or Magellan's ships first circumnavigated the globe. We are at the verge of some of our greatest adventures. Just what is out there? If you want to know more about space, I've provided a special section at the end of the book that will tell you more about our planets and the stars. The next time you stand under the night sky and look up at the infinity of space you can wonder all the more.

Mike Ashley
January 1996

Introduction: Space Explorers Start Here

DOUGLAS HILL

N ext time you're out on a clear night, looking up at the stars that fill the sky from horizon to horizon, think about this.

You're looking at the stars of our own galaxy. And in that galaxy, scientists believe, there are several *million* planets (which we can't see) that could support human life.

Not to mention millions of other planets possibly able to support life that *isn't* human.

And then, far beyond the edges of our galaxy, there are probably millions and millions of other galaxies. Each with millions of planets . . .

All that, the idea of the *universe*, might make you feel a bit small and unimportant. But if you're a science fiction reader (or writer), looking up at the night sky may give you another feeling as well.

It's a feeling that's called "a sense of wonder." Not just because the stars are wonderful, but because they make science fiction people start to wonder, to ask questions. What's out there, they (we) ask, on all those planets we can't see? More especially, *who's* out there?

If there are other planets with intelligent beings on them, what would those beings be like? Friendly and kind and funny, like ET? Or some sort of threatening horror, to remind you that "in space, no one can hear you scream"?

That kind of wondering comes naturally to science fiction fans. But they usually don't just ask what other worlds would be like. They go on to ask, what if those worlds are like *this* . . . or *this* . . . or *this* . . . ?

It's one of the first and oldest questions of the human imagination, and it's the basic question that gets every science fiction story started. *What if . . .?*

Of course science fiction asks that question about more than space and other worlds. Science fiction should really be called *future fiction*—and there will surely be a great many remarkable things besides space travel in any sort of future that's ahead of us.

But, all the same, the humans of the future probably will be in space, perhaps out among the farthest stars. It's simply the way we are, the way we've always been. All through our history, brave and curious people just *had* to wander off across the open sea, on clumsy canoes or flimsy rafts or leaky sailing ships, to have a look at what might lie over the horizon. In our future history to come, exactly the same sort of people will just have to fly off in rusty spaceships, for exactly the same reason.

It might well turn out for those future explorers that the worlds and creatures that they discover in space are not at all like anything in any science fiction story ever. So those explorers in their spaceships might smile and shake their heads if in their future they ever read the stories in this book.

If so, it won't matter. As yet, humans haven't gone out past the moon, and our unmanned ships have only just begun to venture out of the solar system. For now, we still have to do our exploring among the stars in other ways. In stories, in fictions.

But in fact, when we do go on those inner journeys, by means of science fiction, we'll always be starting from *exactly* the same place that those actual space explorers of the future will start.

From wondering *what's out there*? From asking *what if . . .*?

In their days to come, the future explorers will fire up their spaceships to go and look for the answers.

In our days, now, we simply fire up our imaginations—and open a book like this.

Happy exploring . . .

Douglas Hill

To See the Stars

LAWRENCE SCHIMEL & MARK A. GARLAND

"Can you believe how dark this is?" Jerina asked, holding her hand before her face and unable to see it.

"Shh," Mitchell hissed back. He stared up at the stars displayed on the inside of the exhibit's domed ceiling, listening to the lecturer in his earphones. ". . . generally lasting anywhere from six to twelve hours in most places of old Earth, there were some spots in which night lasted for a full six months, followed by an equal period of daytime.

"As most of you are learning this week, our Dyson sphere was constructed to harness all the solar energy that was escaping out into space. This allowed us to stop using other, dangerous sources of energy, such as nuclear fusion. In the next room . . ."

The lights switched on and the stars winked out. "I wish we could see them for real," Mitchell said aloud.

"No, you don't!" Jerina scolded. "That would be the *last* thing you'd ever see, and you know it. Besides, you'd freeze to death out in the darkness – because there wouldn't be any sunlight." She shivered at the thought. "Come on. I don't want to miss the nuclear exhibit. I hear the holographs of Chernobyl are spectacular."

Mitchell nodded. It was well known that if you went

outside the Dyson sphere (which nobody could) and if you did find yourself face to face with the universe, the pull from the stars would drag you away. You would fall helplessly forever and ever.

So far as Mitchell knew, no one had been outside the Dyson sphere in two thousand years. No one who had lived to tell about it. For all of that, though, questions remained . . .

Jerina had never been on the tour before; he had practically grown up here. His father was the institute's senior trustee. By secretly using his father's codes, Mitchell had found places he was certain no one was supposed to know about.

The tour included the space exhibits and a holovideo showing how all the planets, moons, rocks, dust, and countless comets had been combined to make the Dyson sphere's thin shell of solar panels, like a giant egg with the sun as its yolk. A strip around the middle was thick enough to live on, an area many times the surface of old Earth.

"Were there ever any missions to other stars?" someone asked.

"No," the guide replied. "We sent probes to all the neighboring stars and there is no life. Here is where the human race belongs, safe from foolishness and the cold, empty depths of space."

"Why weren't the people who built the sphere sucked away by the pull from the stars?" Mitchell asked, as he always did.

"Many were," the guide replied, frowning. "But the pull is much stronger now than it was then, thousands of years ago. No one could survive such an attempt today."

The tour proceeded to the artifacts room, where

hundreds of antiques were kept, including tools and equipment used to build the sphere. There was even a mock-up of the living quarters on a space station. In one glass case in the corner hung a row of perfectly preserved pure white space suits. Mitchell was quite familiar with one of them . . .

"Hey, come on!" Jerina called, waiting for him. "We'll miss the rest!"

"Maybe not," Mitchell said.

"What do you mean?" Jerina asked.

He had thought about it for years; with his father's codes he could get into the institute any time he wanted. But he'd always been too young, too little, too scared. And he needed the right person to . . . help.

"I mean," Mitchell said, "we might be coming back."

At 22:00 his bedroom lights dimmed and the windows turned opaque, throwing the room into near darkness. Mitchell rolled on to his side and stared at the blank window. *If I were living on old Earth,* he thought, *I would see stars when I looked outside.* If he looked at the sky now, he would see only the bright sun shining down.

Mitchell had watched all the video-disks about sunsets in the library, but he still couldn't imagine the possibility of no sun at all. In the videos the sun looked as if it fell out of the sky! He wanted to see the sun move through the sky, see twilight, when the sky was balanced between day and night.

And the moon! Oh, to have a moon up in the sky!

Parts of the Dyson sphere were made from pieces of the moon. Would living in one of those areas make him the man in the moon? According to the video-disks, people had thought the craters of the moon's surface looked like a face. And children believed the moon was made of cheese! Did they think it had been put out in orbit to keep it fresh, where space would act like a giant vacuum-sealed refrigerator?

They also called the moon blue sometimes, when it shone pearly white as always. Colors on old Earth had nothing to do with reality, it seemed. Or had they?

There was no way for him to know, just as there was no way to know what it was like to see the stars for real. You would first have to find a way out of the sphere, and everyone knew that all the spacelock exits had been sealed centuries ago. Then you would have to find a way to stay alive in space long enough to get a look around. And everyone knew that was impossible, too . . .

But Mitchell had tried the space suit in the artifacts room, charging it with power and fluids and oxygen culled from his school lab supplies. He'd even constructed a small receiver that operated on the suit's radio frequency.

And in one of the very secret places he had been to lately, he was pretty sure, he had found something else that still worked, too . . .

Mitchell needed just one more thing: help. He wasn't sure Jerina would go along with his plan, or if he could trust her, but as he closed his eyes and tried to sleep, he decided it was worth a try.

"You're crazy!" Jerina said. "You'll be sucked away by the pull. You want me to help you kill yourself!"

"The space suits protected them when they built the sphere," Mitchell argued. "And there aren't supposed to be any working spacelocks anymore, but I've found one!"

Jerina twisted her mouth, interested. "So?"

"So maybe what they say about the pull isn't quite true, either. Maybe it was just a story created to keep people from wanting to leave, only people have been saying it for so long everyone believes it. All I know is, I've got to find out. And I need you to help me."

Jerina looked scared, but the flicker in her eye was definitely getting brighter. "I don't have to go outside too, do I?"

"No," he said. "You just have to open the spacelock."

"The stars are going to suck you away," Jerina said quietly, "and then your father *and* my father are going to kill me."

"Maybe," Mitchell said. "But when he finds out I've been using his codes, mine's going to kill me anyway." Mitchell looked away. "So, will you help?"

"Okay," she told him, beginning to grin. "I'll do it."

The suit worked perfectly. Mitchell was too short for it, really, and barely strong enough to move the metal joints, but he could move his arms enough to operate the external controls, and he could see through the faceplate if he stood on tiptoe. He had hooked a steel cable to the suit, a tether line of designer carbon that he was sure must be a hundred times stronger than anything they had used back when the sphere was built.

"Start the sequence," he said over his suit radio. Jerina stood at the spacelock's control console, nervously waiting. They'd left the room lights low, so that an increase in energy consumption would not be detected until the lock actually started to operate. After that, there wasn't much that anybody could do. Not until Mitchell came back inside, assuming he did . . .

Jerina touched the console and one entire wall of

the little room slowly opened, revealing a long, empty corridor.

"Okay," Mitchell said. "I'm going in." He lumbered forward, teetering in the huge, bulky suit and fighting against its weight. "Now!" he cried. The door closed again and he was completely alone. "Can you still hear me?" he asked.

There was silence, then at last Jerina's voice said, "Yes." Mitchell looked down the dimly lit corridor and watched the outer door start to open, right to left.

"It's working," he panted, anxious now, shaking. He rushed toward the wall, groping for something to hook his tether onto. The wall was completely smooth. The outer door opened further, then disappeared altogether, a square of utter blackness and countless, genuine stars. Mitchell was floating, being pulled slowly out toward space, and there was nothing he could do to stop it!

As he drifted free of the Dyson sphere into the void, Mitchell twisted his head from side to side, desperately looking for a handhold. Rows of fist-sized metal rings lined the outer surface beside the opening. Mitchell reached out with the cable's hook, trying for the nearest ring, and missed. He tried again, straining, even though there was nothing to push against. This time the hook caught.

Through the edge of the suit's visor Mitchell watched as the line uncurled for forty meters, then went taut. He held his breath and braced himself, waiting for the line to give, for the stars to pull him away with a suction not even the strongest materials could withstand.

He waited, suspended above infinity at the end of the line, and nothing happened.

"I'm okay," he told Jerina. "The line is holding." He could hear her heave a great sigh of relief as he turned his attention to the stars. Billions of them. Brilliant, filling the universe with fierce, sparkling white light.

Then he felt the pull growing strong, stronger than anything he could have imagined. Strong enough, he knew now, to sever the finest tethers, to overcome the greatest obstacles, to ultimately break any bonds that a human might ever know or imagine . . .

"What are you mumbling about?" Jerina asked, the sound of panic in her voice. "What's happening?" Mitchell realized he had been thinking out loud.

"The pull," he explained, "it's real. But the stars aren't pulling on the outside of me, they're pulling on the inside, inside my mind, inside every part of me."

"You're sounding crazy now," Jerina said. "Are you all right?"

"No, I'm not," Mitchell said with a grin. "But it's nothing to worry about."

"Are you coming back inside?" Jerina urged him.

"Yes," Mitchell replied, "but only for a while. Jerina, I want you to try it."

He heard Jerina gasp. "You said I wouldn't have to!"

Mitchell smiled and started pulling himself back in.

The Long Night

JOHN CHRISTOPHER

They were five days out from the Base when the caterpillar stripped a track. Dugmore was driving. They had entered a wide ravine spectacularly divided between sunlight and shadow, cold black and blinding white. Although the line of demarcation ran roughly along the center, Dugmore kept within the sunlit area to avoid putting extra strain on the relays.

Ahead he noticed a dip in the ravine floor—a medium-sized crater that took up the entire width of the ravine. He studied the obstacle as they approached. Both the dip and the ascent on the far side were well inside the caterpillar's potential—and since there was no way around and going back would involve a long detour, he drove on.

The caterpillar reached the lip of the crater, nosed down. Suddenly there was a screech of tracks trying to grip and failing, a sensation of sliding. Corfield was thrown against him. They wound up in a heap on the floor, knocked about but undamaged.

They donned suits and went out to examine the damage. It was easily found. The left-hand track was broken and stripped, a limp tail that trailed behind the caterpillar. They touched helmets to speak, a grotesquely romantic gesture, Dugmore always thought.

Corfield said: "Think you can manage it?"

His voice was small and tinny; even normally it was high-pitched for a man so massive. Dugmore said:

"Nothing to it. Go and amuse yourself."

Of course, Corfield could have done the work, just as Dugmore could carry out the necessary mineralogical surveys; but this was basically Dugmore's field, just as the other was Corfield's. It was simple enough—a straightforward job of welding and reassembly. Before getting the tools, he straightened his back and had a look at the surrounding scene. The caterpillar had slid to the bottom of the crater, which was filled with loose rock and gravel and dotted with boulders. All very dead, bleakly devoid of life.

Inside, he had a shot at raising Cape Canaveral before picking up the welder. No good. Direct communication with Base had, of course, been out since they dropped below the horizon. After that, signals had to be bounced through the link stations back on Earth. The sunspot interference had come in first on the morning of the third day, and on the next contact, when they should have had Tokyo, there was nothing but howls, whistles, and bangs. The regulations ruled that you turned back on losing touch, but this particular edict was honored mainly in the breach—had been broken, in fact, by the last probe as well. The point was that the caterpillar was pretty much an independent entity: air and water, with recycling, would last a couple of months; food concentrate half as long again.

There were other considerations as well. One was that they had been waiting a long time for the chance to get out of the underground tunnel that was Base. Another was that their's was the fourth probe, heading south as the previous ones had gone west, north, and east and there was a certain amount of rivalry as to distance covered. Probe 2 had done best, but they were ahead of them now. They had little difficulty in making up their minds to carry on. The following day they got through to Shannon, though only in Morse: radio transmission was still impossible.

"Day" was a misleading word. The probes set out from Base at the lunar daybreak, traveled away with the rising sun, and then, as it began to slip from the zenith, made their way back. Seven Earth days each way. But they continued to live on a twenty-four-hour clock, taking turns to have the six hours' sleep that was as much as anyone needed on the moon.

If anything went wrong, they could easily survive the fourteen-day lunar night. They would stay warm and snug in their caterpillar, and could listen again to the music tapes or re-read the flimsy rice-paper books. It would be a bit boring but that was something they were used to. There were no hazards: no storms, no monsters. A dead world, in which nothing changed, nor had changed for hundreds of thousands of years. The most interesting thing any previous probe had turned up had been a high-temperature streak in the tufa that covered the greater part of the ground area, the high temperature being ten degrees above calculation.

They, of course, had discovered Corfield's invisible worms. Dugmore smiled at the thought.

They stopped at specified intervals to take specimens. Usually Corfield brought back two or three cores, but the last time he had taken the cutter and sliced out a much larger section, a piece of rock about two feet square and a couple of inches thick. On Earth, it would have been quite a weight, but he hefted it

11

easily. Too easily even for the moon. When he carried it through the lock, Dugmore said:

"A hefty chunk of real estate, that. You planning to take it back to Joan for that rock garden of hers?"

"What would you say it was?"

Dugmore looked at it. A section of typical ore-bearing basalt, except that instead of ore veins it had . . . well, holes. In parts it looked as though worms had crawled through the rock, an unlikely notion to say the least.

"Metalliferous," he said, "without the metal."

Corfield nodded. He looked excited.

"Typical iron-bearing rock. I'd swear to that. But without iron. Almost as though it had been leached out."

"Doesn't iron oxidize?"

"Where there's oxygen, it can."

"Then maybe the moon had an atmosphere at one time."

Corfield considered the point. "A rather selective one. We've come across plenty of exposed iron ore elsewhere."

"Then there's life on the moon after all. The rock-eating lunar worm. *Vermis lunaris corfieldis*. OK to move on, or do you want more from here?"

Corfield was studying the rock. He said abstractedly: "Sure, move on."

For an hour Dugmore bent over the welder with Corfield checking occasionally to see how things were going. He thought it was time then to have a break for food. He went in and opened a self-heating can of high-protein, low-residue mush, chicken and ham flavor. He was not sure whether the texture or the flavor inspired more nausea. But it was nourishing. They had been well assured of that.

Corfield followed him in. "How long now?" he asked.

"Another hour, I should think."

"Fair enough. You picked an interesting spot to bust a track."

"More worms?"

"By the dozen, from the looks of it. A good place for an iron mine, except that it's been surface-mined already. And with high efficiency. I've found a couple of pockets where the iron content assays staggeringly high. The rest is holes where the iron ought to be."

Dugmore plugged in a tape of the musical *Royal Scot*.

"You can have yourself a ball with it. A short one, anyway. We need to get on, since it's turnaround tomorrow."

Corfield, whose taste was for string quartets, grimaced as the overture belted out.

"I think I'll get out there right away."

The job in fact took another two and a half hours to finish. In that time, the line dividing sunlight from shadow had shifted fractionally away from them. At the top of the rise there was a boulder—about three feet in diameter—one edge gleamed now in the sun's marginally more vertical ray. They went inside, Corfield taking the tiller. It was his turn for driving, and Dugmore was tired, anyway. His sleep period was almost due, and he was in favor of that.

The caterpillar jerked forward and stopped. There was a higher whine from the engine. The wheels were turning, but the tracks were not gripping—you could hear the stones spinning under them. Corfield gave her more power, and the tracks bit. The caterpillar moved up, skidding and sliding sideways. They were climbing the slope. Then she stopped again, with a more decisive feel to it.

Dugmore took over—there was nothing to worry about but she might need coaxing. He revved high before he let in the clutch. She bounded and covered about half of the remaining distance to the top. She stuck there, however. The pitch was a little too steep with this kind of loose scree. Only a little, but that was enough.

Corfield said: "Now what?"

"I suppose we could wait to get through, and then wait for a rescue party."

"Three weeks. Any brighter suggestions?"

"Yes," Dugmore said. "We'll get the block and tackle staked in up above, and hook the spare motor to it. Run a hawser around the caterpillar. Pull and push at the same time. Dead easy."

Corfield nodded. "You're the boss."

Working in their suits, it took over an hour. At least, Dugmore reflected, there was no need to worry about getting caught by the dark. The sun would not start setting for another twenty-four hours. When it was ready, Corfield went up to handle the winching part, while Dugmore stayed in the caterpillar. He was near the edge of exhaustion.

He had told Corfield to start the spare motor first and to gun the caterpillar as soon as he felt the hawser taking the strain. Corfield did so. The caterpillar moved serenely up the slope, poised on the lip, and came onto level ground.

Corfield was visible a few yards ahead. Dugmore signaled to him to stop the engine, cutting his own at the same time. He heard the hawser grate against the

side of the caterpillar, shifting position. There was a
harsh tearing spang of metal. It sounded expensive.

Corfield came in through the lock. He said:

"Bad luck. It's the . . ."

"I know," Dugmore said. "The track's snapped again."

Corfield nodded. "At the weld."

Dugmore took a grip on himself and breathed out
heavily.

"Ah well—back to the workbench."

Dugmore's eyes were aching, their fatigue made worse
by the blinding whiteness of vacuum light reflected
from volcanic dust. Both his reflexes and his judgment
were impaired by fatigue. He fumbled things. He had
to redo the first weld he made. Corfield stood and
watched for a time and then, to Dugmore's relief,
wandered off, examining the terrain. Corfield stayed

in view, of course: that was one rule no one ever broke. Later he went back to the caterpillar to watch Dugmore add the final touches. He bent his head, making contact.

"All right now?"

"It had better be."

They went in through the lock. Dugmore said:

"Try the radio again?"

"Yes."

"No luck?"

"I heard something. Garble."

"No matter. We're on our way."

"You look shot," Corfield said. "You're overdue for the bunk. I'll take her off."

Dugmore finished removing his suit. "She's all yours. I don't think I'll need earplugs."

He had put his own cocoon in the narrow recess of the bunk. He slid into it, turning his face to the blankness of the wall. Drowsily he heard Corfield making the necessary connections. The engine started, a good healthy note. Clutch in. Something was wrong. The engine whined on a higher note for a moment, then stalled. Dugmore was filled with a murderous rage—against the caterpillar, Corfield, himself. He heaved himself up and out, and began dressing.

Corfield asked: "Shall I try her again?"

"I'll have a look outside first."

"You don't want to try her yourself?"

"No."

"I'll come out with you."

He did not bother to reply to that.

He examined the track he had mended first. He could see nothing wrong. He went to the other side. The trouble was plain. A boulder was jammed in the tracks, wedged in the space between wheel and body. Visible, all right—but possible? He pulled at the boulder for a moment, then drew back as if stung.

The rock was hard, but not rock-hard. There was resilience there.

Corfield's helmet touched his. Corfield said: "What is it?"

"You tell me. Not stone, anyway. Feel it." He saw Corfield touch it, then the expression of surprise behind the visor. "The main thing is getting it clear. I'm going in for a crowbar."

When he came back Corfield was lying prone staring at the boulder. Crouching was difficult in a suit. Dugmore wedged the crowbar in and heaved. Nothing happened. If it had somehow been wedged in during that last ascent, then it should have been forced out again. He tried again. The thing was in solid. Corfield touched heads with him.

"Hang on while I get the drill."

While he waited for Corfield's return he decided there was something wrong with the shape as well. It was too regular, too close. The surface gleamed with a faintly bluish sheen in the sunlight. He hit it with his hand—it yielded ever so slightly.

Corfield put the edge of the drill against the thing and started up. There was no sound, but a faint vibration transmitted through the rock to the soles of his feet. He ran it for several seconds, and switched off. Dugmore stared at the place where he had drilled. Not the faintest sign of penetration.

Corfield's head bent down to his. "Let's go inside."

Dugmore nodded, pulled at the crowbar to free it. He had to put his weight behind it. The odd thing was

17

that it felt like overcoming adhesion rather than ordinary jamming.

When they were back in the cabin Dugmore said:

"You're the metallurgist—what is it and how did it get there?"

Corfield looked dazed. "It's not metal, nor rock either."

"Then what?"

Corfield held out the drill. "I had the diamond head on. Didn't touch the thing—yet it gives when you press it—just a little."

"Go on."

Corfield said slowly: "Two things emerge. One is that it has a different molecular structure from anything we've ever come across."

"The other?"

"It could be alive."

"On the moon? No air, no water—how?"

Corfield picked up the crowbar that Dugmore had put back in its box.

"Look at this."

Dugmore stared at the crowbar. For 40 centimeters from the end—the part that had been pressing against the boulder—there was a discoloration, a kind of blue smear. He looked more closely. Just barely visible, there was pitting.

"Metal?" he asked. "Are you suggesting it eats metal?"

"It would explain some things."

"The worms, you mean? A bit on the large size, to get into those holes."

"I don't know. I'm going out to have another look at it. You could try raising Cairo again. Or Manchester might be coming in by now."

"And tell them what? That we've found the local inhabitants, and that they chew iron filings and excrete rust?"

"I think it might be a help to have them send someone out from Base with another caterpillar."

"In case we can't pry our little friend loose?"

"Just in case."

Dugmore applied himself to the radio. Cairo offered a gale of noise. On the Jodrell Bank frequency it seemed a little better. R/T was obviously out of the question, so he keyed and waited. There was nothing. He was still straining to pick up an intelligible signal when Corfield came back in.

He shook his head in answer to Corfield's unspoken query, and said:

"What about our little friend?" Dugmore asked.

"Siderophagous," Corfield said, "and siderotropic. Polymorphous with it. I suspect its natural shape is a sphere, which is the most conservative of energy. But if you put iron-containing material near it, it throws out a pseudopod toward it, fastens on, and starts absorbing."

"At what rate?"

"A slow one, fortunately. It's slow altogether, which I suppose is what one would expect."

Dugmore closed down the set. "If it's slow, and that size, why didn't we notice it before? I mean, you've been busy checking the local territory. You didn't spot a bluish sphere, a couple of feet across?"

"I saw it all right, only it wasn't a bluish sphere then. It was a boulder, lying on the lip of the crater. At least, the boulder is now missing, so that's my guess."

Dugmore wrinkled his brow, remembering. "That can't be right. I remember that stone: there was only the one. It was nothing like a sphere, and didn't have that sheen. A chunk of rock."

"Try a cut with Occam's Razor. The boulder miraculously removed as well as our lunarian sphere fastening on to the caterpillar? Better two improbabilities than one."

"I don't get it."

"Nor do I—but I'm feeling my way toward something. That section was in shade when we arrived. Let's suppose the thing inactivates during the lunar night—goes to sleep until the sun touches it again. Then it wakes up and starts looking around for food. It can obviously mine iron out of rock pretty effectively. But the caterpillar offers more attractive scope. Something like one of us back home finding a flying saucer composed of T-bone steak."

"The thought's too poignant. It's a good theory, but there's one thing against it."

"What's that?"

"If it tends toward a sphere shape as a means of conserving energy, surely it would remain in that form during the dormant period? That boulder was a pretty jagged piece of stone."

Corfield shrugged. "Protective mimicry perhaps. Who cares? What matters is that we've found life—or pseudo-life, at least." He had the look of a child who's just discovered that Father Christmas is real after all. "It's fantastic."

"Yes," Dugmore said, "I can see that. I'll start cheering as soon as we've pried the darn thing loose."

They weren't worried, not yet. The thing did not look menacing, did not appear likely to become a threat. Corfield tried various metal objects in contact with it and thereby established that it displayed tropism only for iron and its alloys. The higher the iron content, the more rapid the rate of absorption, the highest rate being, Corfield calculated, slightly less than a thousandth of an inch per hour, something like a fiftieth of an inch per day. The caterpillar's plating was half an inch, which meant they had twenty-five days before the thing ate its way through.

On the other hand, the problem of freeing the track from its clutches remained obdurate. Various attempts at prying or pushing it out got nowhere.

After an hour of this, Dugmore thought of heat. It could plainly take extreme temperature changes, but a touch of oxyacetylene flame was somewhat different from the sun's radiant energy, even in vacuum. He set up the welder and directed the torch at that part of the sphere farthest away from the caterpillar. In a short time, the blue turned to orange and then to cherry-red. Nothing else happened. Corfield had another go at levering it out, with no result. Dugmore held the torch steady in one spot and the red brightened to a yellowish white. But that was absolutely all. Corfield touched a part of the sphere away from the flamed area. He made a gesture of negation, and another toward the airlock. Dugmore switched off and followed him back in to the caterpillar.

Corfield was excited again. He said:

"Quite a different molecular structure, obviously. Do you realize that a few inches away from the point you were burning the temperature was absolutely normal?"

Dugmore stashed the welder away. He said:

"I say it's spinach, and I say the hell with it. Look, I'm beat. I'm going to get in the sack. Wake me if it sprouts wings and starts lifting us off toward Tycho."

21

Corfield said abstractedly: "Sure. I wonder if it would respond to magnetism?"

"You find out. You might also have another shot at getting through to Base. I have a feeling maybe we are going to need help. Try Manchester again—or Shannon."

Corfield woke him with the usual hemidemisemitasse of coffee and steaming tin of scrambled egg with diced ham mush. Sitting up, Dugmore asked:

"Any luck?"

"No. It was an odd thing with the magnet, though."

"How so?"

"It started putting a tendril out and then stopped and withdrew."

"You should have carried on. You might have gotten it confused."

"I didn't think of that."

Dugmore reached for his sponge and began rubbing himself.

"Don't take it to heart."

"But I mean it. It might . . ."

"Forget it. What about the link? Any luck?"

"None."

"Cape Canaveral should be in by now."

"I tried them. Nothing."

Dugmore sighed. "We're still on our own, then, coping with our ravening monster. No other bright ideas?"

"I set up the camera to record it."

"That should win a prize for action movies."

"Single-frame at minute intervals. Do you think electricity might touch it?"

"We could try. Or tickle it with a feather, maybe."

They manhandled the generator outside, hooked it up to the transformer, managed to boost the output to two thousand volts. Dugmore held a contact against the sphere, which seemed distinctly larger, bulging out more obviously from the track, and nodded to Corfield to apply the juice. This time, it didn't even change color. When Corfield cut and came over to touch helmets, he asked:

"You sure it was getting through?"

"It was getting through, all right."

"Let's go in and think again. Might be worth trying Berkeley, too."

Corfield tried to get through to Berkeley. The static sounded louder than ever, a storm of sound. There was no point in persisting. As he switched off, Dugmore said:

"This is the turnaround point, by the way. I just checked the clock. We ought to be on our way home by now."

"We've got a day in hand."

"Yes."

For the first time, Dugmore felt uneasy. If they did not get started on the return journey within twenty-four hours, the chances were that they were not going to make it—they would have to spend the lunar night in the open. And suddenly that was a prospect not just of boredom but of something else . . .

He started looking for tools. Corfield asked:

"What do you propose doing?"

"I'm going to dismantle the track on that side. We might be able to do more if we can get a clear approach to it."

It was not an easy job under the best of conditions;

23

working in a suit made it harder. Dugmore sweated heavily and had to break off after a couple of hours and go inside to rub down. He stood the suit in the dehumidifier and had another try at radio communication, with the same result as before. Corfield had tried half an hour before. He realized he was beginning to get nervous.

An hour later he was again soaked with sweat—but he had the track off. The thing was exposed, a flattened blue spheroid pressed against the metal side of the caterpillar.

It was bigger than he had thought, more than a meter across. He saw at once that the exercise had been futile. It clung tightly to the metal as though part of it. All the same, he tried driving aluminum wedges in at the side. No luck. When he tried it with a steel chisel it yielded; yielded—and held. First he tried to pull it out, then to knock it out with a hammer. Neither attempt succeeded. When he had first tried to remove it, it had not gripped the crowbar like that. Their beast had grown stronger.

They went inside for a conference. Corfield said: "It's not going to budge, is it?"

"No. There's something else."

"What?"

Dugmore said: "If adhesion can change, maybe absorption can."

Corfield nodded slowly. "I'll check that."

"While you're doing it, I'll try to raise Hawaii."

"It's been a long time for a sunspot flare, hasn't it?" Corfield said.

"Yes."

If they managed to put through a call for help it would take six days for a relief caterpillar to get to them, and that meant both parties spending the lunar night in the open. All the same, it would be a comforting thought to know that help was on the way.

He called Hawaii, went on calling. Through the bubble he could see the globe of the Earth, a pale disc against the brightly hazed black of the sky. Late evening there. Maybe people were walking by the sea, watching moonlight on the waves.

He listened to the crackle of the ether. Maybe the whole world was dead. He broke off as Corfield came back in.

"Well?"

He really did not need to ask. Corfield's face told him. But not exactly how bad. Corfield said:

"Double."

That meant twelve days instead of twenty-five; presumably it would inactivate during the night. Six days for the relief tractor to get out here. It was going to be close. One could live for forty-eight hours in a suit, but no longer.

Corfield said: "And, of course, if it's variable, then it could go on varying. We don't know that it's reached it's maximum."

"No." The chill of fear for a moment was the chill of the airless vacuum outside. "I see that."

"I've had an idea, though," Corfield said. "We've been trying force on it. Persuasion might be more rewarding."

Dugmore said bitterly: "Promise it we'll take it back to Earth and feed it cannonballs?"

"We could have a shot at luring it. We've got stuff in here with a higher iron content than the hull. Those tools, for instance. It might find a purer food source more attractive. If we could lay a trail away from the caterpillar . . . I agree it sounds unlikely. On the other hand . . ."

"Sure," Dugmore said. "On the other hand, anything is better than nothing. I'll start collecting the gear."

They used the crowbar as the final link. Dugmore closed the gap with it. As it approached the blue spheroid, the surface pulsed and a tendril rose out of it. It reached the bar and started moving along it—not fast, but the movement was quite perceptible. From the far end it went on to a metal jack and from there to various tools placed end to end. The trail ran more than six meters. The filament, Dugmore saw, was thickening, first along the crowbar and then over the jack. And the spheroid itself looked slightly smaller. Crazy as the idea was, maybe it was going to work. But something else was happening: a lump of the same slightly gleaming dark blue as the rest swelled under the tendril and flowed along it to the crowbar. The nucleus? It moved to the jack, enveloped it. Then, between the crowbar and caterpillar, the tendril thinned and parted. The ends retreated from each other into their parent spheres.

That made two of them.

Dugmore persuaded Corfield to get some sleep, and made him take a pill to ensure that he did. Listening to Corfield's deep, even breathing, Dugmore felt loneliness as a physical presence. More for something to do than out of real hope he fiddled with the radio, found the Tokyo frequency relatively quiet. Switching to transmit, he sent the call-sign LUN5. The burst of staccato dots at the end sounded like nails in a coffin.

Listening in afterward, he thought he heard a signal, but it was so weak that it might have been his imagination. He transmitted again, and listened again. This time the static was back, and there was no hope of picking anything up.

Dugmore spent the rest of Corfield's sleep period outside with the monsters. He tried all the things that they had tried before. When none of them worked, he stood and looked at the two spheroids. The new one seemed to be growing faster than its parent. A function of infancy, or of a pure iron diet from "birth"? He was not interested, he found, in such academic questions. His attention was focused solely on survival.

Corfield woke. They ate more mush and rehearsed about the situation. Neither of them came up with anything new. Their tempers were frayed and they began snapping at each other. Dugmore felt that he was more to blame, but he could not do anything to cool himself out. His nervous tension was such that he could not stop himself. In the end, Corfield went outside and he concentrated on the radio. Static, nothing but static. He continued to search the dial hungrily and hopelessly. When Corfield came back in, Dugmore didn't bother to look up. But Corfield said:

"I checked the rate of absorption of the new one, to see if the higher iron content made a difference. It does. The rate's up."

"Write a book about it."

"And then I checked the first again. Its rate's up, too."

Dugmore stared at him. "Are you sure of that?"

"I double-checked. At the new rate it will be through the hull in four days, give or take the odd hours."

27

"So even if we get through, and they sent a relief caterpillar out . . ."

"Yes," Corfield said. "Too late."

He found himself cursing insanely, a string of vituperation against the spheroids, the moon, Corfield, the indifferent millions who worked or played two hundred and fifty thousand miles across space. Corfield let him run on until exhausted, and then said:

"I think I may have the answer."

Hope paralyzed him. He waited, staring. Corfield said:

"If it's got a mind at all, it must be of a pretty primitive order—and it seems to be activated by sunlight. Perhaps the reverse is true. When the sun goes down, maybe it reverts to that pseudo-boulder form. Unfortunately, the way this ravine runs, it will be another five or six days before the sun is off it—unless we provide an artificial night, rig up a sunshade."

"It can't be as simple as that."

"Worth trying, don't you think?"

Dugmore looked around the cabin. "We can rip the bunk out for a start. Use the sides as supports."

It was ridiculously easy. Nothing happened until the last ray of sunlight was obscured, and then it all happened at once. The spheroid seemed to shrivel and fell away from the caterpillar. Once again it was an ordinary, irregularly shaped chunk of rock. Felt like it, too. Dugmore prodded it with his glove. Not yielding any more; just a rock.

He put both hands down on it, heaved. He rolled it along to the point where the natural shade took over, left it. Then they went to deal with the other one.

Dugmore said: "I can't think why it took us so long to work it out. It seems so obvious."

"I've always been a bit weak on the obvious," Corfield said.

"Not as weak as I am." He paused, considering this. "I wonder if I would have thought of it, before that damned thing chewed its way through. I'm not at all confident I would."

Through the bubble he could see the remaining segment of the sun's disc. Otherwise no different from what it had looked like at the zenith; there were no spectacular sunsets here.

They were still in the same place. There were two reasons for that. In the first place, it had taken longer than they expected to put the damage right: the erosion had made the track difficult to fit. By the time the caterpillar was ready to go they were in communication with Base again.

Their report of the spheroids, as they had expected, had caused quite a stir. The relief tractor would head toward them at the next lunar daybreak, carrying a lightproof, iron-free container in which the two lumps of pseudo-rock could be crated. Meanwhile, they were to stay and keep watch. There was obviously no danger now, and in any case they could not have returned to base in the four days' light that remained and they had more than adequate supplies to sit the night out.

The tape that was being played was some quartet of Beethoven's; one of the later ones, Dugmore guessed, because it made even less sense to him than most. But he was not irritated by it, nor by the prospect of hearing it a dozen more times. Relief from the fear of death was a great mollifier; even several days later it came over him, a wave breaking and showering him with a fine spray of awareness of the joy of living.

Corfield looked happy, too. He sat staring out through the bubble with a remote half-smile on his broad face. His wife had come through on R/T from Cape Canaveral that morning, and told him all was well—she was expecting to have the baby sometime during the next week or two. They were, Dugmore gathered, a very contented couple. Lucy had not come through to him, but she scarcely would, with a divorce pending. He found he did not worry about that any more. What were those lines?

The world is so full of a number of things,
I am sure we should all be as happy as kings . . .

The world was up there, waiting. The sun was creeping down, the long slow shadows were creeping toward them. Soon only starlight and earthlight would remain. A long night, but day at the end of it.

The Hunters

WALT SHELDON

The spaceship lay in the valley, just as reported. Lon and Jeni could see it from the ridge.

Lon finally said, "We'll keep going. We'll go further into the hills. Chara Canyon—there's a stream there."

"And when they reach Chara?"

Lon turned slowly. Her eyes were unblown tinder, smoking, not yet aflame. They wouldn't flame. That was her way, quiet and patient and always there behind him, following where he led. She was his wife. She had followed from the shining city when the bombs from space began to fall and the great black columns of smoke were monuments in the sky. She had skinned her hands helping with the cabin logs, washing clothes in the stream; she had bloodied them butchering game.

They were not alone. There were others who had fled to the great mountains, the spine of the continent, but they were scattered among the slopes and canyons, and stayed close to their cabins and mud huts and caves.

"When they reach Chara—" Lon shrugged.

"I know, I know. I shouldn't have said that. It's too big to think about."

He thought: When it's this big the mind doesn't accept. You keep on doing whatever you were doing.

A twinkle of light down the slope caught his eye. It was only a few hundred yards below. His eyes darted in that direction, and he squinted and saw the figures moving up toward them. The light had been a reflection—the sun catching one of their strange weapons.

"Come on, Jeni!"

"To the cabin?"

"No, no. We'll have to leave the cabin—they'll discover it in a day or so. Chara Canyon—"

They started north. He glanced back once more at the thing in the valley, there on the dry plain. It was longer than a city block, projectile shaped, mirror bright. It was about what he had expected: the radio reports in the past month had been full of descriptions of the others. One by one the radio reports had stopped as the cities had fallen.

They kept to the ridge, but stayed within the tree shadows. It was cooler in the shadows. They did not run, but walked with long strides.

By looking left Lon could catch shuttered glimpses of the sky and the big round valley that stretched away to the west. He could still see the hunters once in a while, coming diagonally up the slope, as if to cut them off. Faintly, at times, he could hear their throaty voices.

At the north end of the ridge Lon and Jeni headed downslope. The mouth of Chara Canyon, a break in the mountains to their right, was only a mile or so ahead. They heard the report of a weapon, releasing echoes that tumbled all through the hills. The report came from the ridge top behind them, and they knew the hunters were following.

At the bottom of the slope they came to a dry streambed. Lon jumped across, then held out his hand for Jeni. She missed. She fell, twisting her ankle.

"Oh, Lon!"

"You've got to keep going, darling—you've got to keep going!"

"Yes. I know."

He helped her along, with his hand around her waist. He saw how she kept the pain from showing. She quirked her lips in a funny way each time her injured foot touched ground, but kept her face rigid otherwise.

He stared at that face with his usual quiet wonder. Her features were still small and delicate; still fine porcelain. There was that same compassion about her, after everything that had happened. He remembered what she had said nearly a year ago when the invading things first came out of the sky. Aircraft had lanced upward to meet them, firing . . . several of the things had been destroyed. Lon and Jeni had seen one explode over the city. It made a great orange ball in the air, and the ball grew and turned over and over, and smoke curled around it like shriveled skin. Jeni said: "Those poor things, those poor creatures in there . . ."

And then they had fled. They were luckier than most. Lon had worked for an aircraft plant and owned a small plane. They flew west, flying at night so the shining projectiles wouldn't find them; they begged and stole fuel and sometimes, Lon swore, they conjured it up. They crashed upon landing in the mountains, and had used parts of the plane to start their cabin.

Another shot sounded, and this time it was terribly near. He dared to turn his head. The hunters were halfway down the shoulder of the ridge. They gestured and called to each other.

33

"In here!" He led Jeni into a grove of white-barked trees.

Jeni's lips were tight, but a whimper forced its way through.

He held her more tightly, lifting. His heart stuttered violently. His legs ached. Jeni—fragile Jeni—was heavy.

He stumbled, and she fell with him. They lay there, at the roots of a white-barked tree, in each other's arms, and they looked into each other's eyes and knew they couldn't go on.

They heard the shouting voices.

She said, "I don't feel anything. Funny. I'm not angry or afraid or anything."

They clung to each other suddenly. He ran his lips along her cheeks and hair and he wiped the tears from her cheek with his own and he murmured things

without really hearing them.

"I'm glad we're together," said Jeni.

They heard the breaking of the underbrush.

Abruptly, he stood. He faced the approaching sounds and made fists at his sides. His eyes were wild. "Damn you! Damn you! Damn you!" he cried.

"It's their way," said Jeni. "They're hunters. It's their way."

There was no anger in her voice.

A creature emerged from the white-barked trees. He stood there and stared at Lon, and stared at Jeni upon the ground. He seemed a little frightened himself. He lifted his weapon.

Lon stared back, taking in every strange detail. It was his first close look at one of these invaders from the planet called Earth, which was third from the sun and had one moon.

He waited for the noise of the weapon, wondering if he would hear it.

Asteroid 745: Mauritia

DONALD A. WOLLHEIM

It's a rather strange thing to be expected to tell a ghost story out here in interplanetary space. The captain has asked me to do this rest period and I'm a man who obeys orders. He says you passengers asked for a ghost story this time and, what's more, you want a ghost story of space.

Now, that's not an easy thing to do. Ghosts and space travel do not quite hit it off with each other. Ghosts belong to the old world, the air-bound, land-bound, sea-bound world, a world where people were dominated by ugly castles and power-mad little men with twisted minds, and where the spirit was warped and bent by the desires of little, land-locked souls. Dirt and lust and night fright: those are the things that called forth ghosts. We haven't had much of that these past seventy years, thank heavens.

Somehow, out here in the spaces between the stars, between the worlds, there's no room for that sort of horrible thing. There's fright, sure, for there's lots of danger between the stars. There's eeriness, sure, on those strange planets and bits of asteroidal rock. But there are no ghosts of twisted little minds, generally speaking.

Nonetheless, I do know one incident which I consider a true ghost story of space. I can't account for it any other way. The whole thing fits the ghost pattern, though of course we didn't realize it at the time.

It was many years ago, when I was only a junior hand aboard a prospector ship poking around the asteroids. We had been out for a month, had a few more days to go before heading back to base on Juno. We were all a bit restless, because thus far we had had no luck. We'd made landings on three asteroids so far, without being able to get a worthwhile bite out of our Geigers. Chief Braun was in an ugly mood and we were all hoping we'd strike something on this fourth and last landing.

We were angling to make our hook-down on this last rock we had closed in on. Asteroid 745 it was, Mauritia by name, an average size for the type, perhaps thirty-two kilometers in diameter. From our radars and scopes it checked up as moderately spherical, primarily rock, no atmosphere, of course—you don't expect any—probable outcroppings of metal, iron for sure, according to the reflected rays, but otherwise nothing to get excited about.

Braun swore he'd have us all transferred to base jobs if we didn't turn up something this time. He was never a pleasant man to work with, and I almost wished he'd make good his threat. He was excitable, given to sullen periods and violent dislikes. In fact, I think he was a trifle nuts. He was wild about a certain ancestor he claimed to have. A character named Hitler, who lived about two hundred years ago and figured in one of the last two or three world wars.

This Hitler figured as a sort of superman of that benighted century. He'd made himself dictator of Germany—at that time the four German states were one country—and set out to conquer the world. Did a lot of damage, too, if I remember my history lessons. He was killed when his capital in Berlin was captured. Or so the books claim, anyway.

Now this Braun claimed to be a direct descendant of his. He had a long story that he claimed he had heard from his father who'd heard it from his mother. This Hitler was supposed to have died childless, but according to Braun he had one child, who was given to his wife's family to raise and who took his wife's family name, which was Braun.

Anyway, it all seems downright silly today, but if a man's got a bug on a thing like this, I suppose it helps his ego. Just why he should think it means something to be the descendant of one of those twentieth-century military nuts I don't know, but then I'm not Braun.

Whatever the case, Braun sure tried to act like his ancestor. He had books about this dictator, he had pictures, he raised a little toothbrush moustache like this character had, and in general he raised hell. He didn't dare try to rake up any of that old conqueror's race nonsense, because that's against the law, and the one thing this Braun bully was afraid of was getting his record muddied. He'd probably have tried it if he dared.

So Braun lined us up when we'd completed our landing and secured the ship to the rocky plain about us. He read us the riot act, said we had better be sure we returned with some evidence of ore, said he'd keep his radio tuned in to our helmet phones and he wanted us to keep ours turned on. We were to report everything to him as we progressed, and he wanted to hear our Geigers clicking.

So the four of us prospectors humped out of the port in our suits, with our junk tacked on all around, and sailed our way off in all four directions. In spite of carrying a small mountain of equipment, we still weighed practically nothing and had to be careful how we bounded along. Braun stayed behind, alone. He was going to sit by the transmitter and heckle us. This had happened before, and it undoubtedly gave him a sense of power.

What I liked to do in a case like that was to get completely around the planetoid and turn off my helmet. I could claim that I couldn't receive him through the planetoidal core. He mightn't believe me, but he couldn't prove it, could he?

Anyway, I did get about four miles away, beyond a ridge of rock, when I got some slight ticks on my counters. You are bound to get something, but unless it comes in strong it's never worth the effort to the Syndicate. Still, it's well to report these things. Besides, when you get a few ticks you may find a strong streak near it.

So I settled down, magnetized my land shoes, and started walking slowly about the vicinity, poking and probing. You can't imagine what it is like unless you have tried it. You may have seen photos and even movies of asteroid prospectors at work, but you have to be there to get the full effect.

You are out of sight of any living or moving thing. You are alone in a completely bleak landscape, all gray and black rock, with infinitely deep crevices, with nasty meteor scars that look like old-time battlefield shell holes. Above, the sky is dead black and filled with cold stars and occasional moving ones, passing asteroids. There is nothing, simply nothing, friendly or calming about the scene. It is a scene of permanent, perpetual death.

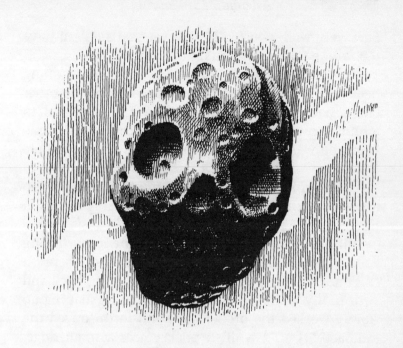

In the midst of this, you stalk slowly about, waiting
for a series of clicks to sound in your ears. Also hearing
Braun yap at you. He's sitting back there in the ship,
listening to the sounds of our breaths over his pickup,
hearing the slight clicks, and talking to us, urging us to
greater effort, as if that could possibly do any good.

All this was going on in my ears as I strolled back
and forth. I could hear him talking to the three other
fellows. Incidentally, none of them had any more luck
than I did.

Then I heard Braun swear. "Who's that coming back
to the ship without notifying me?" he yells. There's no
answer. He calls each of us separately and we all claim
we're working. I heard each man reply myself. But
Braun is still swearing.

"One of you is lying or else is crazy! I see you coming

back very well, you fool! Whoever you are, you have left your equipment! You'll pay for it!"

I was a bit puzzled. I wondered who was coming back to the ship and why. Perhaps one of the other chaps had forgotten something and didn't want to admit it over the phones. Perhaps there was something he wanted to tell Braun in secret. It made me nervous.

Braun's voice sounded again in my earphones. "Who are you? Identify yourself! Any nonsense, and you'll never see space again!"

Still I heard no answer. At this moment my ticking prober sounded a bit quicker. I paid no more attention to Braun's ravings against the man coming back and bent to my work. My streak seemed to be shaping up now. I worked the prober back and forth, traced the radioactivity to a whitish pocket near a small ridge. The white was frozen gas of some sort.

I unpacked my heater and melted the mass away. Underneath was a metallic outcropping that was surely radioactive. I unpacked my digging equipment and set out to blast off a chunk for further analysis. While I was working I heard Braun still ordering the returning man to identify himself and to explain what he was doing.

I leaned on my tools a moment and listened, for what was going on was quite unusual. Why should a man return—and without his stuff? Did he have an accident?

"Yes, the spacelock is open, you dunderhead!" Braun was fuming. "Come in, come in, so I can report you! Did you break your communicator? You'll pay for it!"

In my helmet phone, I heard Braun get up from his seat and start the pump of the spacelock. Idly I poked a loose rock with a tool, saw the rock fly off and vanish from the impact of my light stroke against its near-weightlessness.

The pumping sound of the lock ceased. I heard the inner door click open. Braun's voice roared out, "Who are you? How did you get here? Where is your space-suit?"

There was no answer that I could hear. "You don't need a spacesuit!" shouted Braun, a little high-pitched. "How is that possible? How did you get here?"

Again, I heard no sound in reply. But Braun's voice, still higher in pitch, a trifle on the hysterical side, came again. "It's a lie! It's a trick! You can't be stand-ing here! What did you say your name was? You look funny! You dress funny!"

No reply. But this time, after an interval, I heard Braun, apparently in a corner of the room, shouting hysterically, "Your name is Mauritz, Leopold Mauritz. Yes, yes. But what do you want of me? And why is your head so lopsided? What has happened to your skull?"

I heard a sound of rushing about, as if Braun was trying to hit something or somebody. Then there was a hissing sound as of air escaping, then silence.

I tripped my helmet phone on, called in. There was no answer. The line was dead.

Staking out my find, I hastily loaded my equipment and started back.

When I came within sight of the ship, the other three men were also arriving. We stood side by side before the lock and conversed by means of direct contact.

What we saw was this: The spacelock was open, the air had escaped, and Braun was lying half in and half out, dead from strangulation. That was all. How the lock had got open I can't say, except that Braun in his frenzy must have operated the hand switch from the inside without checking the outside controls. I find it hard to believe that Braun would do that, for he was much too experienced a hand.

But then if Braun had not done it, who had? There was no one else around. We four were the sum total of living things on the planetoid Mauritia. I checked with the others. They had all heard Braun's strange conversation. None of them had heard any answers.

It is down in the records that Braun died of a mental fit. We all four testified to what we had heard and the infallible lie detectors bore us out completely. None of us had returned to Braun. But Braun was dead, cold and blue and frenzied of face.

That's the extent of my ghost story. I didn't see any ghost. I didn't hear any ghost. But it is my opinion that Braun saw and heard one.

Why a ghost there, and why did it pick on Braun? Now that's a question folks always ask me when I tell this yarn. I gave it a lot of thought, and once when I had a leave on Earth I did some research.

I found that this planetoid, number 745, was first discovered about 1928 by an amateur astronomer named Leopold Mauritz. He named it after himself, Mauritia. Now this man Mauritz was a fairly successful businessman in his hometown, which was Berlin in Germany. But he also happened to be of the Jewish religion, which was one of the things this German superman-character, Hitler, hated.

I couldn't find very much on Mauritz, except one final item. He jumped out of a window and killed himself in 1934. He was driven to suicide by the persecution and the lunatic laws set up by this Hitler.

I also think that Braun's story of being a direct descendant of that old dictator must be correct. A ghost—if it was a ghost—couldn't make a mistake, could he? Not on the ghost's own personal world, anyway.

City of Ancient Skulls

SIMON CLARK

BANG!
The ship was going to crash. There was no doubt about that. The only question was: how hard would we hit? And, if we survived the crash, did this gray, forbidding planet that was now rushing up to meet us have an atmosphere we could breathe?

BANG!

The force of the explosion threw me against the cargo bay door; my head struck it, almost breaking my horn. Quickly I curled my long tail around a steel support spar to anchor me securely and stop me from being dashed against the walls.

"The ship's breaking up," called N'Catra from the passageway. "I'll call the captain. We might need to jettison the cargo pod."

"How long before we crash-land?"

"We can't tell. Guidance system and main computer went down when we hit the space debris."

BANG-BANG-BANG . . .

A series of convulsions ran through the ship. I hung on tight. N'Catra looped his tail around a steel spar. I noticed a trickle of blood staining his beautiful gold mane black.

N'Catra looked at me sympathetically. "I'm so sorry about this, Jantrey. This time last week you were still in school; now, on your first deep space haul, we've run into this kind of trouble." His tail flicked forward and touched my cheek gently in a gesture of friendship. "But don't worry, Jantrey. We've transmitted distress signals. The rescue ship will collect us within a few days."

BANG!

This time the tremendous explosion was followed by the sound of metal ripping; the sound was like a huge beast in agony.

From the speaker came the stark command: "Attention, crew. Abandon ship. Immediately proceed to escape pods. Repeat, proceed to escape pods and abandon ship."

N'Catra moved fast, his gold mane bristling with determination. "You heard the captain, Jantrey. Into the escape pod."

"But there's only room for one; what will—?"

"Don't worry about me. I'll make it to the main escape pod in time."

"But what about—?"

"Remember your training, young Jantrey. Also, activate Bright Spark on the escape pod's computer. That will advise you."

Before I knew it, N'Catra had used his tail and hands to push me through the hatch and into the tiny escape pod. I looked back to see his concerned eyes and his tail wave me good luck before he hit the release button. The hatch snapped shut. I felt a thump as the pod blasted from the ship.

I managed to fasten the restraints as the pod spun furiously away from the ship and down to the gray clouds that blanketed the unknown world below.

*   *   *

I'd been on the surface of that forbidding world for maybe an hour before I activated Bright Spark. Instantly a point of blue light appeared and seemed to play like a light from a torch on the inside wall of the pod.

"Bright Spark, is the atmosphere breathable?"

Bright Spark's voice whispered back at me, "Have all your lung implants been completed?"

"Yes."

"Then atmosphere is tolerable. However, high oxygen content will irritate your eyes and throat. Use of methane spray every three hours is recommended."

"What happened to the ship?"

"Data stream cut short prior to landing suggests ship detonated in high atmosphere."

My eyes widened in horror. "The crew? Did they—?"

"Crew abandoned ship before detonation. They have safely landed in . . . Sorry . . . Am receiving information update. The main life pod was damaged on landing. Danger warning. Breathable air reserves are low."

"But they all have lung implants. They can leave the ship."

"They are unable to do so. Hatch jammed on landing. They are unable to exit pod. Breathable air reserves falling to critical levels."

"If someone doesn't get them out of the pod, they'll all die."

"Affirmative."

"Come on, we've got to help them."

I opened the pod's hatch and hauled myself out. All around me was a landscape of dirty gray powder. In the distance a mountain range of the same dirty gray rose toward dirty gray clouds. There were no trees or plant life of any kind.

Bright Spark followed. "I advise extreme caution," it said, hovering above my shoulder. "This world is unknown to us. We don't know if there are life forms that might be dangerous."

"I've got to save the crew. They're my friends."

"Advise a pause to consider future actions, junior rating Jantrey. You only graduated from school last week. You are inexperienced and—"

"Do you expect me to sit here and wait for my friends to suffocate to death?"

I set off at a brisk trot with Bright Spark bobbing along behind me like a ball of blue light.

Bright Spark told me in which direction the main escape pod lay with the crew trapped inside.

We'd been walking less than two hours when we reached the ruined city.

"Caution," Bright Spark warned. "It may still be inhabited."

"It's not. See for yourself."

"I regret I cannot. I lack high-definition vision. Describe, please."

"It consists of a large number of ruined buildings. They are gray in color; most have been reduced to rubble; oh, and they possess tall oblong doorways."

"Anything else?"

"Yes," I said in awe as I approached. "It is full of skulls."

I thought at first that this must have been a battleground, but as I picked up one of the skulls that littered the ground like fallen fruit, I realized the truth.

"They are the heads of androids," I said to Bright Spark. "If you look inside the skulls you can see the

remains of imaging equipment and electronic components."

"An alien technology?"

"Definitely. See, the skulls have two forward-facing
eyes, unlike our two forward-facing and one upward-
facing."

Bright Spark paused. "I have information update
from main escape pod computer. Breathable atmosphere reserves falling rapidly. If we are unable to reach
the pod and release the crew within five hours, they
will die."

I moved on through this weird alien city of ancient
skulls. And all the time, I wondered: How could I save
my friends?

Bright Spark told me that it would take three hours
to reach the escape pod on foot. Then I would have a
mere two hours to somehow break through the magna-
steel walls of the capsule. But how could I do that with
my bare hands? All I could hope for was that somehow
I could repair the airlock mechanism and open it without having to force a way in.

I walked through the deserted streets that were littered with the artificial android skulls. Everywhere was
the same dull gray; from the gray concrete walls to the
gray powder beneath my feet. Bright Spark, an electric-
blue blob of light, skipped along; it was the only splash
of color in that drab landscape.

"Maybe we could find some tools?" I suggested.

"Possibility of tools in buildings; problem is that
search for tools will delay your arrival at main pod
landing site."

"I'll have to risk it. I'll need something to break into
the pod."

I stopped here and there to search at random amongst

those bleak gray buildings. Most had been half-filled by that drifting gray powder. Some contained the remains of furniture.

Whoever had deserted this city of skulls must have left a long, long time ago.

After finding no tools of any description we reached the edge of the city. I was just thinking I would have to resort to trying to batter a way into the pod using stones when I saw a low, flat building.

This seemed more promising. It looked intact. I pushed in the crumbling door. It fell to the ground with a sound like a book being snapped shut.

Inside, complete darkness.

"Caution," said Bright Spark, hovering by my ear, "there may be unseen hazards inside."

"I'll risk it," I said, trying to sound confident. But the truth was I was scared half to death by the forbidding darkness, not knowing what might lurk within.

And what might leap out at me.

But the moment I set foot inside the building I must have triggered a sensor, because lights flickered and came on to illuminate a long corridor lined with rooms. Instead of a door, each room was sealed by a large piece of transparent material.

I walked slowly along the corridor, looking through the transparent screens into the rooms.

Bright Spark said, "Arrangement of rooms suggests this is some kind of store or warehouse."

There were more skulls on the floor, but in the storerooms the androids were almost complete.

"Type of android suggests manufacture by humanoid species. Two forward-facing eyes, two arms, two legs—"

"But no tail," I said, gently tapping the glass with the tip of my own tail.

As I tapped, one android sitting on a chair raised its yellow head and spoke:

"Hey, man, eat my shorts."

The words were meaningless. "Can you translate?" I asked Bright Spark.

"The android invited you to devour an article of clothing."

Puzzled, I shook my head, then asked the android, "Can you hear me?"

The yellow head twitched. "Don't have a cow, don't have a cow, don't . . . have . . . a . . . ckkk . . ."

The yellow head slumped, the eyes closed.

Bright Spark said, "Its power levels are exhausted."

"But why are these androids so well preserved?"

"These have been sealed in rooms that contain pure nitrogen. Therefore the rate of decay has been greatly reduced."

An idea occurred to me. "If we can find one of these androids that is still in working order it might be able to show us where to find some tools."

I hurried along the corridor. Some of the transparent screens were broken. Once the planet's oxygen-rich atmosphere had entered the rooms the androids had rusted away to shreds of synthetic skin and plastic skulls.

But at last I found a room where there were two figures sitting at a table. I tapped on the glass with my tail.

The larger of the two figures looked up, smiled, and said: "Allow me to introduce us. This is Mr. Laurel. And I'm Mr. Hardy. We're delighted to make your acquaintance."

The cold wind blew, stirring up the gray dust. The two

androids—their names were meaningless to me . . .
Laurel and Hardy told me they could take me to the
escape pod in their wheeled vehicle. They called it a
car. A box of tools stood in the back.

Hardy said to me, "Now, good sir, if you would be so
kind as to sit in the front, I'll help my friend, Mr.
Laurel, to start the motor."

"Hey, Ollie. You want me to crank the handle?"

"No, Stanley. I'll do it. You sit in the driver's seat and
pump the pedal."

"Which pedal?"

"Why, the gas pedal, of course."

"What about the brake, Ollie?"

"Leave the brake, Stanley."

"But I thought it should—"

"Stanley. Don't touch the brake."

"But—"

"Ah, ah, now do as I say and pump the gas pedal."

The thin android shrugged and began pressing a
lever on the floor with his foot.

The big android, Hardy, gave a nod and cranked a
handle on the front of the car. Instantly the car, which
was facing downhill, rolled forward. It knocked the
android flat on his back. He held on to the front end of
the car, which dragged him downhill.

"Ow . . . ooooooooooo!"

The car jolted across the rough terrain; the big android
yelled with every bump. Laurel, in the driver's seat,
wrenched at all the controls he could reach. Appalled
by this disaster, I jumped into the front seat. Laurel
struggled with the steering wheel; he didn't seem to
know how to steer the vehicle.

"Let me try," I called, leaning forward to help steer.

Instead of sitting back to give me a chance to put my

hands on the steering wheel, he immediately grabbed the steering wheel, ripped it clean off the column, and handed it to me.

Now the car was careering out of control. Hardy was still being dragged along yelling.

We're going to crash, I thought. With me hurt who'll rescue the others? Flying above my shoulder was Bright Spark. "What do we do?" I shouted. "How do you stop this thing?"

Laurel said, "To stop it, you use the brake."

"Why didn't you use the brake, then?"

"Nobody asked."

He pulled a lever at the side of the car and it skidded to a stop.

Then the round face of Hardy appeared above the front of the car. It was covered with dust. His bowler hat was flattened. He stared hard at his friend, who scratched the top of his head. "I didn't mean to do it, Ollie, honest. I tried to tell you about the brake. You wouldn't . . . I thought . . . I was going to . . ."

Stanley started to cry.

I whispered to Bright Spark, "What do you think of these androids? Their behavior seems so strange."

"A sign in the room where they were stored said LAUREL & HARDY—THE KINGS OF COMEDY."

"What is COMEDY?"

"The word is not translatable, therefore I am unable to inform you of its meaning. The word KINGS is clear enough, however; we must assume these two androids represent two rulers from that culture's history."

By now the two had managed to start the car's primitive motor. It coughed and clattered, sending out clouds of blue smoke. Hardy replaced the steering wheel on its column and soon we were riding across that gray landscape in the direction of the escape pod, the car's wheels leaving furrows in the dust.

Bright Spark said to me, "Breathable atmosphere in pod reaching danger level. If they are not released within the hour, they will die."

As soon as I saw the pod as we approached in the car I realized what the problem was.

The pod, shaped like a cylinder, had landed in a cleft between two rows of rocks. In fact, the cleft might have been what was left of an ancient river bed. The water was gone, but the old rocky banks flanked the shiny magna-steel walls of the pod.

Once Hardy had stopped the car I raced across to where the pod lay. I saw that the escape hatch was actually undamaged. The reason they couldn't open it from the inside was because the hatch was pressed hard against a bank of boulders.

"We need to move those rocks," I said.

Bright Spark added, "The occupants of the pod must be released in one hour. Otherwise they will suffocate."

I communicated to the Laurel and Hardy androids through Bright Spark, so translation was automatic. "Mr. Laurel, Mr. Hardy, it's vital we move these rocks from the pod. Will you be able to help me?"

Hardy said, "Why, most certainly. It'll be our pleasure, won't it, Stanley?"

"It sure will." The thin man gave such an emphatic nod of the head that his hat fell off. "But first, Ollie, can I have a banana?"

"A banana? What for?"

"I'm hungry. I didn't have any breakfast because you sat in the milk."

"And why did I sit in the milk?"

"I didn't know you were going to sit on the chair just as I rested the jug of milk there."

Hardy looked exasperated. "Well, we don't have any bananas. We have apples, grapefruit, cherries, oranges, and pears. Now what will you have?"

Stanley scratched his head. "I'll have a sad suma."

"*Sad suma*? You don't mean a sad suma, you mean a satsuma."

"Yes, one of those little oranges that you get at Christmas."

"Well, we don't have any."

"What other fruit don't you have?"

Ollie looked thoughtful and ticked them off on his fingers. "We don't have rhubarb, melon, grapes, pineapple, gooseberries, blackberries, strawberries . . . doh!" Suddenly, Hardy hit Stanley with his hat. "What fruit *don't* we have? It's not important to know the fruit we *don't have*. So what piece of fruit would you like?"

"A banana."

"Doh!" Ollie hit Stanley again, and soon both were swiping each other with their hats. Then they chased one another around the car.

"Their behavior is most infuriating," I said to Bright Spark. "From what you translated they argued about food. Now they are fighting?"

"Correct. But you must remember they are androids, which are robotic versions of the anthropoid life forms that created them. They were obviously intended for some kind of automated museum display. Although they can think independently, it appears that every so often they lapse into some kind of dramatic scene that is stored in their memory cells."

"Well, I can't wait for them to stop their routine. I'll begin without them."

I'd no sooner begun to hack at the mound of rocks with a pick taken from the back of the car than I heard N'Catra's voice crackling through Bright Spark.

"Jantrey, the atmosphere is now poisonous. Of the twenty-five of us, six are already unconscious. Have you reached the pod yet?"

"Yes, N'Catra, I'm here." I shivered with fear from mane to tail tip. "Don't worry, I'll get you out . . . I'll get you all out."

"In the name of the Shining Akkron, please be quick . . . we will not live much longer."

I began to hack furiously at the boulders. It was harder than I expected. The gray dust had cemented all the stones together, so I had to shatter each one in turn.

The two androids had stopped chasing one another now.

"Humph! Bananas indeed," Ollie said to Stanley. "You see this good gentleman has had to begin his work without us." He turned to me. "I'm sorry, sir. How discourteous of us to allow our private disagreements to hinder your own selfless endeavors."

Stanley asked innocently, "Are we digging for oil?"

"No, Stan," said Ollie. "Why, this man is digging the foundations of a house. Now we must move this pile of rocks that are in the way."

I whispered to Bright Spark, "A house. Doesn't he understand what the pod is, and who's inside?"

"No. What we are seeing is a mixture of pre-programmed memories interacting with new information that the optical sensor is relaying into the electronic brain."

"You mean everything's getting mixed up and they

don't really understand what we're doing?"

Bright Spark gave a little jig. "Precisely."

Stan Laurel said, "You know, Ollie, I've been thinking."

"You've been thinking!"

"Instead of digging the rocks away, why don't we just pull them away with the car?"

Ollie gave a stern frown. "What was that you just said?"

"I said . . ."—Stanley took off his hat and scratched the top of his head—". . . why don't we tie a rope around the car . . . Drive the rocks away . . . pulling the car from the house . . . so we can . . . I mean drag the house from the rocks . . . then the car will be none the wiser . . ."

Ollie's stare hardened. "Why, Stanley . . . that's the most sensible idea I've heard you have. You mean we tie a rope around the rocks, tie the rope to the car, then drive the car away, pulling the rocks with it?"

Stan Laurel looked puzzled. "Do I?"

"You do, my friend, you do."

The two tied a rope around the boulder that jammed the hatch door shut, tied it to the car, then Stan Laurel climbed in.

Hardy stood in front of the car and beckoned Stan to drive slowly forward to take up the slack. Then the car would tug the big boulder away from the escape pod.

Disaster struck.

Stan revved the car too hard and lost control of it. It lurched forward toward Ollie, who stood right in its path. I was too slow to stop what happened next.

The car raced in the direction of Hardy, who yelled in horror. Stan put his hands over his eyes, not wanting to see the effects of such an accident.

But just then the rope snapped tight. The car stopped dead in its tracks. Stan was catapulted from the car. He turned somersaults in the air before landing on top of Hardy. Both went sprawling in the dust.

Hardy sat up, then said heavily, "Are you trying to ruin the only hat I've got left?"

I could waste no more time. I attacked the pile of rocks with the pick, but progress was agonizingly slow. The Laurel and Hardy androids lent a hand, doing their clumsy best with a small hammer and chisel. Ollie held the chisel point to the rocks while the thin one hit the end of the chisel. The pieces they dislodged were no larger than a baluka bean.

Bright Spark urged, "Condition red, danger. Atmosphere within pod can no longer support life. If the rocks holding shut the hatch aren't removed within the next three minutes the crew will begin to die."

Desperately I hacked at the stubborn boulders. I had to save my friends, but I knew it would take a whole day to move these rocks. I had minutes.

Stan said, "This gentleman's awful keen to build his new house. Look how fast he's working, Ollie."

Hardy nodded. "Excuse me, sir, why such a big hurry?"

At last I told them the truth. I didn't know if they would understand or not but I had to get them to work faster. "My friends are trapped in there."

"Trapped in this big tin can?"

"Yes. If I don't free them within two minutes they will all be dead."

Both looked at each other seriously. Ollie picked up the chisel and held it to the rocks. "You know what this means, Stanley?"

"I certainly do."

"Right, Stan." He positioned the chisel so the point rested against a rock. "Now, when I nod my head, you hit it."

"When you nod your head I hit it, Ollie?"

"That's what I said."

"Is that a good idea?"

"Listen to me, Stanley. I'll nod my head and you hit it, okay?"

"Okay, Ollie."

Hardy nodded his head.

Stanley hit Ollie's head with the hammer, denting the bowler hat.

I was growing weary of their peculiar antics now. In a minute, my friends would be dead within the pod. Furious, I was ready to shout at the androids. But then a strange thing happened.

Instead of complaining about being hit over the head with the hammer, Hardy shook hands with Stan Laurel and said to him, "Good work, that should do the trick. Well . . . so long, old friend. We've been together for many, many years."

Stanley smiled sadly, "Through thick and thin."

"Through good times and bad."

"You don't regret anything?"

"I regret nothing," Ollie said, giving a little wave of his finger. "In fact, if I had my wish, we'd do it all over again."

"Perhaps in some other place we will, Ollie."

Hardy smiled. "That's the spirit. One day we'll be reunited again, Sons Of The Desert forever more."

"Bye bye, Ollie." Stan wiped away a tiny tear that trickled down his cheek.

"Farewell, Stan, old friend."

"What's happening?" I whispered to Bright Spark, confused. "Why's he climbing up the mound of rocks?"

Stan hurried forward, a look of concern on his face. With a beckoning gesture, he grabbed my arm and started to pull me away from the rocks that held the pod hatchway shut.

I saw Hardy had sat down with his back to the largest rock.

"Bright Spark," I said, "I don't understand. What's he sitting there for?"

Bright Spark's voice crackled. "I suggest we move away quickly."

"Why? What's wrong?"

Laurel still pulled me along by the arm.

Bright Spark said, "Stan hitting Hardy on the head with the hammer was deliberate. The concussion has damaged the sensor that regulates the android's power plant."

"It means—"

"It means my sensors indicate we have less than twenty seconds before detonation."

Suddenly I wanted to call back to the big, friendly android to shut down its power and save itself, but Laurel was almost carrying me at a run away from the pod, his big feet slapping the gray dust into clouds.

"Fifteen seconds to detonation," said Bright Spark.

"Keep running," urged Stan. "Faster . . . faster . . ."

We ran toward a mound of stones.

"Ten seconds . . ."

In a way, I wanted to look back and see Hardy sitting there in his bowler hat. I wanted to see that affection-ate but shy wave he gave with just his fingers. But I couldn't look back, I just concentrated on running toward that mound of stones.

"Eight seconds to detonation," droned Bright Spark as it flew beside us.

We hit the mound of loose stones and scrambled up them, hand over hand, panting. We reached the top and tumbled over and over down at the other side. At the bottom of the slope we paused. It seemed so quiet. Maybe it hadn't worked. Maybe in two minutes we would see Hardy's face appear over the top of the mound to announce that—

First came the flash.

It splashed a golden light on the underside of the gray cloud. Then came a roar like thunder; the ground shook and above us a blast of air drove the gray dust high into the sky like a gray, boiling fog.

For a second or so we sat in complete silence. Then at last I knew I had to return to the pod. Bright Spark and Stan followed slowly behind.

For a moment, as I stood on the mound of stones, and looked in the direction of the pod, I could see nothing but the white dust fog hanging in the air.

Nothing moved.

Dead silence.

Then my heart quickened. I didn't know why. I stood on tiptoes looking hard into that white fog.

Then I did realize why. I let out a huge whoop of joy.

One by one shapes were moving in the white fog. Then I saw N'Catra. He looked weak, but when he saw me he straightened and waved with both arms and his tail.

I raced down toward my friends, hugging each in turn. They were all safe. The blast had dislodged the boulders. Instantly, they'd been able to open the hatch and escape the poisonous atmosphere of the pod. By the moment they were growing stronger as they gulped down the fresh air.

That explosion . . . The moment I realized what it had cost to save my friends, a sadness filled me. I remember Hardy sitting there so calmly, his back to the rock, knowing his sacrifice would save many lives. I know he was a robot, an android, but he had acted with a greater altruism than I've ever known from a flesh-and-blood creature. I saw Stan Laurel walk slowly up. He saw something on the ground and picked it up. It was Ollie's bowler, still dented from the hammer blow. Stan gently blew the dust from it and held it to his heart.

Eight days later we boarded the rescue craft. During that time, Stan had helped us build shelters to protect us from this gray planet's icy nights. He'd hardly spoken, though, and his friend's bowler hat was rarely far from his hands.

Now it was time to say goodbye. We said our farewells. Stan Laurel's face was expressionless. He gave a tiny wave of the hand and turned to walk away, alone, across the gray featureless desert.

Already the figure was tiny when we lifted off for home. As I watched him through the observation window, I gave the little finger wave that I'd learned from Hardy. I swallowed. My future lay with my family and friends on a warm and friendly home planet.

Far below, Stan Laurel was now a speck the size of a single period. His future, whatever it might be, lay down there. And I prayed to the Shining Akkron that some day he would find a new friend, somewhere in that city of ancient skulls.

Derelict

RAYMOND Z. GALLUN

I t drifted there in space, to the right of the Sun, its spherical hull half illumined and half in shadow. No native of the solar system could have guessed either at its age or its origin. Battered, lifeless, desolate, and forlorn, it betrayed a kinship both with the remote past and with the distant stars against the sharp pinpoints of which its bulk was limned.

Jan Van Tyren should have felt a surge of enthusiasm over his discovery of this derelict vessel of the void. Yet he did not. Within him there was room for little but the gnawing ache of grief. Listlessly preoccupied, he stood before the periscope screen of his own trim craft, watching with only a shadow of interest the spheroid pictured in it.

His big, loose body seemed to droop without animation before his instruments. A tuft of yellow hair protruded, cynical and slovenly, from beneath his leather helmet. All the strength had been drained out of him. His blue eyes were clouded, as if he gazed less at reality than at some horror of memory.

He had seen blood often during his years with the Jupiter company. He'd seen death and revolt. Such things were incidental to colonization, to progress. But Greta and little Jan—they had been safe. That anyone, even the horrid Loathi of the Jovian moon,

Ganymede, might harm them, had seemed inconceivable. His young wife, his baby—murdered. The torturing vision of what had happened had been with him for days now. Three? Four? He didn't want to recall anything related to that vision.

He didn't want to forget it either. Nor was it possible to forget. He kept hearing the weird screams of the Loathi echoing inside him; he kept seeing their long, keen beaks, and their batlike bodies swooping crazily out of the Ganymedean night. Here, where no one could observe, he allowed himself the relief of a silent snarl. The look on his gaunt, weatherbeaten face was not an expression of hatred. He was past hatred. He was numb and lost, like an engine without a governor.

That was why he was out here in the void, with the cold stars around him. He was trying to escape from— he wasn't completely sure what. He was going back to Earth to paint pictures and to seek in its mellow atmosphere of peace something that was lacking in the cruel environment of Joraanin, the outpost of which he had been master. He was quitting cold—returning home to heal his soul.

Small wonder then that even a spaceship that had floated without aim across the light-years, perhaps from another galaxy, could not awaken in him a spark of real enthusiasm. Mystery and the promise of adventure no longer had any direct appeal.

Yet Jan Van Tyren was still a creature of habit. Though his mind was caught up in a maelstrom of pain, still the automatic part of him continued to function with some semblance of normalcy. He was an artist; so, almost unconsciously, the channels which his hobby had established in his brain began their intended work—taking note of form and color.

He saw the contrasts of light and shade playing their bizarre tricks with the details of the great globular hull. He saw the deep grooves that stray meteors had scored in a crisscross pattern on the lusterless gray shell of the derelict.

He took note of the slender rods projecting like the prongs of a burr from the vessel's form, and of the rows of windows that met his gaze blankly, as if they were eyes that wondered in an uncomprehending way what he and his flier might be. All this could have been a picture that a man might paint, starkly beautiful against the black background of the universe.

Then too, Jan Van Tyren was an engineer by profession; and though he wished to leave such matters buried in the past, once more the habit of long experience had its way. Something deep in Jan's being, detached from his other thoughts, wondered what marvels of invention and science a survey of the derelict might reveal.

These combined forces gave to him that small thread of interest. Life had no strong purpose any more, and he was in no hurry to continue the two months of continuous flying that would bring him across the etheric desert to his native planet.

Van Tyren's hands flashed over controls with careless ease, as if they moved without the guidance of his brain. The spaceboat turned, beginning the graceful curve that would bring it alongside the spheroid. Across the periscope screen, stars reeled; then Jupiter appeared, a tiny belted bead millions of miles away. Around it were the specks of radiance that were its moons.

Finally the derelict came back into view, gigantic and near. It appeared to be some three hundred feet in diameter. The feeble light of the distant Sun shone on

it, revealing in its lower hemisphere a ragged rent whose depths were shrouded in shadow.

Jan steered his flier into a position from which he could get a better glimpse of the interior of the spheroid, beyond the torn opening in its shell. Spear points of light pierced the thick shadows there, revealing crumpled masses of metal. But there was sufficient room for his purpose.

Without considering the possible danger of the move, and in fact quite indifferent now to such danger, Jan worked the guide levers and throttle of his craft. There were sharp bursts of incandescence from its rocket vents. It turned, swaying; then glided into the hole in the side of the derelict and came to rest amid the wreckage.

With what might have been a fragment of his old active spirit, Jan Van Tyren donned space armor. But his memories were still with him. He cursed once. No, it was not really a curse; the fury was lacking. There was only anguish in it. It was like the whimper of a big dog with a thorn in its foot.

He climbed through the airlock, and for a minute stood quietly, viewing his surroundings. Somewhere gravity plates continued to function in this ancient wreck, for he had weight here—perhaps one-third Earth-normal. Junk was everywhere in the cavernous interior, distorted and crumpled grotesquely. Yet the metal was bright and new.

Whatever colossal weapon had ripped the globular vessel open like this might have done so within the hour or a billion years ago, as far as anyone could tell from visual inspection. There was no air; oxides didn't form; nothing moved, nothing changed. There was no sound in Jan's ears save the rustle of his own pulse. It was as if time had stopped in this minute speck of the universe. Only the derelict's aura of desertion, and the memory of the countless meteor scorings on its outer shell, suggested to Van Tyren its vast age.

Meteors are too rare to constitute a menace in the traveled lanes of the solar system, and in the interstellar void they are rare indeed. Lifetimes might go by before one of those minor collisions took place; and yet here on the wreck they were numbered in thousands.

Rearing from the debris was a stairway. Jan learned later to think of it by that term, though it was not a stairway such as men would find convenient to use. It was a pillar, fluted spirally after the fashion of the threads of a screw. At regular intervals pegs were set along these threads, to provide a grip for some kind of prehensile member.

The pillar swept upward to meet a broad roof. Sunlight, stabbing in from space, awoke an opalescent gleam on the metal surfaces of this queer means of ascent to whatever lay in the bulk of the derelict overhead.

Jan took hold of the pegs on the fluted column, and with easy surges hoisted his loose, muscular frame toward the top. Beside the place where the pillar joined the ceiling was a trapdoor. He fumbled with the lever that latched it. It slid aside, allowing him to pass through into a tiny square compartment that appeared to have the function of an airlock—for there was another, similar, trapdoor in its roof.

The lower entrance had closed beneath him, and now he unfastened the valve over his head and climbed into the chamber above.

Dust and silence and motionless mechanical grandeur reminiscent of the tomb of a dead Cyclops—that in brief was a description of the place. It was much larger than the room below. Through windows along one wall the sun shone, gilding inert engines whose monstrous forms seemed capable of generating sufficient power to tear a planet from its orbit. Huge cylinders of opalescent metal reared upward. Flywheels, which on Earth would have weighed hundreds of tons, rested in their pivot sockets. Cables, wires, and pipettes ran between colossal, generatorlike contrivances. Crystal tubes stood in webby tripods or were supported in framework attached to the ceiling; but no energy flowed in the delicate filaments that formed their vitals, and there was no way for a man to tell what purposes they were intended to fulfill.

Between the windows massive rods were mounted, pointing through the external wall of the sphere, as the weapons of a battleship would do. Whatever the race that had been responsible for this outlay, it was certain that it had been a race of fighters.

Jan Van Tyren, browsing listlessly among these wonders of another solar system, obtained his first direct hint of what the owners of the ship had been like. Sinuous patches of gray ash, contorted so as to still portray the agonies of death, sprawled here and there on the floor. Brown flakes, resembling bits of parchment, were mixed with the ash—the remnant, probably, of chitinous exoskeletons.

The crew of the derelict had been slain. The pitted plating of the floor around the remains of each of their bodies showed that clearly. Something hot and corrosive had blasted them out of existence. They had battled valiantly, but they had been overcome.

Jan saw a silvery object lying beside one of the areas of ash. He picked it up. A mummified fragment of flesh, suggestive of the foot of a bird, clung to it, its three prehensile toes curved fiercely around the grip and trigger button of the small weapon.

Yes, those unknowns had fought as men would do; but they had failed. Van Tyren's set face exhibited a fleeting sneer as he hurled the object aside.

He went on with his explorations. The dust of remote mortality swirled up in the path of his careless feet, filling the sunbeams from the windows with eddying motes. There was air here to support the motes; but whether it was breathable after the passage of ages seemed hardly probable.

Jan paused before a switchboard. His gauntleted hand fumbled hesitantly over a dial at its center. He turned the dial to the right. A faint vibration was transmitted to his fingers. He turned the dial more, not knowing if his act was perhaps altering a detail in the normal course of destiny. The vibration increased. He stood back, waiting.

Beneath the framework mounting of the switchboard was a cabinet of smooth, tawny material. The front of it opened now, revealing a darkened interior. From the opening a slender head was thrust, swaying with rhythmic cadence from side to side. It had a single eye, as expressionless as the lens of a camera, which in truth the orb seemed to be.

There was no mouth in evidence, nor any need of one; for this thing, though it presented characteristics commonly associated with living creatures, yet was marked with the unmistakable stamp of the machine. The triangular head had the purple gloss of the other metallic objects in the room. The intricate appendages that projected around its throat, forming a sort of frilled collar, were of the same substance. Beneath them the slender length of the thing was revealed as it crept in serpentine fashion from the cabinet. Its body was composed of thousands of glistening segments, as minutely tooled as the parts of a watch.

The monster was in full view now, its head raised to the level of Jan's eyes. Instinctively he had backed away, though somehow the idea of danger did not occur to him. Perhaps he had left normal caution behind him on Ganymede.

For a time, nothing more happened. The triangular head continued to sway from side to side, but that was all. Van Tyren stood statuesquely, his feet spread wide apart in bullish defiance directed not so much against this amazing fabrication as against his own aching memories. Even the tangible truth of this fantastic episode could not wholly smother the agony of the recent past.

Presently the serpentine robot turned and glided off among the surrounding maze of machines. With a grace that was at once beautiful and abhorrent it writhed its way to an apparatus at the center of the room. Its glittering appendages touched controls skillfully.

A blast of air surged from vents high up on the walls. Jan felt the thrust of it against his armor and saw the ashes of the derelict's dead crew go swirling away into other vents along with the lifeless vapor that had been sealed for so many eons in this tomb of space.

In response to some further manipulation of dials and switches on the part of the robot, a light, restful blue began to burn in a crystal tube above Jan's head.

He looked up at it, and it seemed to exert a soothing, hypnotic influence upon him. He did not even protest when the unknown that he had freed returned to his side and made a gentle attempt to remove his space armor. His own fingers closed on the fastenings and helped those delicate metallic members to complete the task.

Free of the cumbersome attire, he stood eagerly in those cool, blue rays. They appeared to probe to every corner of his being, drawing all the ache and tension out of his tortured nerves.

The grief in his mind blurred to a diffused sweetness. At first he was almost terrified. It was sacrilege to let the thought of his wife and son fade away from him so. Then, no longer wishing to think, he surrendered completely to the healing, Lethean influence of the rays.

The air around him was now cold and refreshing. He sucked in great lungfuls of it. He flexed his muscles indolently, and at last his rugged face broke into a smile. Somewhere music whispered—exotic music out of a time and region too distant to fathom.

The automaton was gliding here and there with no sound except a soft, slithering jingle. It was putting things in order, inspecting and readjusting this device and that. Jan wondered how many thousands of millennia had gone by since any of those machines had been called upon to function. He wondered too at the unfathomable kindness of his queer host, and whether it had read his mind, learning of the pain that had crushed him.

But the rays made him inclined to accept rather than to question, and for a while he did not pursue his ideas further. He was in no hurry. He had not a care or responsibility in the universe. There was plenty of time for everything.

After perhaps an hour under the tube of the blue light, Jan Van Tyren realized that he was hungry. Little food had passed his lips since the quick departure from Ganymede. He put on his space suit again, descended through the airlock by which he had entered this chamber, and shinned down the spirally fluted pillar. Before he had reached the bottom the robot was descending above him, its flexible, snake-like body sliding easily in the spiral grooves. The thing had deserted its tasks to follow him.

Jan proceeded to gather certain food articles from the store of concentrated rations aboard his spaceboat. But before he had collected what he wanted, the automaton was beside him, trying to help. Jan attempted to shove those gleaming claws away, but they were persistent; and finally, in a mood to accept the gentle suggestion, he capitulated, allowing the robot to take several containers from him.

"I think I know what you are." Jan chuckled inside his oxygen helmet. "You were made to take care of the various small wants of the people who manned this ship. Now that there isn't anyone else to play servant to, you've picked me as your boss."

He collected a few other articles—the sleeping bag of his flier, several astronomical instruments and the case containing his artist's equipment—and thrust them into the waiting arms of the robot.

"Might as well take this stuff along too," he said, "so I won't have to climb down again and get it."

He paused to see what the friendly mechanism would do next. The result was just faintly amusing. After a moment of uncertainty it approached him. A stubby member which was part of the frill of appendages around its throat elongated itself like a telescope, coiled its metal length around his waist and hoisted him easily off his feet. Then the serpentine monster made its weaving way to the stair and commenced to ascend with its new master and the bulky equipment.

"Hey!" Van Tyren protested. "This is making a good thing too good! I'm not a cripple!"

But even though the automaton might have possessed a means of divining the telepathic waves of the thoughts behind Jan's words, still it had its way with him.

The man, hardened and self-reliant though he had always been, accepted the mild, emasculating yoke of a monster of which he really knew nothing quite as trustingly as a child accepts the love of its mother. The blue ray was not penetrating his body here, but its care-effacing power still persisted. And he had no thought of the possibly dangerous consequences of the spell.

He remembered the Mercurian who had valeted one of his friends of his student days. Khambee was the Mercurian's name—a curious elf whose unobtrusive yet insistent indulgence was much the same as that of this mechanical slave.

"Khambee the second," Van Tyren pronounced good-naturedly, bestowing the nomen on the automaton that bore him. "It fits you."

In the chamber of wonders beyond the airlock, Jan set out his meal and ate, while Khambee watched with his camera eye, as if to learn the intricacies of the task.

Then he crept through an opening in the wall and returned with a bowl containing cubes of a golden, translucent compound that emitted a pleasant odor.

He set the bowl beside the man.

Van Tyren took one of the cubes, tasted it, and devoured it without considering that, to his earthly system, the substance might be poisonous. But he experienced no ill effects. The food was slightly fibrous, but sweet and tasty. He consumed more of it with relish.

The blue rays from the tube on the ceiling poured their lulling effulgence over him. The whisper of music, thin and threadlike and soothing, worked its magic upon his senses. Jan crouched on the floor, his head nodding against his knees.

So he remained for a long time, neither awake nor quite asleep, his brain and nerves pervaded by a deliciously restful quasi-consciousness. Khambee had disappeared, perhaps to attend to some obscure matter in another part of the vessel.

Such was the beginning of Jan Van Tyren's adventure on the derelict. As yet he gave the future no attention, living each careless moment as it came; thinking, but not too deeply. Never before had the instinct of the empire-builder in him been so completely submerged.

Just to amuse himself he set up his astronomical instruments and took minute observations of both Jupiter and the stars at intervals of an hour to discover what sort of path the derelict was following. The angular change in the positions of those celestial landmarks told the story.

The vessel was a moon of the planet Jupiter, swinging around it slowly in an immense orbit many millions of miles across. Probably it had been doing so for eons before men had considered seriously the problem of traffic between worlds.

The fact that it had never been discovered until he had stumbled upon it was easy to explain. Without guidance it would be simpler to find an individual grain of sand on a beach than to locate so small a satellite in the vastness of the etheric desert.

Now, however, with distances and velocities measured perfectly, there would be no trouble in estimating where the vessel would be at a given second. Jan fumbled with the paper on which he had made his calculations, and then carelessly tossed it aside.

Like the good servant he was, Khambee, who happened to be present, picked it up and placed it in a little case fastened at his throat.

Looking at the stars gleaming so gloriously in the ebon firmament had given Jan Van Tyren an inspiration.

"Men are fools," he confided to Khambee. "Trouble and misfortune are all the reward they get for their struggles. It was the same with the serpent-folk who made you. Those of them who formed the crew of this vessel were killed—murdered.

"Why can't we escape from all that sort of nonsense, Khambee? Why can't we fix up this ship so that it can travel out to the stars? What an adventure that would be! Vagabonding from one planet to another without any responsibilities, and without ever returning to the solar system! That would be something worthwhile, Khambee."

Jan was only talking for companionship's sake, attempting to give an idle dream a semblance of reality. He did not believe that what he spoke of was possible. There was the matter of food, water, and energy. It seemed unlikely that this decrepit derelict's supply of each was sufficient for such a venture.

However, Khambee had greater powers at his command than Van Tyren could guess. And there had been built into the inorganic frame of him an astute understanding that penetrated the very motives and purposes animating flesh, bone, nerves, and brain tissue.

He appeared to listen attentively to the rustling thought waves of his human master. Then, impelled by the complex urges which the genius of his creator had stamped indelibly into the metal and crystal intricacies of his being, he returned to the tasks which he was meant to do.

And Jan Van Tyren, who had established and bossed Joraanin, the Ganymede colony, continued with his idle play. He slept, he ate exotic foods, he wandered about the ship, he dreamed; but most of all he painted, setting up his easel wherever whim might suggest. And the marvels around him seemed, by their very aura of strangeness, to direct and control his skillful fingers.

He painted great engines with shafts of sunlight twinkling on them; he studied the highlights that shifted elusively in the hollow grooves of the pillars that the sinuous folk of long ago had used as stairways, and he transferred the forms of those stairways to canvas.

He painted Khambee at work with a flaming welding tool, slim, efficient, and almost noiseless. He even painted scenes and subjects of Earth and Ganymede—pleasant reminiscences, for all that was unpleasant had been shoved far into the background of his mind.

A white collie of his childhood. A jagged mountain jutting out of the red desert of Ganymede. Greta, blond and pretty and smiling. Little Jan with his stiff, yellow curls. Such were the subjects of his pictures. He thought of his wife and child, but only of the happy incidents of their lives together.

The horror was blurred and distant. The blue rays saw to that. And so a will not his own, and perhaps not even Khambee's, but belonging to a serpentine monster dead for ages, controlled Jan Van Tyren.

At odd moments he watched space, and felt the yearning pull of the stars. Thus many days must have gone by. He did not bother to keep track.

The time came when he was aroused from slumber by a throbbing sound, soft but eloquent, of titanic forces at work. He crept out of his sleeping bag and stared at the source of the disturbance. Huge flywheels were spinning. He felt a powerful thrust as the ship's propulsive equipment took hold for a fraction of a second.

Then Khambee, worming his slender shape like a weaving shuttle here and there among the machinery, broke the contacts of massive switches. The activity died to silence once more. But the test had been made and Jan sensed that it had been successful.

He hurried forward. "We've got enough power, then?" he demanded huskily. "Have we?"

For an answer the robot opened the side of a cylindrical arrangement, and with the clawed tip of an appendage pointed to the maze of coils and crystal that glowed with heat inside.

Jan studied the apparatus intently for several minutes. Much of it was beyond his grasp; but there were places where tangible fact corresponded with human theory. Energy from the cosmic rays that exist everywhere in space. Limitless, inexhaustible energy! The engines of the vessel were worked by it.

"I see," Van Tyren commented quietly. "The power problem is solved. Have we enough food, air, and water?"

Khambee led him through the labyrinths of the ship to a place where he had never been before—a hall lined with vast, transparent tanks, most of them filled with a clear liquid that had been sealed up for ages. There was water enough here to make the ship a little world, independent of outside sources, since none could escape from the sealed hull.

Farther down the corridor were other tanks filled with preserved food supplies, and beyond them were extensive chambers where odd, bulbous things were growing under the intense light of great globes.

Were those growths plants of some kind, or artificial cultures to be classified somewhere between the organic and the inorganic? Their color was deep green. Was it chlorophyll, or a substance analogous in function to the chlorophyll of green plants? Perhaps it did not matter. Here food was being produced under the action of the intense light.

Carbon dioxide, piped to these chambers from all parts of the craft, was being split up by those queer growths, and the oxygen in it was being freed to refresh the atmosphere of the ship. Khambee had started a process that had been dead for uncounted millennia; now it could go on indefinitely.

Nourishment, water, and oxygen—everything essential to life had been taken care of.

"Speed?" Jan questioned. "Can we build up sufficient speed to travel between the stars without making the trip endless?"

It was an important query. No man-built ship could have reached the outer galaxies in a lifetime, though there were experiments in progress that in a decade or so might produce promising results.

Khambee's tactile appendages swung toward a huge power-distributor tube nearby in a gesture of confidence.

Jan was satisfied. "Then we're going," he said. "There's not much left for me here in the solar system."

His voice was steady, but the thrill of adventures to come made his heart pound and sent tingling prickles through his scalp muscles.

Khambee the unfathomable offered no protest, yet his actions indicated that there was work still to be done.

He clutched his master's arm and drew him along gloomy passages to a storeroom filled with various machinery parts and other supplies. Here he selected a great sheaf of metal plates, and bore it back to the airlock that opened into the wrecked compartment where Jan's spaceboat was housed. The silvery length of him passed through it, lugging the heavy load.

Jan Van Tyren donned his airtight armor and followed.

For several hours he watched the slave-robot patch the great rent. During that time the effects of the blue ray must have worn off; for presently, of his own volition, he tried to help, holding the massive plates steady while his snakelike henchman welded them into place with a flame tool. Khambee accepted the assistance without protest.

Jan was more his own self now—cool, dominant, purposeful, making ready for a venture that no man had yet attempted.

At last the job was finished. The wreckage of an ancient battle was neatly cleared away, the jagged hole was covered, and only an oval door was left, through which the flier might pass when necessary.

The eye lens of the robot met Jan's gaze briefly. "All is prepared," it seemed to say.

Van Tyren nodded, his weatherbeaten face grim, hard, smiling. "Good!" he commented.

He shinned up the spiral pillar. Khambee was close behind, but he did not offer to help.

Nor did he go immediately to the controls of the engines. Instead he drew the man to a broad, white screen, which was part of a complex apparatus near by. He snapped switches and twirled dials expertly.

Pictures appeared in the screen—bleak, rolling desert and tortured gorges. Then an oasis where there was water, and where the radioactive ores underground provided enough heat to permit the growth of vegetation. At its center was a little, rough city under a crystal dome. Joraanin, the Ganymede colony!

Around it men and loyal Loathi were entrenched, fighting off hordes of rebel Loathi that circled on batlike wings above, their long beaks gleaming. The revolt was still in progress. A strong hand was needed there to end this chaos and death. Yes, needed. The bensonium mines —

Jan Van Tyren stood with the oxygen helmet in his hands, his mouth puckering pensively. A thousand thoughts swarmed in his brain; problems which he was sure he'd thrashed out before. Impressions of courage, of fear, of loyalty, and of love. The Loathi. Greta. Little Jan. Revenge. No, not revenge—constructive co-operation. That was his policy. But he didn't have a policy any more, did he? An empire-builder. But he'd given up empire-building. Or had he?

Jan's eyes roved the gleaming, segmented form of Khambee beside him. All at once truth came out of the muddle. He saw one of the robot's purposes clearly at last. Khambee had been the slave of a fighting race. A worker, and when the occasion demanded, a healer. He, Van Tyren, had been healed and freshened. His sense of responsibilities to come had returned, and he was ready for them now.

"I suppose I could still choose to leave the solar system, and you would obey me," he said. "But you probably knew all along what my final choice would be. Return to your cabinet, Khambee. I'm going back to Joraanin—alone. It's my job."

Khambee helped him gather his various possessions together and carry them down to the spaceboat. The exit door of the compartment rolled aside. Sunlight stabbed inward, causing the automaton's body to reflect a thousand shifting, iridescent colors.

Just as Van Tyren was entering the flier, Khambee thrust a paper into his hands. It was the paper on which Jan had recorded his astronomical measurements and had calculated the orbit and velocity of the derelict.

He felt more than ever that Khambee could read his innermost thoughts. There was a bit of tightness in his throat then.

"Thanks, Khambee," he said very seriously. "This might be useful. I may want to come back sometime. I may need to come back."

The flier was in space. Jan Van Tyren hummed a tune that was lost in the growl of the rockets. Ahead lay Jupiter and its satellites. Beyond them the bright stars seemed to smile.

A Walk in the Dark

ARTHUR C. CLARKE

R obert Armstrong had walked just over two miles, as far as he could judge, when his torch failed. He stood still for a moment, unable to believe that such a misfortune could really have befallen him. Then, half maddened with rage, he hurled the useless instrument away. It landed somewhere in the darkness, disturbing the silence of this little world. A metallic echo came ringing back from the low hills: then all was quiet again.

This, thought Armstrong, was the ultimate misfortune. Nothing more could happen to him now. He was even able to laugh bitterly at his luck, and resolved never again to imagine that the fickle goddess had ever favored him. Who would have believed that the only tractor at Camp IV would have broken down when he was just setting off for Port Sanderson? He recalled the frenzied repair work, the relief when the second start had been made—and the final debacle when the caterpillar track had jammed.

It was no use, then, regretting the lateness of his departure: he could not have foreseen these accidents, and it was still a good four hours before the *Canopus* took off. He *had* to catch her, whatever happened; no other ship would be touching at this world for another month.

Apart from the urgency of his business, four more

weeks on this out-of-the-way planet were unthinkable.

There had been only one thing to do. It was lucky that Port Sanderson was little more than six miles from the camp—not a great distance, even on foot. He had had to leave all his equipment behind, but it could follow on the next ship and he could manage without it. The road was poor, merely stamped out of the rock by one of the Board's hundred-ton crushers, but there was no fear of going astray.

Even now, he was in no real danger, though he might well be too late to catch the ship. Progress would be slow, for he dare not risk losing the road in this region of canyons and enigmatic tunnels that had never been explored. It was, of course, pitch-dark. Here at the edge of the galaxy the stars were so few and scattered that their light was negligible. The strange crimson sun of this lonely world would not rise for many hours, and although five of the little moons were in the sky they could barely be seen by the unaided eye. Not one of them could even cast a shadow.

Armstrong was not a man to bewail his luck for long. He began to walk slowly along the road, feeling its texture with his feet. It was, he knew, fairly straight except where it wound through Carver's Pass. He wished he had a stick or something to probe the way before him, but he would have to rely for guidance on the feel of the ground.

It was terribly slow at first, until he gained confidence. He had never known how difficult it was to walk in a straight line. Although the feeble stars gave him his bearings, again and again he found himself stumbling among the virgin rocks at the edge of the crude roadway. He was traveling in long zigzags that took him to alternate sides of the road. Then he would stub his toes against the bare rock and grope his way back on to the hard-packed surface once again.

Presently it settled down to a routine. It was impossible to estimate his speed; he could only struggle along and hope for the best. There were four miles to go— four miles and as many hours. It should be easy enough, unless he lost his way. But he dared not think of that.

Once he had mastered the technique he could afford the luxury of thought. He could not pretend that he was enjoying the experience, but he had been in much worse positions before. As long as he remained on the road, he was perfectly safe. He had been hoping that as his eyes became adapted to the starlight he would be able to see the way, but he now knew that the whole journey would be blind. The discovery gave him a vivid sense of his remoteness from the heart of the galaxy.

On a night as clear as this, the skies of almost any other planet would have been blazing with stars. Here at this outpost of the universe the sky held perhaps a hundred faintly gleaming points of light, as useless as the five ridiculous moons on which no one had ever bothered to land.

A slight change in the road interrupted his thoughts. Was there a curve here, or had he veered off to the right again? He moved very slowly along the invisible and ill-defined border. Yes, there was no mistake: the road was bending to the left. He tried to remember its appearance in the daytime, but he had only seen it once before. Did this mean that he was nearing the pass? He hoped so, for the journey would then be half completed.

He peered ahead into the blackness, but the ragged line of the horizon told him nothing. Presently he found that the road had straightened itself again and his spirits sank. The entrance to the pass must still be some way ahead: there were at least four miles to go.

Four miles—how ridiculous the distance seemed! How long would it take the *Canopus* to travel four miles? He doubted if man could measure so short an interval of time. And how many trillions of miles had he, Robert Armstrong, traveled in his life? It must have reached a staggering total by now, for in the last twenty years he had scarcely stayed more than a month at a time on any single world. This very year, he had twice made the crossing of the galaxy, and that was a notable journey even in these days of the phantom drive.

He tripped over a loose stone, and the jolt brought him back to reality. It was no use, here, thinking of ships that could eat up the light-years. He was facing nature, with no weapons but his own strength and skill.

It was strange that it took him so long to identify the real cause of his uneasiness. The last four weeks had been very full, and the rush of his departure, coupled with the annoyance and anxiety caused by the tractor's breakdowns, had driven everything else from his mind. Moreover, he had always prided himself on his hardheadedness and lack of imagination. Until now, he had forgotten all about that first evening at the base, when the crews had regaled him with the usual tall yarns concocted for the benefit of newcomers.

It was then that the old base clerk had told the story of his walk by night from Port Sanderson to the camp, and of what had trailed him through Carver's Pass, keeping always beyond the limit of his torchlight. Armstrong, who had heard such tales on a score of worlds, had paid it little attention at the time. This planet, after all, was known to be uninhabited. But logic could not dispose of the matter as easily as that. Suppose, after all, there was some truth in the old man's fantastic tale . . .?

It was not a pleasant thought, and Armstrong did not intend to brood upon it. But he knew that if he dismissed it out of hand it would continue to prey on his mind. The only way to conquer imaginary fears was to face them boldly; he would have to do that now.

His strongest argument was the complete barrenness of this world and its utter desolation, though against that one could set many counter-arguments, as indeed the old clerk had done. Man had only lived on this planet for twenty years, and much of it was still unexplored. No one could deny that the tunnels out in the wasteland were rather puzzling, but everyone believed them to be volcanic vents. Though, of course, life often crept into such places. With a shudder he remembered

89

the giant polyps that had snared the first explorers of Vargon III.

It was all very inconclusive. Suppose, for the sake of argument, one granted the existence of life here. What of that?

The vast majority of life forms in the universe were completely indifferent to man. Some, of course, like the gas-beings of Alcoran or the roving wave-lattices of Shandaloon, could not even detect him but passed through or around him as if he did not exist. Others were merely inquisitive, some embarrassingly friendly. There were few indeed that would attack unless provoked.

Nevertheless, it was a grim picture that the old stores clerk had painted. Back in the warm, well-lighted smoking room, with the drinks going around, it had been easy enough to laugh at it. But here in the darkness, miles from any human settlement, it was very different.

It was almost a relief when he stumbled off the road again and had to grope with his hands until he found it once more. This seemed a very rough patch, and the road was scarcely distinguishable from the rocks around. In a few minutes, however, he was safely on his way again.

It was unpleasant to see how quickly his thoughts returned to the same disquieting subject. Clearly it was worrying him more than he cared to admit.

He drew consolation from one fact: it had been quite obvious that no one at the Base had believed the old fellow's story. Their questions and banter had proved that. At the time, he had laughed as loudly as any of them. After all, what *was* the evidence? A dim shape, just seen in the darkness, that might well have been an oddly formed rock. And the curious clicking noise that had so impressed the old man—anyone could imagine such sounds at night if they were sufficiently over-wrought. If it had been hostile, why hadn't the creature come any closer? "Because it was afraid of my light," the old chap had said. Well, that was plausible enough: it would explain why nothing had ever been seen in the daylight. Such a creature might live underground, only emerging at night—darn it, why was he taking the old idiot's ravings so seriously! Armstrong got control of his thoughts again. If he went on this way, he told himself angrily, he would soon be seeing and hearing a whole menagerie of monsters.

There was, of course, one factor that disposed of the ridiculous story at once. It was really very simple; he felt sorry he hadn't thought of it before. *What would such a creature live on?* There was not even a trace of vegetation on the whole of the planet. He laughed to think that the bogey could be disposed of so easily—and in the same instant felt annoyed with himself for not laughing aloud. If he was so sure of his reasoning, why not whistle, or sing, or do anything to keep up his spirits? He put the question fairly to himself as a test of his manhood. Half-ashamed, he had to admit that he was still afraid—afraid because "there *might* be some-thing in it, after all." But at least his analysis had done him some good.

It would have been better if he had left it there, and remained half-convinced by his argument. But a part of his mind was still busily trying to break down his careful reasoning. It succeeded only too well, and when he remembered the plant-beings of Xantil Major the shock was so unpleasant that he stopped dead in his tracks.

91

Now the plant-beings of Xantil were not in any way horrible. They were in fact extremely beautiful creatures. But what made them appear so distressing now was the knowledge that they could live for indefinite periods with no food whatsoever. All the energy they needed for their strange lives they extracted from cosmic radiation—and that was almost as intense here as anywhere else in the universe.

He had scarcely thought of one example before others crowded into his mind and he remembered the life form on Trantor Beta, which was the only one known capable of directly utilizing atomic energy. That too had lived on an utterly barren world, very much like this . . .

Armstrong's mind was rapidly splitting into two distinct portions, each trying to convince the other and neither wholly succeeding. He did not realize how far his morale had gone until he found himself holding his breath lest it conceal any sound from the darkness about him. Angrily, he cleared his mind of the rubbish that had been gathering there and turned once more to the immediate problem.

There was no doubt that the road was slowly rising, and the silhouette of the horizon seemed much higher in the sky. The road began to twist, and suddenly he was aware of great rocks on either side of him. Soon only a narrow ribbon of sky was still visible, and the darkness became, if possible, even more intense.

Somehow, he felt safer with the rock walls surrounding him: it meant that he was protected except in two directions. Also, the road had been leveled more carefully and it was easy to keep to it. Best of all, he knew now that the journey was more than half completed.

For a moment his spirits began to rise. Then, with

maddening perversity, his mind went back into the old grooves again. He remembered that it was on the far side of Carver's Pass that the old clerk's adventure had taken place—if it had ever happened at all.

In half a mile, he would be out in the open again, out of the protection of these sheltering rocks. The thought seemed doubly horrible now and he already felt a sense of nakedness. He could be attacked from any direction, and he would be utterly helpless . . .

Until now, he had still retained some self-control. Very resolutely he had kept his mind away from the one fact that gave some color to the old man's tale—the single piece of evidence that had stopped the banter in the crowded room back at the camp and brought a sudden hush upon the company. Now, as Armstrong's will weakened, he recalled again the words that had struck a momentary chill even in the warm comfort of the Base building.

The little clerk had been very insistent on one point. He had never heard any sound of pursuit from the dim shape sensed, rather than seen, at the limit of his light. There was no scuffling of claws or hoofs on rock, nor even the clatter of displaced stones. It was as if, so the old man had declared in that solemn manner of his, "as if the thing that was following could see perfectly in the darkness, and had many small legs or pads so that it could move swiftly and easily over the rock— like a giant caterpillar or one of the carpet-things of Kralkor II."

Yet, although there had been no noise of pursuit, there had been one sound that the old man had caught several times. It was so unusual that its very strangeness made it doubly ominous. It was the faint but horribly persistent *clicking*.

The old fellow had been able to describe it very vividly—much too vividly for Armstrong's liking now.

"Have you ever listened to a large insect crunching its prey?" he said. "Well, it was just like that. I imagine that a crab makes exactly the same noise with its claws when it clashes them together. It was a—what's the word?—a *chitinous* sound."

At this point, Armstrong remembered laughing loudly. (Strange, how it was all coming back to him now.) But no one else had laughed, though they had been quick to do so earlier. Sensing the change of tone, he had sobered at once and asked the old man to continue his story. How he wished now that he had stifled his curiosity!

It had been quickly told. The next day, a party of skeptical technicians had gone into the no-man's-land beyond Carver's Pass. They were not skeptical enough to leave their guns behind, but they had no cause to use them, for they found no trace of any living thing. There were the inevitable pits and tunnels, glistening holes down which the light of the torches rebounded endlessly until it was lost in the distance—but the planet was riddled with them.

Though the party found no sign of life, it discovered one thing it did not like at all. Out in the barren and unexplored land beyond the pass they had come upon an even larger tunnel than the rest. Near the mouth of that tunnel was a massive rock, half embedded in the ground. And the sides of that rock had been worn away *as if it had been used as an enormous whetstone.*

No fewer than five of those present had seen this disturbing rock. None of them could explain it satisfactorily as a natural formation, but they still refused to accept the old man's story. Armstrong had asked them if they had ever put it to the test. There had been an uncomfortable silence. Then big Andrew Hargraves had said: "Hell, who'd walk out to the pass at night just for fun!" and had left it at that. Indeed, there was no other record of anyone walking from Port Sanderson to the camp by night, or for that matter by day. During the hours of light, no unprotected human being could live in the open beneath the rays of the enormous, lurid sun that seemed to fill half the sky. And no one would walk six miles, wearing radiation armor, if the tractor was available.

Armstrong felt that he was leaving the pass. The rocks on either side were falling away, and the road was no longer as firm and well-packed as it had been. He was coming out into the open plain once more, and somewhere not far away in the darkness was that enigmatic pillar that might have been used for sharpening monstrous fangs or claws. It was not a reassuring thought, but he could not get it out of his mind.

Feeling distinctly worried now, Armstrong made a great effort to pull himself together. He would try to be rational again; he would think of business, the work he had done at the camp—anything but this infernal place. For a while, he succeeded quite well. But presently, with a maddening persistence, every train of thought came back to the same point. He could not get out of his mind the picture of that inexplicable rock and its appalling possibilities. Over and over again he found himself wondering how far away it was, whether he had already passed it, and whether it was on his right or his left. . . .

The ground was quite flat again, and the road drove on straight as an arrow. There was one gleam of consolation: Port Sanderson could not be much more than two miles away. Armstrong had no idea how long he had been on the road. Unfortunately, his watch was not illuminated and he could only guess at the passage of time. With any luck, the *Canopus* should not take off for another two hours at least. But he could not be sure, and now another fear began to enter his head—the dread that he might see a vast constellation of lights rising swiftly into the sky ahead, and know that all this agony of mind had been in vain.

He was not zigzagging so badly now, and seemed to be able to anticipate the edge of the road before stumbling off it. It was probable, he cheered himself by thinking, that he was traveling almost as fast as if he had a light. If all went well, he might be nearing port Sanderson in thirty minutes—a ridiculously small space of time. How he would laugh at his fears when he strolled into his already reserved stateroom in the *Canopus*, and felt that peculiar quiver as the phantom drive hurled the great ship far out of this system, back to the clustered starclouds near the center of the galaxy— back toward Earth itself, which he had not seen for so many years. One day, he told himself, he really must visit Earth again. All his life he had been making the promise, but always there had been the same answer— lack of time. Strange, wasn't it, that such a tiny planet should have played so enormous a part in the development of the universe, should even have come to dominate worlds far wiser and more intelligent than itself!

Armstrong's thoughts were harmless again, and he felt calmer. The knowledge that he was nearing Port Sanderson was immensely reassuring, and he deliberately kept his mind on familiar, unimportant matters. Carver's Pass was already far behind, and with it that thing he no longer intended to recall. One day, if he

A Walk in the Dark

ever returned to this world, he would visit the pass in the daytime and laugh at his fears. In twenty minutes now, they would have joined the nightmares of his childhood.

It was almost a shock, though one of the most pleasant he had ever known, when he saw the lights of Port Sanderson come up over the horizon. The curvature of this little world was very deceptive: it did not seem right that a planet with a gravity almost as great as Earth's should have a horizon so close at hand. One day, someone would have to discover what lay at this world's core to give it so great a density. Perhaps the many tunnels would help—it was an unfortunate turn of thought, but the nearness of his goal had robbed it of terror now. Indeed, the thought that he might really be in danger seemed to give his adventure a certain piquancy and heightened interest. Nothing could happen to him now, with ten minutes to go and the lights of the port already in sight.

A few minutes later, his feelings changed abruptly when he came to the sudden bend in the road. He had forgotten the chasm that caused his detour and added half a mile to the journey. *Well, what of it?* he thought stubbornly. An extra half-mile would make no difference now—another ten minutes, at the most.

It was very disappointing when the lights of the city vanished. Armstrong had not remembered the hill that the road was skirting; perhaps it was only a low ridge, scarcely noticeable in the daytime. But by hiding the lights of the port it had taken away his chief talisman and left him again at the mercy of his fears.

Very unreasonably, his intelligence told him, he began to think how horrible it would be if anything happened now, so near the end of the journey. He kept the worst of his fears at bay for a while, hoping desperately that the lights of the city would soon reappear. But as the minutes dragged on, he realized that the ridge must be longer than he imagined. He tried to cheer himself by the thought that the city would be all the nearer when he saw it again, but somehow logic seemed to have failed him now. For presently he found himself doing something he had not stooped to, even out in the waste by Carver's Pass.

He stopped, turned slowly round, and with bated breath listened until his lungs were nearly bursting.

The silence was uncanny, considering how near he must be to the port. There was certainly no sound from behind him. Of course there wouldn't be, he told himself angrily. But he was immensely relieved. The thought of that faint and insistent clicking had been haunting him for the last hour.

So friendly and familiar was the noise that did reach him at last that the anticlimax almost made him laugh aloud. Drifting through the still air from a source clearly not more than a mile away came the sound of a landing-field tractor, perhaps one of the machines loading the *Canopus* itself. In a matter of seconds, thought Armstrong, he would be around this ridge with the port only a few hundred yards ahead. The journey was nearly ended. In a few moments, this evil plain would be no more than a fading nightmare.

It seemed terribly unfair: so little time, such a small fraction of a human life, was all he needed now. But the gods have always been unfair to man, and now they were enjoying their little jest. For there could be no mistaking the rattle of monstrous claws in the darkness *ahead of him.*

Protected Species

H. B. FYFE

The yellow star, of which Torang was the second planet, shone hotly down on the group of men viewing the half-built dam from the heights above. At a range of eighty million miles the effect was quite Terran, the star being somewhat smaller than Sol.

For Jeff Otis, fresh from a hop through space from the extra-bright star that was the other component of the binary system, the heat was enervating. The shorts and light shirt supplied him by the planet coordinator were soaked with perspiration. He mopped his forehead and turned to his host.

"Very nice job, Finchley," he complimented. "It's easy to see you have things well in hand here."

Finchley grinned sparingly. He had a broad, hard, flat face with tight lips and mere slits of blue eyes. Otis had been trying ever since the previous morning to catch a revealing expression on it.

He was uneasily aware that his own features were too frank and open for an inspector of colonial installations. For one thing, he had too many lines and hollows in his face, a result of being chronically underweight from space-hopping among the sixteen planets of the binary system.

Otis noticed that Finchley's aides were eyeing him furtively.

"Yes, Finchley," he repeated to break the little silence, "you're doing very well on the hydroelectric end. When are you going to show me the capital city you're laying out?"

"We can fly over there now," answered Finchley. "We have tentative boundaries laid out below those pre-colony ruins we saw from the 'copter."

"Oh, yes. You know, I meant to remark as we flew over that they looked a good deal like similar remnants on some of the other planets."

He caught himself as Finchley's thin lips tightened a trifle more. The coordinator was obviously trying to be patient and polite to an official from whom he hoped to get a good report, but Otis could see he would much rather be going about his business of building up the colony.

He could hardly blame Finchley, he decided. It was the fifth planetary system Terrans had found in their expansion into space, and there would be bigger jobs ahead for a man with a record of successful accomplishments. Civilization was reaching out to the stars at last. Otis supposed that he, too, was some sort of pioneer, although he usually was too busy to feel like one.

"Well, I'll show you some photos later," he said. "Right now, we—say, why all that jet-burning down there?"

In the gorge below, men had dropped their tools and seemed to be charging toward a common focal point. Excited yells carried thinly up the cliffs.

"Ape hunt, probably," guessed one of Finchley's engineers.

"Ape?" asked Otis, surprised.

"Not exactly," corrected Finchley patiently. "That's common slang for what we mention in reports as

Torangs. They look a little like big, skinny, gray apes; but they're the only life large enough to name after the planet."

Otis stared down into the gorge. Most of the running men had given up and were straggling back to their work. Two or three, brandishing pistols, continued running and disappeared around a bend.

"Never catch him now," commented Finchley's pilot.

"Do you just let them go running off whenever they feel like it?" Otis inquired.

Finchley met his curious gaze stolidly.

"I'm in favor of anything that will break the monotony, Mr. Otis. We have a problem of morale, you know. This planet is a key colony, and I like to keep the work going smoothly.

"Yes, I suppose there isn't much for recreation yet."

"Exactly. I don't see the sport in it myself but I let them. We're up to schedule."

"Ahead, if anything," Otis placated him. "Well, now, about the city?"

Finchley led the way to the helicopter. The pilot and Otis waited while he had a final word with his engineers, then they all climbed in and were off.

Later, hovering over the network of crude roads being leveled by Finchley's bulldozers, Otis admitted aloud that the location was well-chosen. It lay along a long, narrow bay that thrust in from the distant ocean to gather the waters of the same river that was being dammed some miles upstream.

"Those cliffs over there," Finchley pointed out, "were raised up since the end of whatever civilization used to be here—so my geologist tells me. We can fly back that way, and you can see how the ancient city was once at the head of the bay."

The pilot climbed and headed over the cliffs. Otis saw that these formed the edge of a plateau. At one point their continuity was marred by a deep gouge.

"Where the river ran thousands of years ago," Finchley explained.

They reached a point from which the outlines of the ruined city were easily discerned. From the air, Otis knew, they were undoubtedly plainer than if he had been among them.

"Must have been a pretty large place," he remarked. "Any idea what sort of beings built it or what happened to them?"

"Haven't had time for that yet," Finchley said. "Some boys from the exploration staff poke around in there every so often. Best current theory seems to be that it belonged to the Torangs."

"The *animals* they were hunting before?" asked Otis.

"Might be. Can't say for sure, but the diggers found signs the city took more of a punch than just an earthquake. Claim they found too much evidence of fires, exploded missiles, and warfare in general—other places as well as here. So . . . we've been guessing the Torangs are degenerate descendants of the survivors of some interplanetary brawl."

Otis considered that.

"Sounds plausible," he admitted, "but you ought to do something to make sure you are right."

"Why?"

"If it *is* the case, you'll have to stop your men from hunting them; degenerate or not, the Colonial Commission has regulations about contact with any local inhabitants."

Finchley turned his head to scowl at Otis, and controlled himself with an obvious effort.

"Those *apes*?" he demanded.

"Well, how can you tell? Ever try to contact them?"

"Yes! At first, that is; before we figured them for animals."

"And?"

"Couldn't get near one!" Finchley declared heatedly. "If they had any sort of half-intelligent culture, wouldn't they let us make *some* sort of contact?"

"Offhand," admitted Otis, "I should think so. How about setting down a few minutes? I'd like a look at the ruins."

Finchley glared at his wristwatch, but directed the pilot to land in a cleared spot. The young man brought them down neatly and the two officials alighted.

Otis, glancing around, saw where the archeologists had been digging. They had left their implements stacked casually at the site—the air was dry up here, and who was there to steal a shovel?

He left Finchley and strolled around a mound of dirt that had been cleared away from an entrance to one of the buildings. The latter had been built of stone, or at least faced with it. A peep into the dim excavation led him to believe there had been a steel framework, but the whole affair had been collapsed as if by an explosion.

He walked a little way farther and reached a section of presumably taller buildings where the stone ruins thrust above the sandy surface. After he had wandered through one or two arched openings that seemed to have been windows, he understood why the explorers had chosen to dig for their information. If any covering or decoration had ever graced the walls, it had

103

long since been weathered off. As for ceiling or roof, nothing remained.

"Must have been a highly developed civilization just the same," he muttered.

A movement at one of the shadowed openings to his right caught his eye. He did not remember noticing Finchley leave the helicopter to follow him, but he was glad of a guide.

"Don't you think so?" he added.

He turned his head, but Finchley was not there. In fact, now that Otis was aware of his surroundings, he could hear the voices of the other two mumbling distantly back by the aircraft.

"Seeing things!" he grumbled, and started through the ancient window.

Some instinct stopped him half a foot outside.

Come on, Jeff, he told himself, *don't be silly! What could be there? Ghosts?*

On the other hand, he realized, there were times when it was just as well to rely upon instinct—at least until you figured out the origin of the strange feeling. Any spaceman would agree to that. The man who developed an animal's sixth sense was the man who lived longest on alien planets.

He thought he must have paused a full minute or more, during which he had heard not the slightest sound except the mutter of voices to the rear. He peered into the chamber, which was about twenty feet square and well if not brightly lit by reflected light.

Nothing was to be seen, but when he found himself turning his head stealthily to peer over his shoulder, he decided that the queer sensation along the back of his neck meant something.

Wait now, he thought swiftly. *I didn't see quite the whole room.*

The flooring was heaped with wind-bared rubble that would not show footprints. He felt much more comfortable to notice himself thinking in that vein.

At least I'm not imagining ghosts, he thought.

Bending forward the necessary foot, he thrust his head through the opening and darted a quick look to the left, then to the right along the wall. As he turned right, his glance was met directly by a pair of very wide-set black eyes that shifted inward slightly as they got his range.

105

The Torang about matched his own six feet two, mainly because of elongated, gibbonlike limbs and a similarly crouching stance. Arms and legs, covered with short, curly gray fur, had the same general proportions as human limbs, but looked half again too long for a trunk that seemed to be ribbed all the way down. The shoulder and hip joints were compactly lean, rather as if the Torang had developed on a world of lesser gravity than that of the human.

It was the face that made Otis stare. The mouth was toothless and probably constructed more for sucking than for chewing. But the eyes! They projected like ends of a dumbbell from each side of the narrow skull where the ears should have been, and focused with obvious mobility. Peering closer, Otis saw tiny ears below the eyes, almost hidden in the curling fur of the neck.

He realized abruptly that his own eyes felt as if they were bulging out, although he could not remember having changed his expression of casual curiosity. His back was getting stiff also. He straightened up carefully.

"Uh . . . hello," he murmured, feeling unutterably silly but conscious of some impulse to compromise between a tone of greeting for another human being and one of pacification to an animal.

The Torang moved then, swiftly but unhurriedly. In fact, Otis later decided, deliberately. One of the long arms swept downward to the rubble-strewn ground.

The next instant, Otis jerked his head back out of the opening as a stone whizzed past in front of his nose.

"Hey!" he protested involuntarily.

There was a scrabbling sound from within, as of animal claws churning to a fast start among the pebbles. Recovering his balance, Otis charged recklessly through the entrance.

"I don't know why," he admitted to Finchley a few minutes later. "If I stopped to think how I might have had my skull bashed in coming through, I guess I'd have just backed off and yelled for you."

Finchley nodded, but his narrow gaze seemed faintly approving for the first time since they had met.

"He was gone, of course," Otis continued. "I barely caught a glimpse of his rump vanishing through another window."

"Yeah, they're pretty fast," put in Finchley's pilot. "In the time we've been here, the boys haven't taken more than half a dozen. Got a stuffed one over at headquarters, though."

"Hmmm," murmured Otis thoughtfully.

From their other remarks, he learned that he had not noticed everything, even though face to face with the creature. Finchley's mentioning the three digits of the hands and feet, for instance, came as a surprise.

Otis was silent most of the flight back to headquarters. Once there, he disappeared with a perfunctory excuse toward the rooms assigned him.

That evening, at a dinner that Finchley had made as attractive as was possible in a comparatively raw and new colony, Otis was noticeably sociable. The coordinator was gratified.

"Looks as if they finally sent us a regular guy," he remarked behind his hand to one of his assistants. "Round up a couple of the prettier secretaries to keep him happy."

"I understand he nearly laid hands on a Torang up at the diggings," said the other.

"Yep, ran right at it bare-handed. Came as close to bagging it as anybody could, I suppose."

"Maybe it's just as well he didn't," commented the assistant. "They're big enough to mess up an unarmed man some."

Otis, meanwhile and for the rest of the evening, was assiduously busy making acquaintances. So engrossed was he in turning every new conversation to the Torangs and asking seemingly casual questions about the little known of their habits and possible past, that he hardly noticed receiving any special attention. As a visiting inspector, he was used to attempts to entertain and distract him.

The next morning, he caught Finchley at his office in the sprawling one-story structure of concrete and glass that was colonial headquarters.

After accepting a chair across the desk from the co-ordinator, Otis told him his conclusions. Finchley's narrow eyes opened a trifle when he heard the details. His wide, hard-muscled face became slightly pink.

"Oh, for —! I mean, Otis, why must you make something big out of it? The men very seldom bag one anyway!"

"Perhaps because they're so rare," answered Otis calmly. "How do we know they're not intelligent life? Maybe if you were hanging on in the ruins of your ancestors' civilization, reduced to a primitive state, *you'd* be just as wary of a bunch of loud Terrans moving in!"

Finchley shrugged. He looked vaguely uncomfortable, as if debating whether Otis or some disgruntled sportsman from his husky construction crews would be easier to handle.

"Think of the overall picture a minute," Otis urged. "We're pushing out into space at last, after centuries of dreams and struggles. With all the misery we've seen in various colonial systems at home, we've tried to plan these ventures so as to avoid old mistakes."

Finchley nodded grudgingly. Otis could see that his mind was on the progress charts of his many projects.

"It stands to reason," the inspector went on, "that some day we'll find a planet with intelligent life. We're still new in space, but as we probe farther out it's bound to happen. That's why the Commission drew up rules about native life forms. Or have you read that part of the code lately?"

Finchley shifted from side to side in his chair.

"Now, look!" he protested. "Don't go making *me* out a hard-boiled vandal with nothing in mind but exterminating everything that moves on all Torang. *I* don't go out hunting the apes!"

"I know, I know," Otis soothed him. "But before the Colonial Commission will sanction any destruction of indigenous life, we'll have to show—*besides* that it's not intelligent—that it exists in sufficient numbers to avoid extinction."

"What do you expect me to do about it?"

Otis regarded him with some sympathy. Finchley was the hard-bitten type the Commission needed to oversee the first breaking-in of a colony on a strange planet, but he was not unreasonable. He merely wanted to be left alone to handle the tough job facing him.

"Announce a ban on hunting Torangs," Otis said. "There must be something else they can go after."

"Oh, yes," admitted Finchley. "There are swarms of little rabbit-things and other vermin running through the brush. But, I don't know —"

"It's standard practice," Otis reminded him. "We have many a protected species even back on Terra that would be extinct by now, but for the game laws."

In the end they agreed that Finchley would do his honest best to enforce a ban, provided Otis obtained a formal order from the headquarters of the system. The inspector went from the office straight to the communications center, where he filed a long report for the chief coordinator's office in the other part of the binary system.

It took some hours for the reply to reach Torang. When it came that afternoon, he went looking for Finchley.

He found the coordinator inspecting a newly finished canning factory on the coast, elated at the completion of one more link in making the colony self-sustaining.

"Here it is," said Otis, waving the message copy. "Signed by the chief himself. 'As of this date, the apelike beings known as Torangs, indigenous to planet number and so forth, are to be considered a rare and protected species under regulations and so forth et cetera.'"

"Good enough," answered Finchley with an amiable shrug. "Give it here, and I'll have it put on the public address system and the bulletin boards."

Otis returned satisfied to the helicopter that had brought him out from headquarters.

"Back, sir?" asked the pilot.

"Yes . . . *no!* Just for fun, take me out to the old city. I never did get a good look the other day, and I'd like to before I leave."

They flew over the plains between the sea and the upjutting cliffs. In the distance Otis caught a glimpse of the rising dam he had been shown the day before. This colony would go well, he reflected, as long as he checked up on details like preserving native life forms.

Eventually the pilot landed at the same spot he had been taken to on his previous visit to the ancient ruins. Someone else was on the scene today. Otis saw a pair of men he took to be archeologists.

"I'll just wander around a bit," he told the pilot.

He noticed the two men looking at him from where they stood by the shovels and other equipment, so he paused to say hello. As he thought, they had been digging in the ruins.

"Taking some measurements, in fact," said the sunburned blond introduced as Hoffman. "Trying to get a line on what sort of things built the place."

"Oh?" said Otis, interested. "What's the latest theory?"

"Not so much different from us," Hoffman told the inspector while his partner left them to pick up another load of artifacts.

"Judging from the size of the rooms, height of doorways, and such stuff as stairways," he went on, "they were pretty much our size. So far, of course, it's only a rough estimate."

"Could be ancestors of the Torangs, eh?" asked Otis.

"Very possible, sir," answered Hoffman, with a promptness that suggested it was his own view. "But we haven't dug up enough to guess at the type of culture they had, or draw any conclusions as to their psychology or social customs."

Otis nodded, thinking that he ought to mention the young fellow's name to Finchley before he left Torang. He

111

excused himself as the other man returned with a box of some sort of scraps the pair had unearthed, and strolled between the outlines of the untouched buildings.

In a few minutes he came to the section of higher structures where he had encountered the Torang the previous day.

"Wonder if I should look in the same spot?" he muttered aloud. "No . . . that would be the *last* place the thing would return to . . . unless it had a lair thereabouts –"

He stopped to get his bearings, then shrugged and walked around a mound of rubble toward what he believed to be the proper building.

Pretty sure this was it, he mused. *Yes, shadows around that window arch look the same . . . same time of day —*

He halted, almost guiltily, and looked back to make sure no one was observing his return to the scene of his little adventure. After all, an inspector of colonial installations was not supposed to run around ghost-hunting like a small boy.

Finding himself alone, he stepped briskly through the crumbling arch—*and froze in his tracks.*

"I am honored to know you," said the Torang in a mild, rather buzzing voice. "We thought you possibly would return here."

Otis gaped. The black eyes projecting from the sides of the narrow head tracked him up and down, giving him the unpleasant sensation of being measured for an artillery salvo.

"I am known as Jal-Ganyr," said the Torang. "Unless I am given incorrect data, you are known as Jeff-Otis. That is so."

The last statement was made with almost no inflection, but some still-functioning corner of Otis's mind interpreted it as a question. He sucked in a deep breath, suddenly conscious of having forgotten to breathe for a moment.

"I didn't know . . . yes, that is so . . . I didn't know you Torangs could speak Terran. Or anything else. How —?"

He hesitated as a million questions boiled up in his mind to be asked. Jal-Ganyr absently stroked the gray fur of his chest with his three-fingered left hand, squatting patiently on a flat rock. Otis felt somehow that he had been allowed to waste time mumbling only by grace of disciplined politeness.

"I am not of the Torangs," said Jal-Ganyr in his wheezing voice. "I am of the Myrbs. You would possibly say Myrbii. I have not been informed."

"You mean that is your name for yourselves?" asked Otis.

Jal-Ganyr seemed to consider, his mobile eyes swiveling inward to scan the Terran's face.

"More than that," he said at last, when he had thought it over. "I mean I am of the race originating at Myrb, not of this planet."

"Before we go any further," insisted Otis, "tell me, at least, how you learned our language!"

Jal-Ganyr made a fleeting gesture. His "face" was unreadable to the Terran, but Otis had the impression he had received the equivalent of a smile and a shrug.

"As to that," said the Myrb, "I possibly learned it before you did. We have observed you a very long time. You would unbelieve how long."

"But then —" Otis paused. That must mean before the colonists had landed on this planet. He was half afraid it might mean before they had reached this sun system. He put aside the thought and asked, "But then, why do you live like this among the ruins? Why wait till now? If you had communicated, you could have had our help rebuilding —"

He let his voice trail off, wondering what sounded wrong. Jal-Ganyr rolled his eyes about leisurely, as if disdaining the surrounding ruins. Again, he seemed to consider all the implications of Otis's questions.

"We picked up your message to your chief," he answered at last. "We decided time is to communicate with one of you.

"We have no interest in rebuilding," he added. "We have concealed quarters for ourselves."

Otis found that his lips were dry from his unconsciously having let his mouth hang open. He moistened them with the tip of his tongue and relaxed enough to lean against the wall.

"You mean my getting the ruling to proclaim you a protected species?" he asked. "You have instruments to intercept such signals?"

"I do. We have," said Jal-Ganyr simply. "It has been decided that you have expanded far enough into space to make necessary we contact a few of the thoughtful among you. It will possibly make easier in the future for our observers."

Otis wondered how much of that was irony. He felt himself flushing at the memory of the "stuffed specimen" at headquarters, and was peculiarly relieved that he had not gone to see it.

I've had the luck, he told himself. *I'm the one to discover the first known intelligent beings beyond Sol!*

Aloud, he said, "We expected to meet someone like you eventually. But why have you chosen me?"

The question sounded vain, he realized, but it brought unexpected results.

"Your message. You made in a little way the same decision we made in a big way. We deduce that you are one to understand our regret and shame at what happened between our races . . . long ago."

"Between —?"

"Yes. For a long time, we thought you were all gone. We are pleased to see you returning to some of your old planets."

Otis stared blankly. Some instinct must have enabled the Myrb to interpret his bewildered expression. He apologized briefly.

"I possibly forgot to explain the ruins." Again, Jal-Ganyr's eyes swiveled slowly about.

"They are not ours," he said mildly. "They are yours."

The Cage

A. BERTRAM CHANDLER

Imprisonment is always a humiliating experience, no matter how philosophical the prisoner. Imprisonment by one's own kind is bad enough—but one can, at least, talk to one's captors, one can make one's wants understood; one can, on occasion, appeal to them man to man.

Imprisonment is doubly humiliating when one's captors, in all honesty, treat one as a lower animal.

The party from the survey ship could, perhaps, be excused for failing to recognize the survivors from the interstellar liner *Lode Star* as rational beings. At least two hundred days had passed since their landing on the planet without a name—an unintentional landing made when *Lode Star*'s Ehrenhaft generators, driven far in excess of their normal capacity by a breakdown of the electronic regulator, had flung her far from the regular shipping lanes to an unexplored region of space. *Lode Star* had landed safely enough; but shortly thereafter (troubles never come singly) her pile had gone out of control and her captain had ordered his first mate to evacuate the passengers and those crew members not needed to cope with the emergency, and to get them as far from the ship as possible.

Hawkins and his charges were well clear when there was a flare of released energy, a not very violent explosion. The survivors wanted to turn to watch, but Hawkins drove them on with curses and, at times, blows. Luckily they were upwind from the ship and so escaped the fallout.

When the fireworks seemed to be over, Hawkins, accompanied by Dr. Boyle, the ship's surgeon, returned to the scene of the disaster. The two men, wary of radioactivity, were cautious and stayed a safe distance from the shallow, still-smoking crater that marked where the ship had been. It was all too obvious to them that the captain, together with his officers and technicians, was now no more than an infinitesimal part of the incandescent cloud that had mushroomed up into the low overcast.

Thereafter the fifty-odd men and women, the survivors of *Lode Star*, had degenerated. It hadn't been a fast process—Hawkins and Boyle, aided by a committee of the more responsible passengers, had fought a stout rearguard action. But it had been a hopeless sort of fight. The climate was against them, for a start. Hot it was, always in the neighborhood of 85° Fahrenheit. And it was wet—a thin, warm drizzle falling all the time. The air seemed to abound with the spores of fungi—luckily these did not attack living skin but throve on dead organic matter, on clothing. They throve to an only slightly lesser degree on metals and on the synthetic fabrics that many of the castaways wore.

Danger, outside danger, would have helped to maintain morale. But there were no dangerous animals. There were only little smooth-skinned things, not unlike frogs, that hopped through the sodden undergrowth, and, in the numerous rivers, fishlike creatures ranging in size from shark to tadpole, and all of them possessing the bellicosity of the latter.

Food had been no problem after the first few hungry hours. Volunteers had tried a large, succulent fungus growing on the boles of the huge fernlike trees. They had pronounced it good. After a lapse of five hours they had neither died nor even complained of abdominal pains. That fungus was to become the staple diet of the castaways. In the weeks that followed other fungi had been found, and berries, and roots—all of them edible. They provided a welcome variety.

Fire—in spite of the all-pervading heat—was the blessing most missed by the castaways. With it they could have supplemented their diet by catching and cooking the little frog-things of the rain forest, the fishes of the streams. Some of the hardier spirits did eat these animals raw, but they were frowned upon by most of the other members of the community. Too, fire would have helped to drive back the darkness of the long nights, would, by its real warmth and light, have dispelled the illusion of cold produced by the ceaseless dripping of water from every leaf and frond.

When they fled from the ship, most of the survivors had possessed pocket lighters—but the lighters had been lost when the pockets, together with the clothing surrounding them, had disintegrated. In any case, all attempts to start a fire in the days when there were still pocket lighters had failed—there was not, Hawkins swore, a single dry spot on the whole accursed planet. Now the making of fire was quite impossible: even if there had been present an expert on the rubbing together of two dry sticks he could have found no material with which to work.

They made their permanent settlement on the crest of a low hill. (There were, so far as they could discover, no mountains.) It was less thickly wooded there than the surrounding plains, and the ground was less marshy underfoot. They succeeded in wrenching fronds from the fern-like trees and built for themselves crude shelters—more for the sake of privacy than for any comfort that they afforded. They clung, with a certain desperation, to the governmental forms of the worlds that they had left, and elected themselves a council. Boyle, the ship's surgeon, was their chief. Hawkins, rather to his surprise, was returned as a council member by a majority of only two votes—on thinking it over he realized that many of the passengers must still bear a grudge against the ship's executive staff for their present predicament.

The first council meeting was held in a hut—if so it could be called—especially constructed for the purpose. The council members squatted in a rough circle. Boyle, the president, got slowly to his feet. Hawkins grinned wryly as he compared the surgeon's nudity with the pomposity that he seemed to have assumed with his elected rank, as he compared the man's dignity with the unkempt appearance presented by his uncut, uncombed gray hair, his uncombed and straggling gray beard.

"Ladies and gentlemen," began Boyle.

Hawkins looked around him at the naked, pallid bodies, at the stringy, lusterless hair, the long, dirty fingernails of the men and the unpainted lips of the women. He thought, I don't suppose I look much like an officer and a gentleman myself.

"Ladies and gentlemen," said Boyle, "we have been, as you know, elected to represent the human community upon this planet. I suggest that at this, our first meeting, we discuss our chances of survival—not as individuals, but as a race —"

"I'd like to ask Mr. Hawkins what our chances are of being picked up," shouted one of the two women members, a dried-up, spinsterish creature with prominent ribs and vertebrae.

"Slim," said Hawkins. "As you know, no communication is possible with other ships or with planet stations when the Interstellar Drive is operating. When we snapped out of the Drive and came in for our landing we sent out a distress call—but we couldn't say where we were. Furthermore, we don't know that the call was received —"

"Miss Taylor," said Boyle huffily, "Mr. Hawkins, I would remind you that I am the duly elected president of this council. There will be time for a general discussion later.

"As most of you may already have assumed, the age of this planet, biologically speaking, corresponds roughly with that of Earth during the Carboniferous Era. As we know, no species yet exists to challenge our supremacy. By the time such a species does emerge— something analogous to the giant lizards of Earth's Triassic Era—we should be well established —"

"*We* shall be dead!" called one of the men.

"We shall be dead," agreed the doctor, "but our descendants will be very much alive. We have to decide how to give them as good a start as possible. Language we shall bequeath to them —"

"Never mind the language, Doc," called the other woman member. She was a small blonde, slim, with a hard face. "It's just this question of descendants that I'm here to look after. I represent the women of childbearing age—there are, as you must know, fifteen of us here. So far the girls have been very, very careful.

We have reason to be. Can you, as a medical man, guarantee—bearing in mind that you have no drugs, no instruments—safe deliveries? Can you guarantee that our children will have a good chance of survival?"

Boyle dropped his pomposity like a worn-out garment.

"I'll be frank," he said. "I have, as you, Miss Hart, have pointed out, neither drugs nor instruments. But I can assure you, Miss Hart, that your chances of a safe delivery are far better than they would have been on Earth during, say, the eighteenth century. And I'll tell you why. On this planet, so far as we know (and we have been here long enough now to find out the hard way), there exist no microorganisms harmful to man. Did such organisms exist, the bodies of those of us still surviving would be, by this time, mere masses of suppuration. Most of us, of course, would have died of septicemia long ago. And that, I think, answers *both* your questions."

"I haven't finished yet," she said. "Here's another point. There are fifty-three of us here, men and women. There are ten married couples—so we'll count them out. That leaves thirty-three people, of whom twenty are men. Twenty men to thirteen (aren't we girls always unlucky?) women. All of us aren't young—but we're all of us women. What sort of marriage set-up will we have? Monogamy? Polyandry?"

"Monogamy, of course," said a tall, thin man sharply. He was the only one of those present who wore clothing—if it could be called that. The disintegrating fronds lashed around his waist with a strand of vine did little to serve any useful purpose.

"All right, then," said the girl. "Monogamy; I rather prefer it that way myself. But I warn you that if that's the way we play it there's going to be trouble. And in any murder involving passion and jealousy the woman is as liable to be a victim as either of the men—and I don't want *that*."

"What do you propose, then, Miss Hart?" asked Boyle.

"Just this, Doc. When it comes to our mating we leave love out of it. If two men want to marry the same woman, then let them fight it out. The best man gets the girl—and keeps her."

"Natural selection . . ." murmured the surgeon. "I'm in favor—but we must put it to the vote."

At the crest of the hill was a shallow depression, a natural arena. Around the rim sat the castaways—all but four of them. One of the four was Dr. Boyle—he had discovered that his duties as president embraced those of a referee; it had been held that he was best competent to judge when one of the contestants was liable to suffer permanent damage. Another of the four was the girl Mary Hart. She had found a serrated twig with which to comb her long hair, had contrived a wreath of yellow flowers with which to crown the victor. Was it, wondered Hawkins as he sat with the other council members, a hankering after an early wedding ceremony, or was it a harking back to something older and darker?

"A pity that these blasted molds got our watches," said the fat man on Hawkins' right. "If we had any means of telling the time we could have rounds, make a proper prizefight of it."

Hawkins nodded. He looked at the four in the center of the arena—at the strutting, barbaric woman, at the pompous old man, at the two dark-bearded young men with their glistening white bodies. He knew them both—Fennet had been a Senior Cadet of the ill-fated *Lode Star*; Clemens, at least seven years Fennet's senior, was a passenger, had been a prospector on the frontier worlds.

"If we had anything to bet with," said the fat man happily, "I'd lay it on Clemens. That cadet of yours hasn't a snowball's chance in hell. He's been brought up to fight clean—Clemens has been brought up to fight dirty."

"Fennet's in better condition," said Hawkins. "He's been taking exercise, while Clemens has just been lying around sleeping and eating. Look at the paunch on him!"

"There's nothing wrong with good healthy flesh and muscle," said the fat man, patting his own paunch.

"No gouging, no biting!" called the doctor. "And may the best man win!"

He stepped back smartly, away from the contestants, stood with the Hart woman.

There was an air of embarrassment about the pair of them as they stood there, each with his fists hanging at his sides. Each seemed to be regretting that matters had come to such a pass.

"Go *on*!" screamed Mary Hart at last. "Don't you want me? You'll live to a ripe old age here—and it'll be lonely with no woman!"

"They can always wait around until your daughters grow up, Mary!" shouted one of her friends.

"If I ever have any daughters!" she called. "I shan't at this rate!"

"Go on!" shouted the crowd. "Go on!"

Fennet made a start. He stepped forward almost diffidently, jabbed with his right fist at Clemens's unprotected face. It wasn't a hard blow, but it must have been painful. Clemens put his hand up to his nose, brought it away, and stared at the bright blood staining it. He growled, lumbered forward with arms open to hug and crush. The cadet danced back, scoring twice more with his right.

"Why doesn't he *hit* him?" demanded the fat man.

"And break every bone in his fist? They aren't wearing gloves, you know," said Hawkins.

Fennet decided to make a stand. He stood firm, his feet slightly apart, and brought his right into play once more. This time he left his opponent's face alone, went for his belly instead. Hawkins was surprised to see that the prospector was taking the blows with apparent equanimity—he must be, he decided, much tougher in actuality than in appearance.

The cadet sidestepped smartly . . . and slipped on the wet grass. Clemens fell heavily on to his opponent; Hawkins could hear the *whoosh* as the air was forced from the lad's lungs. The prospector's thick arms encircled Fennet's body—and Fennet's knee came up viciously to Clemens's groin. The prospector squealed, but hung on grimly. One of his hands was around Fennet's throat now, and the other one, its fingers viciously hooked, was clawing for the cadet's eyes.

"No gouging!" Boyle was screaming. "No gouging!"

He dropped down to his knees, caught Clemens's wrist with both his hands.

Something made Hawkins look up. It may have been a sound, although this is doubtful; the spectators were behaving like boxing fans at a prizefight. They could hardly be blamed—this was the first piece of real excitement that had come their way since the loss of the ship. It may have been a sound that made Hawkins look up, it may have been the sixth sense possessed by all good spacemen. What he saw made him cry out.

Hovering above the arena was a helicopter. There was something about the design of it, a subtle oddness, that told Hawkins that this was no earthly machine. From its smooth, shining belly dropped a net, seemingly of dull metal. It enveloped the struggling figures on the ground, trapped the doctor and Mary Hart.

Hawkins shouted again—a wordless cry. He jumped to his feet, ran to the assistance of his ensnared companions. The net seemed to be alive. It twisted itself around his wrists, bound his ankles. Others of the castaways rushed to aid Hawkins.

"Keep away!" he shouted. "Scatter!"

The low drone of the helicopter's rotors rose in pitch. The machine lifted. In an incredibly short space of time the arena was to the first mate's eyes no more than a pale green saucer in which little white ants scurried aimlessly. Then the flying machine was above and through the base of the low clouds, and there was nothing to be seen but drifting whiteness.

When, at last, it made its descent, Hawkins was not surprised to see the silvery tower of a great spaceship standing among the low trees on a level plateau.

The world to which they were taken would have been a marked improvement on the world they had left, had it not been for the mistaken kindness of their captors. The cage in which the three men were housed duplicated, with remarkable fidelity, the climatic condition of the planet upon which *Lode Star* had been lost. It was glassed in, and from sprinklers in its roof fell a steady drizzle of warm water. A couple of dispirited tree ferns provided little shelter from the depressing precipitation. Twice a day a hatch at the back of the cage, which was made of a sort of concrete, opened, and slabs of fungus remarkably similar to that on which they had been subsisting were thrown in. There was a hole in the floor of the cage; this the prisoners rightly assumed was for sanitary purposes.

On either side of them were other cages. In one of them was Mary Hart—alone. She could gesture to them, wave to them, and that was all. The cage on the other side held a beast built on the same general lines as a lobster, but with a strong resemblance to a kind of squid. Across the broad roadway they could see other cages, but not what they housed.

Hawkins, Boyle, and Fennet sat on the damp floor and stared through the thick glass and the bars at the beings outside who stared at them.

"If only they were humanoid," sighed the doctor. "If only they were the same shape as we are, we might make a start towards convincing them that we, too, are intelligent beings."

"They aren't the same shape," said Hawkins. "And we, were the situations reversed, would take some convincing that three six-legged beer barrels were men and brothers . . . Try Pythagoras' Theorem again," he said to the cadet.

Without enthusiasm the youth broke fronds from the nearest tree fern. He broke them into smaller pieces, then on the mossy floor laid them out in the design of a right-angled triangle with squares constructed on all three sides. The natives—a large one, one slightly smaller, and a little one—regarded him incuriously with their flat, dull eyes. The large one put the tip of a tentacle into a pocket—the things wore clothing—and pulled out a brightly colored packet, handing it to the little one. The little one tore off the wrapping and started stuffing pieces of some bright blue confection into the slot on its upper side that, obviously, served it as a mouth.

"I wish they were allowed to feed the animals," sighed Hawkins. "I'm sick of that damned fungus."

"Let's recapitulate," said the doctor. "After all, we've nothing else to do. We were taken from our camp by the helicopter—six of us. We were taken to the survey ship—a vessel that seemed in no way superior to our own interstellar ships. You assure us, Hawkins, that the ship used the Ehrenhaft Drive or something so near to it as to be its twin brother . . ."

"Correct," agreed Hawkins.

"On the ship we're kept in separate cages. There's no ill treatment, we're fed and watered at frequent intervals. We land on this strange planet, but we see nothing of it. We're hustled out of cages like so many cattle into a covered van. We know that we're being driven *somewhere*, that's all. The van stops, the door opens and a couple of these animated beer barrels poke in poles with smaller editions of those fancy nets on the end of them. They catch Clemens and Miss Taylor, drag them out. We never see them again. The rest of us spend the night and the following day and night in individual cages. The next day we're taken to this . . . zoo . . ."

"Do you think they were vivisected?" asked Fennet. "I never liked Clemens, but . . ."

"I'm afraid they were," said Boyle. "Our captors must have learned of the difference between the sexes by it. Unluckily, there's no way of determining intelligence by vivisection —"

"The filthy brutes!" shouted the cadet.

"Easy, son," counseled Hawkins. "You can't blame them, you know. We've vivisected animals a lot more like us than we are to these things."

"The problem," the doctor went on, "is to convince these things—as you call them, Hawkins—that we are rational beings like themselves. How would they define a rational being? How would *we* define a rational being?"

"Somebody who knows Pythagoras's Theorem," said the cadet sulkily.

"I read somewhere," said Hawkins, "that the history of man is the history of the fire-making, tool-using animal . . ."

"Then make fire," suggested the doctor. "Make us some tools, and use them."

"Don't be silly. You know that there's not an artifact among the bunch of us. No false teeth even—not even a metal filling. Even so . . ." He paused. "When I was a youngster there was, among the cadets in the interstellar ships, a revival of the old arts and crafts. We considered ourselves in a direct line of descent from the old windjammer sailormen, so we learned how to splice rope and wire, how to make sennit and fancy knots and all the rest of it. Then one of us hit on the idea of basketmaking. We were in a passenger ship, and we used to make our baskets secretly, daub them with violent colors, and then sell them to passengers as genuine souvenirs from the Lost Planet of Arcturus VI. There was a most distressing scene when the Old Man and the Mate found out . . ."

"What are you driving at?" asked the doctor.

"Just this. We will demonstrate our manual dexterity by the weaving of baskets—I'll teach you how."

"It might work . . ." said Boyle slowly. "It might just work . . . On the other hand, don't forget that certain birds and animals do the same sort of thing. On Earth there's the beaver, who builds quite cunning dams. There's the bowerbird, who makes a bower for his mate as part of the courtship ritual . . ."

The Head Keeper must have known of creatures whose courting habits resembled those of the Terran bowerbird. After three days of feverish basketmaking, which consumed all the bedding and stripped the tree ferns, Mary Hart was taken from her cage and put in with the three men. After she got over her hysterical pleasure at having somebody to talk to again she was rather indignant.

It was good, thought Hawkins drowsily, to have Mary with them. A few more days of solitary confinement would surely have driven the girl crazy. Even so, having Mary in the same cage had its drawbacks. He had to keep a watchful eye on young Fennet. He even had to keep a watchful eye on Boyle—the old goat!

Mary screamed.

Hawkins jerked into complete wakefulness. He could see the pale form of Mary—on this world it was never completely dark at night—and, on the other side of the cage, the forms of Fennet and Boyle. He got hastily to his feet, stumbled to the girl's side.

"What is it?" he asked.

"I . . . I don't know . . . Something small, with sharp claws . . . It ran over me . . ."

"Oh," said Hawkins, "that was only Joe."

"*Joe?*" she demanded.

"I don't know exactly what he—or she—is," said the man.

"I think he's definitely *he,*" said the doctor.

"What is Joe?" she asked again.

"He must be the local equivalent of a mouse," said the doctor, "although he looks nothing like one. He comes up through the floor somewhere to look for scraps of food. We're trying to tame him —"

"You encourage the brute?" she screamed. "I demand that you do something about him—at once! Poison him, or trap him. Now!"

"Tomorrow," said Hawkins.

"Now!" she screamed.

"Tomorrow," said Hawkins firmly.

The capture of Joe proved to be easy. Two flat baskets, hinged like the valves of an oyster shell, under the trap. There was bait inside—a large piece of the fungus. There was a cunningly arranged upright that would fall at the least tug at the bait. Hawkins, lying sleepless on his damp bed, heard the tiny click and thud that told him that the trap had been sprung. He heard Joe's indignant chitterings, heard the tiny claws scrabbling at the stout basketwork.

Mary Hart was asleep. He shook her.

"We've caught him," he said.

"Then kill him," she answered drowsily.

But Joe was not killed. The three men were rather attached to him. With the coming of daylight they transferred him to a cage that Hawkins had fashioned. Even the girl relented when she saw the harmless ball of multicolored fur bouncing indignantly up and down in its prison. She insisted on feeding the little animal, exclaiming gleefully when the thin tentacles reached out and took the fragment of fungus from her fingers.

For three days they made much of their pet. On the

fourth day beings whom they took to be keepers entered the cage with their nets, immobilized the occupants, and carried off Joe and Hawkins.

"I'm afraid it's hopeless," Boyle said. "He's gone the same way . . ."

"They'll have him stuffed and mounted in some museum," said Fennet glumly.

"No," said the girl. "They couldn't!"

"They could," said the doctor.

Abruptly the hatch at the back of the cage opened.

Before the three humans could retreat, a voice called, "It's all right, come on out!"

Hawkins walked into the cage. He was shaved, and the beginnings of a healthy tan had darkened the pallor of his skin. He was wearing a pair of trunks fashioned from some bright red material.

"Come on out," he said again. "Our hosts have apologized very sincerely, and they have more suitable accommodation prepared for us. Then, as soon as they have a ship ready, we're to go to pick up the other survivors."

"Not so fast," said Boyle. "Put us in the picture, will you? What made them realize that we were rational beings?"

Hawkins' face darkened.

"Only rational beings," he said, "put other beings in cages."

Intelligent Life Elsewhere

STEPHEN BOWKETT

W hat we took to be a rocky hill, ancient and crumbling, turned out to be a temple.

When my father realized what we were looking at—the sheer size and wonder of it—he cried. The whole band of us—Dad, Commander Keel, Lee-Ann and me, sat on the grassy slope looking down into the little valley: just staring as the thought sank in that, at last, mankind had discovered another intelligent civilization, far out on the very fringes of explored space.

We had traveled to the Sadalsuud System aboard the Research Ship *Anubis*. Dad had named her himself, after the Egyptian god who helped to preserve the remains of the dead. It seemed very apt, because Dad's work had always been as an archeologist for the Earth Cluster Exploration Organization. His whole life was one of discovery, of caring for races now vanished, of finding out *why*. During the past thirty years he had met with some success in discovering traces of primitive alien species, but this looked to be his greatest triumph yet. . . . I was proud to be his daughter.

"This is bound to be the crowning glory of your career, Professor Spring," said Keel. He was the military administrator assigned to our expedition. Keel was a huge man, clad in battle gray, the left side of his body a mass of gleaming bionics. I guessed that he did not care one way or the other about Dad's career. Keel was only interested in expanding Earth's frontiers in space—and making sure no one stood in the way of that aim. I despised him as much as I admired my father.

Dad nodded slowly and got to his feet. "Yes, thank you, Commander. Perhaps it will. At least now I ought to be able to get funding from the ECEO to mount a full-scale excavation of the site."

"It's very exciting," added Lee-Ann. She was Dad's most brilliant student, doing field work with us as part of her studies in offworld archeology at Beijing University. Lee-Ann was small and delicate, with beautiful blue-black hair and eyes the color of opals. I'm sure she loved and respected my father almost as much as I did. He certainly admired her . . . which sometimes made me just the tiniest bit envious . . .

Lee-Ann suddenly turned to me with one of her beaming, charming smiles. "You must be very proud, Becky. What a marvelous time we'll all have exploring this place!"

And she was so thrilled, she clapped her hands together and jumped up and down, like a little girl going to the seaside.

"The knowbots must go in first," Keel said, making the suggestion sound like a demand. And, even as he spoke, his internal electronics issued their instructions, and a swarm of sleek black machines swished overhead and sped down towards the temple.

"Knowbots," as we called them, were smart machines; seek-and-scan robots with the ability to decide for themselves whether to move forward, fight, run, or self-destruct. Dad hated them. They were used by the military and had nothing to do with the scientific purpose of the expedition. Their usual job was just to see if it was safe to send soldiers into a war zone.

Not to be outdone, my father used his wrist-keypad to transmit instructions to our three videodroids, Eeny, Meeny, and Miny. Their function was simply to look, to photograph, to sample the air and radiation background, and a hundred other things that would help us to form an impression of what lay inside the huge and ancient building. The videodroids were tools for exploration, nothing more.

They glided by moments later like bright silver dragonflies, winging down through the warm summer afternoon to disappear into the shadows of the temple. We used our laptop holoscreens (which we nicknamed "handscreens") to pick up what the 'droids were seeing. And the pictures were utterly breathtaking. There were decaying towers and minarets, massive stone walls that seemed built to last for eternity; strange metal carvings and twisted sculptures, melted by centuries of rain.

"Just look at that . . ." breathed Carl, Dad's assistant, shaking his head in amazement and disbelief. Now on the monitors there loomed the statue of a beast, as powerful as a lion but fifty times larger. A single spiral horn jutted out from its forehead, like a unicorn's horn, and its alien eyes were made of glittering blue jewels the size of my body.

"I've got the strangest feeling it's looking at me," Lee-Ann whispered, faintly afraid. "Haven't you?"

"Its eyes are so real . . . staring . . ."

"They're certainly staring at *something*," Dad added, and he frowned, rubbing his chin. "Meeny, swing one-eighty degrees and dip to scan the woodland floor, please."

I grinned, as I always did when my father said please to a 'droid.

Meeny did as he was told, pivoting on his jets, swooping low to look at the ground.

Something glimmered there, we saw; something all but covered by leaves, tantalizingly hidden from view.

Dad keyed in another command. Eeny appeared and began to sweep across the clearing, the downdraft from the jets blasting leaves and twigs and earth aside. Gradually, the whole area in front of the lion-unicorn turned silver as a huge metallic expanse of floor was revealed.

"Look there!" Carl yelped in his astonishment. "It's a mass of writing!"

"Runic . . . Symbolic . . ." Dad pressed for a hard copy from his laptop, then set to work on the symbols at once with a stylus. "Now if I can just decode the major characters . . ."

I looked across at Carl and Lee-Ann, and shrugged. That was Dad's afternoon taken care of. He'd be absorbed in his work for hours—and would not proceed with any further exploration until he'd cracked the runic code.

Which left the rest of us with time to read or talk or sunbathe. Carl decided to work on his tan. I played chess with Lee-Ann (though she always beat me hands down!). And Commander Keel, having nothing better to do it seemed, dismantled and polished his gun.

Sadalsuud, the orange-red star of this system, dropped down toward the mountains, turning their towering peaks the color of rusty iron. Evening came on. Lee-Ann told me the name Sadalsuud was an old Arabic word meaning "the luckiest of lucky stars." "And I guess it is, Becky," she went on, smiling warmly. "For this discovery will surely make us all famous. It'll go down in history."

"I suppose you're right," I replied. "The trouble is, history has a way of often being wrong."

Lee-Ann had no answer for that. We played another game of chess. She won effortlessly.

Shortly afterward, Commander Keel withdrew most of the knowbots and sent them scouting up in the hills. We kept a few on-station, together with the videodroids, just in case. There came a time when the dusk shone violet across the sky. The lights of all the machines blazed on—and a sudden fierce light sparked in my father's eyes.

"I've done it," he said quietly, looking up from his work: and then, on a rising note of excitement, "I've done it!"

"What's that?" Keel grunted grumpily. He'd been staring away into the distance.

"I've translated the runes—at least, enough of them to know that the creatures who built this place did not live on this planet. And this building is neither a temple nor a tomb, but rather a way-station; a stopoff point to thousands of other worlds."

"Is that all the words say, Dad?" I wondered. He grimaced a little in frustration.

"That's all I've managed to read. And I'm amazed I've been able to decipher anything, but there are similarities between this script and ancient Mayan lithoglyphs that . . . Anyway, never mind. The way-station part I'm sure about. The rest isn't so clear. But I think it may be a welcome . . ."

"You're not positive?" Keel asked. He was leaning

close, tiny status lights blinking down the darkened side of his face. My father shook his head.

Keel shrugged.

"Then it could be a warning, Professor. Couldn't it?"

Whether welcome or warning, nobody could take action until we'd beamed a report back to the ECEO Headquarters on Alrakis II, and to Keel's military overlords on Earth. Out of the thousand planets that mankind had explored, a little under half had harbored life, but none, until now, had revealed any signs of intelligent beings. The orbital survey had failed to trace the presence of advanced aliens on this world, and we might easily have missed this ancient complex . . . We might so easily have passed it by and moved on . . .

But now, having made the discovery, both Commander Keel and my father were agreed on the need for caution, though for very different reasons. All of us knew how important our next actions would be, and that we could not afford to make any mistakes.

We camped out on the hill under a sky that swarmed with stars, drifting in and out of sleep, alternately listening to the soft swish of the breeze through the valley woodland and the whispered secrets of our dreams. Once, deep in the night, something woke me—a thought, or a nocturnal bird perhaps—and I gazed down at the vast shadow of the alien temple. I still called it that, because of its decayed magnificence. Down there among the trees, the identification lights of the knowbots sparkled like fallen stars; all green, indicating safety.

And much later, a little before dawn, an immense blue moon rose behind the encampment and flooded the whole valley with a ghostly turquoise glow. By straining my eyes to the limit, I could just make out the shape of the lion-unicorn guarding the sealed portals of the structure, its eyes burning with a glacial fire.

And I wondered then if that was what the temple-builders themselves had looked like.

Soon after dawn, a Beta-Space message arrived advising us to proceed, but with extreme caution. A small fleet of military support ships was on its way, and Keel also called down a hundred of his troops from *Anubis* to accompany us as we made our first approach in person.

My father led the way, his tall, thin figure straining forward eagerly as we descended through the trees toward the valley clearing. As we reached it, the morning sky filled with harsh thunders and a troopship swept in from the mountains, disgorging soldiers like dandelion seeds as they paraglided swiftly down toward us, landing with gentle precision fifty meters away.

The foremost of the troops saluted Keel and marshaled the rest of the men. They were wearing full body armor, and looked more like deadly matte-black robot machines than human beings. All were carrying weapons.

"Right, let's move it!" Keel snapped, grinning suddenly at us. "I feel *much* better about this now."

My father sighed, wearily. " 'We came in peace,' " he quoted, remembering the wise and ancient promise, " 'for all mankind . . .' "

The temple complex was even more imposing up close. I felt like an ant crawling beside a skyscraper of towering stone.

While my father continued working on translating

the runic hieroglyphs as we uncovered them, Lee-Ann, Carl, and I searched the perimeter for an entrance that did not seem to be sealed for eternity. And we found one not an hour later; a five-meter tall doorway set deep within arches of rock, the door itself made of some dark green metal that Carl was unable to mark, even with his hand laser or diamond drill.

We hurried back to the clearing to report the news, a walk around the base of the temple took us twenty minutes. Meanwhile, we discovered, Commander Keel had been busy. He'd instructed the knowbots to enlarge the valley clearing, each knowbot overseeing three auto-excavators. These big halftrack vehicles, part bulldozer, part tank, took little time in dredging the soil away from the remainder of the vast runic tablet set solidly in the ground. Trees were uprooted as the air whirled with late summer leaves, and moths disturbed from their daytime quiescence. Those moths were as big as sparrows, furry-bodied with blackberry eyes. Beautiful, and terrified.

That's when I thought how *wrong* we were to interfere with what might have been a sacred place to the lost people who constructed it: perhaps we were defiling a memorial to their dead.

I guess Dad thought so too. He stood at the edge of the huge silvery field, which, after the efforts of the auto-excavators, now looked like a great mirror reflecting the sky. Amber leaves were tangled in his unkempt gray hair, and there was a look of something like anguish in his eyes. He glanced at me, and quoted a bit of poetry we both knew; softly whispering the words from Thomas Hardy's "An Ancient to Ancients":

" 'Where once we danced, where once we sang / The

floors are sunken, cobwebs hang . . .' Until the army arrives, eh, Becky?"

I smiled at him, understanding his mixed feelings. In remembering past greatness, it was *necessary* to disturb it. I knew that Dad wouldn't mind so much if the disturbance didn't involve soldiers' boots . . .

The knowbots, hanging in the air with their hoverjets hissing, ordered the excavators away. Troopers in their black bodyshells marched forward to take up position around the temple. Commander Keel, surveying the scene from the hillside, roared out his orders: "Come on, you pathetic excuses for soldiers—move it AT THE DOUBLE!", his words booming like thunder from his chromium throat.

"It's a question," Dad said.

Late afternoon. He had finished transcribing the symbols in the clearing, and was now able to read the inscriptions that Carl had found in the green metal door.

"And do you have the answer?" Lee-Ann wondered softly. I saw a smile touch his lips, and knew that he had.

Dad nodded.

"We are being asked the galactic coordinates for a number of stars visible both from here and from our home planet. I presume that this lost race possessed the secret of space travel—perhaps Beta-Space travel at paralight speeds—and I suspect that if we supply the answer, this temple will allow us to enter and examine its secrets. . . . Allow us to journey to the farthest reaches of the galaxy . . . and maybe beyond."

"But how do we *communicate* the answer?" Carl

asked. "There's no sign of a computer terminal or surveillance cameras. *There's no one to talk to!*"

"No, wait," interrupted Lee-Ann. She pointed to the carving of the lion-unicorn above the doorway, a replica of the giant statue we'd already seen. Small, exquisitely made, its tiny jeweled eyes twinkling. "We've already noticed how the eyes seem to be staring at us . . ."

Dad laughed aloud as we realized what she was saying. He dug into his bag and pulled out a flashlight.

"Galactic coordinates," he explained, "like any number system, can be reduced to binary code—torch on for one, off for zero. It may take some time this way . . ." He grinned. "But I think it will be worth the effort."

Flashing the message into the lion's eyes actually took my father four hours. By that time the evening had arrived, together with the support ships Commander Keel had requested. We heard the distant rumbles in the upper atmosphere as the landing craft dropped down from orbit. The violet dusk sky was filled with torn and fading rainbows where the fleet had appeared out of Beta-Space. Within ten minutes, the ships had touched down, crushing trees like straws as they settled into position.

Floodlights were swiftly set up as the darkness deepened. The clearing became busy with troops, knowbots—and a number of mankind's most dangerous fighting machines, the Deathdroids. They were much bigger than the human soldiers in their armor, who, I thought perversely, looked like the Deathdroids' children.

Commander Keel strode across to us, looking rather

arrogant now that he had a greater force under his control.

"Professor. You say you have beamed the entry codes into the temple's computer network?"

Father shrugged. "Well, I'm assuming it has built-in automatics—though of course we can't be certain. On the other hand, if the lost race of Sadalsuud under-stands galactic mapping, then it follows that they are—or were—a highly advanced civilization."

"And yet the temple hasn't opened," Keel pointed out, his face twisting into a rather unpleasant, sneer-ing smile—as though he was looking forward to seeing my father fail.

"It has not," Dad agreed, disappointedly. "But I'll continue working and, perhaps, tomorrow —"

And that's when we heard the scream, shrill and agonized, echoing back through the dark woodland glades.

A trooper in trouble.

With a clatter of metal and a sleek whine of servos, the Deathdroids swung themselves to face the source of the cry. Dad sent his nearest videodroid—Miny—to take a closer look. We watched on his handscreen as the gloomy undercanopy of trees swooped by. The temple doorway came into view—and it was open now, a faint red light glowing from the depths of a passageway beyond. There was no sign of the soldier.

"Miny," Father said, "move forward and check —"

A brilliant white flash came from the doorway. We heard the explosion crash back through the trees. The handscreen fizzed and went blank.

Behind us, watching over our shoulder, Keel's face looked grim. His internal circuity was working: 'droids and soldiers were mobilizing to his radioed commands.

"You know what you've done here, don't you?'
he grated angrily. Father's face looked shocked and
pale. "You've triggered an alarm! These aliens are still
around—somewhere. And now they know we've arrived. We've told them, through our answers, that
we're a threat."

"But—Commander—" Dad opened his hands. "These
beings are intelligent. They built this beautiful temple
. . . These intricate carvings . . ."

"Get real!" Keel snapped. "*We* built beautiful tem-
ples, too. People painted the Mona Lisa *and* constructed
the neutron bomb . . . Beauty and terror from the same
human hands."

"I—don't—believe . . ." Father whispered.

That's when the skies opened, and the aliens poured through.

Night turned to day—a wonderful, terrible, multi-colored morning—as a swarm of ships burst out of Beta-Space. They engaged the orbiting Earth vessels in combat at once. And we retaliated. Lasers crisscrossed the skies. Ships exploded and came tumbling through the atmosphere like ruined, spinning comets of fire.

Ground fighting also began. Armored creatures emerged from the temple doorway, guns blasting. The Deathdroids roared and spat flame. Trees erupted into splinters and dust. Rocks shattered into powder. Fires swept through the woods. The hills looked like cut-out silhouettes set against the blazing horizons . . .

"Let's get out of here!" Carl yelled above the awful din, his voice shrill with fear. My father looked absolutely stunned, as though this wasn't—couldn't be—happening.

Lee-Ann, terrified and lost, began running for cover. A flower of flame blossomed beside her. I saw her body hunker down before it was engulfed. And I screamed . . . screamed until Carl came and hugged me, then took my arm and led me shuddering to safety.

In the middle of the clearing, we saw Commander Keel was standing, directing his men and machines. He was holding his cleaned and polished smartgun, which he waved in the air and then began firing randomly towards the temple, blasting away huge chunks of sculptured stone.

"Listen up, guys!" his machine voice boomed. "Let's have ourselves a bug hunt!"

I do believe he was happy.

*　　*　　*

We rest now, high up in the hills, away from immediate danger. Carl has been wounded in the arm. My father's breathing is ragged and fast. The shock has hit him hard, and he's barely conscious. I'm OK, I suppose, for now at least . . .

Below us the fighting continues. Above us too, right across the heavens, as Keel's forces do battle with the creatures we hoped to discover, and to understand.

And as I sit here, crouched in the rocks, I think I *do* understand . . .

I'm looking at the handscreen, at an image transmitted by Eeny. He's in the thick of the fighting, damaged, hanging in the scorched branches of a tree. There are fires burning all around him; flashes of blinding light; dreadful explosions . . . Crippled machines are lying everywhere: one Deathdroid is scuttling in a circle like an injured ladybird. An alien warcraft arrives to crush it.

Troops are surging forward. Lights gleam and flicker on the polished surfaces of their armor. The aliens fight back and gain ground . . .

Yes, I understand, as I glance from alien to man, and from man to alien, and from alien to man again. But already it is impossible to say which is which.

Hally's Paradise

DOUGLAS HILL

Hally Kenner paused at the top of a low rise, took a deep breath of the cool air, and gazed around at the landscape, as he had done several times that morning.

It's ideal, he thought, as he had also done several times that morning. *A fine planet. A fine place to live, and to die.*

He strode away down the slope, through thick, knee-high brush and out on to a sweep of open land covered with a purplish growth that was more like moss than grass. Its soft springiness under his boots made him feel more light of foot than he had felt for years. For, although he was lean and straight-backed, Hally's hair was gray and thinning, and his face was deeply lined by some sixty years of a hard and dangerous life.

But he had left that life behind him, now—to start a new life, on this planet. This ideal planet.

He knew that most other people would not have found it ideal. They would have used words like *bleak* and *dull*. The rolling plain of moss seemed to go on forever, interrupted only by swaths of the thick, feathery brush, like ferns—and by an occasional range of low, bare, rock-clad hills. The place even lacked any interesting life forms to break the monotony. The

largest creatures Hally had seen looked like slugs covered with shell, half a meter wide, slow-moving, entirely harmless.

But all the things that would make the planet seem dull and empty and boring to most people were the things that made it ideal for Hally. He had had enough excitement and danger in his life. Now he wanted just what he had found on this world—silence, and emptiness, and peace.

But as he strode along over the rich moss, the silence was broken—by a snuffling sound from a cluster of brush nearby, followed by a hoarse coughing like a human with a heavy cold. A smile tugged at the corners of Hally's thin-lipped mouth. *I'm not the only one*, he thought. *Skitter thinks this place is ideal too.*

Skitter was a creature called a wiryz, from a planet on the far side of the galaxy. He had been Hally's faithful companion since the day Hally had found him, a tiny, abandoned cub. Now, fully-grown, Skitter was a thigh-high bulk of gray fur and muscle, with a long triangular head that displayed two pairs of eyes and a mouthful of sharp black teeth, serrated like a saw. He also had eight legs, like every wiryz, and moved in jerky, high-speed bursts that had given him his name.

Hally's smile broadened as he heard Skitter's cough deepen into a resonant roar. That roar, combined with the solid bulk and the sharp teeth, could make a wiryz seem fearsome. But in fact the creatures were vegetarians, not hunters, and certainly not fighters. Skitter was gentle, playful, good-natured, and a complete coward.

Just then, Hally guessed that Skitter was trying to play with one of the slug-things, which would be ignoring him totally. But if the slug showed the slightest sign of aggression, Hally knew, Skitter would turn and run as fast as his eight legs could carry him.

For an instant Hally glimpsed the big creature, charging through the brush. As always, when he was happy, Skitter's mouth was gaping wide in a foolish grin that exposed all of his shiny black saw-teeth. For Skitter,

who had spent much of his life cooped up in spaceships, all this wide-open land was clearly a joyous
paradise.

And for me too, Hally thought, *it's as near to paradise
as I could find.* But that, he knew, really had little to do
with the nature of the planet itself. It had to do with
the total absence of other people.

Hally had known a great many people in his life.
But he had liked few of them, and had loved none.
And in the end he had come alone, except for Skitter,
to spend the last years of his life on a planet that
offered him peace, not people. Because peace was something that Hally Kenner had almost never known,
through all his sixty years.

In his youth, Hally had been a drifter, wandering from
planet to planet of the League of Human Worlds,
looking for adventure. He had found plenty of that—
but he had also found, on all of those colonies, that
people were still people. Wherever they went in the
galaxy, they took with them all the old human fail-
ings, all their greed and fear, envy and ignorance. And
wherever Hally went, in all the hundreds of planets of
the League, he found the same old human drift toward
ugliness, misery, destruction, violence.

What was perhaps worse, Hally had found that he
too had the human capacity for violence. And the
skills that went with it had come swiftly and easily to
him. So his own drifting had led him, almost naturally, to earn his living with those skills—as a mercenary soldier.

Over the years, his reputation had grown and spread
throughout the League of Human Worlds. And when
the League had finally fallen apart in a welter of cor-

ruption and treachery, the mercenary warriors of those
planets came into their own. The catastrophic Wars of
the League had shattered humanity's dream of colonizing the galaxy. But they had made the name of
Hally Kenner into a legend.

Yet Hally had gained no satisfaction from his fame,
or from the use of his fighting skills. He had fought to
earn his living, because it was the thing he did best.
But all those years of destruction and death had turned
him grim and bleak and cold, sickened by what mankind was capable of doing to itself. And so, finally, he
had quit.

He had used all his savings to buy and equip a small
space cruiser. And then he and Skitter had set off for
the farthest reaches of the galaxy. His plans had formed
so completely in his mind that it was as if they had
always been there, waiting for him to notice. He intended to find an uninhabited planet, far from the
Human Worlds, and spend the rest of his life on it, in
peace.

And when he had wandered into this region, and
had found this planet, it seemed as if it too had been
waiting for him.

It was called Gammel V on the star charts. It was
chill and bare and empty, but able to support human
life. It was the kind of world that the League might
once have colonized. But the League was now in ruins,
and humans would be doing no more colonizing for a
century or more—by which time it would no longer
trouble Hally. So he had landed his ship on a patch of
solid rock within one of the ranges of low hills.

The landing had been the day before, and he had
spent the rest of that day taking what he needed out of
the ship. He had brought a small dome-shelter of pre-

fab plastic, solar-powered recycling equipment that provided food and water, and a few other items—including his nova-gun, the only weapon that he had packed. He had carried all that equipment out on to the rolling plain, and had set up his home in a gentle fold of land, about two kilometers from his ship. And then, this morning, he had come out to look at his surroundings.

He and Skitter each had years of life left. And he was sure they would be good years. He could already feel peace settling around him in the absence of people, with their uglinesses and violence. And he would not be bored. He would think, and dream, and play with Skitter, and wander—and it would be enough. He had a whole world to investigate and explore. His world.

I came looking for a hermitage, he thought wryly. *And I found a paradise.*

By midday Hally had circled halfway around the perimeter of the low hills where he had landed his ship. The walk had given him an appetite, so he decided to return to his dome-shelter by crossing over the hills, and along the way taking another look at their bare, rocky ridges and the gravelly clefts between them.

Soon he had climbed easily up one of the steeper slopes, and was angling downward into a dusty gully. As he walked along it, the gully deepened, its far side becoming an almost sheer wall of low cliffs. Hally felt pleased. The cliff walls would offer the enjoyment of a little rock-climbing, and they were also split and broken here and there by the gaping dark mouths of caves, just waiting to be explored.

But there was no hurry. He could come back next day, or next week. He could explore every centimeter of the gully, and all the others like it among the hills. It could take him months, maybe a year, if he went about it slowly and thoroughly. And that thought made him feel even more happy and peaceful.

But then, as he moved around a bend in the gully, he stopped short, breath hissing between his teeth with shock. And almost all thought was driven from his mind.

Ahead of him, in the cliff face, was the entrance to another cave. And in that opening stood something that told Hally he was not the first space traveler to have landed on Gammel V.

A statue.

It was about a meter and a half high, sculpted from a substance that was rough-textured like stone, but gleaming like metal. Clearly it had been there for a long time, so that wind and weather had had their eroding effect on the surface. But there was more than enough to show Hally that it had not been carved by humans.

It was a statue of a being of some sort. Vaguely humanoid, with two thick legs, a long narrow torso, four multi-jointed arms, a head like a large oval lying on its side. The arms were upraised, and the head was tilted up toward the sky. And the broad feet rested not on a plain pedestal but on a carving of a machine of some sort. It was vaguely a hemisphere, with strange protuberances sprouting from it. And Hally felt certain, though he could not have explained why, that it was some kind of spacecraft.

A light wind moaned around him as he stood in the gully, rooted, amazed, staring. And as he stared he shivered, not from cold but from the eerie feelings that the statue caused within him.

Humans had found only a few other intelligent species among the stars. All of them had been at a more primitive stage of development, without space flight. And none of them had looked anything like this sculpted figure.

Again Hally shivered. It was not just the alienness of the statue, nor its obvious great age. From it came a feeling of dignity and strength, but also a terrible loneliness, a deep, soul-wrenching sadness. It affected Hally much like some objects he had seen on old Earth—broken statues of ancient gods, crumbling memorials to long-forgotten heroes. But this statue was more awesome, because it was more mysterious.

In the distant past—perhaps before humanity had come out into space—alien beings must have passed this way, left this statue, and then departed. What they were, where they went, why they had left the statue—these were mysteries that Hally knew he would never solve.

But then, as he stared at the alien sculpture, another thought entered his mind. An unworthy thought, but a very human one. A temptation.

Back on the Human Worlds, he knew, there were museums and wealthy people who specialized in collecting artifacts from alien planets. Such artifacts were often worth a great deal.

And for this statue, with all the mystery of its origin, a man could literally name his own price.

He stepped slowly forward, letting his fingers slide over the harsh surface of the sculpture. If he were to take it back and sell it, he would be rich. As rich as any of the Lords of the Nebulae. And then he could . . .

Abruptly he turned away, shaking his head angrily. Without looking at the statue again, he stalked rapidly away along the gully, as if trying to get away from the temptation that the alien object presented. But as he hurried on through the hills, those thoughts continued to clamor in his mind. Thoughts of great wealth, unending luxury for all the years that were left to him.

The dream of living out his life on Gammel V, alone and in peace, faded away. Part of his mind was telling him that a spartan life on a bleak deserted planet was no life for a tired old warrior. Far better, his thoughts were saying, to find comfort and rich pleasure on one of the lush resort planets untouched by the Wars of the League, attended by servants, surrounded by all the delights that wealth could buy. And all he had to do was to load the statue into his ship and take off.

Such thoughts were still swirling and whispering in his mind as he came down out of the hills, on the far side. He was half-jogging now, as he crossed the two kilometers of rolling mossy plain to the cleft of land where his dome-shelter stood. But though his mind was clouded by the temptations, lost in dreams of wealth and luxury, he was still Hally Kenner, with all his lifetime of training and battle-hardened skills.

So as he approached his little dome, he stopped suddenly, hairs on his neck prickling with the reflex awareness of danger.

Something had been tampering with the dome. He had locked its narrow door out of habit, and only his thumbprint could open it. But the plastic around the lock was deeply scarred and gashed, as if something had been trying to break in. And the gashes looked as if they had been made with knives, or claws.

He wheeled slowly, in a balanced crouch, studying the empty landscape, grimly wishing that his nova-gun was not stowed away inside the dome but clipped to his belt as it had always been for so many years. The thick brush on the slopes around the dome seemed to have become dark and ominous, as if it were hiding a host of unseen, unknown enemies.

And then he froze, rigid as if he too had become a statue carved from stone. Behind him he had heard the one sound he had thought he would never hear again.

Another human voice.

"Stay where you are, old man," the voice said, in a rough growl, "and you won't get hurt."

Though Hally remained blank-eyed and unmoving, a mixture of emotions swept through him like a storm. Shock, wariness, a clear awareness of danger, and a sudden clench of shame that he, of all people, should have walked into an ambush. And with those feelings came a cold swelling anger, and outrage.

It was bad enough that a stranger should have taken him by surprise. It was far worse that any stranger, any other human, should be there at all, on Hally Kenner's world.

Ignoring the voice's order, but keeping his hands motionless, Hally turned, slowly and carefully.

He saw three men, in stained and crumpled coveralls, stepping out from behind the far side of the dome. Each had a nova-gun on a belt-clip, and one also had a heavy knife jutting from his boot. They were standing well apart from one another, to make three separate targets. Hally knew that if he lunged at them bare-handed, he would probably get only one before the other two fired. Twenty years ago, he thought sourly, I might have gotten two—but the third would kill me just as dead.

None of these thoughts, none of his flaring emotions, showed on his face as he stared at the three men.

"Saw your ship land yesterday," the man in the center said. He was the owner of the rough voice, probably the leader. Heavily built, coarse features made coarser by smears of dirt and several days' growth of beard. "Took us till now to get here," he went on, grinning. "Nice place you made for yourself."

Hally said nothing, just watched them stonily. He knew their kind well enough. A trio of drifters, probably criminals wanted on several planets. What ugly mischance had brought them here?

As if aware of the question in Hally's mind, the leader of the trio answered it. "Our ship came down a few days ago. Malfunction—useless. Figured we were stuck on this ball of nothing forever. Real nice surprise to see you coming down. What I can't figure is what you're *doing* here."

"Who cares?" one of the others said sharply. "Where's your ship, old man?"

Still Hally said nothing. And the leader shifted one hand slightly toward his gun.

"We'll find it, sooner or later," he said. "But you can save us some trouble—and stay alive—by telling us."

Hally knew that the trio would kill him at once without a second thought. So he jerked his head slightly, towards the hills. "Over that way. About two kilometers."

"Good," the leader said, his grin widening. "Now you can step over here and open up your dome, so we can see what else you got."

Hally's mouth tightened, but again he knew that he had no choice. He stepped forward, watchfully. And as he did so, the leader's eyes narrowed.

157

"I got the feeling I've seen you before," he said. "What're you called?"

"Hally Kenner," Hally said quietly.

He saw the slight widening of the eyes, the tensing of the jaw, on all three men. Clearly they knew the name, and the reputation that went with it. But then the leader's grin slowly returned.

"Course," he said. "The great Hally Kenner. I was in one of your star troops one time—must've been fifteen years ago. Just a kid then, I was, a recruit. You remember? Creel's the name, Lann Creel."

"No," Hally said with blunt honesty. "I don't remember. But I don't think you'd have been in my troop for long."

As one of the others snickered, Creel's grin became a snarl. "That's right. You chucked me out, for stealing." His laugh was vicious and ugly. "And here we are, and I'm still stealing. Only it's your ship, now. And you can sit on this nothing planet for good, Mister Hally Kenner, and think about the old days . . ."

But then the tirade stopped—because it had been interrupted. By a hoarse, coughing roar.

Over the top of the slope at one side of the dome, Skitter came lolloping on his eight wiryz legs, glittering black saw-teeth exposed in one of his most foolish grins.

Automatically, all three men whirled towards the unexpected sound. They saw a huge gray-furred beast, fanged mouth gaping, charging toward them with a terrifying roar. Instantly their hands flashed to the nova-guns at their belts.

But just as instantly, Skitter skittered. With all the awareness of a true coward, the wiryz sensed the fear and aggression in the three humans even before they had touched their guns. Wild panic turned Skitter into a fleeing, eight-legged blur. And the three nova-rays seared harmlessly through the air as Skitter vanished back over the top of the slope.

"What in starfire was that . . .?" one of the men began.

But he was interrupted by a vicious curse from Lann Creel, the leader. Creel had swiftly swung back toward the gray-haired man who had been standing silently before them.

But Hally Kenner was no longer there.

In the fraction of a second that the men had taken to turn, see Skitter, and fire, Hally had simply vanished. There was no sign of him, no sound of his movement, anywhere around.

"Come on!" Creel yelled wildly. At a headlong run, the threesome dashed away up the other slope, in the opposite direction from Skitter.

And lying full-length in the thick brush nearby, Hally listened to their departing footsteps with a small cold smile. When Skitter's arrival had given him the chance he needed, he had simply taken three swift strides and dived head first into the nearest cluster of the fernlike brush. Then he had slid away, belly-down, with a stealth that did not rustle a single feathery leaf, through the shadowy heart of the dense growth.

As he lay there, listening to the fading sound of three pairs of running feet, he heard a low snuffle behind him. Turning his head, he saw Skitter, all four eyes wide and fearful, edging nervously toward him. He reached out to stroke the rich gray fur, feeling the wiryz's trembling subside.

"Still," he murmured. "Still."

Obediently Skitter lay down, tucking his legs under him. The brush would keep him hidden, Hally knew, even if the three men doubled back. Which was not very likely.

"Stay still," he told Skitter. Then he rose and moved toward his dome.

A moment later he emerged from it, his nova-gun clipped to his belt. And there was a cold glint in his eyes, like the sun on ice, as he climbed warily up the slope toward the hills where his spaceship stood.

He moved with instinctive care, making full use of the natural cover on the brush-covered slopes, then of the even better cover among the jutting stony ridges of the hills. Yet he moved at speed, in an easy lope, drifting across the terrain like a shadow. He was hardly aware of how all of his old skills had come smoothly into action. What he was doing was simply second nature to him, using the abilities that had kept him alive through hundreds of similar pursuits, through hundreds of other alien landscapes.

Several minutes later he was tucked into a rocky crevice on one side of a broad, flat plateau. In the center of that open area his cruiser rested on its landing gear, angled upward, pointing at the sky. The three men had not yet reached the plateau—but within moments Hally heard their approach, heard their voices from a nearby cleft.

"I still think we should've stayed and looked in that dome," one of them was saying. "It could've been full of good stuff."

Lann Creel's reply was a vicious snarl. "You want to go back, with Hally Kenner out there somewhere, you go ahead."

"He's an old man, Creel," the third one said. "We could've hunted him down—there's three of us."

"Old, maybe," Creel spat. "But he's still Hally Kenner. You saw how he disappeared. We'd never find him, if he didn't want to be found. And then it'd get dark, and he'd come and find *us*. Remember, I've seen what he can do. So we'll find his ship, and get out of here while we still can—and be glad of it."

The sound of his voice had grown louder as the three men had drawn nearer to the plateau. And then Hally drew back into the crevice, for he had seen them—crouching at the edge of the plateau, staring nervously around, no more than thirty meters away. But clearly they saw nothing except an empty expanse of bare rock, and the silent spaceship in the center.

"There it is," he heard Creel say. "And it looks like we got here first. But he'll be coming after us, probably with a gun. Let's move."

Hally heard their boots crunch on rock, and edged carefully forward. The three were moving out on the plateau now, heads twisting around as they kept a wary eye on the barren rock around them. Silently Hally raised his gun, sighting along the bulbous barrel. In their nervousness the trio had bunched together, and he could drop them with a single fiery blast.

His finger began to tighten on the firing stud. He felt no scruples about killing from ambush. Killing was killing, neither heroic nor admirable however it was done. And he was coldly, grimly ready to finish off these men. They would have murdered him just as readily, he knew. And they were trespassers, intruders into the perfect peace and emptiness of his ideal planet.

But then he hesitated, lowering the gun, as a new thought came to him. If he fired, the men would *still*

161

be intruders. Their corpses would be there, on the planet, even if Hally buried them as deeply as he could dig. He would always be aware of them, as other presences that did not belong, shattering his isolation.

And at that moment the realization of what he was thinking jolted him, like a physical blow.

Ever since the three men had appeared, he had not given a thought to the alien statue in the cave. He had not even felt a second's worry that the trio might discover the statue, and take it from him. Nor had he been even briefly troubled by the threatened theft of his ship.

His anger and outrage, his cold determination to kill, had been caused solely by the fact that the men were *there*, intruding on his paradise.

Slowly, with amazement, he shook his head. He recalled all those dreams of wealth and luxury that had entered his mind as he had stood staring at the alien sculpture. What had been happening to him at that moment? How could he, Hally Kenner, have ever thought such thoughts, felt such inane temptations?

Great wealth might bring comfort and luxury, but at a price far greater than money. Hally had met many rich people, and had found them all to be empty, greedy and fearful. Empty because they acquired things too easily, and so drew no pleasure from them—greedy because they always wanted to acquire more—fearful because the Worlds were full of dangerous ·folk who wanted to take the things of the rich away from them.

He shook his head again. How could he have thought that he could ever go back among the worlds of people, where he would find nothing but violence and ugliness, and a rich man's self-indulgence? How could he have dreamed that there would be contentment and peace in a life like that?

He suspected that even if he had given in to the temptation, he might have come to his senses some time. But by then it might have been too late—he might have been too old, too weakened by soft living, to make a real life for himself on a world like Gammel V. So, in a way, the three intruders had done him a service.

Smiling a thin smile, he looked across the plateau, at the three nervous figures who had now almost reached the cruiser.

You can have the ship, he said to them silently. *I'll have the planet. And I've got the best of the bargain.*

He watched without moving as the trio hastily fumbled for the outer control to the airlock, then scuttled into the ship. Within seconds a spume of fiery gases burst from the ship's stern—and within minutes more the cruiser was lifting from the plateau on an eruption of flame, howling up into the cold blankness of the sky.

Still and silent as the rock around him, Hally watched the ship climb until it disappeared. He felt no sense of loss, since the ship would be of no further use to him. And its theft removed any chance that he might, at some later time, give in to the temptations that the statue offered. He felt almost grateful to the three thieves.

And he felt such overpowering relief that they were gone from the planet, that he would not have minded if they had taken all his possessions.

Of course, he thought, they might come back and try to steal the rest of his equipment. But he doubted it, since they had been in such a towering hurry to get away from him. And if they *were* stupid enough to come back, he told himself firmly, they wouldn't take him by surprise a second time.

Nor was there much chance that they would tell other people in the Worlds about finding Hally Kenner alone on a distant planet. Too many questions might be asked, about *how* they had found him. And the questions might uncover their theft of the ship, and the fact that they had left him there, apparently marooned.

He clipped his gun back on to his belt and turned quietly away, heading back towards his dome-shelter. First of all, he intended to call Skitter out of his hiding-place in the brush, and to reassure the wiryz that all was well, that the danger was gone—that there would probably never be any more danger for either of them, ever again.

Then we'll go and have another look at that statue, he decided, as he strode peacefully along. *And tomorrow, we'll go for a really long walk, and look at some more of our world.*

Our paradise.

Scrutiny

WILLIAM F. TEMPLE

Three hundred parsecs from Earth, five planets circled a white dwarf star. One bore life—but nothing more complex than moss. Three others were as barren as this long voyage of spaceship *Ulysses* had so far proved to be. *Ulysses* was searching for intelligent life in the universe other than mankind.

The fifth planet promised it. It displayed forests, mountains and, far more importantly, towns, thinly scattered. The captain named the planet Promise and put *Ulysses* into close orbit around it for scrutiny.

At last his verdict was: "Maybe I should have named it Puzzle. There's the town and there's the steeple—but where are all the people?"

"Away on holiday," said Leo, his lieutenant, not seriously.

The captain took him seriously. "But where? All the towns, large or small, look completely deserted."

"They've taken to the hills," said Bruce, a crewman. "Someone tipped them off that the Earth people were coming—and they'd read about us in the monster magazines."

The captain ignored that and stared again at the scanner screen. Presently he remarked: "Whoever they are, they're redeveloping their towns like mad. Look at all those great stacks of building materials and those cleared sites."

Leo shrugged. "It's not all that much different from home. Take New York—was there ever a time when it wasn't being rebuilt—feverishly rebuilt, I mean?"

"Maybe not. But the New Yorkers stay on the job. They don't put down their tools and vanish like this lot. It's odd—their buildings and artifacts look so much like ours. They must be humanoid. Note the designs of their cars—most of them wouldn't look out of place on our motorways."

"Yes, Skip, the cars that happen to be in one piece. Have you noticed how many aren't? Just standing there in the street with half their guts out. Wheels, manifolds, gears, pumps piled along the pavements. Don't these people have any garages for repairs?"

The captain sighed. He was baffled and yet relieved. "We've found life, anyway. After all this time. Even if they're mad, they're alive."

"Are they?" Leo queried. "Or are they robots?"

"You'll soon have the opportunity to find out— you and Bruce. I'm sending you both down in the Module . . ."

The Module landed in sand scrubland on the fringes of a small town. Gravity was two-thirds G. The atmosphere was clear and thin—composition as yet unknown but probably lethal to them: they'd never yet come upon breathable air away from Earth. They would take a sample back for analysis. Meantime, they donned spacesuits.

They could detect no animal life in the scrubland. The sky was mauve. Tall against it the nearer buildings stood, less than a mile off. Nobody had come to greet them.

Leo reported all this by radio to the captain. *Ulysses* had moved out to a stationary orbit, too distant to observe detail. Leo added: "Since they won't come to us, we're now going to look for them. In—good Lord!"

While speaking, he was gazing out through a port— and the sudden and inexplicable happened: the outer door of the Module's airlock swung open. Yet there was nobody outside—nor inside—the airlock.

Bruce had also seen it. "That just can't happen," he said, also on the radio net.

"What can't? What's going on there?" the captain called.

It was Leo who answered. "Maybe someone *has* come to meet us. If so, he's an invisible man. Could be all the townsfolk are invisible."

Next moment, the inner door of the airlock fell inward on them. They skipped back and it clanged on the floor. The pins of its hinges, which had somehow pulled out, rattled beside it. The denser air in the cabin swooshed out into the planetary atmosphere. Only their suits saved them from near-suffocation at best, death at worst.

"Hey, Skipper, something's—" Leo's urgent radio call was suddenly swamped and obliterated by a fierce, rising hum. It was as though a gigantic bee had gotten into the cabin. It went on. He tried to shout above it. He could hear no reply.

But Bruce's voice, very faint, came through the buzzing. "I can hear you, Leo. Can you hear me?"

"Only just. Can't hear the ship, though. They're drowned out."

"What's causing this blasted interference? And what the devil happened to those doors?"

"I don't know. But look at that console."

Bruce followed the line of Leo's pointing glove.

The holding screws in the panel of the manual guidance console were spinning anticlockwise. They came clean out and floated loosely, as though weightless. Then the panel itself lifted away, trailing wires and transistors, which began to separate and become detached. It was as though a gang of expert but invisible troubleshooters had set to work to dismantle the apparatus. The thin atmosphere became thick with floating components, as though the Module were in a state of free fall. But it was still resting on the sandy soil and the two men were still captives of gravity.

But the Module seemed to be starting, piecemeal, an independent struggle against that gravity.

Floor bolts began popping up like champagne corks. One section of the floor flapped open like a trapdoor.

Bruce exclaimed: "My God, they *are* invisible! They're wrecking us. Let's get out—quick."

He stabbed a gloved finger towards the lift-off button—then froze, realizing his foolishness. Built-in safety devices would prevent the Module from taking off with an open door. Anyway, he couldn't steer it: the manual guidance console was in a hundred pieces.

The radio interference throbbed on. No hope of getting a call for help through it.

Bruce thought: *there's only one chance.* He must get that outer door shut. Then they could lift off, get back into space, and leave all this trouble back at ground level. Away from the interference, *Ulysses* could regain contact, take over, guide the Module back by remote control.

He took one step toward the airlock—and the big red lift-off button flipped into the air like a giant tiddlywink, with a spiral spring chasing it.

So that was that. They'd had it now.

A human scream cut through the fierce hum. It was Leo. "Oh, my hand! Something's got my hand!"

Bruce spun around.

The complex wrist attachment of Leo's right gauntlet was undone and the gauntlet itself was floating away. His fingers were widespread at painful angles. Something was pulling and twisting them. He tried to fight the thing off with his free hand—and then that, too, was caught in an invisible grip, which began to twist it, excruciatingly. He screamed again.

Bruce flung himself forward to help. His ankle caught

an edge of the loose floor section. Off balance, he went sprawling across the radio transmitter. Before he could regain his feet, the faceplate of his helmet began to move fractionally. He thought it had been knocked loose. It hadn't. His whole space-helmet was being rotated, unscrewing.

He clapped both hands to it, tried to force it back into position. He might as well have tried to stop a two-ton flywheel with one finger. The fear of death swept through him and he dropped his hands in despair. The chances were a hundred to one against his surviving in the tenuous, unknown air of Promise.

Beyond that, he couldn't think consciously. What he did next may have been spurred by a deep-level instinct for self-preservation. Or it may have been merely a hysterical reaction.

One hand had fallen athwart the tuning knob of the radio transmitter. His fingers gripped it, began wrenching it around wildly, back and forth. The dial kept passing the silent point. The banshee howl of oscillation sliced through the powerful hum, making even it a secondary noise.

It was as though the shrill note of a police whistle had suddenly halted all traffic, all movement. The drifting components, screws, bolts, lengths of cable hung dead motionless in midair.

Then, unbelievably, Bruce's helmet was screwed back tight again. The unexpected relief left him limp. He let go of the knob. And then dazedly watched time going into reverse—or so it seemed.

All the dismantled apparatus began to reassemble itself. Steel pins slid back into their sockets, dials and buttons fitted themselves back on the panels, the floor bolted itself down, the outer airlock door thudded shut, the inner one re-hung itself.

Leo had passed out from sheer pain, but his gauntlet was back on his hand, wrist attachment sealed.

When complete order was restored, the throbbing hum in the earphones died away rapidly, leaving only the faint hiss of the carrier wave.

The captain came on the net, loud with worry.

"Leo, Bruce, report, report . . . Can you hear me? Report, report . . ."

Bruce had to retune the transmitter to answer. He said, shakily: "Bruce here. I'm okay. I think Leo is too, now, but I'll check that. We can't stay here. It seems the natives don't want us here. I'm bringing the Module back . . ."

The Module's systems had worked perfectly, as though they had never been tampered with. The two men had been back for an hour now. They and the captain were still mulling over their report and its implications.

Ulysses remained in the stationary orbit. Scratching his chin, the captain stared out at Promise. Distance blurred its surface into a common mystery.

He said: "We've come upon many strange things on the trip but nothing like this before. An invisible monster with a hundred hands—or tentacles or whatever."

Leo, now recovered except for residual soreness in his arms, massaged his left wrist and grumbled. "It didn't have enough brain to distinguish between flesh and material. The stupid thing was trying to unscrew my hand and fingers."

"That probably indicates that it can't have encountered organic animal life before it came to Promise," said Bruce. And added, unhappily, "And that doesn't promise much for our chances of encountering any, either."

They had decided that the phenomenon was alien to Promise. That it was an unfortunate coincidence that they and it had begun a scrutiny of the planet at approximately the same time—in their totally different ways. They had met with sentient, intelligent life at last, but it was on a completely different plane from theirs.

"We can't possibly communicate with it," said the captain.

"We've already done so," said Bruce.

The other two stared at him.

"Look," said Bruce, "we're agreed it must be an electromagnetic entity, a sort of knot of pure force. Therefore it's invisible, except for the tangible evidences of its lines of force—the objects it moves along them. It can't hear us because sound waves aren't electromagnetic. It can only perceive us via the electromagnetic spectrum. Whether it 'sees' or 'feels' us is a question of definition. I think it first became aware of us through our radio transmissions. And it came to investigate, out of scientific curiosity."

"You call that communication?" The captain looked doubtful.

"Hardly. No, I meant when, knowingly or not, I sent it a distress signal. Or a cry of pain in its language, if you like. For that's how it interpreted that wild oscillation, which basically is a disturbance of wave movements. It divined it was doing something destructive and wrong. Therefore it immediately restored the *status quo*—and us."

"The thing has a heart? Or, say, a moral sense?" Leo looked incredulous.

172

"Well, more a sense of order. Order is right, disorder is wrong, if you like," said Bruce.

"How can you say that when it's taking the whole darn place apart on Promise?" asked Leo.

"It's doing it in an *orderly* fashion, don't you see? So methodically that we thought the towns were being redeveloped, rebuilt."

"All very well, Bruce," said the captain. "But what's it done to the natural inhabitants of Promise? Pulled them apart methodically, too? It can't put Humpty-Dumpty together again, can it? How many of them has it killed because it couldn't hear them yelling?"

"I expect it did kill some, quite unwittingly," Bruce admitted. "I guess the rest fled into the forests, taking their dead with them. To it they were only more machines, like cars, like the Module. It was doing only what we're doing—exploring, analyzing, scrutinizing, dismantling things to see how they're made, how they work. We analyze minerals—how do we know they're not screaming at us on a wavelength beyond our small section of the spectrum?"

Nobody answered.

Presently, Leo said: "Well, what now, Captain? Do we move on and look elsewhere? Or do we stay in orbit till that thing moves on and looks elsewhere?"

"We stay here," said the captain. "Promise still holds promise—and there looks to be darn little of that in this neck of the universe. When the thing has satisfied its curiosity and gone, the humanoids will return to their towns. Maybe we can help them. Maybe they can help us."

"So be it," said Leo, and turned to look again at the still-mysterious planet. "So long as when that thing moves on, it doesn't come *this* way."

In the Picture

STEPHEN BAXTER

"It seems a pretty friendly planet, Captain," said Rossiter, the biologist. He waved a handful of computer printouts. "There's not a hostile bug in the atmosphere."

Captain Hamilton frowned. "Then it's safe to disembark?"

"I should say so." The rest of the lander's six-strong crew looked at Hamilton expectantly.

Hamilton peered challengingly out of the lander porthole, as if trying to force the planet to give up its secrets. The vista from the porthole was fairly idyllic: gentle, glaciated hills, emerald green; in the valleys nestled small clumps of trees. This was an ordinary-looking terrestrial world, three-quarters ocean, small ice caps, a central tropical zone and two extensive, comfortable temperate zones. Some large animals, no humanoids. The lander from the exploration starship *Falcon* had touched down during springtime in the northern temperate belt.

The sky was blue, the clouds were fleecy, the wildflowers were blooming; and Hamilton hated it. It was the kind of planet you felt you could trust, that made you lower your guard.

Hamilton looked up. A brilliant light crossed the zenith, clearly visible despite the brightness of the day. It was the kilometer-long starship *Falcon*, orbiting the new world.

Hamilton was not a hard man, but he had fought a lot of hard worlds. The acid forests of Bartoldy Four, for instance, hadn't exactly been fun, but at least you knew what you were up against. He had learned that the kind of world to fear most was the kind that welcomed you with open arms.

On the other hand, the lander had left *Falcon* and touched down eight hours ago now, and just about everything that could be learned from inside the lander had been learned. The only way to make further progress was to venture outside.

Hamilton scowled. "All right, we go out."

"Yes, sir!" said Jill Jones, the radio operator. The three civilian scientists—Karla Legrand, the anthropologist, geologist Arthur, and Rossiter, the biologist—looked eager to get to grips with the new world. Hamilton thought they should know better.

He said heavily, "Now listen carefully. This planet looks pretty and nice, just like home. Well, it isn't home, and you will remember that. This is an alien, unknown planet, and you will keep on your guard at all times. All right, Burdon, crack the lock. You stay in the lander."

"Yes, sir," said Burdon, the young pilot, without enthusiasm.

Grumbling about military inflexibility, the three scientists moved about the cramped interior of the lander. Midshipman Jill Jones knew better than to say anything at all.

Three men and two women emerged into the bright landscape, breathing deeply and swinging their arms.

176

After the confines of interstellar spaceflight, such freedom was glorious.

Rossiter walked over to the captain. The biologist was a short, stocky, cheerful man of forty. "Well, Captain? It certainly beats breathing canned ship's air."

"*Falcon*'s air is good enough. And a lot safer, too."

Arthur, the thin, intense, middle-aged geologist, put in, "But not nearly so healthy. This is how I imagine Earth before industrialization and so forth. No people—not a humanoid on the planet. Clean and unspoiled." He spotted a small, worn boulder a few meters away. "Well, now, that's an odd-looking sedimentary . . ."

Hamilton's gaze raked the landscape, and his nostrils drank in the atmosphere. Alarm bells sounded instantly in his subconscious. Something was wrong. Something always was. But what?

Rossiter said thoughtfully, "Funny, isn't it?"

Hamilton said, "What's wrong?"

The biologist smiled indulgently. "Always looking for the hidden dangers, Captain? It's just that—everything seems a little too bright and fresh, somehow. It's a bit too much like an oil painting to be true. There's not a dead blade of grass, for instance; not a flower that isn't in bloom."

"What could that possibly mean?"

"I've no idea. Perhaps it's just a nice planet. Do you see those trees over there? They caught my eye a while ago. I wouldn't have expected to see branch and leaf structures like that. Not here. Those trees would be better suited to a much wetter climate."

Midshipman Jones wandered past, grinning in the sunshine. She wore a small red flower in her lapel. "Pretty, isn't it, sir?"

"Yes, very pretty, Jones."

"It's almost an Eden."

"Yes."

Rossiter peered at the flower, frowning. "Let's have a look at that." Jones handed him the flower. The biologist began to take apart the ruddy petals. "That's funny — "

"Captain!"

Hamilton whirled at Karla Legrand's cry, instantly at a crouch. Then he heard what the anthropologist had heard, a deep, distant, ominous rumbling.

Arthur began, "Hamilton —"

"Stay where you are!"

Then the tremor hit them.

It was over in a second, like a thunderclap.

Hamilton found himself on his back, gazing up at a sky suddenly filled with ugly clouds. *What happened? What did I see in that second, during the quake?*

Experience took over and he was on his feet. "Is anybody hurt?"

He was answered by glazed stares, dull headshaking. All of them had been thrown to the ground.

A heavy rain began to patter down all about them, drop by massive drop.

Rossiter looked about him stupidly. "What happened to that flower?"

Hamilton said, "All right, everyone back to the lander. Legrand, Rossiter—Jones, give Professor Arthur a hand." They set off through rain that rapidly thickened.

"Where did this come from all of a sudden?" muttered Jones. "What happened to the sunshine?"

Hamilton, striding purposefully toward the lander, found Legrand at his side. The anthropologist was a dark, earnest young woman, observant and imaginative. "Captain," she began hesitantly, "did you—see anything during that tremor?"

Hamilton said guardedly, "Such as?"

"Well — " The anthropologist groped for words. "It was as if—everything changed color. The landscape was suddenly black and barren, and the sky was a gray blur." She chewed her lip uncertainly. "It reminded me of—a video tape being run too fast. What do you think? I suppose it must have been some kind of hallucination."

The rain beat down.

"Damage to the lander, Burdon?"

"None, sir. There was a quick jolt—then nothing."

Midshipmen Burdon and Jones distributed towels, blankets, and steaming coffee to the shivering scientists. Hamilton opened a radio channel to the orbiting *Falcon.*

"Get me seismology. Kyle?"

"Yes, sir." The disembodied voice, relayed from the orbiting *Falcon*, sounded puzzled. "Uh, I'm looking at the readouts of the quake now, sir, and frankly I don't know what to make of this."

Arthur, the geologist, said hoarsely, "Beam them through and let me have a look." A teletype began to chatter.

Hamilton said, "Just give me the facts, Kyle. In lay language."

"Well, sir, the quake that hit you was like no quake I've ever come across. There was no center, no secondary wave. The shock seems to have hit the entire planetary surface simultaneously, with equal force."

Arthur looked up from the teletype printout. "He's

right, Hamilton. The planet rang like a bell."

"What caused it?"

Arthur shrugged. "No hypothesis. Speaking as a geologist, I'd have said this was impossible."

"Captain?" The radio spoke again.

"What is it?"

"This is Gough in meteorology. Remember in our preliminary survey we noted that the planet had two small ice caps? Well, it now has two larger ice caps. Not much larger, but there's a definite increase."

"What?"

"Yes, sir. Also, the central tropical belt has contracted, and the two temperate zones have shifted significantly toward the equator."

"How is that possible?"

"I don't suppose it really is, sir. Similar changes on Earth would take of the order of thousands of years."

Hamilton sighed wearily. Impossible earthquakes, impossible ice caps. He looked at his bemused and bedraggled scientists. What next?

The radio crackled to life once more.

"Captain? This is biology. It looks as if Miss Legrand won't be redundant down there after all. Scanners now show a large humanoid community of some two hundred individuals, fifteen kilometers to your west."

Anthropologist Legrand and Midshipman Burdon stood at the top of a low rise, gazing down over the picturesque native village. Both of them were sweating after the hike from the lander, despite the cool grayness of the day. Spaceflight took its toll in unexercised muscles.

Legrand shifted her backpack more comfortably on

180

her shoulders. "Wattle and skin huts, simple but well made."

"They look like something out of the movies," said Burdon. "Very cute, but not very functional for a climate like this."

They began to make their way down the hill. Legrand said, "These people are probably late Stone Age. Possibly some bronze working."

Burdon grunted. "What I want to know is where they came from so suddenly. Why weren't they found by the preliminary surveys? Not to mention those ice caps. I think the captain's right. We ought to get off this planet while we still can."

"Hello," said Legrand. "Here comes a welcoming committee."

A party of three humanoid aliens approached. The aliens were of slight build, about a meter and a half tall. They were hairless, naked, and their skin was dusted with a soft golden coating of fur. Their heads were large and as fragile-looking as porcelain, and their faces were small and exquisitely formed, like the faces of very young children. They smiled at Legrand and Burdon, and each of them had large, wondering yellow eyes.

"Why, aren't they pretty?" said Burdon.

"Yes."

At the words, one of the aliens, slightly taller than the others, stepped forward grandly, pressed a small fist to his chest and said in a high, singsong voice, "Eyeful calipy velepo carp."

Burdon laughed. "And velepo carp to you too, friend! I guess this one's the leader."

Legrand had unslung her universal translator. "Try and keep them talking."

Burdon said, "Uh, Doctor Livingstone, I presume?"

"Copul capuko?" inquired the leader, and suddenly all three aliens were jabbering away excitedly.

Legrand laughed, delighted. "That's great!" she told the aliens. "Just talk into this little box here." The aliens, fascinated by the translator, gathered around the gadget, poking and prying harmlessly at it, melodious sounds pouring from their throats.

Burdon pulled faces at a small child peeking shyly around the corner of a nearby hut. Then he stiffened suddenly. "Hey, what's that noise? Thunder?"

Legrand was peering, slightly puzzled, at the translator. "That's strange . . . It doesn't seem to be making any progress. It should have had enough material to work on by now."

Burdon came over. "Maybe —"

And the second tremor was as unexpected as the first.

"Legrand! Burdon! This is Captain Hamilton. Are you all right? Report, Legrand!" Her wrist radio blared at Legrand, jarring her to full wakefulness. She sat up ruefully, rubbing at bruises. Burdon, also on the ground, was groggy but uninjured.

"Captain? Burdon here. We're unhurt, just a little shaken up."

Legrand looked at Burdon. "Did you see what I saw?"

Hamilton said from the radio, "What's that?"

"It was during the tremor, Captain," said the anthropologist. "It was just like the first time. I was in a landscape of bare black rock, like a lava plain, totally devoid of life. The sky was gray and flickering, and over the ground was—a kind of thick, gray, translucent carpet that seemed to twitch and move rapidly."

Burdon spoke into his own wrist radio. "I had the same impressions, sir."

Legrand said to Burdon softly, "Have you noticed the weather? The clouds have broken up. The sun's shining again."

Burdon looked around. "And another thing," he said. "What happened to our big-domed friends? And the pretty huts?"

From the entrance of rude, inelegant, unadorned huts, small squat aliens, sloping brows covered with shaggy yellow hair, peered hostilely at the two bewildered Earth people.

Hamilton listened to their report, scowling. "All right. Legrand, finish your investigations and get back to the lander as quickly as you can. Hamilton out."

The ship-to-lander radio buzzed. "Captain? Meteorology in *Falcon*. Those impossible ice caps are now two thousand kilometers wider, sir. The other climatic regions have shifted accordingly."

"Explanation?"

"We have none, sir."

Hamilton snapped off the radio and stalked out of the lander into the brilliant sunshine. None of this made any sense at all, and Hamilton didn't like it one bit.

Geologist Arthur approached. "Captain?" The thin, birdlike scientist was looking very pleased with himself. "I think you should take a look at this."

"What is it?"

Arthur presented a lump of grainy rock. "I know you're not a geologist, Captain, but what would you say this is?"

Hamilton disliked guessing games. "Looks like sandstone."

Arthur smiled like a conjurer reaching into a top hat. "Have a look at the internal structure." He pressed his thumbs to the thinnest part of the rock, and it split in two. The brown core of the rock was shot through with fine yellow fibers. "Hamilton, this is not genuine sandstone. It was not formed by geological processes; that is, it's not a real rock. It's not my field, of course, but close examination shows that this stuff bears closer relation to a kind of plastic fiber than to true sandstone. Every specimen I've looked at has been the same—igneous, sedimentary, the lot. All have the same composition as this."

"But that's incredible."

"I suppose it is. It's certainly not geological. The stuff looks and feels like rock—but it's no more the genuine article than is a lump of green cheese. Now, granted I've examined only a small portion of the planet's surface; but since our landing site was chosen more or less at random, the assumption of mediocrity demands that the entire planetary crust be composed of this same sham substance."

Hamilton took a deep, steadying breath. "Let me get this straight. You're telling me that every lump of rock on the planet is actually a kind of plastic mock-up. You make it sound—artificial. But who could have done this . . . and why?"

The geologist shrugged triumphantly. "That's your problem, Captain. It's not my field any more."

Hamilton walked on, lost in thought. After a while, he became aware of Rossiter standing before him. The biologist's customary sturdy cheerfulness was conspicuously absent.

"Captain —"

Hamilton grunted. He found it difficult to focus on the biologist. Plastic rocks?

"Have a look at this." Rossiter squatted beside a clump of violet blooms. "What's wrong with this flower?"

More guessing games, Hamilton groaned inwardly. "Uh, it looks all right to me. Very pretty."

"Hamilton —" The biologist ran a hand through graying hair. "It has no stamens—no pollen-bearing stalks. It has no means of propagation that I can discover. This flower shouldn't be alive, by the rules of biology.

"I've never come across a planet like this. Everything seems to evade classification; nothing fits the usual pattern. There are tropical trees growing in this temperate climate. The flowers bloom all the time— impossible! There is no humus in the soil. In fact, there is no underground animal life—no worms, grubs—so a major section of the life system is missing. Such animals as I've examined show a remarkable lack of detailed internal structure. They're almost homogenous, in some cases—that is, the same all the way through. They bound through the undergrowth, yet not one of them appears to have brains enough to keep breathing—literally. There is no protein base to their cells—in fact, they seem to be composed of a fine plastic. These don't seem like real life forms at all!"

"Then what's your conclusion, Doctor?"

"I have no conclusions, Captain," said the biologist unhappily. "I don't know what to make of this. Biologically speaking, the natural life of this planet shouldn't exist. There is no functional ecosystem—too many vital pieces of the life cycle are missing. No protein base. How life is maintained here is, I admit, a mystery to me. It's impossible. More than that, it is unreasonable. Ridiculous!"

Hamilton said, "Professor Arthur has been telling me some very odd things about the rocks on this planet. Now you tell me that the plants and animals shouldn't be alive at all." He sighed. "And yet here we are, standing on a sunny hillside and birds sing and the grass grows beneath our feet!"

"I know, I know!" wailed Rossiter.

"Doctor, would you join myself and Professor Arthur for a long, cool drink? We've a lot of thinking to do."

Karla Legrand sat in the dust, sweating profusely in the heavy sunlight. Opposite her squatted a surly, ugly alien. Legrand was hot, sticky, bored and irritable. It had taken her the best part of two hours to get the confidence of this creature. The pretty, friendly beings who had welcomed them before the tremor had vanished completely.

"All right, let's try it again." Legrand pressed the button of the universal translator, and the yellow-haired, shaggy alien looked on curiously. "Now, you speak into this little box here."

At length, the alien said grudgingly in a low, gravelly voice, "Ungh-ug agruba. Kakachigug. Grop." Grunting conclusively, he lapsed back into sullen silence.

Legrand sighed and pressed the process button on the translator. After a while, the translator flashed up its results.

The anthropologist scratched her head. It was the same conclusion as before. The aliens had well-developed voice boxes and a good range of sounds—but as a language, their jabber showed up completely null. There was no pattern; there seemed to be no identifiable words. The aliens' speech was a mere string of sounds, not a usable means of communication.

But it sounded like a language, Legrand thought. Could that, somehow, be its purpose?

Burdon came into view, walking dispiritedly toward Legrand. The anthropologist's alien tutor got to his feet and, after a few insulting grunts and gestures, disgustedly loped away.

The lander pilot flung himself down beside Legrand. "I'm getting sick of this planet. None of it makes any sense."

Legrand offered him a water bottle. "Drink?"

"Thanks. What a place—this is more like midsummer than early spring. I think I preferred the rain."

"Don't tempt fate."

"There seemed to be plenty of tools around the village—stone axes, arrowheads, simple plows. The odd thing was, I never once saw a villager using anything. They seem to just stand about all day looking native. They have their plows, and skins of grain, but I saw no evidence of actual agriculture—no obvious fields, for instance, although I walked quite a way out of the village. All the tools seemed brand-new—clean and sharp, as if they'd never been used."

Legrand told him about the natives' lack of language. "What do you think? It all seems to tie in, somehow. This can't be a real, functioning village at all. On the surface, things appear complete—a tribal system, language, tools, agriculture. But scratch a little deeper . . .

"You get the impression that they shouldn't last a week. It's almost as if they're play-acting. Actors filling a role, not real humanoids at all—or like the idealized characters in a movie."

"But how? And why? Where does the grain come from? Is it for our benefit?"

"I don't know."

Abruptly, a low rumbling filled the air, and the ground gave a premonitory tremble. Legrand leapt to her feet.

Burdon said, "I think —"

And the third tremor was on them.

Legrand fought to keep her balance on the shifting, rubbery surface the ground had become. The world had become a shock of black and gray; the village and its surroundings had vanished, to be replaced by a skeletal, ebony landscape, hard and bleak, over which there lay a ghostly layer of grayness that flickered in intensity and texture, too quickly for the eye to follow. Patches of greater opacity congealed and disappeared; gigantic shapes loomed out of the chaos and vanished, quick as blades.

At last, the tremor was over. The world was solid once more, and a sun beat down.

Groggily, she struggled to raise her head. She made out the slumped form of Burdon a few meters away; and from the shadows of nearby trees, great yellow eyes stared out at her.

Captain Hamilton, in the lander, listened to Legrand's report by radio.

"There's another thing, Captain," said Legrand. "After this latest tremor, the natives seem to have regressed again. The village now looks more like a campsite—a huddle of crude shelters about a central fire site. And as for the aliens—I've seen one of them trailing his knuckles on the ground, not walking properly upright. Uh, Midshipman Burdon thinks perhaps we were thrown a good distance by the tremors, and have observed three different villages."

"And what do you think?"

"I don't know. I don't see how that's possible."

"All right, Legrand. Pack up your stuff and get back to the lander as fast as you can. Hamilton out."

Hamilton snapped on the ship-to-lander link. "This is Hamilton. Report."

"Kyle in geology, Captain. The third quake was of the same type as the others. It was by far the most severe, and the longest. Uh, six hours separated the first and second tremors; two and a quarter hours separated the second and third. Captain, I suggest you get off that planet before it shakes you off!"

"Thank you, Kyle. The next time I need your advice, I'll ask for it. Give me meteorology."

"Gough here, sir. Those ice caps are four thousand kilometers broader than they were an hour ago, Captain."

"Any opinions?"

"I guess you could say we're working on it, sir."

"Keep me posted. Hamilton out." Hamilton sighed wearily and rubbed his eyes. He would have sold his soul for a hot bath and a cup of real Denebian coffee.

Leaving Midshipman Jones watching an old video movie flickering across a computer access screen, Hamilton moved into the main cabin of the lander and joined the two scientists at the bare central table.

They reviewed the facts. There was a community of aliens that had clean, unused tools but that showed no inclination to use them, speech but no language, grain but no agriculture. The planet's surface was constructed of some plastic-like substance, everywhere the same, formed into semblances of rocks, mountains, valleys. The natural life was composed of a similar substance, and should not have been able to grow and move; yet it did so, in an apparent imitation of reality. There were incongruities such as the presence of tropical trees in temperate climes. Periodically, a shock hit the entire surface of the planet, leaving climatic patterns drastically and instantaneously altered, the aliens regressed.

Rossiter puffed out his cheeks. "Quite a list."

Arthur folded his hands complacently. "This is not strictly my field, of course —"

"Nor mine, naturally!" put in the biologist.

"— but I do have a theory that explains at least some of these facts."

"Well?"

"Imagine an ancient, vanished civilization, nevertheless long-lived. Perhaps Legrand's aliens are their degenerate descendants. These people, in the course of their history, gradually replace the raw materials of the planet's crust with industrial products—plastics. Waste. Eventually, the entire planetary surface would be composed of artificial substances."

"But," said Rossiter, "why should the stuff heap itself into convincing-looking rocks and mountains? And how do you explain the apparently living things? No, there's much more to it than that. There has to be a deliberate, designing intelligence behind all this."

Hamilton said thoughtfully, "All these things have the appearance of the originals, but there is a—flatness about them. A uniformity of substance; a lack of detail." He groped for metaphors. "Like two-dimensional photographs, perhaps, or—or a facade . . . The plants and animals cannot move of themselves, so to speak. They must follow set patterns, imitating originals.

Shapes congealing out of some medium, to ape the real thing . . ." He stopped. A pattern was forming in his mind.

Rossiter said, "This whole planet must be a kind of model. A dynamic, detailed, working image of an entire world."

Hamilton said abstractedly, "I think you're almost there, Doctor. But what about the quakes? The ice caps, the changing aliens?"

Rossiter said thoughtfully, "It's almost as if, during those tremors, we were slipping abruptly through tens of thousands of years. Instantaneous time travel, leapfrogging into a past when the ice caps were much more extensive than at present—perhaps a complete Ice Age. Legrand has caught glimpses of her alien people at progressively earlier stages of their evolution." The biologist's round face suddenly blanched. "Good Lord, you don't think we've actually —"

Arthur snapped on an intercom. "Wake up in there, Jones. Get me astronomy on *Falcon*. Lufferty? I want you to fix me today's precise date, purely from astronomical considerations: positions of stars, and so on. Don't argue, just do it." They waited for the reply. Hamilton reflected that he hadn't needed to ask that question; he already knew the answer with an inner certainty.

The answer, when it came, was no surprise to Hamilton. "Good news, gentlemen," Arthur said. "External evidence shows that it's not we who have slipped in time. We have been stationary, while the planet has flowed past us, so to speak."

Hamilton thought, of course not. The picture was coalescing.

The silence in the lander was broken only by the tiny babble of Jones's old video.

And the fourth and greatest tremor hit them completely without warning.

The vision of the black, pulsating landscape dropped from Legrand's eyes, and she was on her knees in the dirt. The pack on her back, freshly strapped in place, weighed heavily. Burdon lay unmoving. Legrand looked up. Four or five yellow-haired, brutish, apelike creatures bounded gracelessly away from her, chattering and squabbling. From somewhere, her name was being called. She had time to cry, "Captain . . ." before the dust came up to hit her, and the world spun away.

A voice sounded from the radio. "Captain? Meteorology. Those ice caps are four and a half thousand kilometers wider, sir. We respectfully suggest —"

Coughing, Hamilton staggered to the control console of the lander, and snapped off the radio. He began pushing buttons. "Strap yourselves down!" he called. "We take off in thirty seconds. Emergency lift procedure, Jones. We'll home on Legrand's wrist radio and pick them up."

"Yes, sir."

The lander lurched sickeningly into the sky.

"It all adds up," Hamilton said. "Of course the planet's surface is artificial, and its purpose is clear. It was Jones's old video that was the key.

"Think of a television screen, by analogy. The screen is a representation of reality in two dimensions. A series of flat images move over the screen in an imitation of the real world. But the images themselves are not the reality—the images are only transient patterns

192

of light, unreal and devoid of substance. A television flower may appear to be alive and growing, Rossiter—but it is only a patch of light.

"Now think of the planet's surface. Objects had weight and form and texture—yet were all composed of the same sham substance. The flowers appeared to grow, and yet they were only lumps of plastic. Through an unknown medium—in which those plastic shapes are the equivalent of the television screen's patches of light—these things moved in an imitation of the real world. Of course the flowers had no intrinsic means of growth, Rossiter—they were merely representations, projected, three-dimensional images. Gentlemen, the surface of that planet is no more than—by analogy—a television screen!"

Arthur whispered, "Ah. Ah, yes. I see."

The lander lurched through atmospheric turbulence, and a smile glanced across Hamilton's face. "Marvelous images, though. They even responded to our presence—you could pick the flowers; Legrand's aliens responded to her. A superb representation of reality. It wasn't perfect, of course. The internal structure of the rocks and vegetation left a lot to be desired. There were inconsistencies: the idealization of the humanoids, and so on. Well, there's always artistic license, I suppose. And as for the flowers without pollen, the tropical trees in temperate climes—what producer, working within a tight budget, hasn't cut the corners on props when he could? Especially if the audience wouldn't know the difference."

"And the tremors?" asked Arthur. "The bizarre landscape, the time shifting?"

"It's obvious in retrospect. The projectionist was just rewinding the videotape! The black lava plain is

In the Picture

the real surface of the planet. The flickering fog is the false cinematic surface; flickering because thousands of years of history are being flicked back in seconds. A looming shape that disappears in an eyeblink? A great spreading tree being sucked back to the seed through centuries of stately life. A transient smudge on the horizon? A great city shrinks, buildings leaping from rubble, back to its mud village beginnings.

"It was all just a video film, gentlemen. From the state of the props and scenery, I would say just a cheap made-for-TV movie. Nothing spectacular."

Arthur sighed. "Ah, but think of the technology behind it! The camera? Actors? Plot? The audience!"

Rossiter said, "But why have we lifted, then? What's the danger?"

Hamilton wrenched at a lever; the lander shot through a bank of thin cloud. "The planet's being rewound to a Hollywood Ice Age," he said. "I don't relish the thought of being crushed by a glacier. Especially not by a cheap plastic imitation!"

The tiny lander arced high over the blue pool of atmosphere, and far off, on the northern horizon, was a fine, bladelike line of pure white.

Quinquepedalian

PIERS ANTHONY

I t lay there, an indentation in the soil, one centimeter deep and three meters in diameter. It was flat, it was smooth, and the sand and the dirt were twined with rotted leaves and stems in a marbled pattern. The edge, cut sharp and clean, exposed a miniature stratum leading up to the unpressed forest floor, and spoke of the weight that had stood on that spot, molding the earth into the shape of its fundament.

It was the mark of a foot, or a hoof, or whatever it is that touches the ground when an animal ambulates. One print —

Charles Tinnerman shook his head somberly. A single print could have been a freak of nature. This was one of many: a definite trail. They were spaced twenty or thirty feet apart, huge and level; ridges of spadiceous earth narrowed toward the center of each, rounded and smooth, as though squirted liquidly up between half-yard toes. Some were broken, toppled worms lying skew, scuffed when the hoof moved on. Around the spoor rose the forest, in gargantuan splendor; each trunk ascending gauntly into a mass of foliage so high and solid that the ground was cast into an almost nocturnal shadow.

At dusk the three men halted. "We could set up an

arc," Tinnerman said, reaching behind to pat his harness.

Don Abel grunted negatively. "Use a light, and everything on the planet will know where we are. We don't want the thing that made that"—he gestured toward the trail—"to start hunting *us*."

The third man spoke impatiently. "It rains at night, remember? If we don't get close pretty soon, the water'll wash out the prints."

Tinnerman looked up. "Too late," he said. There was no thunder, but abruptly it was raining, solidly, as it must to support a forest of this type. They could hear the steady deluge flaying the dense leaves far above. Not a drop reached the ground.

"The trees won't hold it back forever," Abel remarked. "We'd better break out the pup tent in a hurry —"

"Hey!" Fritz Slaker's voice sang out ahead. "There's a banyan or something up here. Shelter!"

Columns of water hissed into the ground as the great leaves far above overflowed at last. The men galloped for cover, packs thumping as they dodged the sudden waterfalls.

They stripped their packs and broke out rations silently. The dry leaves and spongy loam made a comfortable seat, and after a day of hiking the realization was bliss. Tinnerman leaned back against the base of the nearest trunk, chewing and gazing up into the bole of the tree. It was dark; but he could make out a giant spherical opacity from which multiple stems projected downward, bending and swelling for thirty-five meters until they touched the ground as trunks four meters in diameter.

Don Abel's voice came out of the shadow. "The

monster passed right under here. I'm sitting on the edge of a print. What if it comes back?"

Slaker laughed, but not loudly. "Mebbe we're in its nest? We'd hear it. A critter like that—just the shaking of the ground would knock us all a meter into the air." There was a sustained rustle.

"What are you doing?" Abel asked querulously.

"Making a bed," Slaker snapped.

"Do you think it's safe?" Abel asked, though his tone indicated that he suspected one place was as unsafe as another. After a moment, the rustle signified that he too was making a bed.

Tinnerman smiled in the dark, amused. He really did not know the other men well; the three had organized an AWOL party on the spur of the moment, knowing that the survey ship would be planetbound for several days.

The bark of the tree was thick and rubbery, and Tinnerman found it oddly comfortable. He put his ear against it, hearing a faint melodic humming that seemed to emanate from the interior. It was as though he was auditing the actual life-processes of the alien vegetation—although on this world *he* was the alien— and this fascinated him.

The other two were soon asleep. Sitting there in silence, the absolute blackness of a strange world's umbra pressing against his eyeballs, Tinnerman realized that this outing, dangerous as it was, offered him a satisfaction he had seldom known. Slaker and Abel had accepted him for what he was not: one of the fellows.

Those footprints. Obviously animal—yet so large. Would a pressure of seven tons per square meter depress the earth that much? How much would the total creature weigh?

Tinnerman found his pack in the dark and rummaged for his miniature calculator. The tiny numbers fluoresced as he set up his problem: 144 times the square of 4.5 times pi divided by 20. It came to about 460 tons per print. And how many feet did it have, and how much weight did each carry when at rest?

He had heard that creatures substantially larger than the dinosaurs of ancient Earth could not exist on land. On an Earth-type planet, which this one was with regard to gravity, atmosphere, and climate, the limits were not so much biological as physical. A diminutive insect required many legs, not to support its weight, but to preserve balance. Brontosaurus, with legs many times as sturdy as those of an insect, even in proportion to its size, had to seek the swamp to ease the overbearing weight. A larger animal, in order to walk at all, would have to have disproportionately larger legs and feet. Mass cubed with increasing size while the cross section of the legs squared; to maintain a feasible ratio, most of the mass above a certain point would have to go to the feet.

Four hundred and sixty tons? The weight on each foot exceeded that of a family of whales. Bones should shatter and flesh tear free with every step.

The rain had ceased and the forest was quiet now. Tinnerman scraped up a belated bed of his own and lay down. But his mind refused to be pacified. Bright and clear and ominous the thoughts paraded, posing questions for which he had no answer. What thing had they blundered across?

A jumping animal! Tinnerman sat up, too excited to sleep. Like an overgrown snowshoe rabbit, he thought—bounding high, hundreds of meters to nip the lofty greenery, then landing with terrific impact. It could be quite small—less than a ton, perhaps, with one grossly splayed balancing foot. At night it might sail into a selected roost . . . or *onto* . . .

He turned his eyes up to the impenetrable canopy above. In the flattened upper reaches of the banyan . . . a nest?

Tinnerman stood, moving silently away from the bodies of his companions. Locating his pack a second time he dug out cleats and hand spikes, fitting them to his body by feel. He found his trunk, shaping its firm curvature with both hands; then he began to ascend.

He climbed, digging the spikes into the heavy bark and gaining altitude in the blackness. The surface gradually became softer, more even, but remained firm; if it were to pull away from the inner wood the fall would kill him. He felt the curvature increase and knew that the diameter of the trunk was shrinking; but still there was no light at all.

His muscles tensed as his body seemed to become heavier, more precariously exposed. Something was pulling him away from the trunk, weakening his purchase; but he could not yet circle any major portion of the column with his arms. Something was wrong; he would have to descend before being torn loose.

Relief washed over him as he realized the nature of the problem. He was near the top; the stem was bending in to join the main body of the tree, and he was on the underside. He worked his way to the outside and the strain eased; now gravity was pulling him into the trunk, helping him instead of leaving him hanging. Quickly he completed the ascent and stood at last against the massive nexus where limb melded into bole.

Here there was light, a dim glow from overhead. He mounted the vast gnarled bulk, a globular shape ten meters in diameter covered with swellings and scars. It was difficult to picture it as it was, a hundred feet above the ground, for nothing at all could be seen beyond its damp mound. Although it was part of a living or once-living thing, there was no evidence of foliage. There was no nest.

The center of the crude sphere rose on to another trunk or stalk, a column about three meters in diameter, pointing straight up as far as he could see. He was not at the top at all. The bark here was smooth and not very thick; it would be difficult to scale, even with the cleats.

Tinnerman rested for about ten minutes, lying down and putting his ear to the wood. Again the melody of the interior came to him, gentle yet deep. It brought a vision of many layers, pulsing and interweaving; of tumescence and flow, rich sap in the fibers. There was life of a sort going on within, either of the tree or in it.

He stood and mounted the central stalk. Quickly he climbed, spikes penetrating at fingers, knees and toes, bearing him antlike up the sheer column without hesitation. The light above became brighter, though it was only the lesser gloom of a starless night on a moonless planet. Ahead the straight trunk went on and on, narrowing but never branching. Huge limbs from neighboring trees crossed nearby, bare and eerie, residual moisture shining dully; but his climb ignored them. Fifty feet; seventy-five; and now he was as high above the bole as it was above the ground. The stem to which he clung had diminished to a bare five-foot diameter, but rose on toward the green upper forest.

Tinnerman's muscles bunched once more with strain. A wind came up; or perhaps he had come up to it. At this height, even the slightest tug and sway was alarming. He reached his arms around the shaft and hung on. Below, the spokes of other trees were a forest of their own, a fairyland of brush and blackness, crossing and recrossing, concealing everything except the slender reed he held. Above, the first leaves appeared, flat and heavy in the night. He climbed.

Suddenly it ended. The trunk, barely a meter through, expanded into a second bole shaped like an upside-down pear with a two-meter thickness, and stopped. Tinnerman clambered onto the top and stood there, letting his weary arms relax, balancing against the sway. There was nothing else—just a vegetable knob two hundred feet above the ground. All around, the dark verdure rustled in the breeze, and the gloom below was a quiet sea.

No branches approached within twenty feet of the knob, though the leaves closed in above, diffusing the glow of the sky. Tinnerman studied the hollow around him, wondering what kept the growth away. Was this a take-off point for the hidden quarry?

Then it came to him, unnerving him completely. Fear hammered inside him like a bottled demon; he dared not let it out. Shaking, he began the descent.

Morning came, dim and unwilling; but it was not the wan light filtering down like sediment that woke the explorers. Nor was it the warmth of day, soaking into the tops and running down the trunks in the fashion of the night water.

They woke to sound: a distant din, as of a large animal tearing branches and crunching leaves. It was

the first purposeful noise they had heard since entering the forest; as such, it was unnatural, and brought
all three to their feet in alarm.

The evening deluge had eradicated all trace of the
prints leading up to the giant structure under which
they had taken shelter. Beneath it the spoor remained,
as deep and fresh as before; one print near the edge
was half gone.

Slaker sized up the situation immediately. "Guaran-
tees the trail was fresh," he said. "We don't know
whether it was coming or going, but it was made
between rains. Let's get over and spot that noise." He
suited action to word and set off, pack dangling from
one hand, half eaten space-ration in the other.

Abel was not so confident. "Fresh, yes—but we still
don't know where the thing went. You don't look as
though you got much sleep, Tinny."

Tinnerman didn't answer. They picked up their packs
and followed Slaker, who was already almost out of
sight.

They came up to him as he stood at the edge of an
open space in the forest. Several mighty trees had
fallen, and around their massive corpses myriad little
shoots were reaching up. The sunlight streamed down
here, intolerably bright after the obscurity underneath.
The noise had stopped.

There was a motion in the bush ahead. A large body
was moving through the thicket, just out of sight,
coming toward them. A serpentine neck poked out of
the copse, bearing a cactus-like head a meter in diameter. The head swung toward them, circularly
machairodont, a ring of thirty-centimeter eyestalks
extended.

The men froze, watching the creature. The head

moved away, apparently losing its orientation in the silence. The neck was smooth and flexible, about three meters in length; the body remained out of sight.

"Look at those teeth!" Slaker whispered fiercely. "That's our monster."

Immediately the head reacted, demonstrating acute hearing. It came forward rapidly, seven meters above the ground; and in a moment the rest of the creature came into sight. The body was a globular mass about three meters across, mounted on a number of spindly legs. The creature walked with a peculiar caterpillar ripple, one ten-foot leg swinging around the body in a clockwise direction while the others were stationary, reminding Tinnerman of the problems of a wounded daddy-long-legs. The body spun, rotating with the legs; but the feet managed to make a kind of precessional progress. The spin did not appear to interfere with balance or orientation; the ring of eye-stalks kept all horizons covered.

Slaker whipped out his sidearm. "No!" Tinnerman cried, too late. Slaker's shot smacked into the central body, making a small but visible puncture.

The creature halted as if nonplussed, legs rising and falling rhythmically in place. It did not fall. Slaker's second bullet tore into it, and his third, before Tinnerman wrested away the gun. "It wasn't attacking," he said, not knowing how to explain what he knew.

They watched while the monster's motion gradually slowed, huge drops of ichor welling from its wounds. It shuddered; then the legs began pounding the ground in short, violent steps, several at a time. Coordination was gone; slowly the body overbalanced and toppled.

The great mouth opened like a flower, like a horn, and emitted an ear-shattering blast of sound, a tormented cry of pain and confusion; then the body fell heavily on its side.

For a moment the three men stood in silence, watching the death throes. The creature's legs writhed as though independently alive, and the head twisted savagely on the ground, knocking off the oddly brittle eyestalks. Tinnerman's heart sank, for the killing had been pointless. If he had told the others his nighttime revelation —

From the forest came a blast of incredible volume. Tinnerman clapped both hands over his ears as the siren stridence deafened them with a power of twelve to fifteen bels.

It ended, leaving a wake of silence. It had been a call, similar to that of the creature just shot, but deeper and much louder. There was a larger monster in the forest, answering the call for help.

"Its mate?" Abel wondered out loud, his voice sounding thin.

"Its mother!" Tinnerman said succinctly. "And I think we'd better hide."

Slaker shrugged. "Bullets will stop it," he said.

Tinnerman and Abel forged into the brush without comment. Slaker stood his ground confidently, aiming his weapon in the general direction of the approaching footfalls.

Once more the foghorn voice sounded, impossibly loud, forcing all three to cover their ears before drums shattered and brains turned to jelly. Slaker could be seen ahead, one arm wrapped around his head to protect both ears, the other waving the gun.

The ground shook. High foliage burst open and

large trees swayed aside, their branches crashing to the ground. A shape vast beyond imagination thundered into the clearing.

For a moment it paused, a four-legged monster thirty meters high. Its low head was four meters thick, with a flat, shiny snout. A broad eye opened, several feet across, casting about myopically. A ring of fibers sprouted, each pencil-thick, flexing slightly as the head moved.

Slaker fired.

The head shot forward, thudding into the ground ten meters in front of him. The body moved, rotating grandly, as another member lifted and swung forward. They were not heads, but feet! Five feet with eyes. The monster was a hugely sophisticated adult of the quinquepedalian species Slaker had killed.

The man finally saw the futility of his stand, and ran. The towering giant followed, feet jarring the ground with rhythmic impacts, hoofs leaving three-meter indents. It spun majestically, a dance of terrible gravity, pounding the brush and trees and dirt beneath it into nothingness. As each foot lifted, the heavy skin rolled back, uncovering the eye, and the sensory fibrils shot out. As each foot fell, the hide wrinkled closed, protecting the organs from the shock of impact.

The creature was slow, but its feet were fast. The fifth fall came down on the running figure, and Slaker was gone.

The quinquepedalian hesitated, one foot raised, searching. It was aware of them; it would not allow the killers of its child to escape. The eye roved, socketless, its glassy stare directed by a slow twisting of the foot. The circle of filaments combed the air, feeling for a sound or smell, or whatever trace of the fugitives they were adapted to detect.

After a few minutes the eye closed and the fibrils withdrew. The foot went high; plummeted. The earth rocked with the force of the blow. It lifted again, to smash down a few feet over, leaving a tangent print.

After a dozen such stomps the creature reversed course and came back, making a second row ahead of the first. This, Tinnerman realized, was carpet bombing; and the two men were directly in the swath.

If they ran, the five-footed nemesis would cut them down easily. If they stayed, it would get them anyway, unless one or both of them happened to be fortunate enough to fit into the diamond between four prints. The odds were negative. And quite possibly it would sense a near miss, and rectify the error with a small extra tap.

They waited, motionless, while it laid down another barrage, and another. Now it was within fifteen meters, mechanically covering the area. Behind it a flat highway was developing.

Saturation stomping, Tinnerman thought, and found the concept insanely funny. Man discovers a unique five-footed monster—the Quink—and it steps on him. Would the history books record the irony?

He saw the answer. He gave a cry and lurched to his feet, flinging his pack aside and plunging directly at the monster.

The foot halted, quite fast on the uptake, and rotated its eye to cover him. It gathered itself, crashed down, an irresistible juggernaut. The earth jumped with its fury; but Tinnerman, running in an unexpected direction, had passed its arc.

He halted directly under the main body of the

quinquepedalian. If his guess was correct, it would be unable to reach him there. It would have to move—and he would move with it.

Far above, the main body hovered, a black boulder suspended on toothpicks. Above that, he knew, the neck and head extended on into the sky. A head shaped like a pear—when its mouth was closed. The first foot turned inward, its eye bearing on him. It hung there, several meters above the ground, studying him with disquieting intelligence. It did not try to pin him. Balance, Tinnerman judged, was after all of paramount importance to a creature two hundred feet tall. If it lost its footing, the fall of its body would destroy it. So long as it kept three or four feet correctly positioned and firmly planted, it could not fall; but if it were to pull its members into too small a circle it could get into serious trouble. Several hundred tons are not lightly tossed about.

The quinquepedalian moved. The feet swung clockwise, one at a time, striking the ground with an elephantine touch. The bars of Tinnerman's cage lifted and fell, crushing the terrain with an almost musical beat; the body turned, gaining momentum. The feet on one side seemed to retreat; on the other they advanced, forcing him to walk rapidly to keep himself centered.

The pace increased. Now the feet landed just seconds apart, spinning the vast body forward. Tinnerman had to break into a run.

Small trees impeded his progress; every time he dodged around an obstruction, the hind feet gained. On an open plain he might have been able to outrun the monster; but now it had maneuvered him onto rough ground. If it didn't tire soon, it would have him. In time it could force him over a cliff that its own legs could straddle, or into a bog. Or it might forget him and go after Abel—and he would have to stay under it, not daring to place himself outside its circle. His respect for it mounted; he was in the eye of a hurricane, and would soon have to find some other place of safety.

Tinnerman studied the pattern of motion. At this velocity, the individual feet did not have time for more than peremptory adjustments; the maintenance of forward motion dictated an involved but predictable pattern. One foot had to vacate the spot for the next; he was not sure whether two feet ever left the ground at the same time, but could see sharp limitations. If he were to cross a print just vacated —

He timed his approach and took off to the side, almost touching the ascending foot. It twisted in flight, its eye spotting him quickly; but it was unable to act immediately. It struck the ground far ahead, casting up debris with the force of its braking action, and the following member lifted in pursuit.

Tinnerman ran straight out at breakneck speed. He had underestimated Quink's versatility; the second foot went after him much more alertly than an ordinary nervous system should have permitted. In a creature of this size, many seconds should have elapsed before the brain assimilated the new information and decided upon a course of action; yet the feet seemed to react promptly with individual intelligence. This thing was far too large and far-flung for the operation of any effective nervous system—yet it operated most effectively.

The shadow of a leg passed over him, and Tinnerman

thought for a detached moment that he had been caught. But the impact was eight meters to his rear. The next one would get him, unless—

He cut sharply toward a medium-large tree at the edge of the clearing. He dared not look; but he was sure the creature behind was milling in temporary confusion. It could not dodge as fast as he—he hoped.

He reached the tree and ducked behind its five meter diameter, feeling safe for the moment.

Quink brought up before the tree. One foot quested around the side, searching for him. He could see its enormously thick hoof, completely flat on the underside: polished steel, with a reddish tinge in the center. Probably natural coloration; but he thought of Slaker, and shuddered.

The wooden skin drew back, uncovering the eye. The ankle above the hoof widened, the skin bunching in a great roll. He knew now that it settled when the foot rested, coming down to make contact with the ground. He had rested against that swelling last night; he had climbed that leg. . . .

As though satisfied that it could not reach him so long as he hid behind the tree, the quinquepedalian paused for an odd shuffle. Tinnerman peeked around the trunk and saw the legs bunched together in a fashion that destroyed some previous theories, then spread out in a trapezoidal formation. One foot hung near the tree, supporting no weight, and seemingly overbalancing the body somewhat. Then the near foot hefted itself high, swinging like a pendulum, and threw itself against the tree with resounding force.

The entire trunk reverberated with the blow, and a shower of twigs and leaves fluttered down from the upper reaches. The foot struck again, higher; again the tree quaked and loosed a larger fall of detritus. Tinnerman kept a cautious eye on it; he could be laid low by a comparatively small branch.

The single foot continued its attack, striking the tree regularly about fifteen meters above the ground. At that height the foot was about the same diameter as the tree, and the weight behind it was formidable. Yet such action seemed pointless, because damage to the tree would not affect the man behind it.

Or was he underestimating Quink again?

The pounding ceased, and he poked his head cautiously around once more. Was the thing retreating? Somehow he did not expect it to give up easily; it had demonstrated too much savvy and determination for that. It was a remarkable animal, not only for its size.

Three legs stood in a tripod, while two came up simultaneously. Tinnerman's brow wrinkled; it did not seem possible for it to maintain its balance that way. But it was acting with assurance; it had something in mind.

The two feet rose, together, one held just above the other. In awe, Tinnerman watched the lofty body topple forward, unable to stand upright in such a position. Suddenly the two feet thrust forward with staggering power; the entire body rocked backward as they smashed into the tree. And this time the timber felt it. A gunshot explosion rent the air as the fibers of the trunk split and severed, wood splaying; and the large roots broke the ground like sea monsters as the entire tree hinged on its roots.

Now Tinnerman could see how the clearing had been formed. The parent opened a hole in the forest, so that the baby could feed on the little saplings. As the vegetation grew, so did the child, until tall enough to reach the foliage of full-sized trees.

A few more blows would fell this one. Tinnerman waited for the next impact, then fled, hidden from view, he hoped, by the tilting trunk. The creature continued its attack, unaware that the real quarry had gone.

Tinnerman picked up the trail, human prints this time. Abel should have escaped during the distraction, and would be heading for the ship.

The mighty forest was quiet now, except for a slight rustle ahead. That would be Abel. Tinnerman moved without noise instinctively, disinclined to interrupt the medication of the great trees' eternal beauty. And knew that he was a fool, for the forest hardly cared, and the quinquepedalian, with all its decibels, would not worry about the distant patter of human feet.

"Don," he called, not loudly. Abel turned at once, a smile on his face.

"Tinny! I'm glad you got away." He too was careful of his volume; probably the monster could not hear, but it was pointless to ask for trouble. "You seemed to know what you were doing. But I was afraid you had not made it. I would have waited for you if —"

"I know, Don." Abel was no coward; if there had been any way to help, he would have done so. When dealing with the quinquepedalian, loitering was futile and dangerous; the person involved either got away or he did not. The most practical recourse was to trek immediately for the ship, so that at least one person would live to tell the story.

"Ship takes off in twelve hours," Abel said, shaking his pack into greater comfort. "If we move right along, we can make it in six hours. Can't be more than twenty miles."

"Going to make a full report, Don?" Tinnerman was uneasy, without being certain why.

"Fritz was killed," Abel said simply.

Tinnerman put out a hand and brought him to a stop. "We can't do it, Don."

Abel studied him with concern. "I'll give you a hand if you got clipped. I thought you were OK."

"I'm all right. Don, we killed that thing's baby. It did what any parent would do. If we report it, the captain will lift ship and fry it with the main jet."

"Code of space, Tinny. Anything that attacks a man —"

"It didn't attack. It came to the defense of its child. We don't have the right to sentence it."

Abel's eyes grew cold. "Fritz was my friend. I thought he was yours too. If I could have killed that monster myself, I'd have done it. You coming along?"

"Sorry, Don. I have no quarrel with you. But I can't let you report Quink to the captain."

Abel sized him up, then took off his pack. He didn't ask questions. "If that's the way it has to be," he said evenly.

Don Abel was a slow man, cautious in his language and conservative in action. But he had never been mistaken for a weakling. His fists were like lightning.

Tinnerman was knocked back by two blows to the chin and a roundhouse on the ear. He held back, parrying with his forearm; Abel landed a solid punch to the midriff, bringing down his guard, and followed that with a bruising smack directly on the mouth. Tinnerman feinted with his left, but got knocked off his feet with a body check before getting a chance to connect with his right.

He rolled over, grasping for the feet, and got lifted by a blinding knee to the chin. His head reeled with a red haze; and still the blows fell, pounding his head and neck, while Abel's foot stunned the large muscle of the thigh, aiming for the groin.

Tinnerman's reticence fell aside, and he began to fight. He bulled upward, ignoring the punishment, and flung his arms around the other man's waist. Abel retaliated with a double-handed judo chop to the back of the neck; but he held on, linking his forearms in a bearhug, pulling forward. Abel took a fistful of hair, jerking Tinnerman's head from side to side; but slowly the hug lifted him off his feet.

Abel was free suddenly, using a body motion Tinnerman hadn't met before, and once again fists flew.

It took about fifteen minutes. Abel finally lay panting on the ground, exhausted but conscious, while Tinnerman rummaged in the pack for first aid. "I knew you could take me," Abel said. "It had to be fast, or that damn endurance of yours would figure in. You ever been tired in your life, Tinny?"

Tinnerman handed him the sponge to clean up the blood. "Last night I climbed the Quink," he said. "I stood on its head—and it never made a motion."

"Quink? Oh, you mean the monster." Abel sat up suddenly. "Are you trying to tell me —?" A look of awe came over his face. "That thing with the legs, the big one—you mean we slept under —" He paused for more reflection. "Those tracks — it does figure. If it hadn't been so dark, we would have seen that the monster was still standing in them! That's why there were leaves under there, and a couple of prints from the front feet. It must have been asleep . . ." His mind came belatedly to grips with the second problem. "You *climbed* it?"

Tinnerman nodded soberly. "It couldn't have slept through that. I used the spikes . . . I didn't catch on until I saw the way the leaves had been eaten around the head. All it had to do was open its mouth—but it let me go. Live and let live."

Abel came to his feet "OK, Charlie—we'll wait six hours before heading for the ship. That'll give us time to look this thing over. Don't get me wrong—I haven't made up my mind. I may still tell the captain . . . but not right away."

Tinnerman relaxed. "Let's see what we can learn," he said. He reassembled Abel's pack, then glanced up.

The foot was there, poised with Damoclesian ponderosity five meters above their heads. The eye was open, fibrils extended. The quinquepedalian had come upon them silently.

"Split!" Tinnerman yelled. The two men dived in opposite directions. Once more the ground bounced with concussion as he raced for the nearest tree. He slid around it, safe for the moment.

A glance back showed the monster hauling its foot back into the air. Only half of Don Abel had made it to safety. Then the huge hoof hovered and dropped, and the grisly sight was gone. There was only another flat print in the earth.

Abel might have been fast enough, if he hadn't been weakened by the fight. Just as Slaker would have been more careful, had he been warned. The quinquepedalian was the agent; but Tinnerman knew that he was the cause of the two deaths.

Now Quink approached the tree, spinning in her stately dance, hoofs kissing the shadowed ground without a sound. She stood.

Why hadn't she crushed them both as they fought, oblivious to the danger above? She must have been there for several minutes, watching, listening. One gentle stomp, and vengeance would have been complete. Why had she waited?

Fair play?

Was this thing really intelligent? Did it have ethics of its own—her own?

The familiar foot came around the trunk, perceptors out. He stood calmly, knowing that he was safe from immediate harm. He stooped to pick up a handful of dirt, tossing it at the light-sensitive area. The eye folded shut immediately, letting the earth rattle over the bare hide. Fast reflexes.

Too fast. An animal of this size had to be handicapped by the distance between brain and appendages. It was manifestly impossible to have an instantaneous reflex at the end of a limb thirty meters long. No neural track could provide anything like the speed he had witnessed.

Tinnerman moved to the other side of the trunk, as though getting ready for a dash to another tree. The foot swung around at once, intercepting him from the other direction. There was no doubt that it learned from experience, and could act on it immediately.

But how could that impulse travel from eye to brain and back again so quickly? Usually, an animal's eye was situated quite close to the brain, to cut down neural delay. Unless Quink had a brain in her foot —

The answer struck him stunningly. There *was* a brain in the foot. There had to be. How else could the pedal members be placed so accurately, while maintaining perfect balance? There would be a coordinating ganglion in the central body, issuing general orders concerning overall motion and order of precedence for the lifting of the feet; there could be another small brain in the head, to handle ingestion and vocalization. And each foot would make its own decisions as to exact placement and manner of descent. Seven brains in all—organized into a mighty whole.

The foot-brains could sleep when not on duty, firmly planted in the ground and covered by a thick overlap of impervious skin. They were probably not too bright as individuals—their job was specialized—but with the far more powerful central brain to back them up, any part of Quink was intelligent.

"Creature of the forest," Tinnerman said to it in wonder. "Quinquepedalian, septecerebrian—you are probably smarter than I." And certainly stronger. He thought about that, discovering a weird pleasure in the contemplation of it. All his life he had remained aloof from his fellows, searching for something he could honestly look up to. Now he had found it.

Eleven hours later, on schedule, the ship took off. It would be three, four, five years before a squat colony ship came to set up frontier operations.

Quink was stalking him with ageless determination and rapidly increasing sagacity. Already she had learned to anticipate the geometric patterns he traced. He had led her through a simple square, triangle, and star, giving up each figure when she solved it and set her body to intercept him ahead. Soon she would come to the conclusion that the prey was something more than a vicious rodent. Once she realized that she was dealing with intelligence, communication could begin.

Perhaps in time she would forgive him for the death of her child, and know that vengeance had been doubly extracted already. The time might come when he could walk in the open once more and not be afraid of a foot. At night, while she slept, he was safe; but by day —

Perhaps when the colonists came, they would be greeted by a man riding the mightiest steed of all time. Or by the quinquepedalian, carrying its pet. It did not matter who was ascendant, so long as the liaison was established.

"Creature of the forest," he said again, doubling back as he perceived her bulk in wait at an intersection of the triquetra pattern. For a moment he stood and looked at her, so vast and beautiful, spinning in the dance of his destruction. "Creature of the forest," he said, "Thou art mighty."

"Thou art mightier than I." There was an answering blast, bels in magnitude, like a goddess awakening beyond the horizon.

The Lonely Alien

SYDNEY J. BOUNDS

C adet Kirsty Hammond hit bottom with the breath knocked out of her. She sprawled facedown with one leg twisted under her. She spat out leaves and small twigs and tried to get up. Pain shot through her ankle.

"Ouch!"

Pale orange light filtered through a canopy of leafy branches and the smell reminded her of cats. She looked up. The sides of the pit were steep and her ankle wouldn't bear her weight; she wasn't going to make it without help.

That meant trouble. Going off exploring alone on an alien planet was strictly against regulations. And to fall into a hole . . . Senior Cadet Paul Scully was going to laugh his head off. And then report her to Lieutenant Ash.

Kirsty sighed. There was nothing else to do; she'd have to call the landing party and take her punishment. As she reached for her radio transmitter she heard movement in the pit. She sucked air and froze. She was not alone. She might have fallen into the lair of some wild animal.

"I'm not scared," she told herself. "I'm a cadet in the space service. I'm going to be the first woman to captain a starship and I'm definitely not afraid of anything!"

And, suddenly, she wasn't. A feeling of friendliness,

like a fleecy blanket, invaded her mind and calmed her.

From the shadows at the far end of the pit padded a small furry creature; an inquisitive animal with delicate paws and a pointed black-and-white face. It purred, and Kirsty relived a memory of a kitten she'd had when she was young.

"Merlin," she whispered.

"Merlin," echoed a small voice inside her head. "Abandoned. Lonely."

The kitten, if it was a kitten, snuggled into her arms and purred. It must be, she thought, telepathic.

"Together?" asked a small voice hopefully.

Kirsty wished that were possible; she felt a unique bonding with the tiny creature. But regulations insisted that live animals from other worlds were never brought aboard a starship.

She sighed and switched on her transmitter. "Cadet Hammond calling to request help."

A young male voice snapped back at her. "Scully here. Keep transmitting so we can track you."

Merlin explored her uniform, sniffed at her red hair and tasted her freckles. He seemed to approve.

A light shone into the pit, a rope snaked down, and two cadets slid to the bottom.

"Trust you to make trouble," said the senior cadet. "Why they allow girls into the service is beyond me."

He, too, would be on the carpet for allowing her to break away from the landing party.

The cadets looped a rope around her waist. "Haul away!"

"I'm not helpless," Kirsty protested. "I've only twisted my ankle."

"So you'll be carried," Scully said sourly, "and report to Lieutenant Ash aboard *Endeavour*."

Kirsty was wondering what had happened to Merlin when a small voice warned, "Best not to draw attention to me."

As they approached the starship's shuttle, Kirsty said, "Can't we overlook this, Paul? I don't want to get you into trouble."

Scully looked angry. "You should have thought of that before. Your transmission was monitored."

The shuttle lifted, and Kirsty realized she had somehow acquired an extra piece of equipment; she now had two laser cutters attached to her belt.

"It's me," Merlin said. "I mimic things."

The shuttle docked with the starship in orbit, and Kirsty hobbled out.

"Escort her to sick bay," Scully ordered. "I have to report."

Doc Wilson greeted her with a beaming smile. "And what has my favorite patient been up to this time? You do seem to get into more trouble than any other cadet."

"I don't mean to, Doc."

Kirsty sat on the examination table while he inspected and then bandaged her ankle. "Just a sprain. Keep off it for a few days. Light duties only, then report back to me."

The door opened and Lieutenant Ash, I/C cadets, walked in. "I suppose there's no hope it could be fatal this time, Doc?"

"Not a hope. More lives than a cat ... what was that? It sounded like a miaow!"

Ash grinned. "No cats aboard *Endeavour*, Doc." He turned to Kirsty, his face grave.

"Why is it always you, Cadet Hammond? Independent action is to be encouraged but, at seventeen, you should have some sense of responsibility. An officer

has to learn to take orders as well as give them. You are confined to your cabin until further notice."

Frowning, he tapped into the personnel file. "I see you have a navigation exam coming up. That exam will be brought forward, and you'll take it in your cabin."

"Yes, sir," Kirsty said meekly, and limped away.

In her cabin, with the door shut, Merlin reappeared. The catlike alien prowled around, sniffing at everything.

"I hope you're satisfied," Kirsty said. "I could get into big trouble if anyone sees you."

Merlin wound about her ankles, purring. "Navigation, yes?"

"Yes, and if I pass, promotion to lieutenant is automatic."

Ash's voice sounded over the intercom. "Your first paper is coming on-screen now. Good luck, cadet."

Kirsty sat down at the keyboard, waiting. "Merlin! What are you —?"

The alien had changed form again, mimicking a computer tape, and plugged itself into the navigation computer.

"Navigation is easy, Kirsty. Just print out what I tell you . . ."

To the annoyance of Senior Cadet Paul Scully, Kirsty passed the navigation exam with the highest score recorded by any cadet.

"Now I'm on my way," she said.

"Now we're on our way," a small voice corrected.

Lieutenant Kirsty Hammond snapped on her seat belt as a siren wailed its final warning. Crew sections reported:

"All holds secured . . . Port shuttle clear."

The captain's voice was calm and controlled: "Chief engineer, I want maximum acceleration."

The starship *Endeavour* broke out of orbit on her mission of mercy. G-forces pressed Kirsty into her seat at the navigator's console. Beside her Lieutenant Jordan, the pilot, watched his own screen. Behind them, in the command chair, the captain could survey the whole of the bridge.

The main screen showed the port shuttle falling

away to its base; then there was only the star-studded void before them.

Kirsty studied her read-outs and said, "Exit window clear."

Acceleration pressure continued to build up until it reached the permitted maximum. Normally, a starship made a more sedate leavetaking, but, on this trip, time was a governing factor.

The distant colony of Crusoe was in trouble. Plague had struck down the small population and the only treatment, a rare blood serum, was in short supply. The *Endeavour* had been diverted to pick up a batch of the serum and rush it to the dying colonists.

"Isn't this thrilling?" Merlin asked in Kirsty's head.

She glanced down to discover what form the alien had taken, and found she had an extra pouch attached to her belt.

"It'll be more than thrilling if we don't make it in time," she thought. "It'll be a tragedy." In seventy-two hours the colony on Crusoe would cease to exist.

"Lieutenant Hammond." Jordan, the pilot, was speaking. "This is your chance to see some old-fashioned 'seat-of-the-pants' piloting. A bit different from the textbook stuff!"

Kirsty was studying for her pilot's exam; an essential if she were one day to captain her own starship.

Acceleration ended and *Endeavour* coasted. She unbuckled and stood behind Jordan to observe.

The captain had decided to risk the Maze, a hazardous region of subspace that could not be plotted with accuracy and was usually avoided. But it was a short cut. Normally a navigator could plot an entry into subspace, with the exit of choice. In the Maze conditions changed haphazardly and a successful crossing was up to the pilot's skill and experience.

"Proceed when ready," the captain said.

"Aye, sir."

Jordan watched the readouts from the navigation computer, waited with his hand poised—then moved the toggle that took the ship into subspace.

The screen went crazy.

The region known as the Maze was a vortex of deadly energies with reefs of antimatter. Failure to find a safe path between the appalling energies involved meant instant destruction.

On-screen Kirsty saw a pyrotechnic display of sparkling colors; swirling rainbows that blossomed and shrank and blossomed again.

"This could be dangerous," Merlin remarked, and vanished.

Seconds later, Jordan toppled to the deck, unconscious. Kirsty slid into his seat; someone had to take over quickly and she was nearest. Her hands hovered over the control console and she concentrated. She knew the theory . . .

What she had to do was keep in a black lane. Bursts of color were to be avoided at all cost. The changes came fast, confusing her. She was vaguely aware of Doc Wilson bending over the still form of the pilot.

Suddenly, Merlin was back with her, his presence a comfortable feeling in her mind.

"Stay calm," he said. "You can do anything with my help."

The black lane she was following narrowed and a kaleidoscope of energies threatened the ship. Just in time she took another pathway. It was exhilarating, and her reactions were on a hair trigger.

The Maze kept switching randomly; now she entered an area of geometric shapes; triangles and squares and circles, gaudy with dazzling color. Each represented enough energy to reduce *Endeavour* to its component atoms.

Down the side of the pilot's screen ran two columns of computer figures; time elapsed aboard ship and an estimated position in the real world. She seemed to be on course, if that was the right expression; lucky might be a better word.

"Not lucky," Merlin said. "With my help, you're seeing one second ahead all the time —"

Kirsty was startled. "How?"

"Subspace does not follow the laws of normal space-time. I can take advantage of this. Now concentrate."

The sinuous black thread split and she took the left turn, praying it was not a dead end. This wasn't called the Maze for nothing.

The screen filled with explosions of color till she felt dizzy; the black lane shrunk almost to a pinhead, then fanned out.

She remembered Crusoe and the people depending on her and clung on like a fly in the webwork between dimensions, following an ever-changing path.

She was following a strand of the web, darting like an arrow towards the bull's-eye. Then, ahead, she saw the gray wall that marked the boundary of subspace. Her hours of practice at the pilot's mock-up had paid off. She felt her concentration flagging.

"Steady," Merlin warned. "Now!"

She squeezed the toggle that brought *Endeavour* into normal space, with the main screen showing the purple-and-yellow globe of Crusoe. She sagged in her seat, wet with sweat.

She glanced at the clock. Sixty hours! They had arrived in time.

"Well done, Hammond," the captain said. "I think I can say you've passed your practical; your promotion to pilot first class is assured." He paused, and added, a bit reluctantly, Kirsty thought: "You may even make it to starship captain one day. Off duty now and relax."

Jordan, looking shaken, took his seat to orbit Crusoe while a shuttle flew the vital serum down to the planet. He smiled at her. "A whole lot of people down there owe you their lives."

"And Merlin," she thought. She went to her cabin and flopped out, feeling dead beat.

Merlin stretched out beside her on the bunk.

"Were you responsible for what happened to Jordan?" she asked.

"He has an allergy to a particular scent. I simply gave him enough to knock him out temporarily."

She stared at the alien. "When are you going to show me your true shape?"

"True shape?" Merlin yawned. "What true shape? I use anything handy that's around, or take an image from your head. What more do I need? It's all the same to me. Any shape at all is my true shape. Like this . . ."

Kirsty Hammond found herself looking at her mirror image.

Status Extinct

ERIC BROWN

Jessica Ball sneezed as her ship came in to land.

She blew her nose and dropped the tissue in the waste chute. She could not believe it. Modern science had developed starships to send her to the edge of the galaxy in search of intelligent life, and yet there was still no cure for the common cold.

She sat in the darkness of the command cabin, sniffed, and felt sorry for herself. She stared through the viewscreen as the ship touched down with a gentle bump. For as far as she could see, the world was covered in a thin layer of snow. Gray, leafless trees, like umbrellas stripped of their covering, dotted the hilly terrain. The sky was gray, and low on the horizon a tiny sun burned orange. Even as she watched, a new fall of snow began.

She decided to call the planet Winterworld.

"Computer," she said. "Any more information on those life forms you scanned earlier?"

She stared at the screen in front of her. Seconds later, the words appeared: LIFE FORMS TOO DISTANT FOR ACCURATE ANALYSIS: THEY ARE SMALL, SLOW-MOVING, WARM-BLOODED . . . NO FURTHER INFORMATION AVAILABLE.

"Can you tell if they're intelligent?"

The reply flashed up on the screen: NO FURTHER INFORMATION AVAILABLE.

Humankind had been exploring the stars for fifty years, and not one species of intelligent alien had been found. It seemed that only humankind existed, alone in the universe. Jessica often thought that humanity was like a child growing up without playmates, lonely and in need of company.

We need to find intelligent aliens, she told herself. Humanity needs playmates.

"Computer, what's the atmosphere like out there, and the temperature?"

She read the screen. ATMOSPHERE: NINETY-EIGHT PERCENT EARTH-NORMAL, TEMPERATURE: FIVE DEGREES BELOW ZERO, ADVISE USE OF ENVIRONMENT SUIT.

"I'll do that, computer," Jessica said.

She broke her suit out of storage and climbed into it, then ran checks on the air supply and radio links. She would go out for a short exploratory walk lasting no more than thirty minutes, collecting samples of soil and plant life for computer to analyze. Later, after she had returned and slept, she would take the buggy out and explore further afield.

Before she sealed her helmet, she blew her nose for the last time. She had taken anti-influenza pills for the past twenty-four hours, but still felt no better. Her head ached and her throat was sore. She told herself that she was being weak: here she was, an intrepid pilot-explorer, complaining about a common cold.

She stepped into the airlock, and then walked down the ramp to the surface of Winterworld.

She crunched over the frost-hard ground, climbing a low hill toward a stand of bare, gray trees. Her footsteps shattered the silver leaves of a thistle-like plant that covered the surface of the land. She knelt and clumsily picked up the broken leaves in her gloved fingers, then dropped them into her samples bag.

She climbed the hill, and at the top turned to survey the view. Her orange and white ship was the only splash of color in the gray landscape. Beyond the ship to the south, a vast plain stretched away to a distant sea. She turned and looked north: the hills climbed, became foothills, then rose to become high, snow-covered mountains.

She looked down the hill, into the valley. Fifty me-ters away she saw a low bush decorated with yellow flowers. She decided to collect a sample of the flowers, then return to the ship.

She was halfway down the hill when she lost her footing. Her boots shot out from under her and she crashed painfully onto her back, sliding down the hillside like a runaway toboggan.

Too late, she saw the drop before her. She tried to grab hold of passing plants, tried to slow her slide. She screamed as the hillside disappeared beneath her and she fell through the air. She hit the ground with an impact that knocked the breath from her lungs, tore her suit, and smashed the faceplate of her helmet. She rolled over and over, pain shooting through her body.

She came to a stop at the bottom of the ravine. She lay on her back, staring up into the gray alien sky. When she tried to move, the pain became too much and she passed out.

She came to her senses.

The pain and the cold were too much. Her helmet was shattered, her suit torn. The cold invaded, freez-ing her body. She tried to move, sit up. An incredible pain shot up her right leg, making her cry out. She

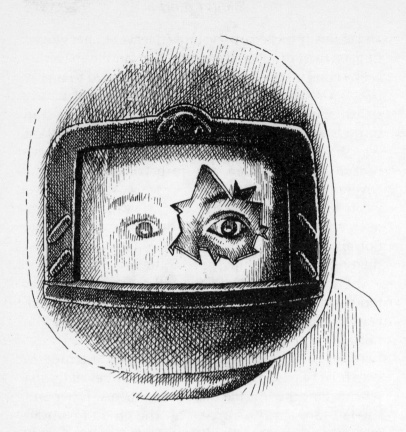

looked down the length of her body. Her leg below the knee was bent at an awkward angle—obviously broken.

Very well, she told herself: she must not panic. This was an emergency, but there was a way out. She would contact the ship, tell the computer to send out the buggy by remote control. It would home in on her signal, locate her, and carry her back to the ship. There, she would spend some time in the healer unit and her leg would be mended. Simple.

She pulled the radio from the chest of her suit, and then stared at it in dismay. The device had been crushed in the fall and was mangled and useless.

Not to worry . . . she carried a spare radio, in case of emergencies. The trouble was, the backup radio was in a pouch on her right boot.

As she sat up and tried to reach forward, pain shot up her leg. It was if someone was hacking at her shin bone with an ax. She cried out, gritted her teeth, and reached out again. This time, she managed to reach her boot and pull the radio from its pouch.

Her sense of triumph lasted just five seconds.

Her fingers, numb with cold, fumbled the radio. It dropped from her grasp. She reached out for it as it slid away from her, but she was too slow. In panic, she watched it skitter away over the frost-hard ground, down the ravine, and out of sight.

Jessica lay back and screamed with desperation.

She tried to clear her mind, consider what to do next. She could not move. The pain from her leg was too intense. Every time she tried to drag herself up the ravine, she felt herself slipping into unconsciousness. But the simple fact was that if she failed to get back to the warmth of the ship, she would be dead in hours.

Also, she was breathing the atmosphere of this planet, and she had no idea what alien viruses might be poisoning her system. She decided that this, at the moment, was the least of her worries.

Her first priority was to get back to the ship.

She sat up, steeled herself, and, using her arms to push herself up the hillside, moved about ten centimeters. Then the pain gripped her leg, and moaning in pain, she passed out again.

Jessica opened her eyes.

She was so cold that she could not feel her hands

and feet. She had to clamp her jaw tight shut to stop her teeth from chattering. Carefully, knowing that if she passed out again she might never wake up, she tried to push herself into a sitting position.

It was impossible. She lay on her back, staring up into the sky. What a way to die, she thought; on a lonely planet five hundred light-years from Earth . . .

It was then that she thought she saw movement. Out of the corner of her eye, at the top of the ravine, she saw something move quickly, then disappear. Seconds passed by, and when nothing happened she told herself that she must have imagined the movement.

She saw it again. Something bobbed its head over the edge of the hillside and quickly looked at her, before moving out of sight. She felt a sudden stab of fear. The computer had told her that animals lived on Winterworld. What if those animals were hungry, and decided to make a meal of her?

There was more movement above her. She saw a dozen small, round heads appear over the edge of the hill. They were gray, as bald as emus' eggs, and they were staring down at her. She closed her eyes, opened them again. They were still there.

Seconds passed, and then the creatures climbed over the edge of the hill and moved down the ravine toward her, and Jessica stared in disbelief.

The creatures were not animals—but men. They were tiny, perhaps a meter high and impossibly slim, their arms and legs as thin and gray as gun barrels. Jessica counted twenty of the tiny extraterrestrials. They moved slowly down the slope, as if wary of the strange creature lying at the bottom.

I don't believe it, she said to herself. Aliens—real, live humanoid aliens . . . She decided to call them Thinnies.

234

They approached her slowly, encircling her and moving forward. She stared at the closest being. It had a slit mouth, two holes in a flat nose, and two big, black eyes.

The aliens came within a meter of her and then crouched down on their iron-rod legs, staring at her. From time to time one would turn and speak to the others in a high, whistling voice.

Jessica raised a hand, pointing up the slope. "I . . . need your help."

At the sound of her voice, the Thinnies stood and backed off.

"The ship," she went on, pointing. "Can you get me back to my ship?"

She laughed at the uselessness of her request. They were aliens—how would they begin to understand what she was talking about?

They approached her again, settling themselves into their peculiar squats, all pointy knees and elbows, and regarded her with curiosity.

"Please," she said desperately. "Please do something to help me . . ."

The Thinnies turned and looked up the slope. Two creatures appeared on the edge of the ravine. They climbed down, dragging something after them.

It was a sled—a crude, narrow sled constructed from the wood of the planet's leafless trees.

They had realized what had happened to her, that she had injured herself and needed to be taken back to her ship.

The Thinnies positioned the sled next to Jessica, and then took hold of her body and legs. She grimaced in pain and they lifted her quickly and placed her on the sled.

235

She was too long for the simple vehicle, and her legs trailed on the ground. As all twenty aliens took hold of the ropes attached to the sled and began pulling, Jessica gasped in pain as her broken leg bounced across the frozen ground.

She hovered on the edge of consciousness, the pain increasing with every passing second. They moved down the ravine, and Jessica expected the sled to turn south and head up the hillside toward her ship.

But instead of heading towards the ship, they turned north and dragged her further into the foothills. Jessica cried out in panic. "No! You don't understand! The wrong way! Please . . . please take me back to the ship!"

They ignored her, carried her further into the hills. In the final seconds before the pain became too much and she passed out, she wondered where they were taking her, and why.

She came awake slowly.

The first thing she realized was that she was no longer freezing cold. She was not exactly warm, but she could feel her hands and feet. The second thing she noticed was that she was flat on her back inside some kind of vast chamber.

She raised her head, looked around, then lay back again in disbelief. She was lying in the performance area of a big, circular amphitheater, covered with a great membrane of material through which she could see the gray sky. The amphitheater was full of aliens seated around the sloping banks. Perhaps thousands of the creatures were gathered there, quietly watching her.

"What do you want?" she asked weakly. "What do you want with me?"

An alien approached her, squatted and spoke to her in its high, fluting language. Jessica shook her head. "It's no good—I don't understand you. Just as you don't understand me."

The alien stood, turned, and spoke to the gathering. It reached out a thin, stick arm to another Thinnie standing out of sight behind Jessica's head. She rolled her eyes to see what was happening, and saw one alien pass the other a long, thin implement like a knife.

She closed her eyes. She could not stop herself from crying. She tried to move, to get away, but the pain from her leg, from the rest of her bruised and battered body, kept her flat on her back.

When she opened her eyes, the Thinnie was approaching her with the knife. She wondered why they were going to kill her—to provide food, as a sacrificial offering to their gods, or simply because she was a stranger who had invaded their territory?

She closed her eyes, waiting for the first blow . . .

It never came.

She felt the material of her suit being cut. Other hands pulled away the remains of her shattered helmet. When she opened her eyes she saw perhaps half a dozen Thinnies moving around her, taking away pieces of her suit, removing her gloves, then unzipping her undersuit and taking that away, too.

When she was naked, two Thinnies squatted beside her and began touching her body with their tiny, clawlike hands. They tested her limbs, pressing the bruised areas and touching the cuts. One alien, curious, examined the St. Christopher medallion around her neck.

They stood, spoke to the gathering.

Then they moved to her broken leg. Together, they

lifted the leg and straightened the break, causing Jessica to cry out in agony. They tied her leg to something straight and cold, a splint of wood. They applied some sticky substance to her cuts and bruises, and as they busied themselves about her, Jessica closed her eyes and gave thanks that the first race of aliens discovered by humankind should prove to be so caring and—she could think of no other word for it—*humane*.

They dressed her again in her undersuit, leaving the remains of the outersuit on the ground around her. Twenty of the Thinnies gathered and gently lifted her back on to the sled, and Jessica could have wept with joy.

Lastly, the gathering of the aliens left their seats around the amphitheater and filed past where she lay, examining her with their staring black eyes, their expressions unreadable. She reached out and touched their arms, each as hard and cold as iron. She murmured, "Thank you," even though she knew that they had no way of understanding her gratitude.

Then they pulled her on the sled from the amphitheater, through a village of crude wooden huts, and back in the direction of her ship.

The ride was less painful this time. The splint kept her leg straight and off the ground, and the ointment they had applied to her body eased her aches and pains.

The aliens dragged the sled up the ship's ramp and left her at the top. Jessica sat up, stared at the beings who had saved her life. She raised her hand, and the Thinnies, responding to her gesture, raised their hands also before walking down the ramp and away from the ship.

Jessica dragged herself into the airlock and through the warm ship to the surgery. She climbed into the healer, stripped off her garments, and removed the makeshift splint. She set the healer for three days, then closed the lid over her and lay back. She felt the warmth of the healer as it began its work, and slipped into a deep, peaceful sleep.

She awoke three days later, climbed from the healer, and tested her leg. It was still sore, but she could walk. She sniffed, then sneezed. The healer might have mended her broken leg, but it had done nothing to cure her cold.

She would, she realized, be famous when she returned to Earth with the news of her discovery. Her name would be known on every colony world: Jessica Ball, the first pilot-explorer to contact intelligent aliens. She imagined the vid-stations on Earth, all wanting to interview her, the crowds eager to see the woman who had met the aliens . . . In years to come there would be scientific teams sent to Winterworld to study the Thinnies and their history, to learn their language and customs.

Maybe, one day, a Thinnie might pay a visit to Earth.

But before she left Winterworld, she would return to the Thinnies and thank them, maybe take them a gift.

She took the St. Christopher medallion from around her neck. St. Christopher, the patron saint of travelers. It would make a suitable present for the race that had helped her in her hour of need.

She climbed into her backup suit, took the buggy from the hold, and drove from the ship. She climbed the hill and passed down the other side, moving around the ravine where she had fallen. She accelerated, speeding over the hills to the alien village.

She expected the noise of the buggy to alert them to her arrival, but if it had they did not venture from their huts to greet her. She braked, climbed from her buggy and looked around. The place was deserted. The sun was high in the sky—it was midday. She wondered if they were in their huts, perhaps taking a meal.

She strode across to the first hut, peered inside. It was empty. She moved to the next one, and this too was deserted.

She saw the covered amphitheater in the center of the village. Perhaps the Thinnies were attending a meeting?

She hurried across to the amphitheater, ducked under the skin, and walked down the slope to the central performance area where three days ago the aliens had treated her leg.

Her footsteps slowed when she saw the first aliens, and then all the others sitting and lying around the banked amphitheater. She ran across to the nearest Thinnie, knelt and reached out to touch the tiny being.

It sprawled on the bank, unmoving. All the others, thousands of them, lay on the bank, many clutching each other. She climbed the bank, stopping often to examine an alien she thought might still be alive.

Then she stood, stared around at the amphitheater full of dead aliens, and a terrible thought occurred to her.

She examined the nearest Thinnie. Its eyes were inflamed, its nose-holes blocked with mucus . . .

Then Jessica saw her old suit in the center of the performance area. Slowly, in a daze, she walked towards it, and stopped.

An alien lay next to the suit, its stick-thin arm outstretched.

Protruding from the chest of the suit, pinning it to the ground, was the long, sharp knife the alien had used three days ago to cut away her suit.

She knew what it meant, this knife in her suit. The aliens, unable to get inside the ship to kill her, had symbolically "killed" her suit . . .

For she had brought death to these innocent people; she had spread disease amongst them in the form of the influenza virus, a virus new to them and against which, therefore, they had no protection.

"I'm sorry," she whispered. "I'm so sorry."

She pulled the St. Christopher medallion from her pouch and dropped it into the hand of the dead alien.

Then, weeping, she hurried from the amphitheater, climbed aboard the buggy and drove at speed from the village.

Back at the ship she slumped into her seat before the viewscreen, staring out as the snow fell on Winterworld.

"Computer," she said in a small voice. "Scan for life—the life forms you detected from orbit before landing. Are there any still alive, anywhere?"

Seconds later the reply flashed across the screen: SCANNERS DETECT SMALL ANIMALS, BIRDS, NO SIGN OF ORIGINAL LIFE FORMS.

She readied the ship for lift-off.

As the engines fired, she entered computer's exploration files. She typed in the information:

Planet: WINTERWORLD

Native Fauna: HUMANOID ALIENS—INTELLIGENT

Status: . . .

Jessica hesitated, tears rolling down her cheeks.
At last she typed:
Status: EXTINCT
Then the ship lifted, carrying Jessica Ball away from Winterworld forever.

No Home but the Stars

PETER T. GARRATT

Jim Parker had known no home but the ship, the *John Brunner*. It was his world: Earth was as remote as the Big Bang, and Tau Ceti, the Target Star, didn't feel real yet. But he did know his life had been unusual. Most people spent theirs on planets, and, apart from Great-Grandfather Parker, he had met no one who had ever set foot on one: who had felt real gravity, or smelled unconditioned air, or drunk water recycled by nature.

He still felt strange in the Observatory. It didn't rotate, so he was weightless. He was used to the artificial gravity of the spinning, cylindrical Life Module, not to having none at all. More amazing was the sky. There wasn't any in the Life Module: the portholes were covered since the sight of the stars appearing to move past the ship under the floor made too many people dizzy. Here, black sky and stars that didn't move were all around. Nothing could be seen to move at all. There was nothing in his life that wasn't cramped like the ship or too vast to have a scale, and the sky was *vast*. He could not comprehend the distance of the tiny sharp points, except by thinking that for most the light had been traveling longer than the *John Brunner*. For many, far, far longer.

Ahead, a single star was brighter than the rest. It

didn't have a disk, it was just brighter. It didn't hurt to look at, though Jim knew he would soon have to avert his eyes from it.

"It's quite distinct now." Great-Grand Parker emerged from his cabin, a tiny Life Module with no spin where he could live without weight. "It's starting to look like a landing beacon."

Jim didn't know how to answer. He had never seen a landing beacon. He simply said: "Good morning, Admiral," as he had been taught. His great-grandfather was officially the most senior officer, the oldest and obviously most experienced, though in fact he played no part in the day-to-day running of the ship.

Great-Grand drifted slowly forward in his float-suit. It was padded with airbags in case he bumped into anything, and would turn itself into a vacuum suit if a collision with a meteorite caused the Observatory to depressurize. His face was very thin, and so, presumably was his real body, but the inflated suit was so big it made him look like the methane-man from *Jupiter Rangers*. He was over a hundred years old, the oldest person on the ship by nearly thirty years. All the rest had been born on board.

He indicated that Jim should float with him to the big optical telescope. It was early in the morning on the main shift, and none of the regular observers were about. Some of them had the information wired to labs in the Life Module. Great-Grand insisted it helped him understand the stars to be surrounded by them while he studied. Mind you, he did admit he lived in the Observatory because he feared that spin-gravity would be too much for his old heart and brittle bones. He pointed at the eyepiece and Jim hesitantly looked through it.

Floating against the black sky and the stars was a

dark disk with a silvery crescent down one side. There were colors in the silver, red, orange, and ocher: it looked like an impossibly perfect Christmas tinsel decoration. To one side was a tiny crescent, little larger than the stars, a satellite, he thought.

"It's . . . it's so beautiful!"

"That's Planet Three. We're looking at it and Two." Great-Grand changed the setting. The next planet showed a smaller disk but a larger, pure white crescent. There was a tiny point over the dark part. Another satellite? Great-Grand went on: "Here's Two. Looks to be a bit hot and wet: lots of carbon dioxide, but not much free oxygen. What does that tell you?"

"Er . . . young planet, could be plant life, not much animal?"

"That's most likely. Three is smaller, colder, older. Might be a better bet for a first landing, though. Either's possible if we do decide to colonize. It hasn't been decided."

Jim was shocked. "But I thought the whole purpose of the . . . of this mission of the *John Brunner* was to found a colony!"

Great-Grand made a little bobbing, wiggling movement, as if he was shrugging his shoulders inside the float-suit. "Mission set out eighty years ago, boy. We were young. Didn't like the pollution on Earth. People who could afford to were migrating to L5s, big Life Modules near Earth." He tried to chuckle, a sound between a cough and a tweet. "Big wheels living in big wheels!" He gave Jim an odd look. The pupils of his eyes were covered by silvery lenses, made twenty years ago, six years before Jim was born, and improved recently on instructions from Earth. They had taken all that time to arrive by radio: ten years for the ques-

tion to get there and ten for the answer to return.

"Don't know if we did right by you lot! Wanted to! We didn't want our grandchildren living their whole lives on L5s . . . we set out to find you a planet. I didn't expect to see it, none of us did, felt we were making a big sacrifice. Didn't think about our own kids who'd be old by the time we got here . . . didn't have a way to ask if you wanted to grow up on a ship . . . bit like an L5, come to think about it, except you can't talk to anyone off-ship without a twenty-year thumb-twiddle . . . then expect you to go down to some unexplored place with no experience of anything similar and live our dreams for us!"

Jim felt confused. Everyone else talked about the mission and the colony in which he would one day live. Great-Grand had an ability to disturb: he alone knew about life outside the ship. Jim was the smallest in his age group, short and thin, and recently most of the others had started growing even faster. To make up he worked hard and took extra lessons from people like Great-Grand. "Surely it's just . . . the way things have to be. The colony, I mean—what else could this ship *do*?"

Great-Grand made an agitated fluttering movement toward the control console for the telescopes. Though no one was there, figures were flashing on the display screens. He said in a thin voice: "Study. Collect data and make theories about it, send them back to Earth. People are saying, young people, old to you though, let's just take our time, study this system, refuel, service the ship, then if we don't like this one, maybe go on to another. Most of *them* won't live to see that, of course, but that doesn't seem to worry them . . . dying on the ship."

"It would be awful, coming all this way, then not landing."

Great-Grand gave a bob halfway between a shrug and a laugh. "I never expected to land. I never expected to get this far. This is a deep space vessel and someone's got to stay on it while the rest of you go down on shuttles. If you go down."

Jim took his life for granted, even if it was quiet compared to lives in TVids. In them adventurers could hop from star to star in no time. But they were just fairy tales. He felt the awesomeness of this real adventure, one in which there could be no easy hops. He said: "Wasn't there any other way at all . . .?"

247

"Oh, yes. One. Risky, though. We'd have had to be frozen. No one fancied that. You know why? We'd've been thawed out and woken by machines. We knew about everyday life support. Reckoned we could handle it. But the freezing and the machines, that was new and unknown. No volunteers. No takers for the long cold one and maybe going on forever like mammoths in icebergs but maybe being woken and seeing it all. Some adventurers we were!"

Jim felt for the old man, who had come so far and would now be given a chance to see the things he hadn't been brave enough to seize: but, like Moses, only from a distance.

It was Jim's fourteenth birthday, but the party wasn't his. A big crowd was floating in the Observatory. Senior Captain Ancram wore a gold-braided uniform, his cap chinstrapped to his head. Even Great-Grand wore his admiral's cap, strapped to the top of his floatsuit rather than to his chin. He was speaking, being still Chief Astronomer. He said: "Well, these results speak for themselves. No doubt about it! We've found life!"

Jim's eyes flicked to the red crescent of the third planet on the visual display, then out to the sky. He knew to avoid the tiny, blazing disk of the star, though like the rest he wore mirrored glasses. He found the red planet itself. He could just see that it too was a *shape*, not just a bright point, and that shape was a ruby-red crescent. S-Captain Ancram said: "So! Oxygen, water vapor, probably some open water! It's an old world, a Mars rather than an Earth, but it's bigger and better than Mars. Tell you what! It's a bit like the still-living Mars Victorian astronomers imagined. Let's call it Barsoom!"

"Barsoom, eh?" Great-Grand gave a wheezy chuckle.

"You've got *plant* life. My guess is it's a bit like the upper slopes of the Himalayas, the place they worked out the Yeti couldn't possibly live 'cause there was nothing to live on but moss. I reckon we call it Yetisburg. If there is anything more advanced than moss, it's old, tough and dangerous. It won't want to be challenged for its living space and its moss!"

Ancram looked uneasy. "You really think a Mars-type planet could have evolved dangerous life? Even intelligent life?"

"Could have. Tell you what. We'll know if it has in practice well before we can work out whether it could in theory. Look at this!" Great-Grand keyed something on the control console and Barsoom/Yetisburg was replaced by the image of the unnamed second planet. It was half full, pure white, blazing against the sky and its own dark side. Great-Grand indicated and Jim noticed the tiny satellite, still a point, but visible even though it was above the bright side of the planet. Great-Grand went on: "What about that, eh? Small, not much bigger than this ship, but brighter than the white planet! Lots of metal!"

No one seemed willing to answer, and Jim found himself thinking aloud: "You mean, it's, like, some kind of L5 from, from Bar . . . Yetisburg? Their planet's nearly dead and they're living up there . . . maybe surveying the other one?"

Everyone looked at Jim. His uncles and other relatives shushed, but Great-Grand said: "Birthday boy, eh? Got a brain, coming on. Could go far. Correction. I've come far. He might just stay put, use his brain, make a go of this!"

As the newest Senior Cadet, Jim was surprised to be

the only one allowed on the shuttle. Perhaps it was a reward for the hours he had spent studying while the others were playing stupid games. All the windows of the shuttle had been darkened, lest anyone look directly at the star. He had heard it would be like this, but could never have imagined . . . just as impressive was the white planet. Its vast disk covered half the sky. This close, he could see bands of cloud, tiny variations in the brightness of the white, but no one was studying the planet. Looming ahead was the alien L5, or whatever it was. The one certain thing was that some intelligent being had made it. It didn't resemble any human creation. It looked like a huge dragonfly: the flimsy wings appeared to be solar power panels, and between them was a long, cylindrical hull, a gleaming color between white and silver. It bore no markings, and didn't seem to rotate like a Life Module. At one end was a headlike swelling, and long metal antennas, but it neither broadcast nor responded to signals.

"From this data, it could be dead," Great-Grand remarked. "No way of telling how long it's been up here. Could make even me look like a young 'un!"

"Could that be an airlock?" S-Captain Ancram said. "There, let's call it the 'mouth' position. It's the only thing remotely like a hatch."

The shuttle advanced toward the "head" of the vast alien ship, between the great, silent antennas. It did not seem to have any portholes, let alone an observatory. Jim wondered what kind of beings could live enclosed, entirely dependent on instruments for information, instruments that, whatever they were recording, currently seemed to be transmitting nothing. Could they really be studying the great white planet, planning to eventually land there, without wanting to see it with their own eyes? Without rotation, how would they prepare for the gravitation, so much stronger than that of Barsoom/Yetisburg?

A pioneer, Lieutenant Ralph Bull, was already suited up. He left the shuttle's airlock, air-jetted across the narrow gap to the oval "mouth," which, Jim realized, did look like a hatch. Ralph said over the intercom: "There's one panel. It's more like a single big button. I wonder ..." Jim saw his hand move: then within seconds, the hatch opened outward.

Open, the airlock looked like an eye. The oval opening was about two meters by four, and in the middle of the far wall was a small circular hatch little more than a foot across. Ralph moved in slowly. He said: "There's a similar ... I'll try ..." Then the outer hatch closed as suddenly as it had opened.

"No!" Ancram exclaimed. "What's gone wrong? He could be trapped in there! We should have done a more thorough scan!"

"I thought you said we *can't* scan through the hull," Great-Grand commented drily.

"Not so far. But we shouldn't have taken the risk. *Anything* could be lurking in there. I should have pulled him out while we analyzed ... hold on ..." The hatch was slowly opening again.

Ralph seemed unharmed. He said: "The inner door *did* open, but wasn't big enough for me. There's air inside. That's why we can't have both doors open at once."

"Automatic Virtual Reality Probe, I should think," said Great-Grand. He turned to Jim and spoke on, his voice no longer reedy or wheezy: "This is what I came all this way for!"

"OK." Ancram sounded worried. "We'll send a probe in. Hope that's not a bit rash ... we won't send it too far."

The whole process repeated. Ralph went in with the probe, then a few minutes later returned. The intercom crackled. He said: "It won't allow this probe in. There's a sort of tube or tunnel just beyond the inner door. The probe went in slowly, but it had scarcely gotten beyond the rim of the door when some kind of force blew it out. It happened three times!"

Great-Grand said: "What, it won't let anything in?"

"That's the odd thing. Before that I stretched my arm in, even tried to get in feet-first. I got my legs a *lot* farther in than the probe managed, and there was no problem till my chest stuck on the rim itself. It's as if it's programmed to admit any organic life form but not a pure machine."

Great-Grand asked: "Is there no way anyone could get in there? Maybe a service engineer who's used to squeezing into nooks and crannies of big machines?"

"Not an engineer. Maybe a child."

"That's settled then." Ancram said. "We pull out . . ."

Jim had a vision of a future spent surveying the alien ship. No one would be able to guess what powers it contained, how hostile it might be. If no way into it could be found, Ancram and the others would surely decide to pull out and head on to some further star even he wouldn't live to see. He said: "How about me? I'm small for a Senior Cadet!"

It was strange in the alien airlock. The metal walls glowed wherever Jim shone his helmet-light, though they weren't shiny enough to reflect any actual image. Elsewhere, the walls were dark. There was nothing that resembled writing, no instructions or diagrams, only the oval button by the inner hatch that Ralph had described. Nervously, he pushed it. The first thing that happened was that the outer hatch closed. He had expected that, but alone in the dark with his little helmet-light and whatever creatures had built this odd apparatus, he suddenly wished Great-Grand, like Ancram, had said he was far too young to be here: but Great-Grand was the admiral on a voyage of discovery, and in the end no one, not even Ancram, had been willing to face him down and say nothing should be discovered.

The small, round inner hatch was opening. Beyond, he could see only a tunnel, the same size as the hatch. He thought he could get through it. Tentatively, he stretched an arm in. Nothing pushed it back. He climbed into the tube headfirst. His oxygen pack scraped against the top of the tube, but he could just about pull himself in and along.

He pulled himself awkwardly down the tunnel for a long time. Several times he wondered what would happen if he came to a narrower part, whether he would be able to back out. He could see a little in front, nothing at all behind.

He came suddenly to the end. There was no gravity at all, and by bracing himself against the sides of the tunnel and pulling, he had built up quite a speed. He shot out of the tunnel and found himself floating in the middle of a vast dark space. Momentum was moving him across it, and in the beam of the helmet lamp he could get no idea of what sort of place he was in. At length he bumped into something. He found he was clinging to the point where another, wider tunnel began. He turned back and slowly explored with his light. He saw what looked like couches on the sides of a big cylindrical room. Presumably it would rotate to create gravity when they were occupied, but now not a thing moved. The couches were long enough for a human

No Home but the Stars

adult, but too narrow. In front of each was a dead screen, with what could be controls down the sides.

He felt this was the control room of a ship that nothing was controlling. Whatever it was, it wasn't a permanent L5 colony. He swung the beam of light to the tunnel he had reached. It was opposite the one he had arrived through. He could just see the end. It was bigger: he was able to float down in a standing position. It was much colder than the tunnel or the "control room": he could feel the chill even through his insulated suit. The walls reflected his light in a different way than those of the airlock: they glittered and were divided into segments about the size of the inner entrance hatch. He stopped to examine one of the segments. Then he saw the aliens.

Each segment of the wall was the end of a transparent tube, like a glass sarcophagus. Inside each there floated motionless a creature that resembled a serpent with six short legs. Most looked about two meters long. They had narrow bodies with large heads. On top of each head were stalks with closed eyes, and a slit like the blowhole of a whale. The rear and middle legs ended in webbed feet: but on the front pair, just behind the head, fingers extended from the webbing. They were amphibious creatures, adapted to sea or land, well suited to the likely environment of Planet Two. All were motionless, utterly still.

There were hundreds of segments, each with a glass cylinder. Presumably each contained an alien . . . but why would they live that way, if they were alive? Did they store their dead here?

Suddenly it came to him that they were neither living nor dead. He felt the cold even more bitterly. He realized that these too were interstellar travelers, but,

254

unlike Great-Grand and the others, they had suspended their animation and trusted a machine to wake them. That machine had not done so. What had gone wrong? What dreams, he wondered, had they had and lost?

There was no movement at all save glitters from the beam of his light . . . or was there? Something had caught his eye. He shone the light down the tunnel, then froze, colder than the aliens in their cylinders. Something was moving toward him!

It didn't look like the aliens. Its round body shone like the white/silver metal of the airlock: it had six legs, but these, like a spider's, were long enough to span the tunnel and enable it to move quickly. This must be the thing that had left its creators frozen! What would it make of an intruder?

The thing continued toward him. It wasn't moving as fast as he had at first thought: it advanced at a steady, remorseless pace. In the center of its "body" was a screen like the ones in the "control room": this one, however, was alive. Images flashed across it very quickly. Some were pictures, he thought of aliens like those that were sleeping, but they changed too fast for him to be sure. Much of the time the screen showed rapidly flickering and changing bands of color. There was nothing like the letters or numbers of any human alphabet.

It got steadily closer. It didn't seem to be reacting to his presence, except by being there. He couldn't see any eye, or lens, or any obvious way in which it could study him. He thought an alien image flashed every time a leg touched the end of a glass cylinder, but they changed too quickly for him to be sure. Perhaps this was a routine inspection, one that had happened every so often for more years than he could imagine, while the spider machine waited for a signal it had never been given: or had chosen, for its own reasons, not to notice.

It didn't slow as it got closer. Soon he would be able to touch it, if he dared. That, surely, it would not ignore! He tried to make sense of the colors flashing in sequence across the screen. It was getting harder to make them out . . . he realized the inside of his faceplate was covered with condensation. That wasn't meant to happen: the intense cold around him must be overcoming the temperature-stabilization system of his spacesuit. If he stayed longer, he, too, might join the ranks of the silent frozen: might never be discovered.

He turned and pulled himself back toward the "control room." He could no longer see the spider-machine, and of course he couldn't hear it. He didn't know if it was gaining. He reached the "control room" and without looking back launched himself across. He floated agonizingly slowly, and of course, couldn't speed up. He swung his light toward the tunnel to the airlock, realized he wasn't pointed directly at it, couldn't steer.

Then it hit him. A force like a silent wind. He didn't know what it was. It drove him toward the small tunnel. He raised his arms in a dive position, managed to get into the tube headfirst. The force drove him on down, scraping his helmet and even his precious oxygen cylinder against the sides.

He saw the small hatch opening in front of him, then he was floating in the airlock. He saw the large hatch open, and suddenly there were worried voices on the intercom. He said: "I'm OK! I think! I've seen . . . wonderful things! The aliens . . . they're in there. We . . . you, Great-Grand . . . made the right choice about how to get here! They're sleeping, but what it'll take to wake them, we may never know!"

Jewels in an Angel's Wing

IAN WATSON

D amnably, I'd just been chewed up by a shark. And I'd thought I was doing so well!

As soon as the shark bit through my legs I went into dream-mode. The sensation was sickening, like being eaten in a dream. I felt squeezed and reduced. Maybe that's how a prey often feels when a predator snaps its jaws; natural anesthesia takes over. Except in our case, our bodies go "astral" in dream-mode. With enough effort we can pull free and flee. That feels like wading out of deep, treacly mud. Then you need to find a powerpoint to eat to boost your energy back to a safe level.

No such luck this time. If you're already low on energy after an earlier escape, you've had it. You fade out. You reassemble somewhere else, usually some-where you don't want to be, and you're starving for a powerpoint. Three such fade-outs in succession—don't ask me who does the counting—and you get zapped back to a lower level.

But trying to keep out of harm's way can't work forever, either. The only way you can win through is by risking being eaten time and again. It's a hell of a life.

Am I puzzling you? We were equally puzzled. Be-lieve it. We pretty well knew what to do, but we had no idea why. It was as though we'd lost half or our memories, had them locked away from us.

The first level of existence was radioactive ruins. Scattered throughout a wreck of a city were various safe enclaves—which never stayed safe for long. Radioactivity slowly seeped in, or else the mutants would mount an attack. You had to keep on the move, hunting for new havens that were clean, stocked with food and drink. And you had to collect powerpoints while avoiding the attentions of mutants and clouds of plutonium gas. Powerpoints on this level came in the form of anti-radiation pills, usually to be found in deathtrap buildings, all of them a good distance from the nearest sanctuary and in opposite directions. If you could eat enough pills without being too badly irradiated or mauled by mutants . . . well, I finally managed to, and found myself instantly reassembled on the second level, Ghoul Castle.

With all this rushing about and hiding, we didn't exactly get to hold public meetings, but I'd estimate there were about a hundred of us; and of this number about half had succeeded in escaping from the ruins before I did. So I'm no paragon of agility and quick wits. To start with, in fact, I was quite a slow slob. However, I was persistent and I was capable of cooperating and learning. Indeed, I'd found my ideal partner: Isbeth Anndaughter. Isbeth and I had teamed in the ruins. We covered each other, ran interference for each other. During my successful run that led me to level two, she sidetracked several mutants at great risk to herself. Then before the winning route had time to change, she too ran it solo, gobbling power, and boosted herself out of those ruins to rejoin me.

Of course, I saved Isbeth from close shaves too, but I'd say the balance sheet of debts was in my favor. She must genuinely have loved me, seen in me qualities which she could enhance. Maybe my ability to share. You did come across various individualists who wouldn't cooperate with anyone. Other men and women you met en route would swap experiences briefly. That's how Isbeth and I knew about Ghoul Castle in advance, since some of those latter had already escaped, and been zapped back, and were trying to leave the ruins a second time.

Others—no-hopers—had already given up the struggle. They just dashed from one sanctuary to another in the ruins, hoping not to get caught, hardly even trying for the power pills. Apparently you could sink no lower than the ruins, no matter what.

Ghoul Castle was an immense complex of halls, corridors, towers, battlements, staterooms, galleries, tunnels and dungeons, courts and moats and mazes of sewers—haunted by lethal ghosts, prowled by ghouls and monsters, besieged by barbarians, enchanted by wizards. Jewels were the powerpoints there.

It took Isbeth and myself ages to make it through. How long? Six months, a whole year? It was hard to keep track of time. By the skin of our teeth we avoided being zapped back to the ruins. We learned the ropes— those shifting ropes.

From time to time we met fellow adventurers (or victims), some of whom had already reached the waterworld only to be zapped. So we did learn some advance details of the third level, which Isbeth and I already felt sure must exist. We felt that in our bones, instinctively, along with an urge to reach it.

259

Yet if any of the others had discovered *how* we got into this fix, or who we had been before we all found ourselves in the ruins, they weren't saying.

Unfortunately, ghosts and ghouls homed in avidly on gatherings of more than a couple of persons, which rather set a time limit to more general speculations. The castle was better furnished than the ruins had ever been. Food and drink were definitely superior. If you could keep clear of nastiness, it wasn't too bad a life, merely nerve-wracking. Some of our contacts confided that they intended to hang on in the castle. But that wasn't enough for Isbeth, or for me.

At long last she succeeded in touring the whole vast edifice by the right route, avoiding all pitfalls and evils while consuming the jewels she needed. This time Isbeth took the lead, and I distracted the opposition. As soon as she was translated, out and away, I retraced the circuit and followed her through, on to this submarine level where sharks and squids and other nasty surprises hungered for us. We'd been here quite a while.

When I came back to myself, after being a shark's astral lunch and fading out, miracle of miracles I wasn't far from a total of two powerpoints. Powerpoints on this level were pearls. (Use 'em up, and replacements appeared elsewhere. Same principle applied to sanctuaries and the essentials of life.) After gulping these down, I didn't take more than a few hours to find Isbeth. Soon we were safe in a transparent dome filled with fresh air. Safe, for two or three sleeps, supposing we chose to stay put. Sea water was leaking in slowly, but the dome had two habitable levels. Downstairs was ankle deep in water; upstairs was snug.

We'd slept in a huge cozy sleeping bag. We were feasting on what we'd found in the dome: honeyed figs, sweet dates, coconuts, and a few trays of sushi. And of course we'd also found oxygen packs, for outside use when we quit the dome. Ours not to reason why. That was the way of it. You never saw things pop into existence; you just came across them—or they came across you. However, we were in a reasoning mood.

"Why, Konrad?" she asked me.

"*Where* is a good question too."

"So is *how*."

Outside, a flotilla of violet angelfish the size of shark fins lazed past toward coral cliffs of pink and gold, where weed wafted and a deadly-looking orange medusa bloomed. Isbeth bit into a fig, fed me the rest of it, then asked:

"Who are we, Konrad? Who are we really?"

I mumbled, mouth full.

"We can't be real, you know," she said.

"That's a dangerous assumption."

"Real people don't shift in a twinkling of an eye from a castle to underneath the sea. Real people don't get eaten and find themselves alive again."

"It's a dangerous assumption, Isbeth, because if we don't play everything for real then we'll slacken off. We won't win."

"Win what?"

"Ourselves. Our stolen selves." Yes, that had to be why. In vino veritas. In addition to the food, we had an amphora of fine wine and a couple of golden goblets.

Isbeth was dark and slight and wiry, with magical, deep-set eyes and high cheekbones. I was leaner than

I'd been originally, but in many respects I think her wire was stronger than my new muscle. I wondered how I could change physically, if I wasn't real.

"Maybe we're being tested," I said.

"No one's compelled to strive."

"We compel ourselves."

"Yes! Some of us do."

"Or maybe we're being trained. Odd sort of training, though."

"Trained in initiative." She grinned. "Trained in speed and planning and memory, boldness and caution. Also," she added thoughtfully, "trained not to fear death."

"There has to be a fourth level, doesn't there?"

"Yes—and we'll get to it!"

In fact, despite my recent shark debacle, Isbeth had fared less well than I so far in the waterworld. Nothing terminal as yet. With my help, she'd always managed to recharge before she racked up three successive deaths. But she'd fallen victim to a medusa, an octopus, a poisonous urchin, and other fates too. That wasn't because I let her go ahead into danger. The going seemed tougher. At the same time I was enjoying a run of good luck, or maybe I was developing an instinct. We were still a good team, yet I felt that somehow, in some way, I was pulling ahead.

She glanced down at the level of water seeping in below.

"Listen, Konrad, if I'm zapped back to the castle I'll win through here again—fast. Don't wait for me. Promise to go on ahead. Try to reach the next level."

I nodded. I intended to. Anything extra I could learn might help her too. Somewhere, somehow. Even on different levels, we'd still be thinking as a team.

262

Something awaited. Of that I was sure. Knowledge. Reward. Whatever. Something had to await.

A giant squid squirted its way overhead, its rose and yellow phosphorescent signals flashing incomprehensibly like some flexible control console made of rubber. What long suckery arms it had. What a cruel beak. What big round eyes.

A couple of days later Isbeth got zapped, and I couldn't do a thing to help. She'd already died twice over and reassembled nearby; she absolutely had to recharge. She dived between two great slabs of rock for a power pearl lying exposed on silver sand. Those weren't rocks. They were the two half-shells of a clam larger than any we'd ever seen before. The shells clashed shut on Isbeth. Bubbles gushed from her ruptured tank or face-mask. I watched her exposed feet thrashing in dream-mode. She was still trying to grab that pearl, to pop it in her mouth, give her the zoom to haul herself up out of the clam. She failed. She vanished.

Grief.

Fury.

As the clam began cranking itself open again I dived, snatched the pearl, and thrust myself up and out before the creature was ready to spring shut again.

I found a couple of fellows I knew resting in the next refuge dome. Ivan Koschenko and his black partner Barney Randall. Barney wasn't too welcoming.

"Three of us in one place is like bait, man! We're gonna attract a giant octopus to crack us open."

Barney nursed a particular hatred of octopuses; they seemed to have a special affinity for him.

"My Isbeth's been zapped," I told them.

"Let him stay here an hour or so," said Ivan.

So I stayed. So we talked. Not about Isbeth. What was there to say? She wasn't dead. She was back in Ghoul Castle.

Ivan talked about the surface of the sea.

"What's up there? Why don't we ever swim straight up and take a look?"

"You'd never get there," said Barney. "A big shark would tear you to ribbons, out in the open."

"I'm interested in whether there *is* a surface."

"Maybe," I said, "it's our curiosity that's being tested, and so far we haven't shown enough curiosity."

"Don't get much chance, do we?" snapped Barney. He kept looking out at the submarine landscape in case some menace was creeping close. "When we get caught and go fuzzy —"

"Dream-mode," I said.

"Yeah. That's unnatural. I think we're all models in a big machine. I don't mean like tin soldiers, not that kinda model. I don't know what I mean. I've been robbed of how to know."

"We'll find out on level four," I assured him.

You'll have noted how I started our story halfway through—just the way we had all been started up in the ruins, halfway through our lives with no idea what went before. Now we leap forward a bit, just as I leapt forward soon after that—to the fourth level.

And the fourth level was a starship. I knew right away what a starship was. This wasn't any old starship. It was an interstellar luxury palace, a ritz of a starship patronized by high society, a snobbish, intriguing, catty, star-hopping aristocracy of lords and ladies with whom etiquette was of the utmost importance. Life on board the *Empire Topaz* was an intricate dance of manners, and woe betide you if you stubbed a toe. Deadly as any shark bite, such a gaffe could wreck your status and destroy you. Here, a slap in the face or a snub was death. Dream-mode was the hot melting flush of embarrassment. Powerpoints weren't jewels or pearls this time; we had to collect favors from ladies. Asking one of those fine ladies in the ballroom of the *Empire Topaz* such a question as, "Where are we really? What are you really?" merited a stinging rebuke . . . zap.

Oh, but I got myself deeply involved in all this maze of politeness and innuendo, flirtation and character assassination, and jockeying for status. Perhaps too deeply. What other option was there, unless you merely wanted to stay on the sidelines as some sort of feeble junior midshipman? Besides, the *Empire Topaz* did have its favorable aspects. I was falling in love with the Lady Zania.

Weeks later I turned a corner on B Deck and came face to face with . . .

"Isbeth!"

"Konrad. I just got here. I raced through the castle. The underwater level took longer."

I hustled Isbeth along to a safe cabin where we wouldn't be bothered for a while by partying ladies or scheming beaux, and I filled her in on all that I'd learned. Most of what I'd learned.

When I'd done, she said, "So now we're being taught etiquette the hard way. Etiquette is the final gloss on a professional soldier, I seem to recall! Perhaps we're soldiers, you and I. Officer material. These different levels are the ways we're being taught. Or selected and ranked. Our minds are linked in some type of computer."

Computer. Yes, I knew what that meant. Yes, this starship had a computer to guide her and run her systems.

"The computer could know the real situation, Konrad. We need to reach the computer. That'll be the last initiative test. The recognition of ourselves."

I felt sad. I'd been wasting time flirting, spinning in the social whirlpool while trying to keep my footing and advance, when I could have thought this out for myself.

"Starship," she repeated to herself. "Soldiers. Computers. We're coming across more clues, aren't we? Here's another enclosed world with its own layout and rules and limitations. We're going to raid the computer, you and I, ask it some questions. Even if it *is* only a simulation of itself."

"What was that you said? Simulation?"

"Well, a computer on board this ship can't be any more real than the ship itself. But it may contain authentic data. It may interface."

"Could we be 'simulations' too?"

"Maybe, maybe not. Probably it would be more economical to use real people and put their bodies in stasis while their brains were linked cybernetically."

"Stasis. Cybernetically."

There came a soft knock on the cabin door. We both froze but the knock was repeated impatiently. I had little choice but to open the door.

The Lady Zania stood there.

"Madam." I sketched a bow and made the usual hand flurries. "Utterly delighted! How ever did you find me?"

She stared past me at Isbeth, jealous fury in her eyes.

"My Lady, may I present an old acquaintance, by

name Isbeth Anndaughter? Isbeth Anndaughter, here is the Lady Zania."

With miraculous cool and skill and charm, Isbeth rose to the occasion and bailed me out. Herself too. I don't imagine that Zania was fooled, but an awkward moment which could have toppled headlong into deadly rivalry, vengeance, and disgrace ended instead with Zania linking arms with Isbeth to lead her to the B Deck salon, while I escorted both my ladies. A certain barbed pique was still the undertow to Zania's repartee, but Isbeth simply wouldn't let Zania maneuver her into hostility. Isbeth adopted a wonderfully disarming, flattering frivolity.

And so we partied and danced and made new acquaintances and tasted gourmet canapés and drank champagne and fenced with words. Zania made sure that she introduced Isbeth to all the most dangerous lords and ladies, yet Isbeth hardly faltered. I could sense the strain in my long-time partner, for here were human sharks as smooth and sleek as any sea predator, but far more ingenious. Here were dowager octopuses and young, entangling medusae. Here were old lords like crusty clams who invited being tickled, then snapped shut.

It seemed to take days to disentangle ourselves from the repercussions of that reception on B Deck, which led on to other revels, to casinos and boudoirs and I forget what else. Eventually Isbeth and I pretended to slip away for separate trysts. Together again, alone at last, we fled the passenger section for the starker corridors of crew territory to hunt for the computer room.

Isbeth forbore to discuss, archly or otherwise, my

previous entanglement with Zania; nor was I eager to allude to it. We had other fish to fry.

"We're in an imperial starship on its way to war," I argued. "Strip away all the sophistication of this particular ship, *Empire Topaz*, and underneath is a killing weapon filled with racks of sleeping soldiers being fed with false worlds to train 'em for all contingencies."

"Including courtesy? In case we need to be courteous to the hostile aliens at our destination? In case we need to be diplomats as well as marines? Thus you shall learn the correct way to kiss an alien's hand?"

"Not aliens, no, it can't be that. Humans. This is *Empire* Topaz. We'll be coming up against powerful colonists who have rebelled against the empire."

She laughed, a shade sarcastically.

"It was you who first mentioned soldiers, Isbeth."

"So I did."

Her fingers danced over the keyboard as if with a mind of their own, interrogating. *Who is Isbeth Anndaughter? Who is Konrad Digby? Self-Diagnosis? State of System?*

On the green screen a single repeated word scrolled.

CYBERFUGUE

CYBERFUGUE

CYBERFUGUE

"What the hell does that mean?"

"Let's try to find out." And she typed, *Define.*

Nothing.

Define: Fugue.

FUGUE: A PERIOD OF MEMORY LOSS WHEN AN INDIVIDUAL VANISHES FROM NORMAL HAUNTS. ALSO: A THEME TAKEN UP AND REPEATED REPEATEDLY.

What is level five? she typed.

RADIOACTIVE RUINS.

She turned to me, stunned. "So if we . . . graduate from here . . . we're back in the ruins. There's no other reality! No genuine reality!"

"Maybe we're all dead. Maybe this is hell. Or purgatory."

"Huh. Not so long ago you thought we were on an interstellar battleship, being groomed for command."

"So did you. Almost."

"Something has gone wrong, that's what. Whatever controls us is in a fugue. A cyberfugue. It's looping these scenarios it imprints on us, it's recycling them. The true purpose has been lost."

"Are you remembering more of yourself, Isbeth?"

She shook her head. She said, "Maybe the purpose of these scenarios isn't to train us at all. It's just to occupy us during a huge spaceflight lasting years and years. It's to keep us stimulated so that our minds don't atrophy."

"When we arrive," I asked, "we'll be restored to ourselves?"

"Unless the system really is in cyberfugue. Unless we're locked in, with no way out. Unless that's what the computer's telling us—or rather this simulation, this model here. I'm inclined to believe that's so. I'm going to try and override the program. Crash it."

The periscopes showed ruins. The external Geiger counters chattered like crazy.

We had woken up weak as kittens. It took days to recover, days of sipping special nutrient soups fed us by machine.

We remembered the war, and the automated underground shelter, enormous in its extent, with five levels one below the other, fully stocked for all supposed

269

future needs. Down on level four, the "swimming pools": the algae tanks for our descendants to grow slopfood when the larder got empty. Deepest of all, the nuclear-fusion plant. Enough space for a generation or two to rattle around in. Then it would get a bit more crowded.

We remembered the way our metabolisms had been slowed, how our brains had been linked electronically, how our memories had been suppressed, how we would be given games to play during the next few time-warped centuries . . . until the Earth was habitable once again, or until the machinery was forced to wake us anyway, prematurely; in which case we would have to breed in here and raise kids and they would have to raise kids in turn. Until.

Optimistically, we could sleep through the whole process of the healing of the Earth. A hundred years, three hundred, five hundred. Fifty men and fifty women, the gene pool to rebuild some sort of human civilization or existence.

The computer in the *Empire Topaz* had told the truth. The fifth level was ruins—the ruined, radioactive planet. Without any mutants running about; nothing could survive up there.

And Isbeth, who was a computer whiz, had crashed our survival program. She had woken us all up. No way could we be put back to sleep, in stasis.

Elapsed time: fifteen years. Too soon, far too soon. A century too soon, three centuries too soon.

Isbeth and I agreed that we must blame the machines, otherwise her life might be in danger; and mine too, since I'd helped her.

But if the machines could go so badly wrong chronologically, in what other respects might our sanctuary turn sour? What else might malfunction in the many, endless years ahead?

If only we were back aboard the *Empire Topaz*. Or in Ghoul Castle. Anywhere else.

What a fine environment for despair, for insanity. It was hardly surprising when Barney Randall killed himself. He cut his own throat. I saw him with the knife against his neck. He was down at the end of a corridor. No one else was about but me. I dashed down the corridor towards him shouting, "No!" But he just grinned then sliced a second, bloody grin below that grin.

Without hesitating I raced for help. No, let's be honest, I ran away so as to have witnesses. Otherwise someone might say that I'd killed him myself. I came back with two Hispanic men—Martinez and Cruz, engineers—and a woman doctor, Sandra Macdonald.

"Where's the body, then, eh?" demanded Cruz. "Where's that body?"

"Someone must have . . . removed it."

"Don't be ridiculous," snapped Macdonald. "Where's the blood?"

The floor was spotless.

"But it was here!"

"Don't you try to spook us!" snarled Martinez.

"I'm not. I swear it."

The situation was turning ugly, so I headed for the stairs and went down to the next level.

"Hey, man."

It was Barney. He was leaning against a wall, looking mad. But alive. His throat wasn't grinning redly at me. I had seen him cut his throat.

Barney giggled. "You looking for me? Here I am. Surprise!"

Suddenly he jumped forward and gripped my wrist. "Here's Barney, baby." He was solid, real.

I broke free and fled back up those stairs three at a time, toward the sound of angry voices.

In the meanwhile, Isbeth had arrived. She was arguing heatedly with my three witnesses.

"Isbeth, Barney's down below!" I cried. "I watched him kill himself—and now he's come back to life on another level!"

"You're wrong," shouted Martinez. "Barney made like he was killing himself—that's what you saw—then he ran downstairs. That's it. You were fooled."

"I saw the blood."

"You imagined it! Unless you're in this with the jerk. And her, her too." Martinez faltered.

Barney had followed me. He came up the stairs, grinning maniacally, with that knife or a different one in his hand.

"It doesn't hurt much," he called out. "You go fuzzy. You all know what that's like. Doesn't last long. Try it out." He blundered forward, slashing the blade from side to side.

Isbeth and I escaped into the nearest room, which was full of mothballed tools and spare parts. She had slammed on the lights; I slammed the door and wrestled a crate under the handle. Outside we heard a scream.

Isbeth sagged. Gestured feebly.

"Then this isn't real, either. We're in our sanctuary at last, but we're still dreaming all together, dreaming we're in our ghastly sanctuary. Oh, it'll be ghastly soon. Our enemies won't be mutants or ghouls or sharks. Our enemies will be ourselves. Each other. We'll be a hundred rats in a maze, going mad, killing each other, coming back to life."

"No. Barney has gone mad, that's all. No need for everyone to go mad."

"When we know there's no reality? We've taken a wrong turning, Konrad. We have to get back to the computer on the starship."

"*What?*" I thought she must have gone mad.

"I mean it. We have to use the shaft to the surface. We have to get out into the ruins."

"But the radiation . . . it'll cook us."

"We can't die. Don't you realize? As soon as we get up there, the mutants will appear. They'll start hunting us. Then we'll find our radiation pills. Our powerpoints. We'll jump to Ghoul Castle."

"Oh my God."

"This place, Konrad, this huge nuclear survival shelter—it seems familiar."

"So it should be."

"The layout's familiar, not the place itself. This isn't any nuclear shelter. It never was."

"What is it, then?"

"I keep thinking of the moon. It's as if—" She fell silent, then said, "We'll open up the shaft to the surface."

"Isbeth . . . when you crashed that program, things didn't work out too well. If we bust this shelter open, people aren't going to like it."

"After the first shock they'll be *glad*. It'll be a whole lot better than going slowly, colorfully mad. Better than experiencing the thrills and spills of insanity. I'd rather play hide-and-seek with sharks and ghouls any day. Will you help me?"

I nodded.

"If we get separated, Konrad . . . see you on board the *Empire Topaz*, hmmm?"

True enough, when we got to the surface mutants soon appeared among the ruins of that great dead city. The creatures seemed twice as agile, twice as cunning as before. It was as if they'd only been in first gear earlier on, and now had engaged second gear.

The moon, Isbeth's moon, a ghastly bloated orange of a moon, brooded permanently over the radioactive rubble we ran through, and before long we were meeting other people from the shelter who had made the same decision as us.

But there was worse to come. When I got killed for the third time in succession, torn astrally apart by mutants, and before I popped back to life somewhere else in the ruins, while I was "dead" in a kind of gray in-between limbo, a tendril brushed my mind. That's the best way I can describe the experience.

Fleetingly, foggily, I remembered the moon base: five sublunar levels sunk beneath the Mare Orientalis. I remembered our pastimes, all those interactive computer games we used to play to while away a tour of duty.

I remembered the approach of the aliens: two great spacefaring beings like grotesque, beautiful, ornamental fish a kilometer long, two kilometers high, half a kilometer wide, wrapped round with convoluted sparkling sails and veils, shimmering with powers and forces that we couldn't fathom. All contact with Earth from our transmitter on Nearside was disrupted, lost.

A glimpse: of my colleagues swaying, falling, shriveling as if emptied. I remembered the terrible, sudden

suction of myself . . . away. Of my mind, my soul, my person.

I think I know what we are now, and where we are. We've been collected by one of those aliens. Our minds have been taken. Not copies of us, not analogues, but our very selves, our psyches.

We haven't been taken as scientific samples, nor specimens, nothing like that. How the tendril seemed to preen itself, as it touched me. How it seemed to admire itself. We have been taken as decorations—as psychic jewelry. Jewels on an alien angel's wings. Just as light shifts within a gem, so our adventures scintillate. Ultimately, in a loop.

When the aliens brushed by the moon and removed us, they wondered what would amuse us, what settings would display us to best effect; and they found in our minds what games we played obsessively. So now we live those games.

Probably there are other life forms from worlds of distant stars captured psychically in the being of these aliens, to decorate them: other minds dreaming out their passions. Probably there are alien jewels too.

We're on a starship, in a sense. The journey time may be hundreds of years. Thousands. There are no port-holes or viewscreens as on the *Empire Topaz*. There are no glimpses of our fellow life-form victims—if any—but I assume they must exist. And there are no controls. Does the diamond ring guide the hand that wears it? Does the necklace cause the head to turn?

At least . . . not yet.

Perhaps the computer room of the *Empire Topaz* is the closest to an interface with the energy ganglia of this great alien. Maybe, maybe not. When I reach that computer room again, I hope with Isbeth at my side, maybe we can achieve something subtler, more ingenious than before.

The mutants may be faster. The ghouls may be more dangerous and the sharks less dumb and the fine ladies aboard the *Empire Topaz* more cutthroat. That's reminiscent of the games we played on Moon Base too, with a learner level of difficulty and a professional level. I just hope there are only two levels of difficulty!

Meanwhile, I awake from dream-mode all on my

own amid the glowing ruins. I urgently want a radiation pill. I think I sense that there's one to the northeast.

A rustle. A flurry of rags. A heavy stumble. Already there's a mutant nearby.

And the pocked orange moon glowers down on me, amid a few lonely stars and a vast yawning void.

The Children

CHESTER S. GEIER

It was Sprague who first saw the figures moving through the vast alien forest beneath the cruising jeet. He overcame the massive inertia of his surprise; he pointed and spoke with a quiet intensity.

"Look, Ben! Down there!"

Dagget's ice-blue eyes flared as he peered earthward through the glass-clear transalloy walls of the cabin. In the forest below a score or more of tiny shapes were visible as they crossed open spaces in the network of trees, running to follow the jeet's flight.

"People!" Dagget burst out, awe sharpening the bass timbre of his voice. "And, Phil . . . they look *human!*"

The awe in Dagget's tone found an echo in Sprague's long face. People . . . *human people!* Was it possible? How many habitable planets had been discovered by the interstellar rovers of Earth? Sprague could not begin to remember. But he could remember that few of those planets had been inhabited by intelligent beings, that fewer still had been inhabited by beings even remotely human in appearance.

Here on Hindemuth IV seemed to be a human, or a near-human, race.

The running figures became lost in distance as the jeet soared on through the clear blue-green sky. Sprague turned back to the controls and swung the craft around to retrace its former course at a slower speed. He sent a questioning glance at Dagget.

"Is the camera getting this?"

Dagget briefly inspected one of a number of instruments in a framework behind him. "Still running," he reported. Then, taking a pair of binoculars from a compartment, he fell to an intent scrutiny of the changing terrain below.

"I can see them again," he announced presently. He released a whispered exclamation. "What in space—! Phil . . . they're kids!"

Sprague stared at the other for a moment, disbelieving; then he took the binoculars and peered downward in turn.

Dagget's eyes had not been playing tricks. Magnified now, the moving shapes were indeed those of children; slim brown children, long-haired and unclothed, gesturing up at the jeet in evident excitement. Amid the shadowed green forest setting they had an unreal, elfin appearance—almost like creatures out of fantasy.

"Put the ship down, Phil," Dagget said abruptly. "We've got to give this a first-hand scanning. It . . . why, it's almost the biggest thing that's happened since interstellar travel!"

Sprague shook his head slowly. "This is an alien planet, Ben, and those kids down there are members of an alien race. We can't take chances until we know much more than we do right now. There must be adults around somewhere; we don't know how they'll react to us."

"Guess you're on course there." Dagget's lips took on a sullen curve that denied his spoken agreement.

"The camera is getting all this," Sprague went on.

"We'll check the film when we get back to the ship and see what it shows. We might find something we missed."

"We didn't find the Colonial Administration ship," Dagget returned. "If it's here at all." His resentment was now obvious.

Sprague was aware of it, but for the moment he occupied himself with swinging the jeet around again. Then he said mildly, "The Colonial Administration ship might be here for all you know, Ben."

The other's head swung around in growing ill-temper. "You know blasted well how I feel about this little junket of yours. We've already spent a year in galactic space, searching for the Colonial ship. We covered the area to which we were assigned; headquarters didn't tell us to do any more than that. But instead of hypering back to the System, you take a jump out here, to Hindemuth IV, a planet right in the middle of nowhere."

Sprague lifted his spare shoulders. "I had the idea that the ship might be here, if it wasn't anywhere else."

"Idea!" Dagget snorted. "I call it an attack of space fits."

"Up to a certain limit you're welcome to your own opinions," Sprague answered calmly. He made a slight correction in the jeet's course and went on, "Special Services Division has a habit of expecting considerably more from its members than is stated in orders. It's an official if unwritten rule. You should have thought of that when you volunteered, Ben."

"I was thinking of the nice long vacation between jobs," Dagget grunted. "But now I'm beginning to see I made a mistake. I should have stayed with the Space Force."

"But you didn't," Sprague pointed out. "That's partly the reason why you're here right now, instead of in some pleasure dive back in the System, swilling aphrolac with a bunch of dizzy females."

"Partly?" Dagget questioned. His freckled, muscular features were sardonic; a long-smoldering hostility showed in the hard thrust of his eyes.

"Partly," Sprague said. "The other part is that I happened to remember Special Service agents are often required to use brains in carrying out orders. So when we were briefed on our search for the missing Colonial ship, I decided to do a little checking in Galactic Department archives. I looked up the reports and records of the ship's commander—and came across the name of the sun in this planetary system: Hindemuth. The commander had discovered and named it a number of years back, while running a Mapping Bureau ship; but his find had remained unofficial. The matter was never referred to the Expeditions Bureau, or to authorities in the Galactic Department. It received no attention or publicity whatever, and stayed buried in a mass of other records."

"Something's out of place there," Dagget muttered, grudgingly interested. "The Galactic Department usually doesn't slip up like that. Little things like newly diskovered suns that might have planets are too important to overlook."

"The commander in question *wanted* the matter to be overlooked," Sprague said. "That showed in the way he worded his report and presented his figures. He didn't want to tell all, but at the same time he wanted to play safe in the event that official inquiries were later made."

"What do you suppose was his idea?"

"A likely guess is that he hoped the find would be important, and if important, he wanted to make it into something more than a routine and subordinate capacity."

"But how can you be certain that he made a jump to the Hindemuth system while in command of the Colonial Administration ship?"

"I checked on that, too," Sprague said. "If you take the galactic coordinates of the planet for which the Colonial ship was bound and run them off on a computer for deviations in the Hyper-Drive coordinates, you find that one particular jump will end up in the general neighborhood of Hindemuth."

"All right," Dagget growled. "Say he came here. Where is the ship? Where are the colonists who were aboard? This fourth planet is the only habitable one in the Hindemuth system, and we've already searched most of it. This is the last great island. We haven't found any evidence —"

Dagget broke off; he was suddenly rigid. "The children!"

Sprague shook his head. "I know what you're thinking; but the Colonial ship vanished slightly more than four years ago. There weren't any children aboard. The colonists were all young married couples. And in four years they couldn't have had children as grown as the ones we saw. . . . The children seem to be members of a race native to this world; a race living at a very primitive level of culture. We've seen no buildings, no towns or communities of any sort."

"That puts us exactly where we started from," Dagget pointed out with bleak satisfaction. "I'm glad to hear you finally admit it."

Sprague shrugged. "The instruments might have turned up something this trip. We'll check them as soon as we get back to the cruiser."

The cruiser stood roughly in the center of a small, shallow valley, looking like a slender metal tower as it rested in a vertical position on its massive rear fins. It was not a large craft, as hyper-ships went, yet it dwarfed the approaching jeet.

Sprague touched a stud to send out a radio impulse that would open an entrance hatch in the cruiser's middle section. Deftly, then, he piloted the jeet through the hatch and into a catapult cradle within the parent vessel.

The hatch automatically closed. Sprague and Dagget busied themselves with the instruments inside the jeet, removing the various types of recordings. With these they strode to a small elevator and rode up to the control and living quarters near the cruiser's bow. They reached the large, semicircular room that was used as a headquarters, and here they removed their plasti-leather coveralls, retaining only the short-sleeved shirts and knee-length trunks that were worn aboard ship.

"I'm hungry," Dagget said. "Suppose we have something to eat before getting to work?"

"Eat if you want to," Sprague returned shortly. "I'm going to get started on the data we gathered."

He took a cigarette from a desk humidor, the green-gold tobacco showing through the thin, transparent casing. He puffed the cigarette alight, frowning.

"There's something about this world that bothers me, and I want to get to the nucleus of it. I've seen too many men die on too many worlds to ignore my hunches about this one."

"What do you think is wrong?"

"I don't know. It might be some quality about Hindemuth IV; it might be those kids we saw."

Sprague shrugged impatiently and gathered up the recordings. He strode into the adjoining laboratory.

Dagget followed, his hunger evidently forgotten.

They fell to work with various types of apparatus, moving with skilled swiftness. Sprague concentrated on the camera film; processing this, he inserted it into the projector, setting the editor mechanism so that only certain subjects would be shown on the screen. Then he connected the projector to a self-adjusting magnification device and switched it on.

Colored images raced across the screen. The first were of Hindemuth IV's terrain, a montage of forests and plains, of rivers and hill ranges. Then a scene came sharply into focus, greatly magnified. A group of children stood in a forest glade, staring upward. They wore no clothing. Untrimmed hair rippled about their shoulders: red hair and blond, brown hair and black. In physical appearance all seemed of the same approximate age, which according to Earth standards would have been some ten years.

The children were staring skyward in excitement and wonder. The jeet, which was obviously the focus of their interest, seemed to fascinate and puzzle them.

Then they were running to keep it in sight. Several called and gestured to companions elsewhere in the forest; others appeared, joining the original group; and the swarm of hurrying, slim bodies appeared and vanished between them and the forest floor.

The children were left behind; then they came back into view as the jeet swung around. Again they were running to follow its flight, laughing and shouting.

Finally the children were gone, and the colors in the screen raced without form. Nothing else came into focus.

A frown on his long face, Sprague turned away from the screen. He sent a brief glance at Dagget, who had interrupted his own work to watch.

"Just the children," he said. "No adults, no buildings, no sign of the Colonial ship."

"This children angle doesn't make sense," Dagget muttered. "There would have to be adults somewhere around."

Sprague shook his head in mystification. "We saw no sign of them—and the camera covers a lot of territory. Children as a rule don't stray great distances from their parents." His mouth tightened. "I'm going to crack this if it's the last thing I do. The answer is here, somewhere—and I'm going to find it. . . . Right now, we'll get this work out of the way."

They returned their attention to the recordings that remained. Silence filled the laboratory, a silence that seemed one with the vast, brooding silence of the world outside the cruiser.

Sprague felt the silence. It had a quality of mystery, of lurking threat. It was a thing that seemed to penetrate the walls of the ship by a kind of osmosis. It was like a presence that remained unseen wherever one might turn, watching and waiting.

A gasp from Dagget broke the silence. Sprague glanced at him, dropping a spool of metal tape that unwound itself on the floor with a brittle, whirring noise.

"Ben—what is it?"

Dagget straightened convulsively. "Nothing. I just

thought—nothing. Guess I made a mistake."

Sprague continued to look at the muscular, red-headed man. He had known Dagget too long to mistake the signs—Dagget was hiding something. Dagget looked steadily at a point on the workbench before him, not meeting Sprague's eyes. He rubbed a hand slowly down the side of his trunks.

Sprague crossed the distance between them with slow steps. He saw now that Dagget had been working over a radiation chart, a roll of thin plastic marked with graph lines, over which ran an undulating red trail. The plastic roll had been placed in a translator and pantograph mechanism, which automatically recorded the data on a looseleaf sheet.

Sprague was turning toward the sheet, when Dagget interposed his body with a quick step.

"It was nothing, Phil—just a mistake."

Sprague said sharply, "At ease, Lieutenant!"

Dagget hesitated, his muscular features desperate. Then he nodded at what he saw in Sprague's face.

"Aye . . . Captain."

He stepped away from the workbench.

Sprague ran a quick forefinger down a column of symbols and figures on the sheet. The finger stopped; he drew in his breath, then expelled it in swift, startled words.

"Cosmium! There's cosmium here. The planet's filthy with it. If these figures are right —"

"They can't be!" Dagget said. "It must be some kind of a mistake. Something must have gone wrong with the apparatus."

Sprague shook his head slowly, studying the sheet again. "These radiation figures check perfectly for cosmium—right down to the last decimal place. If

there had been even a slight deviation either way . . .
but there isn't. The figures check. And, great space,
from the intensity of the radiation, this island must be
a regular cosmium treasure trove!"

Dagget said nothing; he stared brooding-eyed
through the broad transalloy viewport in the curving
wall of the semicircular room.

Sprague probed at the red-headed man's expression.
He said softly:

"You tried to hide this cosmium data from me, Ben.
What was the idea?"

Dagget jerked his heavy shoulders. "No idea; just an
attack of space fits, I guess." Then defiance blazed in
his face; he indicated the room with a sudden, savage
sweep of his hand. "We've been boxed up here, more
or less, for over a year. I'm sick of it. I keep thinking of
all the other jobs like this ahead."

"Why don't you quit the Service, then?" Sprague
demanded.

"And take a steady, day-to-day job at a lower salary?
That's no solution." Dagget leaned forward, his ice-
blue eyes bright and fixed. "But the cosmium here, on
Hindemuth IV, *is* a solution. You know how rare the
stuff is. Why, hardly more than a gram or two has ever
been found at any one time. And only one sun system
out of a dozen contains any cosmium, as a rule. A
couple of grams of the stuff are worth a fortune, and
there's more than that here—enough to make us rich a
hundred times over."

Sprague shook his head. "You seem badly mixed up
about this, Ben. The cosmium we've found doesn't
belong to us; it belongs to the Federation. We're repre-
sentatives, not independent agents. We'll get a reward, of course, but—"

"A reward!" Dagget snorted. "A reward would be a piece of vacuum compared to what we could have by keeping the discovery to ourselves. . . . Look, Phil, nobody else knows about Hindemuth IV; the information is buried in Galactic Department records. And nobody knows we came here—nobody will ever have to know.

"We could easily falsify our records, hide every trace of our jump to Hindemuth. It would be simple to extract several grams of cosmium and sell it through agents in the System, keeping our own knowledge and identities hidden. That would be the start; with the money we could put an expedition together and return here."

Sprague shook his head again. "It's too big for us, Ben. If there's as much cosmium here as there seems, the whole thing could too easily get out of control. Farthermore, selling cosmium indiscriminately might all too easily mean that it would get into the wrong hands. The Federation is still young and unstable, and a sudden flood of cosmium is one of the things that would almost certainly upset it and bring on a galactic war.

"The way you propose to handle it, cosmium would get around everywhere except in the one quarter where it's badly needed—in the hands of scientists. They've been doing some wonderful things with the pitiful scraps they've managed to get their hands on. With a good supply to work with, there's any number of miracles they could accomplish for the benefit of the race. And only the Federation could make it available to them cheaply enough and in quantity."

Sprague jerked his hand in a conclusive gesture. "I don't want to throw my rank around, but I will if you make it necessary. My decision stands, and further discussion is closed. . . . If you resist me in any way, Ben, I'll give you a dose of morphelon and take you back to the System in deep-sleep."

Dagget looked at the tall, spare man. Sprague stood very quietly, his long face determined and implacable.

Moving his shoulders as though against an oppressive weight, Dagget turned away. "Time we had something to eat," he said. "I'll get the auto-chef started."

Sprague remained beside the workbench, staring down at the record roll.

That night, while Dagget slept, he moved soundlessly through the cruiser and made certain electronic connections.

Morning sunlight poured in a pale gold stream through the headquarters viewpoint as Sprague and Dagget climbed into their coveralls.

"We'll land and have a close look at the kids this time," Sprague said. "And while we're at it, we'll take check recordings on the cosmium data we got yesterday. We'll also take a last try at locating the Colonial ship."

Dagget nodded equably, but his ice-blue eyes narrowed a moment later as Sprague picked up a small rectangular case.

"A couple of gadgets that might be useful in our interview with the kids," Sprague explained. "Let's go."

They descended to the hatch in the elevator. The jeet waited in its catapult cradle; entering, they adjusted the instruments at the rear of the cabin and then settled themselves in their seats.

Sprague's long fingers moved with swift skill over

switches and buttons. The hatch opened, and with a kind of deliberate, smooth violence, the jeet shot into the outside air, impelled first by the catapult and then by the sibilant roar of its jets.

The cruiser fell away behind and below them, dwindling to toylike proportions and then becoming lost in the distance. The island's expanse resolved into a changing pattern of plains, hill ranges, and rivers. Bright silence lay like a crystal blanket over the scene; a complete, heavy silence, compounded partly of unrelieved wilderness, partly of absent moving life. No birds winged through the clear sky, no animal herds grazed on the rolling plains.

Sprague felt the silence close around him, and its quality of unseen threat fell like a chill over his thoughts. Here, on Hindemuth IV, was cosmium, one of the rarest and most valuable elements unearthed by human science; cosmium in a quantity that meant power, not real and immediate power, but power in the abstract, the power that went with the mere knowledge that cosmium was present on this world. This knowledge could be the exclusive possession of a person or a group, could be an instrument or a weapon.

And the path to either possibility, he knew, radiated invisibly from the minds and desires of two men.

An undercurrent of wonder gathered in him. Cosmium was still a great mystery; scientists had not yet agreed on exactly what it was, or on exactly how it produced its effects. It possessed a strange sort of radioactivity, for while it made its presence known on instruments designed to detect radioactivity, it seemed to bear no relation to the familiar radioactive elements. But scientists had worked wonders with such few bits of cosmium that had come into their hands;

the element produced astonishing and almost supernatural results in the treatment of human ills.

Sprague jerked into alertness as Dagget suddenly
gestured downward. He had been aware in a detached
way that the jeet had reached the forest and was
winging over its vast mottled expanse. He saw now
that Dagget had sighted a group of children in a glade
below, and he sent his hands over the controls, slowing the jeet and swinging it around.

The children were running in pursuit as before, a
tiny trickle of life through the green and shadowed
immobility of the forest; and as the jeet moved in a
semicircle through the blue-green sky, they stopped
and stared upward with eager eyes, awaiting further
developments. It was as though they had sighted a
butterfly or a bird and were at once pleased and puzzled by its antics.

Sprague circled several times, while Dagget watched
intently through the binoculars.

"Just the kids," Dagget announced at last. "No adults
again, no weapons or other artifacts. This group looks
like the same one we saw yesterday."

"We'll land, then," Sprague returned. "And I guess
we'd better pick a spot far enough so the kids won't be
in the way when we come down. They wouldn't know
enough to avoid the jet stream."

He sent the craft skimming above the tops of the trees,
and then, sighting a long clear aisle between the smooth
brownish green boles, he glided to a landing on the
mossy turf. Preparing to leave the cabin, he reached
into a compartment and took out a holstered automatic and belt.

"It might be a good idea to have a weapon handy,"

he said in answer to Dagget's glance. "On a world like this you never know what might happen."

"Maybe I ought to take one, too," Dagget said.

"One gun between us is all we'll need," Sprague said quietly. His eyes locked for a tight, bitter moment with those of the red-headed man.

Dagget shrugged. "All right, Captain."

Sprague buckled the automatic about his waist, gathered up his small case, and followed Dagget out of the jeet. The air in the forest was warm and had a spicy tang. There was a deep stillness, which was underscored without being quite broken by the plaintive rustling of leaves all around in a soft breeze.

Another sound rose above the rustling; the sound of voices. Down the shadowed aisle formed by the trees, running figures appeared. They approached swiftly, and soon they grew distinct as young boys and girls. They laughed and called as they ran, and their long hair flew and their slender arms tossed in unrestrained excitement.

They might, Sprague thought wryly, have been boys and girls on Earth, running to see a circus train that had just arrived. Only he and Dagget were not much of a circus. There was no humor in them—not with cosmium here. Sprague hoped the children would not be too disappointed.

Those foremost in the running band presently slowed to a stop. The others in the rear crowded into them until they too became motionless. Across a mossy gap of some twenty meters, the men and the children gazed solemnly at each other.

The children had a wild look. There were perhaps a score in the group. Their hair was long and tangled about their small flushed faces, and their naked slim bodies were brown and sinewy. With wide eyes and open mouths, curious and yet hesitant, they stared at the men.

Sprague walked forward slowly. The children stiffened; muscles corded in their slender legs as they tensed for flight.

Sprague smiled. "Hello," he said.

The smile seemed to touch the children like a tangible thing; it spread through them like a ripple. Answering smiles appeared on their faces, and a slight blond girl echoed Sprague's greeting in an awkward voice.

"Hel-lo," she said.

The others around her laughed, reassured and delighted by the sound. "Hel-lo!" they said. "Hel-lo!"

The girl stepped closer, and as several of those nearest her moved to follow, the entire group was suddenly jostling and pushing as they swarmed about Sprague. They touched his coverall with exploring fingers, commenting on it in their clear shrill voices. Sprague could not understand them. There seemed a haunting familiarity in their words, but this might have been due to nothing more than the fact that they spoke in human tones.

"You . . . you kids," Sprague said abruptly, with a gentle intensity. "Where is everybody else? Why are you all alone here? How . . . just how can this be?"

The small faces about him turned solemn. The children seemed perplexed and troubled by his tone. They glanced at each other, and for a moment there was an uneasy quiet.

Then swift movements were suddenly audible. The children stared at a point behind Sprague. Alarm shooting an icy-hot flash through him, he whirled.

Dagget was disappearing into the cabin of the jeet. As Sprague started forward the door closed with a muffled thud, and through the transalloy shell he saw Dagget hurry into a seat and send his hands darting over the controls. Then he realized that the jets were partly turned in his direction, and instantly he saw his danger. He flung himself to one side, shouting at the children and waving them away.

Perhaps his harshly urgent voice frightened them, or perhaps they dimly understood; but they scampered to shelter among the surrounding trees. Moments later the jeet took off with a sibilant roar, diminishing swiftly in size as it shot upward into the blue-green sky.

Slowly Sprague emerged from behind the tree trunk where he had taken protection, staring after the jeet with a resigned bitterness. Then he dropped to a squatting position and opened the small case, which he had been keeping clutched under one arm. This contained, among other instruments, a tiny radio set and power unit. He sent out a call to Dagget, which would be picked up by the other's apparatus in the jeet.

"Ben! Can you hear me?"

"I can hear you," Dagget returned. "But it isn't going to do you any good."

"Just what kind of a space-crazy trick do you think you're pulling?" Sprague demanded.

"Space-crazy!" Dagget flashed back. "You're the one who wanted to turn our cosmium discovery over to the Federation. If that's the way you feel, you can stay right here on Hindemuth IV and think of all the fun you're going to miss. I'm taking the cruiser and hypering back to the System. I'll see you later—if you're still alive when I get back."

"Don't be a fool, Ben! You'll never get away with it. Headquarters will give you a thorough scanning over what became of me, and —"

"Headquarters will never touch me. I have the right kind of information, and I know the right kind of people. I'll get all the help I need."

Sprague sighed. "All right, Ben, now I'm going to let you in on a little secret. I've changed the frequency of the cruiser's hatch opening mechanism. You don't know what that new frequency is. If you use the wrong frequency in trying to get into the ship, you'll close a circuit that will set off the engines. The cruiser will take off for space without you—if, of course, you aren't killed by the blast. Remember, Ben, you can guess about the frequency—but you'll have to be right the first time."

Sprague's receiver made a strangled sound, then clicked into silence. He replaced the radio in the case and glanced around at the children, who had slowly approached to watch in puzzled wonder as he spoke to Dagget. They seemed wary and uncertain, as though not yet entirely over their fright. He smiled at them, a wry, tired smile, and then spoke.

"Hello again, kids. I guess we ought to get acquainted, since it appears I'm going to be with you for quite some time. What are your names? Mine's Phil Sprague."

The children said nothing. They smiled back at him, and one of them laughed softly, a glad, comforted sound.

Two days passed. Sprague remained in the forest with the children. He did not know to what lengths desperation might drive Dagget, and there was protection among the trees.

The children seemed delighted with his presence, as

297

though finding in him the fulfillment of some long-felt need. They never strayed far from him, and they watched him anxiously whenever he moved. They followed like so many small frisking shadows, pulling and shoving for the opportunity to be closest at his side, as growing restlessness drove him into aimless walks through the forest.

Food was no problem for Sprague. The children brought fruits and nuts from the forest, and cup-shaped leaves filled with a sweet, milk-like sap. His tests told him that these were edible and nourishing enough, and he knew he could subsist in this fashion for an indefinite period—longer, at any rate, than Dagget, whose only provisions were a kit of emergency rations in the jeet.

The children spent the still, deep nights wherever they happened to be in the forest. They would gather leafy boughs and make mattresses of these, curling up on them like puppies, in groups of three or more. Sprague's comforting nearness was as usual eagerly sought, and he found he did not mind. He felt a kind of bond growing between the children and himself; he was beginning to know them as individuals, to sense the thoughts behind their childish, simple speech. And oddly, concern with Dagget, with the cosmium find, began to recede in his thoughts like problems of another and entirely different existence.

But he was not allowed completely to forget. In the morning of the third day he caught sight of the jeet, far in the sky, cruising over a distant part of the forest. He cautioned the children to remain out of sight beneath the largest trees. He made them understand, and they were quickly amenable, seeing it as a game.

After that he hovered over the radio set, waiting. A few hours later he heard Dagget's voice, heavy with a note of desperation.

"Phil! Are you listening, Phil? I want to talk to you."

"I'm listening," Sprague said. "What's on your mind, Ben?"

"Phil, where are you? We can't go on like this. We've got to get together and talk this over."

"There's nothing to talk over, Ben. I don't see any compromise on this cosmium situation. We can use the discovery your way or my way, but not both at once. . . . And I think my way is best, Ben. When you're ready to agree, I'll tell you how to find me."

Dagget was silent for a long while. Then his radio clicked off.

Sprague sighed and stared emptily into the forest. He felt a touch on his arm; he found himself looking into the worried eyes of the slight blond girl, whose name seemed to be Karreh. He grinned and rumpled her hair, and as she shrieked her delight, he picked up the case and rose, knowing that Dagget might very well have used the radio contact in order to obtain a directional fix. He and the children would have to move to a new spot, and quickly.

He gestured and called to them, using a few of the simple words he had learned. Then he trotted into the shadowed green maze of the forest, and the children followed, laughing and frolicking.

Sprague traveled, with occasional stops for rests, well into the afternoon. The children seemed tireless as they romped through the trees and the undergrowth, their laughing voices weaving an ever-changing pattern of sound. They ate as they went, snatching up the fruits and nuts which were present everywhere in abundance and gathering leaf-cups of milk-like sap during the rest periods.

Sprague himself was not a little surprised to find that he felt no serious fatigue effects. He seemed filled with a youthful vigor almost as boundless as that possessed by the children themselves. It was as though the days he had spent in the forest had given him a new strength and endurance.

The forest gradually thinned out and at last Sprague realized that he and the children had been moving toward one edge of it. He was in doubt about leaving the shelter of the trees, but curiosity impelled him to see what lay ahead. Further, he sensed it might be wise to seek concealment in some less obvious location, one less likely to be searched by an increasingly desperate Dagget.

Sprague paused often to scan the blue-green sky. It was still cloudless, still serene and empty of life. The jeet had not been visible since that morning, and somehow that worried Sprague. He suspected a stratagem on Dagget's part; the other had not resumed radio contact as he would have done in the event that he had realized the hopelessness of his position and decided to give up.

At last Sprague and the children passed beyond the forest's edge and reached the lip of a broad gully where a large stream had once coursed and where now only a thin trickle of water crept. Some change in the land, it seemed, had dammed the stream and sent it flowing in a new direction. Only the gully and the thin trickle within it remained.

Finding a way down to the gully floor, Sprague descended. The children scrambled after him, laughing and unhesitating, agile as mountain goats. They did not understand the sense of peril that drove Sprague; this was an adventure to them, and he was content to let it remain so.

After another short rest, he chose a direction at random and resumed the march, keeping well within the shadows to one side of the gully walls. In this way, a short time later, he came to an obstruction. A landslide or a cave-in brought down the gully wall at this point, filling the channel almost from one side to the other.

Sprague was studying the huge mound of gravel and sand when he saw a gleam of curved metal. He stared at it for a long moment, stunned and disbelieving, a wonder kindling and becoming a vast flame in his mind. Then he was running crazily, clawing his way up the mound, tearing away great handfuls of sand and gravel.

A few seconds later he was certain that he had found the long-lost Colonial Administration ship.

He continued to dig. The children scrambled up the mound to help him, and he motioned to direct their activities. They jostled and laughed, and their slender arms swung as they sent handfuls of debris in a steady shower through the air.

Sprague laughed, too. For this was the answer to the stalemate between Dagget and himself; this was the means of victory. It was Dagget who would now be marooned on Hindemuth IV, since he would meet with immediate frustration in any attempt to enter the cruiser.

Sprague, however, had a ship—if it had not been too damaged to be placed in operation. The possibility sobered him.

He speculated on how the vessel had come to be here. Originally, no doubt, it had been landed in a spot above the gully. Later there had been a cave-in of the supporting earth, caused either by the weight of the ship or by some process of erosion. The vessel had tumbled into the gully, becoming partially buried. It had not been visible from the air, not even to the all-embracing eye of the jeet's camera.

It was one of the children who presently discovered the entrance hatch, and Sprague hurried over from the place where he had been digging. The hatch was open but partially filled with sand, and more digging was necessary before he could enter. Finally he groped his way into the darkness and silence of the ship's interior. The children trooped after him, subdued and quiet with wonder.

He was familiar with the design of this type of ship, and soon he located an emergency light switch station. The lights worked; illumination flooded the stairways and corridors of that immediate section. He found other stations, and a quickening pulse of life now stirred in the vessel's metal carcass.

With the children following in awed muteness, Sprague hurried through the deserted corridors, pausing to glance into compartments as he went. There were no signs of tragedy, nothing to show that there had been an attack, mutiny, or sickness. No remains of bodies were visible anywhere; the compartments were clean and neat, giving no evidence of damage or theft. The ship's passengers seemed simply to have left. And they had left very quietly and calmly, it seemed, taking nothing, disturbing nothing.

Sprague found the captain's cabin, where he at once

fixed his attention on the ship's log. But this did not explain what had become of the passengers and crew. The landing on Hindemuth IV had been made safely, and subsequent entries mentioned nothing more momentous than the fact that cosmium had been reported present on the island. The last entry had been made a week after landing, and discussed only the steps that were being taken to settle the colonists in their new habitat.

The rest was silence. The captain had not again touched the log. Sprague sent a slow glance around the cabin and uneasily wondered why.

He went to the control room. Here again were silence and emptiness. There were no signs of disorder or damage. A glance at the meters and gauges above the pilot's console showed that the reactor furnace had been properly deactivated. A supply of radioactive fuels remained in storage, and automatic devices would easily assemble them to power the Hyper-Drive generators.

He tried the switches and buttons on the console; colored signal lights blinked in response. The ship was still in operating condition. It had not been harmed by the fall into the gully, having been designed to withstand stresses even more serious.

Sprague was satisfied. Everything was ready. He had only to —

He peered around the control room, puzzled. He had a sudden, overpowering feeling of disorientation. He could not remember how or why he happened to be here. The severely utilitarian room seemed strange. He felt that he should be somewhere else entirely; he could not decide where this was. The memories he sought eluded him; they hovered tantalizingly far back

The Children

in his mind, flirting on the brink of awareness, but never crossing it.

He squeezed his eyes shut, standing very still. Somewhere beyond the control room children laughed and children's footsteps pattered through the corridors. And as though dissolved by the sounds, his queer amnesia was gone.

Foreboding remained. He knew that inexplicable sensation would return, for this was not the first time he had experienced it. There had been other instances of late when he had noticed a vagueness in his thoughts, when he had felt his memories becoming dim and unreal. Only now the feeling seemed to be growing in frequency and depth.

He heard the children laugh again, heard their footsteps approach. He turned slowly from the pilot console—and saw Dagget in the control room doorway.

Shock thundered through Sprague. He reached for the automatic in the holster at his side; he became motionless as he saw that Dagget's own weapon was already centered with lethal readiness on his chest.

A group of children had preceded Dagget into the room, their small faces showing delight over his return. But now, as they grew aware of the tense, hostile expressions of the two men, their smiles faded. They stood frozen, sensing that the situation was not quite right, but puzzled over the reason.

"Why don't you go for your gun, Phil?" Dagget asked softly. "I wouldn't mind killing you—not after what I've gone through. I'm going to kill you anyhow, you know."

Sprague was staring at the red-headed man. Dagget seemed queerly changed.

304

"So you traced me here, Ben," Sprague said at last. His voice was bemused; his mind was not on Dagget but on a matter even more important. A pattern, previously bewildering, was now becoming clear.

Dagget smiled thinly. "I got a directional fix on my last radio contact with you. I landed and then used radar to locate the route you and the kids were taking through the forest. I set out after you. I caught up just as you were crawling into the ship."

Sprague's thoughts had a diamond-sharp clarity. Dagget went on, his voice stronger and harsher, yet still he seemed to speak from a distance.

"You kept me from getting the cruiser, Phil—but you aren't going to keep me from getting *this* ship. I've seen enough to be certain it's in working order. I'm going back to the System with my information about the cosmium here—and I'm going back alone."

Sprague shook his head slowly. "You're not going back, Ben."

"Are you going to stop me?"

"No," Sprague said. "Something else is going to stop you, Ben. The cosmium here is going to do that."

"You're crazy! How could cosmium possibly—?" Dagget broke off, blinking, as though to clear an obstructing mist from his eyes. He rubbed the back of his gun hand over his forehead, looked dazed and puzzled. He seemed to have forgotten the weapon he was holding.

"Cosmium," Sprague said, fighting to keep his newfound clarity from becoming lost. "Cosmium is at the bottom of everything. I should have guessed it before, but it became clear only a moment ago—too late, Ben . . . too late."

Dagget blinked, and desperately Sprague went on:

"Ben . . . listen. You've got to understand everything I say. There isn't much time left—I can feel it.

"Ben, cosmium has a powerful effect on life. Scientists back in the System have already learned that much in experiments with small amounts of it. Small amounts—and you and I have been exposed to a greater concentration than has ever existed in any one time and place. As a result one certain effect has become clear: continued exposure to unusually large amounts of cosmium results in a steady reduction or dissipation of bodily mass—most likely as energy. In human beings there is a curious kind of physical regression. I suspect that this reaches equilibrium according to the amount of cosmium to which the body is exposed.

"You've noticed that there is no animal life here, Ben. Because of the highly specialized type of cellular organization needed, animal life never got the chance to evolve. Cosmium made that impossible."

Dagget looked confused and uneasy. "You must be losing your mind," he muttered.

Sprague nodded gravely. "I *am* losing my mind, Ben—and so are you. Just as the colonists lost their minds. A short time after they landed, something happened to them. They . . . *forgot.* They left the ship and never came back. They simply forgot all about it . . . because, you see, in a dissipation of bodily mass the cells are affected, and in the brain this means a loss of memories—amnesia."

"You're trying to trick me!" Dagget whispered. "But it isn't going to work. I'm hypering back to the System in this ship, and you aren't going to stop me. I. . . I'm going to kill you. *Now* . . ."

The weapon in Dagget's hand moved to point

squarely at Sprague. Dagget's finger tightened on the trigger.

"Look at your uniform, Ben," Sprague said. "It's getting too big for you. We've been here almost a week, you know. That was long enough for the cosmium radiation to start working on us."

Dagget looked down at his coverall. He plucked at it, forgetting the weapon in his hand. It fell to the floor.

Dagget smiled in puzzled wonder at Sprague. "Why, it *is* too big!"

The feeling of disorientation swept once more over Sprague. He had been keeping it at bay, but his massive effort of will had finally weakened. He made a tremendous last attempt to drive the dimness back.

"I've got to leave a message before . . . before I forget. I've got to . . . If only—I . . ."

The last attempt failed.

"Too big," Dagget said. He laughed. He stripped the coverall from him and tossed it aside. "I'm hungry," he said.

"There's plenty of good things to eat in the forest," Sprague said. He grinned and hurried impulsively toward the doorway. "Let's eat!"

The watching children laughed. The strangeness of the past several minutes was gone. Everything was all right again. They shouted and called to each other and followed the two bigger children through the ship, through the hatch, and into the gentle dusk outside.

Laughing, jostling, the children ran toward the forest that was home. Among them now were two larger and older than the others. But time and cosmium would take care of the differences. Soon all the children would be the same . . .

Whooo-ooo Flupper!

NICHOLAS FISK

This world is called Positos VI PH. Wow, how I used to hate it!

"We're *prisoners*!" I'd shout. "Never allowed out of this crummy unit!"

"And if we *did* get out, what would we *do*?" squeaked Lollo, my sister. She even waved her fists, which was pretty useless as she's only nine and small for her age. I'm nearly twelve.

We stared out of the unit's window. What did we see? A sort of gray-green blancmange, with some dirty yellow prehistoric-looking trees sticking out. And that's all. "I hate you," muttered Lollo.

I said nothing. What was there to say about Positos VI PH? The name tells you everything. The "VI" means it's a sixth-order world—the smallest sort, the dregs. The "PH" means "partly hostile." In other words, it has a tendency to kill humans. Charming.

"Let's play with the video," I said.

"I'm sick of the video."

"Chess, then."

"You'll only win." She chewed her lower lip for some time, then said, "I'm going out."

"You're not! It's not allowed!"

"I'm going *out*," she repeated. I tried to stop her but she kept putting on more and more outside gear. Even her helmet, although Positos air is breathable. Thick and muggy and smelly, but breathable.

I found myself doing what she was doing—donning boots, suit, bleeper, and three sorts of weapons. It's no good arguing with Lollo. Anyhow, I'm supposed to take care of her. Big brother.

"We're off," she said. Off we went. We followed the tracks of our parents' Ruffstuff at first—the wide, deep tracks of its go-anywhere wheels. Mum and Dad are prospectors. They keep searching for something—any-thing—to sell back home, on Earth. It's a hard way to make a living.

The Ruffstuff's tracks swept off to the right so we kept walking to the left. We didn't want to meet them. We'd get told off. After a time, I said, "Look, Lollo, that's enough. Let's go home." But she just marched on.

We came to the swamp.

Today, it's known as Lollo's Lagoon because she saw it first. "Lagoon" is a bit grand: it's really just a big old swamp, surrounded by droopy trees with their roots half in and half out of the water. And big, mossy, fungus-like growths here and there on the shores. We stood and looked at it. Lollo made a face. I broke off a piece of wood or whatever it is from a tree, if that's a tree, and flung it at one of the huge pancake things like giant water-lily leaves that floated on the surface of the water. There was a damp *plaff!* as the soggy wood hit the soggy pancake. "Good shot!" I was about to say —

When it moved! It rose! It reared up! It sort of humped up in the middle, sucking water with it, shrug-ging sprays of water from its wavy edges! It was alive!

It took off! Its fringe, its edges, became folded-over

hydroplanes. The humped-up middle part was clear of the water. It made an upside-down U shape. Its fringes rippled and it moved. I mean, really *moved*. I fell over backward in the slimy mud.

At first it just zoomed along, hydroplaning. But it had another trick up its sleeves. Suddenly the water inside the hollow of the U seemed to *boil*. Somewhere inside itself, the thing had a sort of jet propulsion.

Now it didn't just move. It accelerated like one of those old twentieth-century water-speed-record break-ers and *hurtled* over the water! It swept around in a huge curve. Lollo's mouth hung open. I gaped. It went so fast, we couldn't believe it. Then *hiss!—surge!—*

vroom!—it headed straight for us like a thousand-mile-an-hour nightmare!

Now we were both on our backsides in the mud. But just as we thought it was going to flatten us, it somehow backpedaled, slowed, cut its jets, rippled its fringes, and turned pink. We stared at it and it seemed to stare at us.

Silence. Then the thing said, "Whooo."

Lollo whooed right back at it. I added a shaky whoo of my own.

The thing—it must have been five meters across—rippled its flanges invitingly and eased right to where we stood. It said, "Whooo?"

You can guess what happened next. Lollo climbed aboard the thing. Her big brave brother followed. The thing said, "Whooo!" and moved.

When we lived Earthside, Lollo and I tried everything: zeta-powered bikes, dune zoomers, no-grav gymnastics, the lot.

You can keep them all as long as you leave us Flupper.

Riding Flupper was Glory, Glory, Glory all the way. Not just the thrill of all that acceleration, all that speed, all that flying water. He was so *nice* about everything. He *wanted* us to be happy aboard him. He showed us the whole lagoon (it is very big), slowing down to let us see the most interesting parts, then hurtled off amid boiling clouds of spray to give us a thrill. He even realized that we might slide off him when he accelerated, and provided us with a vine, like a rope, to hang on to. He held on to the other end, it went underneath him.

Mum and Dad didn't find out about Flupper and us for more than a week. We faked the unit's video to show us "in." That was our only fear—being found out, being told "No! Never again!" Meanwhile, Flupper showed us the deadly thorn bushes that wrapped round their prey like octopuses, then whooshed us off at savage speeds — sometimes so fast he aquaplaned over the water.

There were other Flupper-type lily pads, of course. They seemed to welcome us too. We called one the Clown because he used to follow Flupper, cutting him up and teasing him. All in fun, naturally. Flupper would pretend to skid and go out of control, it was terrific — we'd hang on like grim death to the rope.

We knew we were perfectly safe, of course. But we were wrong.

That day, we were on Flupper doing about a million miles an hour. The Clown was racing alongside and Lollo and I were showing off to him, whooing and waving. Lollo raised one leg and waggled her foot cheekily. Her other foot slipped.

She fell down. The rushing water clutched at one of her legs. The pull of the water tore her off Flupper. For a second I glimpsed her wet, frightened face: then she was hurtling away from me, bouncing over the water like a rag doll, her arms and legs flailing.

She hit the blancmange of the shoreline, bounced over it, and flew sprawling into some bushes. Poison thorn bushes.

She screamed. Loudly at first, then in an awful breathless sobbing way.

Flupper took me to the shore and I ran to Lollo. When I reached her, I stopped dead, appalled by what I saw. She was *red*, red all over. The thorns were cutting her to pieces. The bush wrapped itself tighter and tighter around her and the thorns kept going in.

Then the snake thing came. I had seen the snake things from a distance. This one had a pronglike dagger in its head. I was screaming at Flupper and dancing about in an agony of uselessness. I thought the snake thing wanted Lollo. It didn't. It dug its dagger into the roots of the bush. The bush was of a dirty purplish color. As the dagger went in, the bush turned gray and all its thorns went pale and soft. It died almost instantly. Now the snake thing could go for Lollo.

But it was too slow, or too stupid: I just had time to grab her ankles and pull her away. I towed her over to the muddy shore and flung her aboard Flupper. I was yelling at Flupper to help, to do something, anything. But all he did was to leave the shore and head fast for another part of the lagoon, where the molds and fungi overhang the water. I begged him not to, but he just went on, heading straight for them.

"Home, take me home!" I shouted to Flupper. He took no notice. I could say nothing to Lollo, she had become a silent, horrible, raw red thing. "Not this way!" I shouted. "Home!"

But still Flupper continued in the wrong direction, heading for the grayish clumps of mold and fungi. I hated these growths, they frightened me. And Flupper was not merely heading for them, he was among them! "No!" I screamed. But it was too late: the sticky grayish growths were brushing over Lollo's body, clinging to her, damply caressing her, sticking to her in wisps and clusters.

And Flupper had done this deliberately! I lay down on him and beat him with my fists. I must have been out of my mind . . .

Suddenly it didn't matter anymore. I lay there, head

buried in my arms, knowing that Lollo was dead: I would spend the rest of my life cursing myself and Flupper. Cursing and weeping.

Then Lollo's voice said, close to my ear, "Yuck! I am filthy! All *bloody!*"

I sat up and she was kneeling beside me, picking at herself disgustedly, trying to get rid of the fungi and molds. And—unbelievably—*as I watched, the cuts and stabs in her flesh healed.* "All this *blood,*" she said, in just the same voice she'd have used if she'd spotted chocolate around my mouth. "How disgusting! You'll have to get it off. I can't."

Later, I helped her sponge off the caked blood. It took a long time, there was so much of it. We did it at home back at the unit. We never got rid of the stains on her gear. Those stains gave us away, of course. Dad spotted them and Mum tore us apart. A real tongue-lashing. Almost as bad as the thorn bush, Lollo said.

Our parents wouldn't believe a word we said, so we took them to see Flupper. Dad carried a Trans Vox so that we could talk properly with him. I'm amazed that Lollo and I never thought of using the Trans Vox: it translates almost any language into our language. Soon, everyone was talking away like mad.

A little later—just a few months—we were rich. Rich as you can get!

All thanks to Flupper, of course. And those growths that used to frighten me, the molds and fungi.

You know about penicillin? Alexander Fleming discovered it quite early in the twentieth century. The wonder antibiotic, the great cure-all. Well, *our* molds and fungi (I mean, Flupper's) turned out to be super penicillin, penicillin × 10,000. And Dad and Mum had staked the claim, so they have Galactic Rights.

So we were and are everlastingly rich. "Just think!" Mum said. "We can go back to our proper home! Live Earthside!"

"I don't want to go back home!" Lollo said. "I *won't* go, you can't *make* me go!"

Flupper, of course: she couldn't bear the thought of leaving him. I felt the same.

When we talked to Flupper about it, he said, "Do you know how old I am?" We said no. "I'm 245 Earth years old," he said. "And I've got another 150 to go . . ."

So perhaps Lollo and I won't make so much fuss about going back to Earth. We can always come back. And Flupper will always be there.

"Whooo-ooo, Flupper!"

The Space Butterflies

STEPHEN BAXTER

B urdon felt the familiar lurch as the lander dropped
out of orbit.

He looked up from his instrument console.
Lieutenant Fairbrother was striking a pose, shoulders
back, hands clasped. Burdon peered past her to the
viewscreen —

His jaw dropped. The planet was beautiful.

A dozen Earths could have been laced around its
black equator. Huge towers pierced the atmosphere,
and giant cities sparkled in the light —

What light?

The planet sailed through space alone, far from any
star. But the layer of space around it seemed to churn
as if stirred by a ladle. Gradually Burdon made out
details, and he realized that vast ships were sailing
around the planet, like butterflies with wings a thousand kilometers wide. The reflective wings gathered
up the starlight and splashed it over the cities . . .

"Let's have a status report, Mr. Burdon," said
Fairbrother.

Burdon glared at her back. "I don't think the absolute speedo's working." The absolute speed indicator
gave the lander's velocity relative to the cosmic background radiation—the dull glow all around the sky left
over from the Big Bang. Burdon thumped the indica-

tor's scuffed surface to no avail. "According to this the planet's got zero absolute speed. But we know it's moving at several hundred kilometers a second . . ."

Fairbrother's turret of a head swiveled around toward him. "Don't bring me problems, Mr. Burdon. I want solutions."

Burdon thumped the speedo again. "Fairbrother, for heaven's sake —"

Fairbrother's eyes were wide apart and seemed to target him individually. "Mr. Burdon!" she thundered.

Their wills locked. The moment stretched. Burdon tried to remember that the whole point of him signing up on the *Falcon*'s interstellar voyage of exploration had been to leave his personal weaknesses behind him on Earth. To do more than the nine-to-five routine at the bank—to escape the mess his life had become . . .

Had he gained nothing? Was he going to let himself be dominated by pompous old Fairbrother?

You bet I am, he thought. Burdon dropped his eyes and began the speedo's test routine.

He had traveled light-years and gotten nowhere, he thought gloomily. His faults encased him like a spacesuit. Motion was an illusion —

Burdon snapped out of his introspection.

He checked the speedo again. "Fairbrother, I think the speedo's working after all. It's just that the planet really is stationary."

She frowned. "But we know it's got a velocity of several hundred kilometers a second —"

"In the galactic frame, yes—but the galaxy's moving against the cosmic background. You didn't know that? So are all the nearby galaxies; they're streaming through space like a flock of starry geese."

Her face crumpled with the effort of accepting a new idea. She searched for words. "Why?" she managed.

"Nobody knows. But the point is this planet's motion is an illusion; the galaxy is moving past it."

Fairbrother's eyes flickered skyward. "So helpful," she said dryly. She sat in her control chair. "We'll make for the head of one of those towers."

They crept into the flock of butterflies. Wings flapped over the lander, edged with starlight. They were huge; scaled against Earth's moon they would have looked like moths beating against a light bulb.

The tower was a hollow spire reaching out of the atmosphere. "Look at that." Burdon pointed. "They use the towers to launch the winged things."

A cylinder like a chrysalis squirted up and out of the tower; its shell cracked and tumbled away and magnificent wings began to unfurl. Other butterflies clustered around like parents, bathing the newcomer with focused starlight. Damp-looking wings clutched at the light. "They're using radiation pressure to help it reach orbital velocity," Burdon breathed. "Fantastic —"

Fairbrother took them nosing through the crowd; the mature butterflies scattered nimbly but the "baby" couldn't get out of the way. They made straight for it. Fairbrother extended the grappling arm.

Burdon stared, horrified. "What are you doing?"

She didn't answer. With clinical skill she snipped away the glistening wings. Then she grabbed the helpless central section and began to draw it into the lander.

Fragments of the wings drifted away, crumpling. Mature butterflies sailed around them, agitated.

"Fairbrother, that's brutal."

"Do you want to do an analysis of this thing, Mr. Burdon?"

Burdon, unhappily, went to his console.

Fairbrother brought the butterfly remnant into a lab bay. The monitor showed a clear globe four meters wide. Inside, a mothlike creature thrashed.

It was human-shaped but smoothed out and stretched, a sculpture in hot plastic. It had wings of its own; they were silvery and threw highlights in tantalizing hints of pattern.

It had no mouth. Long fingers worked control threads that led to the forlorn stumps of butterfly wings.

Fairbrother snorted contemptuously. "How primitive."

Burdon watched the wings. "I don't know," he said. "There seems to be a purpose to those reflections. Suppose that's how it communicates?" There was a lot of fast-moving detail. "It must be equivalent to thousands of words a minute. That's a lot of information, Fairbrother —"

She shrugged. "So what? It couldn't even defend itself."

"Military will isn't the only measure of intelligence! How could these creatures have developed spaceflight without a high civilization?"

She smiled. "On Earth there's a spider that builds diving bells out of its webbing. Blind evolution, that's all."

Burdon tried to find the words to shut her up, and failed.

A laser scalpel lanced across the bay and slit open the moth creature's life sac. The delicate wings thrashed in a visual scream as precious gases rushed out.

"Fairbrother, you're such a swine."

"Hm. Interesting mix of trace elements. Almost breathable."

Then she turned her back on the dying alien and moved back to her control chair.

Burdon worked frantically, pumping the lab bay full of a gas mixture. But the alien had crumpled like waste paper and barely twitched.

Burdon felt like climbing in there with it.

The lander plunged toward the atmosphere. Fairbrother hummed as she worked.

They slid over great cities.

A launch tower thrust like a giant's fist from the heart of each city. They sailed over a monstrous well; at its bottom was a ruddy glow. "Geothermal energy," Burdon said. "The source of their power."

"I'm making for what looks like the busiest region," said Fairbrother. Ahead of them, hundreds of butterflies pierced the dusty air with starlight beams.

Something shouldered its way over the horizon: a pyramid jet-black, kilometers tall, and geometrically perfect. Moth creatures swooped over its three faces like flies on the flank of an elephant.

Fairbrother nodded, her hawk eyes unblinking. "Except for the launch towers, the largest structure on the planet. Obviously of religious significance; some kind of temple."

Burdon hesitated. "Well ... I'm not so sure. We don't know anything about this place."

"We'll land here," Fairbrother decided. "We want to have the maximum impact."

"Impact? We're supposed to be scientists, not conquistadors."

But it was too late. Fairbrother set them down hard

at the foot of the pyramid; Burdon watched aliens squirm out of the way. He didn't think they all made it.

"Suit up," said Fairbrother.

"What?"

"Suit up." She started assembling her equipment.

"What kind of expedition is this?" Burdon grumbled. "Shouldn't we fill out the standard reports first? Captain Hamilton will eat us alive when we get back to *Falcon*."

Fairbrother ignored him. Burdon suited up.

Fairbrother strutted onto the surface of the planet.

The pyramid dominated a vast plain littered with moths. The thick air of this huge but light planet was full of them—not truly flying, they glided on their stubby wings, a bit like flying fish.

Their mouthless silence was eerie.

Space butterflies flew over the deep sky, sparkling sheets the size of his hand. They looked like a flock of bony suns.

Fairbrother strode toward the pyramid as if she owned it.

The lander was ringed by curious—or fearful—moths. They parted to let Fairbrother through. Beside their starlit grace she looked absurd in her suit, a lump of clay. "Follow me, Mr. Burdon," she ordered. "They can obviously do us no harm."

Burdon stumbled out of the lander. "Where are you going? What about the atmospheric monitors—the cultural exchange packages —?"

She didn't answer. She towered over the aliens; she walked through them like a hero. After their initial fright, or confusion, the butterflies seemed excited by the novelty of it all. They clustered around her like

faery children, chattering bits of starlight to each other.

In his arms Burdon bore the collection of flimsy rags that was all Fairbrother had left of the butterfly pilot. Burdon walked hesitantly toward the nearest moths. "Here," he said, holding out his burden. "I'm sorry. Perhaps you can do something for it."

A dozen smoothed-over faces peered into Burdon's for a frozen moment. Then they broke into a flurry of glittering wings and fluttered over the casualty.

They definitely seemed to be communicating with their wings, Burdon thought with a part of his mind.

Another part made him turn away in shame.

Burdon set off after Lieutenant Fairbrother.

Burdon reached the base of the pyramid and started to climb. The surface was almost sheer but there was plenty of traction; Burdon climbed with easy bounds in the toy gravity.

Burdon joined a ιane of moths scrambling up the pyramid. Another lane hurried down from the summit, squeezing around them —

One of the down stream fell before him.

Startled, Burdon stumbled and landed on his butt.

Aliens swarmed around them as if directed by a traffic cop. Their wings rippled with concentric circles. Laughter? Embarrassed, Burdon got to his feet.

Burdon stood over the fallen creature. Its slender body trembled and patterns chased each other over its wings, growing ever finer as if focusing. Finally, with an audible click, the patterns froze over a small area at the heart of each wing.

Carefully the moth poked its fine fingers through the fabric of its wings and tore out the patterned areas. There didn't seem to be any pain and the wings started healing immediately. With monkish care the moth rolled up the torn-off pieces and pushed them into fine slots in the side of the pyramid.

Then it got to its spidery feet and hurried off down the slope. Burdon watched it go, bemused.

It was as if the moth had brought some sort of knowledge from the pyramid's summit and had now extruded it from its body.

Burdon knelt awkwardly. The looming face of the pyramid was covered with slots, each stuffed with a wing-fabric scroll.

This whole structure must be a sort of library, stuffed

with knowledge. Could the planet and its people have been redesigned—dedicated to a single purpose, like a vast monastery?

The pieces of the puzzle soared around his mind like the space butterflies.

The planet was stiller than the galaxies, far from the obscuring light of any star. Spaceborne mirrors sailed around it—mirrors big enough to see clear back to the Big Bang. And the very bodies of the little inhabitants had been adapted to serve as recording instruments . . .

Burdon remembered Fairbrother.

She was so far ahead Burdon could only see the wake she left in the stream of moths. Burdon hurried on.

"Fairbrother! Lieutenant Fairbrother! We've got to talk about this!"

"This place is obviously some sort of temple," she transmitted calmly. "We seem to have arrived during a religious festival."

"Fairbrother, you're crazy. Listen to me —"

"We should seize the moment. Take the opportunity." Her voice glinted with self-confidence.

"You've been planning this since you found out how physically weak these creatures are, haven't you?" Burdon panted desperately. "You think you can lord it over the planet."

She laughed at him and stalked on.

Burdon raged at his weakness and tried to run after her. But the more he hurried the more he was scared of crushing fragile limbs beneath his feet.

Burdon battled through the insubstantial obstructions: the aliens, and—still more nebulous—his own inadequacies.

325

"Fairbrother, you're totally wrong about what's happening here. Use your eyes! You haven't stopped to think since we landed.

"This pyramid is the centerpiece of the planet. But it's not a temple. It's a library! Look under your feet. It's stuffed with a million generations' worth of recordings."

Fairbrother was nearing the summit. "Recordings?" she asked absently.

"Face it, Fairbrother. You want to believe you will be treated as a hero here, as a god. Like Cortez, like the conquistadors. The way no one on *Falcon* will treat you. Isn't that it?"

"Shut your mouth, Burdon."

"No!"

Burdon saw her reach the summit of the pyramid. The quality of light changed. The space butterflies sailed into a new formation; their spotlights swooped toward the pyramid, leaving the land bathed in darkness.

Toward the summit the moths were arranging themselves into a formal array. And at the summit itself —

Burdon groaned. "I don't believe it. A throne! There had to be."

Fairbrother squared her shoulders.

"Fairbrother, for the last time, we have to report to *Falcon*. . . . This whole planet's an astronomical observatory. The sky's littered with enormous spaceborne mirrors.

"And these aliens aren't savages. They're not priests— or princes. They're astronomers!" Burdon gestured at the aliens caked over the summit in their patient ranks. "Their whole bodies are recording instruments—they take notes on pieces of their wings."

A scared-looking moth creature sat in the throne,

hopelessly fluttering its wings at Fairbrother. Two others stood to either side, holding a sort of elaborate crown. "You may as well shut your mouth, Mr. Burdon," Fairbrother said reasonably, "because I'm not listening."

She stepped forward and majestically took the silvered crown from the two attendants. They fluttered in protest. Fairbrother reached forward and brushed the third moth from the throne.

"You think that's some sort of king! Wrong! He's a— a—an Astronomer Royal! That's all!"

Fairbrother sat in the throne; it seemed to creak under her weight. She held the crown over her head and surveyed her kingdom, savoring the moment.

Space butterflies in all parts of the sky sent needle beams of concentrated starlight sweeping down at the pyramid. Great rings of light rushed toward Fairbrother. She was at the focus of the planet.

Literally.

"Don't do it, Fairbrother! I'm pleading with you." A rustling crowd still separated them; Burdon struggled forward, trying to force power into his voice. "The bodies of these aliens have been adapted as—as telescope eyepieces. Yours hasn't! You don't know what you're doing—you'll kill yourself . . ."

Fairbrother lowered the crown. It balanced precariously on her helmet.

The light roared in on her –

– and the crown exploded into brilliance, became a bit of starlight.

Fairbrother's head was a ball of flame. She screamed. She slumped from the throne.

The crown fell off and rolled away. The moment of focus passed and the brilliance died.

His eyes watering, Burdon staggered forward.

"Fairbrother! Fairbrother . . . "

When Burdon reached her, Fairbrother was getting to her feet. She said hoarsely, "My suit saved me." She swayed.

Burdon gaped.

The plastic of her helmet had blistered into a monstrous balloon. Fire-extinguishing foam had oozed from her suit's pores and hardened in great bulges. She had a belly like an elephant's.

From above huge foam cheeks her gimlet eyes fixed Burdon. "What's the matter with you?"

Burdon bowed solemnly. "Your Majesty."

The light flickered. The pyramid was covered with moths staring up at them. And the wings of every one of them were covered with flowing concentric circles.

Fairbrother's inflated helmet wobbled uncertainly. "What are they doing?"

"They're laughing," Burdon said harshly. "They're laughing at you. All of them.

"And so am I. Your Majesty."

She stared at him—and then at the ranks of aliens –
– and in that moment something went out of her, a spirit almost visible.

Awkwardly, Burdon took her arm. "Come on," he said. "Let's forget this and get on with our work."

Burdon began to guide her down the pyramid. She crunched as she walked and left behind a trail of foam.

"But I'll tell you this," Burdon said roughly. "I won't be calling you 'lieutenant' again."

The ridiculous head drooped further. Suddenly Burdon felt a lot bigger inside.

"Or maybe I will. What the heck."

Burdon led her through the alien throng to their lander.

The Bells of Acheron

E. C. TUBB

E very planet has an atmosphere, not the one you breathe but the one you feel. Kalturia with its soaring mountains lashed by tumultuous seas, the towering escarpments naked and bare, reflecting the ruby light of a sullen sun in a sky so heavy and brooding that, standing there, you feel like a fly on the face of creation. Lokrush, soft and gentle with its woods and rolling hills, its flowers nodding in scented breezes, the red and green light of its twin suns merging and blending in an eternal kaleidoscope of shimmering wonder. Ragnarok with its snow and ice and incessant electrical storms and, at night, the flaming beauty of the aureoles filling the sky with sheets and curtains of colored fire. Acheron with its Singing Bells.

We covered them all on the Grand Tour, dropping down to spend a day or two days while the passengers stared and marveled, then up again, the grav-drive humming as it lifted us into space, the twisting wrench as the warp jumped us from star to star, then planetfall again and more natural wonders to dazzle the eye and numb the mind. It could have become routine but it was never that. The universe is too big, the worlds too many to ever allow of boredom. So that the crew rivaled the passengers in their eagerness to make planetfall, their reluctance to leave once landed, and, having left, their impatience to land again somewhere new and strange.

Most of us had our favorite worlds. The captain, I knew, loved Almuri with its living crystals; the chief engineer always had to be watched when we reached Homeline with its fantastic seas and equally fantastic fish, and for me nothing could equal Acheron with its Singing Bells.

Holman was talking about them when I entered the lounge. It was his habit to discuss the next world we were to visit, to explain the natural phenomena in scientific terms and to prepare the passengers, in a way, for the wonders to come. It wasn't his job but he had made it so. Accidents were few, sickness rare, and the warp-jump often took as long as several days. Time, for the doctor as for all of us, tended to drag between the stars.

I moved softly about the lounge, collecting empty glasses, cleaning ashtrays, arranging the scattered books and magazines, acting, as always, the perfect steward. I didn't dislike the job, menial though it was. The pay was sufficient, the tips sometimes generous, and the work was not arduous. It served to pass the time and, as long as we visited Acheron, I was content.

"A strange world," Holman was saying. "For some reason animal life never evolved on Acheron and the flora are ascendant. There aren't even any insects."

"No insects?" Klienman frowned. He was a small, balding man who had read much but knew little. "Then how about pollination?"

"The plants are bisexual," explained the doctor. "They are self-pollinating. The winds, of course, scatter the seeds."

"The Bells," said Klienman. "What of those?"

"The famous Bells." Holman paused and looked at his audience. They were all in the lounge, the thirty passengers we carried this trip. Old, mostly, for the Grand Tour is not cheap. A couple of young lovers on their honeymoon held hands and whispered to each other. A fat matron, her bulging throat ringed with diamonds, glared at her son, a gangling, vacuous young-ster who stared with puppy eyes at an attractive ash-blonde. I knew her, Laura Amhurst, a silent, self-contained woman who spoke little and smiled less.

"The Singing Bells of Acheron," continued Holman, and I edged a little closer. "They aren't bells at all, not really. Just a freak of evolution. The dominant plant form is a bush about twice the height of a man when fully grown. It has a continuous seed-cycle and is usually covered with seed pods in various stages of ripeness. The pods are spherical, about an inch in diameter, and each contains a half-dozen seeds."

"How disappointing!" A faded socialite pouted in a manner that had been fashionable when I was born. "I had imagined them to be real bells."

"Seed pods," Klienman snorted in his disgust. "Is that all?"

"That's all." Holman glanced toward me. "Just a freak of nature." He smiled at the others. "But they are rather special at that. You see, there is a high silicon content in the soil of Acheron. So high in fact that no terrestrial plant could survive there."

"Nothing wonderful about that." Klienman seemed determined to make himself unpleasant. "Lots of worlds can't support earth-type vegetation."

"True." Holman paused again and I knew that he was trying to hide his annoyance. Men who knew little and thought they knew all were anathema to him. "The point," he continued gently, "is that the seed pods, because of the absorbed silicon, are in effect fragile spheres of glass. The seeds within them are loose and, when ruffled by the winds, they strike against their containers."

"Like a Japanese lantern," said Laura Amhurst suddenly. "Is that it?"

"Yes," said Holman, and again he glanced toward me. "Exactly like a Japanese lantern. There is absolutely nothing supernatural about the Singing Bells at all."

There was more, much more, a running cross-fire of question and answer with Klienman trying to show off his book-learning and belittle the doctor. Holman was patient. He was, after all, a member of the crew and he refrained from revealing Klienman as the fool he was. Only Laura Amhurst remained silent, *her* ash-blond beauty accentuating her pallor. Later, when the passengers had retired and the ship had settled down for the night, Holman sent for me.

"Sit down, John." He gestured to a chair in his crowded dispensary. "What do you think of the passengers?"

"As usual."

"Meaning not much, is that it?" He didn't really expect a reply and he was not disappointed. "What do you think of the blonde?"

"Laura Amhurst?"

"That's the one." He scowled at a cabinet of instruments. "She's a widow, John, recent too. I don't like it."

I knew what he meant but made no comment.

Some arguments remain evergreen while others pall after the first discussion. To me Acheron was something not to be discussed. I made a point of glancing at my watch and Holman took the hint.

"So you won't talk about it," he said, and his voice held defeat. "Well, I've done what I could and now must hope for the best. But she's a widow, and I've been watching her." He shook his head. "Those damn rumors! Why can't people accept the real explanation?"

"Maybe she will." I rose and stepped towards the door. "You sounded very convincing."

"But not convincing enough, eh, John?" He looked at me from beneath his eyebrows. "I thought not." He sighed. "Well, tomorrow will tell. Good night, John."

"Good night, Doctor." I left him still scowling at the cabinet.

Acheron loomed before us the next morning and the shrill hum of the grav-drive made a singing accompaniment to breakfast. The meal ended as we dropped into the atmosphere, the tables were all cleared before we grounded, the passengers ready to leave as the airlocks opened. Holman, acting for the captain, gave his usual warning.

"There is nothing harmful on this planet," he said. "But there is one great danger. We land at the same spot each trip and you will find well-beaten trails. Do not leave them."

"Why not?" Klienman, as usual, was being awkward. "If there's nothing to hurt us then where's the harm?"

"You may get lost," said Holman patiently. "The bushes are high and it is easy to lose your way. Remain on the beaten paths and you will avoid that danger."

He smiled. "I promise you that you will miss nothing by doing as you are asked."

There was more but he could have saved his breath. They took the warning as they always did, carelessly, indifferently, intent on having their own way. Holman watched them file through the airlock, the escorting crewmen following after a discreet interval. He must have seen my expression for he came towards me, his eyes serious.

"Why don't you skip it this trip?"

"I can't."

"You could if you wanted to," he snapped, then became gentle. "What's the point, John? What good does it do?"

"Please." I stepped away, not wanting to argue. "I have work to do."

The work didn't take long, I saw to that. I hurried through it as I always did when on Acheron, my thoughts elsewhere. Holman was busy when I had finished; three men, Klienman among them, had returned to the ship with badly cut hands. I heard the doctor's voice as he dressed their wounds.

"I warned you," he said. "Silicon is glass and glass is both hard and brittle. What happened?"

"I wanted some of the pods," said Klienman. "I tried to tear off a bunch." He swore, probably from the pain of the antiseptic. "It was like grabbing a handful of knives."

Holman's answer faded to a murmur as I headed toward the airlock. A crewman turned, recognized me, then faced the acres of bushes surrounding the ship. A faint wind was blowing, scarcely more than a breath, but even across the clearing I could hear the Bells.

The sound increased as I ran toward the valley.

It was off the beaten trails but I knew the way. I slipped carefully between the tall bushes and halted only when I had reached the old, familiar spot. Before me the ground fell away into a deep valley, every inch of which was covered with bushes heavy and glistening with their pods. I waited, breathless with anticipation, then, as the wind freshened, it came.

*　　*　　*

335

There are no words to describe the music of the Bells. Others have tried and failed and I am no poet. It is something that has to be experienced to be understood and, once experienced, is never forgotten. The valley, with its thousands of bushes each bearing their hundreds of pods, acted like a sounding board. From it sound rose like a cloud, a multitude of notes ranging all over the aural spectrum, singly and in combination, blending and weaving into an infinity of patterns. Music that held all the sounds there were or ever could be.

A hand fell on my shoulder and I opened my eyes. Holman stared at me.

"John!"

"Leave me." I struggled against his hand. "Why do you interfere?"

"It's late," he said. "I grew worried." He glanced down into the valley and I knew what he meant. "Let's return to the ship."

"No." I stepped away from him. "Leave me alone."

"You fool!" Anger roughened his voice. "How often must I tell you that it's all an illusion?"

"Does it matter?" I looked over the valley. "To me it is real enough. He lives down there, somewhere. I can hear his voice."

"Illusion," Holman repeated. "A dream."

"So you say, but it's all I have." I looked at him. "Don't worry, I believe you."

"For how long?" He swore, savagely, bitterly. "Darn it, John, stop hurting yourself. Your son has been dead for five years now, your ex-wife has remarried. Isn't it time that you stopped wasting yourself and got back to work?"

"Yes." I stepped toward the ship. "Work. I'll be missed."

"Not that work, your real work. Not acting as nurse-maid to a bunch of tourists but doing what you were trained to do." He gripped my shoulders and stared into my eyes. "One day you're going to forget that all this is an illusion. You're going to think it real. Do I have to tell you what happens then?"

"No." I stared down into the valley. "You don't have to tell me."

"Then get some sense, John," he said tiredly. "Go back where you belong. What good are you doing here?"

It was an old argument and one that I'd heard so often, but how could I go back to research? If I did I would lose the opportunity to visit Acheron and the Valley of the Singing Bells and listen to the voice that waited, so patiently, for my return.

The Grand Tour was scheduled for a two-day stop at Acheron, and with good reason. The Bells were at their best only at sunset and dawn, when the morning and evening winds stirred them to vibrant life. A change came over the passengers as the hours slipped past. They became quieter, more thoughtful, less inclined to argue. After the first landing no one tried to collect souvenirs. It wasn't the fear of cuts from the glasslike fronds that stopped them, that could be overcome. Rather, it was a reluctance to despoil the planet of even a little of that which gave rise to such wondrous music.

The second night came and passed all too quickly. Dawn flooded the horizon with flaring streamers of red and gold and, as usual, the morning wind stirred the Bells and filled the air with their incredible beauty. Everyone listened to them. Every member of the crew and every passenger stood in the light of the rising sun and filled their hearts and minds with the beauty of Acheron.

Afterwards, when the ship was readying for take-off, Laura Amhurst was missing. Holman brought me the news, his eyes wide with fear.

"A widow," he said. "The Bells. Darn it, John, you should have been more careful."

"I'm not responsible for passengers once they are outside the ship," I reminded him. "But I think I know where she is."

"The valley?" He had anticipated me. "Are you sure?"

"No, but I met her once heading in that direction." I headed toward the door. "I'll get her."

I raced from the ship and between the bushes, careless of the fronds that slashed my clothing, heedless of the music rising about me, the music created by the wind of my own passage. I left the regular paths and slipped toward the valley. Haste was essential—I had to race the wind and by the time I arrived my body was lacerated and my clothing in rags. My guess had been correct. Laura Amhurst, her eyes closed, her arms extended, was walking directly toward the rim of the valley.

"Laura!" I chased after her, caught her, slapped her face. Her eyes opened and shock twisted her mouth. I talked fast and loud, trying to drown the rising music, fighting the desire to concentrate and listen.

"It isn't real. It's illusion, all of it." I held her close to me, tightly so as to prevent any sudden movement. "Your husband?"

"You know?" Her eyes searched my face. "You do know. The rumors were true. The dead do live here, I know they do."

338

"No." I searched for words to destroy her dream. I had heard them all, a dozen times and more from Holman and others, but still they came hard. "It's a trick of the mind," I said. "You come here and you listen to all the sounds that ever were and from them you pick the ones you want most to hear. The prattle of a dead child, a husband's voice, the laughter and tears of those who are gone. The mind is a peculiar thing, Laura. It can take sounds and fit them with words and make them seem different to what they really are."

"I spoke to him," she said. "And he answered me. He is here, I know it."

"He is not here." I gripped her tighter as she tried to move, knowing that one false step and we would both topple into the valley. "You close your eyes and concentrate and you hear the voice you want to hear. You speak and it answers but all the time you are talking to yourself. You speak and your brain answers, picking words and tones from the sound of the Bells. It is an illusion, less real than a photograph or a recording. The words you hear are from your own memory."

"It was my husband," she insisted. "He was calling to me. I must go to him."

"You can't!" I sweated at the thought of what would happen if she broke away. "Listen to me. You heard his voice or thought that you did and, with your eyes closed, you began to walk toward the sound. But the sound came from the bushes." I shook her. "Do you understand? The bushes!"

She didn't understand.

"Silicon," I said. "Leaves like razors. The valley is covered with them and the ground falls sharply away. Two more steps and you would have thrown yourself among them." I gripped her shoulders and turned her so as to face the valley. "There is a good reason why this place is out of bounds. Too many people act as you acted, believe as you believed." I pointed to where something white gleamed among the pale green vegetation. "We call this place the Valley of the Singing Bells," I said heavily. "A better name would be the Valley of Death."

For a long moment she stared at the bleached bones. The wind had died and only a faint chiming rose from the valley and, when she spoke, her voice seemed very loud.

"You come here," she said. "Why?"

"For the sake of a dream." I told her my reasons. "But now I know that I have wasted five years. Don't do the same, Laura, don't live in the past. Live for the present and the future. Don't try to keep memory awake and hurting. Let the dead rest in peace."

"And you?"

"I'll follow my own advice." I stared for one last time over the glistening expanse of the valley and, for perhaps the first time, saw it as it really was. Not, as rumor had it, the resting place of the departed, the one spot in the universe where they would return and speak in the old, remembered voices to those that had known them, but as Holman had emphasized again and again. The Bells were a natural wonder, no more. They were a freak of evolution utterly devoid of the supernatural, as obvious and as normal as a Japanese lantern.

Laura was smiling as we walked back to the ship. I learned the reason for that smile before we reached Earth.

I had forgotten that Holman was a psychologist. I

had underestimated my own importance. I had discounted the fact that my acquired skill was not to be lightly cast aside. Not by the government who, apparently, still needed me. But wanted me sane.

"It was a trick," said Holman on our last night in space. "I make no excuses—a practitioner does not have to justify his cures. Laura isn't a widow. She is a natural-born actress." He looked sharply at me. "Are you surprised?"

"No," I said truthfully. "I'm not surprised." An intelligent man does not lose all his intelligence because one facet of it is dulled. I had had time to think and little things, seen in a new light, had become obvious. Holman's hints, the coincidence of Laura being missing, even the doctor's hint as to where she could have gone. She had heard me coming, of course, and had timed things well. She had never been in any danger but I hadn't known that. In my anxiety for her I had destroyed my own illusion, faced it and recognized it for what it was. But had found in return something of infinitely greater value.

I smiled down at Holman and left him staring, his eyes perplexed. I could have enlightened him, but that could come later.

Laura was waiting.

Thoughts That Kill

JOHN RUSSELL FEARN

L ike some colossal bird of prey, the spaceship hung
in the ebon void. Six thousand miles distant, a
planet whirled through space, pursuing its own orbit
around its parent sun. Within the vast interior of the
ship was almost an entire world in miniature, complete with every need for its crew.

The voyagers numbered five hundred, the only survivors of a once-mighty race called Man. Kilran, master of the five hundred, stood in silence as he gazed at
a gigantic viewing screen on which swam the magnified image of the planet.

Behind them they had left a dying, exhausted planet,
a planet they called Earth. For generations they had
searched space for another, younger world on which
to live. They had covered light-years in their search for
sanctuary and now, it seemed, their search was at an
end.

.. Like his fellows, Kilran was a small man, pinched
and underdeveloped, seeming almost top-heavy by
reason of his immense and highly-developed head
poised on a skinny neck and shoulders. His entire
cranium was hairless and tight-skinned, overshadow-
ing a face that was a pinched, set mask, expressionless
and inflexibly cold. Centuries of science, a heritage of
supreme achievement, had stamped from him all traces

of natural sentiment and humanity.

He was purely a pitiless intellect, always probing, always searching for new fields to pursue the still unsolved problems tabulated and filed in the recesses of his ultra-developed mind.

His scarcely blinking black eyes, large and hypnotic, gazed with smoldering steadiness into the giant screen and studied the young and lovely planet it depicted. A thriving world covered with dazzling blue oceans and bright green foliage. Here and there a cloud drifted in the dense atmosphere, casting a spot of shadow on the landscape over which it moved.

It looked just like a young Earth. The computer

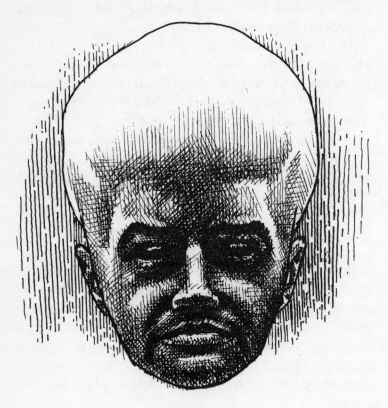

analysis showed it was an uncomfortably hot world, but none the less a possible habitation, one that could soon be adapted.

The gaze of the master scientist shifted and took in details of the curiously designed cities that showed here and there in the clearer portions of the forests. They were low-built and straggling edifices of stone, without order or symmetry, a product of the planet's lowly life form. It was utterly unlike Earth's, semi-plasmic, and obviously little higher in intelligence than Man himself had been in Earth's youth.

Sensing another presence, Kilran looked up from his scrutiny. Ajikon, astronomer-in-chief, had paused beside him. Behind him were the remainder of the five hundred – leathery, big-headed monstrosities utterly unlike the ancestors that had once fought and vanquished and died.

"Well, Kilran?" Ajikon had not spoken aloud. Vocal organs had long since ceased to be used. His highly sensitive brain merely hurled the thought into Kilran's mind.

"A fair world indeed, Ajikon," the master responded. "The more I study it, the more it appeals to me – a world of similar dimensions to our own, habitable, if a trifle warm, and possessing air only slightly denser than that of Earth. It has life, of course, but then . . ." His scar-like lips tightened. "Life! Low in form. Ugly! Plasmic! It can be, will be, destroyed. It is the inevitable law of the cosmos that the fittest must survive. We shall do that, with our highly trained telepathic brains, our thought responses, our vast knowledge. . . . As for those lowly forms . . ." He gestured with contempt to the screen.

"Everything is prepared," Ajikon's thoughts continued smoothly. "Our landing craft are ready. We only await your command before transferring into them the last precious heritages of the Earth."

"Then proceed at once," Kilran ordered. "I am satisfied that this planet shall be our future home. A new Earth! I hereby name this planet accordingly – *Terra Nova*. See to it that every man is at his appointed post, Ajikon."

Ajikon bowed his great head and turned away.

The ruler stood, lost in speculations, planning, devising and scheming with all the power of his mighty brain. There would be vast new accomplishments, and total elimination of all Terra Novan life. Earth brains must and would go on. The intellect of the aliens could not possibly stand against them.

Kilran nodded slowly at last, removed his leathery, warped hand from the viewing rail, and turned to watch the crew's preparations about him.

Within the spaceship there was a gentle stir of activity, efficient but unhurried. Kilran and Ajikon stood together at the major observation window, gazing in silence at the blackness of the void, the eternal stars, the distant sun of this system that would soon be their sun. Below them lay Terra Nova, the world of the future. Kilran smiled as he thought how they would soon dominate the planet and eradicate the meager life forms. If he had any emotion at all, it was of profound contempt for the lesser and ineffectual.

In various quarters of the ship the other Earthlings were at their tasks, some tending the ion drive that powered the ship, others watching computer screens; still others were testing the mammoth device with which they would blast all traces of life from the

planet. Many times in the past Earth had been subjected to the merciless fury of invaders from outer
space in search of new worlds. Now it was Earth's turn
to invade, conquer, and progress.

Presently, Kilran turned from his phlegmatic survey
of space and moved silently across the vast control
room to the observation section. His mummy-like
hands activated a bank of instruments. Meditatively
he studied the screens. He noted in silence the strange
whitish yellow of the alien life form. These beings
seemed to flow rather than walk, like some vast hideous jellyfish. So revolting, yet evidently intelligent
enough to build their own strange cities.

"The more I see of this lowly life," he telepathed to
Ajikon, "the more easy does our victory appear. Interesting that life on Terra Nova never evolved beyond
this quasi-plasmic, semi-fluid stage." He turned from
the screen. "It seems its intelligence, lowly though it
is, must have moved faster than its bodily development. Yet, in another sense, it must be an advantage
to separate or flow together as occasion demands.
Such a state, I imagine, would mean a unity or separa-
tion of intelligence at will."

He became silent for a while, then returned to the
main observation window. Terra Nova was much larger
now. The ship was moving with slowly mounting
velocity, timed to produce an exact replica of earthly
gravitation. Before many hours it would reach the
planet, and then — Kilran's eyes burned a trifle brighter
as he stood in silent, brooding malignance.

As the planet drew closer the great laboratory control
room became abuzz with the busily moving figures,
dominated by the brooding form of Kilran himself,

taking stock of everything, evolving his plan of attack. The telescanners began to reveal a peculiar state of perturbation amongst the Terra Novans. In all directions in the open spaces around their cities they were moving inward toward a rapidly swelling central unit, converging and assimilating with it in the fashion of true protoplasm. From being composed of thousands of individual units that had stretched forth protoplasmic limbs at will, they were now swelling into one solid sea in the approximate center of their major city, overflowing to its boundaries.

Kilran's immense brow furrowed in vague puzzlement as he watched.

"It seems fairly evident they have become aware of our approach," commented Ajikon, standing by his side. "Maybe they have crude telescopes. Considering the immense size of our ship it may even now be visible to them. Evidently by flowing together in that fashion they are seeking safety."

Kilran nodded slowly. "Yes, and by that very act they have simplified matters for us. We have nothing to do but to strike at that one unit." He turned aside and directed his thoughts to the experts congregated around the weapon of destruction. "Be ready to release on full fire when I give the order. We have not much time to go."

It was during the next hour that an odd change began to be perceived amongst the master scientists. At first they scarcely noticed it. Their attention was trained on the rapidly growing globe ahead of them while they waited beside the machine that would rain death and destruction onto the now completely massed life form covering a fair proportion of the planet's land surface. Then there crept into their working efficiency a note of error. The principal control pilots, immovable at their posts, both made simultaneous mistakes in their tasks, and just as quickly recovered, but the slips were noticed by the keen brain of Kilran as he mentally scanned every beat, every rhythm of the lesser minds around him. He turned from his survey of the planet and regarded the two men with his cold black eyes.

"What is the matter?" His thoughts had the icy venom of intolerance, biting contempt for the slightest flaw. "For an instant you both lost control of your minds. What is the meaning of such a retrogressive act?"

The men were silent, half from shame, half from bafflement.

"It must not happen again!" Kilran turned back to the window.

Hardly had he done so than the effect came again – this time with more force. A wave of mental power, so low but so gross that it caused a deep throb of pain, moved through the ship and passed on. The crew gasped at the sudden wrench on their sensitive brains, then fought their way back to balance.

"You felt that, Ajikon?" Kilran queried, his face slightly bewildered. The astronomer nodded. His lean hand was tenderly stroking his immense forehead. The slightest disturbance was sufficient to upset those advanced brains, nurtured as they had been through millennia of evolution. To meet up against a coarse mental force was equivalent to pouring crude oil into a priceless mechanism.

Kilran's tiny mouth tightened into a vicious line as he stared down on the fast-approaching planet's surface. The great white mass of the unified Terra Novans was distinctly visible to the naked eye, like a vast glutinous egg white.

"Can it be possible that such lowly life forms . . . ?" he began, his thoughts appreciable to everyone around him; then he shook his great head impatiently. "No; it is absurd! They cannot possibly do anything against minds like ours. We must have crossed a mentality warp from an unknown source, as we did once before. They are not uncommon in deep space."

He broke off suddenly and began to issue swift instructions for the guidance of the vessel. The pilots responded, but before they could execute the orders, a devastating wave of mentality engulfed them. Their brains rocked under its force; their hands, jerking up in reflex movements under the sudden pain, caused the vessel to destabilize for a moment, flinging several of their companions to the floor.

Kilran spun around just in time to see the two pilots reel from their chairs to the floor, hands clasped wildly to their heads. The mad throbbing in their tortured brains hammered into his own; frantically, his own mind tried to form a coherency out of the impulses. They were in the grip of a searing mental power, and it was slowly engulfing all traces of their normal intelligence.

"Control yourselves!" stabbed his own thought waves, striving for command. "Control, you fools! Control!"

He moved forward quickly, Ajikon by his side, but before either of them could reach the raving pair, they were themselves stricken with the same awful force. It hurled Ajikon to the floor. He writhed in exquisite torture as the waves beat into his mind. Kilran still stood erect, gazing through blurred eyes at the extraordinary sight of his followers toppling in all directions, some of them even sinking into the old emotion of hysteria. The control room began to echo with the sound of wild, insane laughter.

As Kilran struggled to master his brain he felt the ship sweeping out of its approach pattern. With a fierce desperation, Kilran fought for control, his great brow wrinkled in the tremendous effort to offset the supreme torture raging through his brain. To his mystification, they were not thoughts of menace or a deliberate mental attack. That he could have understood. They were instead chaotic, jumbled impulses, incredibly low in meaning, the product of beings dimly evolved and certainly not in possession of the art of directive thought-transference.

He likened the hammering thoughts, increasing now in intensity, to the beating of a myriad of mighty bells in discord, which actually struck against his mentality. The Terra Novans were only intelligent slime, able to fuse or divide at will. They were puzzled by the ship, half afraid – that much Kilran could grasp amidst the beating insanity.

Then he dropped to his knees, holding his head in both tiny hands. Sheer and absolute defeat was biting through him in a million shafts.

"Ajikon!" he signaled desperately. "Ajikon. Listen, if you can." By an enormous effort he held his concentration on the astronomer as he stirred dully and looked up.

"What?" His thoughts were feeble, just like their ancestors would have been in the grip of a lethal nerve gas.

"I believe I understand." Kilran dropped flat as his

351

Thoughts That Kill

brain deflated with growing feebleness. We are too clever. We have overlooked one thing. Our brains, evolved through generations to receive and transmit thoughts, also receive the thoughts of other beings. So far—" He paused, mastering himself by a supreme effort. "So far we have only communicated amongst ourselves; but here we receive the low, terrible thoughts of the planet's inhabitants. Their intellect is so far below us that their thoughts are like a poison to our mentalities. They have converged into one unit for safety, but in so doing all their thoughts have merged into one, and we receive the full impact of a myriad of primitive minds. You – you understand?"

The astronomer nodded weakly. "Yes, and to a brain there is no relief." His thoughts were anguished. "Light you can shut out, sound you can stop, but thought is always there. We can never cease to think, and our brains are too sensitive to stand it."

His huge head sagged and fell backwards. With a low exhalation of breath he relaxed and became still.

Kilran moved slowly, concentration blurred by the raging tumult in him. He gazed about him at the strewn figures of those who had already died. With a sudden return of fierce endeavor, he fought to gain the control board – anything to drive the ship out of this mad chaos. But in that desire he met his physical master too.

Specialization, centuries of brain usage at the expense of the body, had deprived him of almost all power of muscular effort. His little bony limbs sagged weakly under the pressure. Brain, muscles, and nerves were no longer working in intelligent coordination. With the weakest of groans he sank to the floor . . .

Thoughts, memories, bitter regrets, wildly intermingled with the confusions of alien minds, surged through the turmoil. The future, the idea of progress, the intended destruction of these low life forms ... how futile, how impossible! The end of the race of Earth was to be this – mental destruction by creatures thousands of millennia behind in intelligence.

Irony! Cold, merciless irony. The vaguest suggestion of a bitter smile crossed Kilran's face as he sank for the last time.

The space ship whirled on, still following its self-made orbit around Terra Nova. It had provided that world with a satellite. For generations it would continue to circle until the Terra Novans finally found a way to cross space and examine it. Until then – and perhaps not even then – they would never know how they had defeated a ruthless menace, and how the quality of their thoughts had driven the last mighty brains of Earth to their extinction.

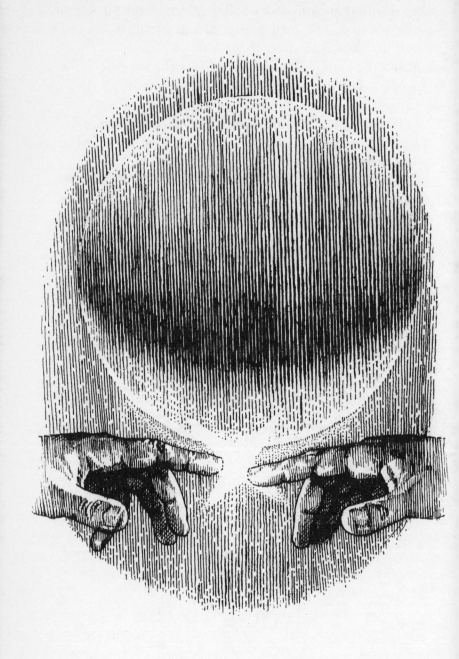

The Chosen

SAMANTHA LEE

Three phases after his father's death Charl was taken to the center to be initiated and sworn in as Headman. It was a great responsibility for a twelve-year-old but there was no one else of the bloodline to take on the job. His father had been killed by a graal monster on his last foray Above and although Charl felt his loss deeply, he had to keep his emotions firmly in check. To hold the Coven together it was essential that a new leader be appointed immediately. Some of the factions were becoming restless.

As was customary, the women led him to the great rock entrance to the Forbidden Palace. And there they left him, naked and afraid. No one but the Headman and the Chief Sorcerer had ever passed beyond this point.

Charl was tall for his age. Taller, at three foot seven, than most of the mutant men he would soon govern. His family had been lucky. Their genes hadn't been too badly affected by the initial radiation and their blood had remained relatively untainted. For twelve generations now, one of Charl's Hearth had held the coveted position of Headman. He had a lot to live up to.

Of course, even Charl's family had its throwbacks. His cousin Grol was one such. Grol's mother had

The Chosen

married a mutant of suspect bloodline against the wishes of the Inner Circle. True, Grol wasn't badly deformed physically, although one leg was considerably shorter than the other and his left eye did work independently of the right, which gave him an extraordinarily shifty look. But his brain had been affected by the wasting sickness and his behavior became more and more erratic as the cells corroded under the creeping contagion of the radiation poisoning. There could only be one end to it. When he became dangerous, Grol would be taken Above and shut out to die where he could do no harm. It was a cruel system but necessary to the survival of the whole.

Charl shuddered and took a deep breath. Then, head bowed and shivering with apprehension, he stepped through the archway and walked toward the High Altar and the veiled thing that stood upon it. The shadows from the sacrificial flames danced and flickered on the rough-hewn walls, stippling Charl's pallid skin and snow-white hair with motes of lava dust.

Before the high Altar stood Azran, Chief Sorcerer of the Clan, his face painted with weird, cabalistic symbols and his wizened body draped around with animal skins.

Azran was older than the oldest in the Coven. He had initiated six Headmen in his time. He had been Chief Sorcerer when Charl's great-grandmother was still a girl. Some said he was immortal. As Charl approached, he held his gnarled hand out in the ritual greeting.

"Why do you enter the Forbidden Place, Charl, Son of Kronak?"

Charl replied in the words of the Formula, as he had been taught.

"I come to bear the anguish, to learn the secrets, to know the truth."

"Hold out your hand."

The boy stretched his arm out before him, mentally screwing up his courage against what he knew was about to happen.

The Chief Sorcerer drew the ritual knife from beneath the grimy folds of his outer garments and sliced it sharply across the boy's upturned palm. Charl watched, fascinated, as the blood began to flow.

"Bear the anguish," Azran intoned, catching the precious crimson liquid in a small, painted gourd. When it was full he placed it tenderly beside the glowing embers of the sacrificial fire.

"This will seal the wound," he said, scooping an evil-smelling salve from the earthenware pot slung at his waist and rubbing it into the boy's palm.

It stung fiercely for a moment but then the bleeding stopped.

"Kneel."

Charl knelt.

The old man picked up the gourd and, bowing his head, offered the brimming vessel in supplication to the enormous covered object on the Altar.

"It is time," he chanted. "I give the blood of this manling into your keeping, a symbol of all that is left of us, all that is pure. May you find him pleasing."

He dashed the contents of the gourd into the heart of the living fire. The flames sizzled and leapt upward. The acrid stench of burning blood caught in Charl's nostrils and made him choke.

357

"Learn the secrets," cried the Sorcerer shrilly. "Accept the divine privileges accorded only to the Leader. Look upon the face of your Gods." He raised his clawed hands and, tearing the covering from the statue, flung it to the ground.

"Behold," he said reverently. "The Chosen."

Charl froze, awestruck and dazzled.

The statue was a work of genius. The two perfect beings, colored to represent life, stood hand in hand, staring blandly down on him. Their limbs were exquisitely proportioned and tanned by a sun that Charl had never seen. Both had the same thick, black, glossy hair. But the most striking feature was their eyes. They shone in the firelight, a rich, glowing gold.

Brought up among deformities and mutations, Charl was overwhelmed. He covered his face with his hands to blot out the statue's soul-piercing stare.

Azran spoke, the harshness of his voice pulling Charl back to his senses.

"It is time to take your vows," he said. "Rise, Charl, Son of Kronak, and repeat after me . . .

"In spite of danger, fire or pestilence . . ."

Charl staggered unsteadily to his feet.

"In spite of danger, fire or pestilence," he said.

"I swear to guard the Coven with my life."

"I swear to guard the Coven with my life."

"And regardless of personal desires."

"And regardless of personal desires."

"To obey the will of the Chosen."

"To obey the will of the Chosen."

"In all things."

"In all things."

"Until the hour of my death."

"Until the hour of my death."

Azran drew a cross in the air above the boy's fore-head.

"It is done," he said with a sigh. "Now it only remains for you to learn the Truth. Come."

The Sorcerer beckoned Charl to follow as he shuffled his way across a well-worn groove in the temple floor to a small sitting area, out of sight of the entrance. He indicated a covered stone bench that jutted out from the wall. Charl sat.

The old man lowered himself to sit beside the boy who was now a man, and arranged his musty animal skin robes around his stick-thin legs. He looked at Charl sideways out of his beady, black eyes, then suddenly he thrust his skeletal features at the boy and hissed hoarsely:

"What I am about to tell you now is known only to myself. It has been passed down from generation to generation since the Holocaust forced our ancestors underground. Only the Sorcerer and the Headman of the Coven have ever looked upon the Chosen or known the Truth. Only they were considered strong enough to bear the burden of such knowledge.

"And now you are a Headman, too, Charl, and young as you are, it is your right to know."

He gripped the boy's arm, his beady eyes glittering in the firelight. "You have seen the Chosen. Our Gods. Perfection in mind and body. The hope and aspiration of our race.

"And do you know why they are our hope? Our aspiration? Not because our worm-eaten blood could ever attain such perfection. That is impossible. But because the Chosen are not Gods."

Charl gasped at such blasphemy, cringing back from Azran's bulging eyes.

"No. Not Gods. Do you hear me? Not Gods. But real beings. Men. They are alive, Charl. They exist."

He slumped back, releasing his grip on the boy's arm.

"Exist?" Charl's voice rose in disbelief. "That cannot be." He rubbed the red weal left on his arm by the Sorcerer's frenzied grasp. "Nothing so perfect can have survived the Holocaust."

The old man raised his hand for silence.

"Hear me out," he said. "You have always believed that when the ultimate bomb was dropped, what was left of mankind, our ancestors, retreated to the caves to escape the polluting disease?"

Charl nodded.

"That is part of the truth," Azran went on, "but not all of it.

"Before the final disaster, humans were not the pitiful creatures we are now. The world was a fine and wonderful place full of marvelous machines and incredible inventions. Humans lived Above in dwellings that reached many miles into the sky. Great racks as wide as twenty tunnels together covered the earth. There were even machines that could fly."

"Fly?" Charl was dumbfounded. "You mean like a bat? But how could that be?"

"I know not," confessed the old man. "The knowledge has long been forgotten. But believe me, for I have seen old manuscripts with pictures that showed that it was so.

"Before our forefathers retreated to this labyrinth, a few children, the brightest and the best, were placed in one of these flying machines and sent to circle the Earth until the contagion had been eliminated and the atmosphere returned to normal. These were the

Chosen. When the time came they were to be recalled, to come back to Earth and people our world again with the beautiful and the strong."

"But what will become of us when they return?" asked Charl blankly.

"Why, we will worship them as we have always done," said Azran. "And they will look after us like the children that we are."

"But when did all this happen?" asked Charl. "And when will they return?"

"It happened many centuries ago," said the Sorcerer, "too many to be recorded." He paused dramatically. "But they will return very, very soon.

"Your father, when he was killed, was on a foray to test the atmosphere. Before he died he managed to get a message to me. The message said 'It is clear.' At least we know his death was not in vain. Because of him the Chosen can come back to us."

Charl looked toward the statue. To him it was inconceivable that he might see them soon in the flesh; like some fairy tale told at his mother's knee.

"But I don't understand," he stammered. "If they are so far away, flying around the Earth in this great machine, how can we call them back?"

The Sorcerer raised a bony hand and pressed it to the wall behind Charl's head.

"Observe," he said.

And as Charl watched, a section of the roughly hewn wall slid back to reveal a small alcove. It was octagonal in shape and the walls, floor, and ceiling were entirely coated in a gray substance the like of which Charl had never seen. He touched it gingerly. It felt cold against his fingers.

In the center of the alcove stood a machine, man-tall and covered in strange knobs and dials. It emitted a peculiar, whining hum and as they approached the whole structure lit up with an eerie pink glow.

"This machine has been here since before the Holocaust," said Azran. "It carries messages to the stars and back. As soon as your father's news reached me I sent word of it to the great ship. They have replied that they will come.

"Alas that Kronak did not live to greet them. The greatest honor ever accorded to a Headman falls on you, Charl. Their ship makes Earthfall, as they call it, tomorrow at the first hour. It is for you to lead the delegation that will welcome them home."

The Sorcerer swayed suddenly and Charl put his arm protectively around the old man's shoulders, steadying him.

"There were times when I thought I would never live to see the Chosen," said Azran. "Only my will has kept my body going. But tomorrow they will be here. Then I can die in peace."

Charl and the old man stood at the top of the hill watching the huge silver vessel descending slowly from a cloudless sky. The morning sunlight glanced off its superstructure, lighting it up like a fireball.

Behind them the entire Coven stood in untidy rows, shading their cave-weak eyes against the glare. They were subdued and uncomfortable away from the familiar dimness of their underground home. But an undercurrent of excitement rippled through the shabby and misshapen crowd. It had been a momentous day. Before he had led them Above, Charl had insisted, against Azran's advice, that every one of his people should look upon the faces of the Chosen. For the first time ever, the whole Coven had seen the Gods they had hitherto worshiped secondhand through their Headman and Chief Sorcerer. In a few more moments they would see them in the flesh.

In the front row Grol grimaced and gibbered as the spaceship came in to land. It settled on the ground as lightly as a bat's wing. The hum of the engines died to a throbbing purr that finally juddered to a halt. Then all was silence.

For a long time nothing happened. The Coven began to grow restive, twittering and muttering among themselves.

"What's the matter?" asked Charl anxiously. "Why don't they come out?"

"Patience," said the Chief Sorcerer. "They will come when they are ready. The world has awaited their return for thousands of years. It can wait a few minutes more."

A hatch lifted in the hull of the ship. Behind it a small, grilled aperture stared balefully at the waiting crowd. Through this opening a voice, hugely amplified but still recognizably human, began to address the assembled throng.

"Greetings," it boomed. "I am Balthasac, Leader of the Chosen, and I speak to you on their behalf.

"Presently we will emerge into the atmosphere of Earth, come to take our places as rulers of a new and perfect society. But before we show ourselves, there are a few things I must explain."

Charl looked uneasily at Azran. There was something ominous in the voice, something that disturbed him. But the old man's expression remained impassive.

"For centuries now we, and our fathers before us,

have been circling the world in the space machine. We have been forced to live in cramped and carefully controlled conditions. Conditions totally dissimilar to those that prevail here on Earth. In space there is no gravity. So for generations the Chosen have lived, bred, been born in a state of weightlessness, or what we call freefall. Because of this our bodies have been forced to adapt to fit the circumstances. Our hearts, for instance, have grown much larger than yours. On the other hand," the voice continued, "parts that were obsolete in space have been reduced in size through lack of usage. I tell you this because you may not find the new breed of man to your taste. But make no mistake. We *are* the new breed. Descendants of the greatest brains our civilization has ever produced. We have come to build a new world."

The tone changed, hardened only fractionally, but the hairs on the back of Charl's neck began to prickle in fear.

"We are powerful and strong," said Balthasac. "And we have weapons to back our enterprise should the necessity arise. So I give you this friendly warning. Do not be foolish. We are your own kind. We do not wish to hurt you. But we are human. And we will survive."

The hatch snapped shut.

Charl turned to the Chief Sorcerer.

"What have we done?" he said.

"Fear not," Azran soothed him. "They are your Gods. They have come to build a new mankind, stronger and better than the old. It is as it should be."

The central section of the ship suddenly swung outward in an arc and a flat platform slid forward about three meters above the ground. Onto this stage, Balthasac and the rest of the Chosen emerged.

There was a stunned silence, then pandemonium. Women screamed, covering the eyes of their children. Men fell to their knees in horror. Mutants they had seen but never anything like this. Only Grol seemed to be enjoying the spectacle. He danced about, giggling and pointing at the creatures on the raised platform and holding his sides in glee.

Balthasac looked like a huge pink slug. Completely hairless, his flaccid flesh pulsed in the warm spring sunshine. He didn't have a head as such, just a bump on the front end of his body on which was superimposed a wide, toothless mouth. Above this two stalk-like protuberances stuck out like horns. The arms, which were thin and muscle-free, ended in a pair of perfectly normal human hands. But the legs and feet had shrunk to tiny prehensile stumps.

As the old man slumped beside him in shock. Charl raised his voice above the shrieks and groans of the Coven.

"Impostors," he cried. "It is a trick. You are some monsters from another world."

On the platform, Balthasac tilted his stalks to get a better view of the speaker.

Charl remembered his vow and his blood ran cold.

The eyes that gazed blandly down on him shone in the sun as they had in the firelight, a rich, glowing gold.

The Chosen had come to claim their inheritance.

365

The Dead Planet

EDMOND HAMILTON

I t didn't look like such a forbidding little world at first. It looked dark, icy, and lifeless, but there was no hint of what brooded there. The only question in our minds then was whether we would die when our crippled ship crashed on it.

Tharn was at the controls. All three of us had put on our pressure suits in the hope that they might save us if the crash was bad. In the massive metal suits we looked like three queer, fat robots, like three metal globes with jointed mechanical arms and legs.

"If it hadn't happened here!" came Dril's hopeless voice through the intercom. "Here in the most desolate and unknown part of the whole galaxy!"

"We're lucky we were within reaching distance of a star system when the generators let go," I murmured.

"Lucky, Oroc?" repeated Dril bitterly. "Lucky to postpone our end by a few days of agony? It's all we can look forward to on *that*."

The system ahead did look discouraging for wrecked star explorers. Here in a thin region at the very edge of the galaxy, it centered around a sun that was somber dark red, ancient, dying.

Six worlds circled that smoldering star. We were dropping toward the innermost of the six planets, as the most possibly habitable. But now, we could clearly see that life could not exist on it. It was an airless sphere, sheathed in eternal snow and ice.

The other five planets were even more hopeless. And we could not change course now, anyway. It was a question of whether the two strained generators that still functioned would be able to furnish enough power to slow down our landing speed and save us from total destruction.

Death was close, and we knew it, yet we remained unshaken. Not that we were heroes. But we belonged to the Star Service, and while the Star Service yields glory, its members always have the shadow of death over them and so grow accustomed to it.

Many in the Star Service had died in the vast, endless task of mapping the galaxy. Of the little exploring ships that went out like ours to chart the farther reaches of stars, only two-thirds or less ever came back. Accidents accounted for the rest—accidents like the blowing of our generators from overload in attempting to claw our way quickly out of a mass of interstellar debris.

Tharn's voice came to us calmly.

"We'll soon hit it. I'll try to crabtail in, but the chances are poor. Better strap in."

Using the metal arms of our suits clumsily, we hooked into the resilient harnesses that might give us a chance of survival.

Dril peered at the rapidly enlarging white globe below.

"There looks to be deep snow at places. It would be a little softer there."

"Yes," Tharn replied quietly. "But our ship would remain buried in the snow. On the ice, even if wrecked, it could be seen. When another ship comes, they'll find us, and our charts won't be lost."

Well, for a moment that made me so proud of the Star Service that I was almost contemptuous of the danger rushing upon us.

It is that wonderful spirit that has made the Service what it is, that has enabled our race to push out from our little world to the farthest parts of the galaxy. Individual explorers might die, but the Service's conquest of the universe would go on.

"Here we go," muttered Dril, still peering downward.

The icy white face of the desolate world was rushing up at us with nightmare speed. I waited tensely for Tharn to act.

He delayed until the last moment. Then he moved the power bar, and the two remaining generators came on with a roar of power.

They could not stand that overload for more than a

few moments before they too blew out. But it was enough for Tharn to swing the falling ship around and use the blast of propulsive vibrations as a brake.

Making a crabtail landing is more a matter of luck than skill. The mind isn't capable of estimating the infinitesimal differences that mean disaster or survival. Use a shade too much power, and you're bounced away from your goal. A shade too little, and you smash to bits.

Tharn was lucky. Or maybe it wasn't luck as much as pilot's instinct. Anyway, it was all over in a moment. The ship fell, the generators screamed, there was a bumping crash, then silence.

The ship lay on its side on the ice. Its stern had crumpled and split open at one place, and its air had puffed out, though in our suits we didn't mind that. Also the last two generators had blown out, as expected, from the overload in cushioning our fall.

"We made it!" Dril bounded from despair to hope. "I never thought we had a real chance. Tharn, you're the ace of all pilots."

But Tharn himself seemed to suffer reaction from tension. He unstrapped like ourselves and stood, a bulky figure in his globular suit, looking out through the quartz portholes.

"We've saved our necks for the time being," he muttered. "But we're in a bad fix."

The truth of that sank in as we looked out with him. This little planet out on the edge of the galaxy was one of the most desolate I had ever seen. There was nothing but ice and darkness and cold.

The ice stretched in all directions, a rolling white plain. There was no air—the deep snows we had seen were frozen air, no doubt. Over the gelid plain brooded

370

a dark sky, two-thirds of which was black emptiness. Across the lower third glittered the great drift of the galaxy stars, of which this system was a borderland outpost.

"Our generators are shot, and we haven't enough powerloy to wind new coils for *all* of them," Tharn pointed out. "We can't call a tenth the distance home with our little communicator. And our air will eventually run out.

"Our only chance," he continued decisively, "is to find on this planet enough tantalum and terbium and the other metals we need to make powerloy and wind new coils. Dril, get out the radiosonde."

The radiosonde was the instrument used in our star mapping to explore the metallic resources of unknown planets. It worked by projecting broad beams of vibrations that could be tuned to reflect from any desired elements, the ingenious device detecting and computing position thus.

Dril got out the compact instrument and tuned its frequencies to the half-dozen rare metals we needed. Then we waited while he swung the projector tubes along their quadrants, closely watching the indicators.

"This is incredible luck!" he exclaimed finally. "The sonde shows terbium, tantalum, and the other metals we need all together in appreciable quantities. They're just under the ice and not far from here!"

"It's almost too good to be true," I said wonderingly. "Those metals are never found all together."

Tharn planned quickly.

"We'll fit a rough sled, and on it we can haul an auxiliary power unit and the big dis-beam, to cut through the ice. We'll also have to take cables and tackle for a hoist."

We soon had everything ready and started across the ice, hauling our improvised sled and its heavy load of equipment.

The frozen world, brooding beneath the sky that looked out into the emptiness of extragalactic space, was oppressive. We had hit queer worlds before, but this was the most gloomy I had ever encountered.

The drift of stars that was our galaxy sank behind the horizon as we went on, and it grew even darker. Our krypton lamps cut a white path through the somber gloom as we stumbled on, the metal feet of our heavy suits slipping frequently on the ice.

Dril stopped frequently to make further checks with the radiosonde. Finally, after several hours of toilsome progress, he looked up from the instrument and made a quick signal.

"This is the position," he declared. "There should be deposits of the metals we need only thirty meters or so beneath us."

It didn't look encouraging. We were standing on the crest of a low hill of the ice, and it was not the sort of topography where you would expect to find a deposit of those metals.

But we did not argue with Dril's findings. We hauled the auxiliary power unit off the sledge, got its little auto-turbine going, and hooked its leads to the big dis-beam projector that we had dismounted from the bows of our ship.

Tharn played the dis-beam on the ice with expert skill. Rapidly, it cut a three-meter shaft down through the solid ice. It went down for thirty meters like a knife through cheese and then there was a sudden backlash of sparks and flame. He quickly cut the power.

"That must be the metal-bearing rock we just hit," he said.

Dril's voice was puzzled.

"It should be twenty-one to twenty-five meters lower to the metal deposits, by the sonde readings."

"We'll go down and see," Tharn declared. "Help me set up the winch."

We had brought heavy girders and soon had them formed into a massive tripod over the shaft. Strong cables ran through pulleys suspended from that tripod and were fastened to a big metal bucket in which we could descend by paying out cable through the tackle.

Only two of us should have gone down, really. But somehow, none of us wanted to wait alone up on the dark ice, nor did any of us want to go down alone into the shaft. So we all three crowded into the big bucket.

"Acting like children instead of veteran star explorers," grunted Tharn. "I shall make a note for our psychos on the upsetting effect of conditions on these worlds at the galaxy edge."

"Did you bring your beam guns?" Dril asked suddenly.

We had, all of us. Yet we didn't know quite why. Some obscure apprehension had made us arm ourselves when there was no conceivable need of it.

"Let's go," said Tharn. "Hang onto the cable and help me pay it out, Oroc."

I did as he bade, and we started dropping smoothly down into the shaft in the ice. The only light was the krypton whose rays Dril directed downward.

We went down thirty meters, and then we all cried out. For we saw now the nature of the resistance which the dis-beam had met. Here under the ice there was thick stratum of transparent metal, and the dis-beam had had to burn its way through that.

Underneath the burned-out hole in that metal stratum there was—nothing. Just empty space, a great hollow of some kind here beneath the ice.

Tharn's voice throbbed with excitement.

"I'd already begun to suspect it. Look down there!"

The krypton beam, angling downward into the emptiness below us, revealed a spectacle that stunned us.

Here, beneath the ice, was a city. It was a great metropolis of white cement structures, dimly revealed by our little light. And this whole city was shielded by an immense dome of transparent metal that withstood the weight of the ice that ages had piled upon it.

"Our dis-beam cut down through the ice and then through the dome itself," Tharn was saying excitedly. "This dead city may have been lying hidden here for ages."

Dead city? Yes, it was dead. We could see no trace of movement in the dim streets as we dropped toward it.

The white avenues, the vague façades and galleries and spires of the metropolis, were silent and empty. There was no air here. There could be no inhabitants.

Our bucket bumped down on to the street. We fastened the cables and climbed out, stood staring numbly about us. Then we uttered simultaneous cries of astonishment.

An incredible thing was happening. Light was beginning to grow around us. Like the first rosy flush of dawn it came at first, burgeoning into a soft glow that bathed all the far-flung city.

"This place can't be dead!" exclaimed Dril. "That light —"

"Automatic trips could start the light going," said

Tharn. "These people had a great science, great enough for that."

"I don't like it," Dril murmured. "I feel that the place is haunted."

I had that feeling, too. I am not ordinarily sensitive to alien influences. If you are, you don't get accepted by the Star Service.

But a dark, oppressive premonition such as I had never felt before now weighed upon my spirits. Deep in my consciousness stirred vague awareness of horror brooding in this silent city beneath the ice.

"We came here for metal, and we're going to get it," Tharn said determinedly. "The light won't hurt us, it will help us."

Dril set up the radiosonde and took bearings again. They showed strongest indications of the presence of the metals we needed at a point some halfway across the city from us.

There was a towering building there, an enormous pile whose spire almost touched the dome. We took it as our goal and started.

The metal soles of our pressure suits clanked on the smooth cement paving as we walked. We must have made a strange picture—we three in our grotesque metal armor tramping through that eerily illuminated metropolis of silence and death.

"This city is old indeed," Tharn said in a low voice. "You notice that the buildings have roofs? That means they're older than —"

"*Tharn! Oroc!*" yelled Dril suddenly, swerving around and grabbing for his beam pistol.

We saw it at the same moment. It was rushing toward us from a side street we had just passed.

I can't describe it. It was like no normal form of life.

375

It was a gibbering monstrosity of black flesh that changed from one hideous shape to another with protean rapidity as it *flowed* toward us.

The horror and hatred that assaulted our minds were not needed to tell us that this thing was inimical. We fired our beams at it simultaneously.

The creature sucked back with unbelievable rapidity and disappeared in a flashing movement between two buildings. We ran forward. But it was gone.

"By all the devils of space!" swore Dril, his voice badly shaken. "What was *that?*"

Tharn seemed as stunned as we.

"I don't know. It was living, you saw that. And its swift retreat when we fired argues intelligence and volition."

"Ordinary flesh couldn't exist in this cold vacuum —" I began.

"There are perhaps more forms of life and flesh than we know," muttered Tharn. "Yet such things surely wouldn't build a city like this —"

"There's another!" I interrupted, pointing wildly.

The second of the black horrors advanced like a huge, unreared worm. But even as we raised our pistols, it darted away.

"We've got to go on," Tharn declared, though his own voice was a little unsteady. "The metals we need are in or near that big tower, and unless we get them we'll simply perish on the ice above."

"There may be worse deaths than freezing to death up there on the ice," said Dril huskily. But he came on with us.

Our progress through the shining streets of that magically beautiful white city was one of increasing horror.

The black monstrosities seemed to be swarming in the dead metropolis. We glimpsed and fired at dozens of them. Then we stopped beaming them, for we didn't seem able to hit them.

They didn't come to close quarters to attack us. They seemed rather to follow us and *watch* us, and their numbers and menacing appearance became more pronounced with every step we took toward the tower.

More daunting than the inexplicable creatures were the waves of horror and foreboding that were now crushing our spirits. I have spoken of the oppression we had felt since entering the city. It was becoming worse by the minute.

"We are definitely being subjected to psychological attack from some hostile source," muttered Tharn. "All this seems to be because we are approaching that tower."

"This system is on the edge of the galaxy," I reminded. "Some undreamed-of creature or creatures from the black outside could have come from there and laired up on this dead world."

I believe we would at that point have turned and retreated had not Tharn steadied us with a reminder.

"Whatever is here that is going to such lengths to force us to retreat is doing so because it's afraid of us! That argues that we can at least meet it on equal terms."

We were approaching the side flight of steps that led up to the vaulted entrance of the great tower. We moved by now in a kind of daze, crushed as we were by the terrific psychic attack that was rapidly conquering our courage.

Then came the climax. The lofty doors of the tower swung slowly open. And from within the building

377

there lurched and shambled out a thing, the sight of which froze us where we stood.

"*That* never came from any part of our own galaxy!" Dril cried hoarsely.

It was black, mountainous in bulk and of a shape that tore the brain with horror. It was something like a monstrous, squatting toad, its flesh a heaving black slime from which protruded sticky black limbs that were not quite either tentacles or arms.

Its triangle of eyes were three slits of cold green fire that watched us with hypnotic intensity. Beneath that hideous chinless face its breathing pouch swelled in and out painfully as it lurched, slobbering, down the steps toward us.

Our beams lashed frantically at that looming horror. And they had not the slightest effect on it. It continued to lurch down the steps, and, most ghastly of all, there was in its outlines a subtly hideous suggestion that it was parent, somehow, to the smaller horrors that swarmed in the city behind us.

Dril uttered a cry and turned to flee, and I stumbled around to join him. But from Tharn came a sharp exclamation.

"Wait! Look at the thing! It's *breathing!*"

For a moment, we couldn't understand. And then, dimly, I did. The thing was obviously breathing. Yet there was no air here!

Tharn suddenly stepped forward. It was the bravest thing I have ever seen done by a member of the Star Service. He strode right toward the towering, slobbering horror.

And abruptly, as he reached it, the mountainous black obscenity vanished. It disappeared like a clicked-off televisor scene. And the black swarm in the city behind us disappeared at the same moment.

"Then it wasn't real?" Dril exclaimed.

"It was only a projected hypnotic illusion," Tharn declared. "Like the others we saw back there. The fact that it was breathing, here where there is no air gave me the clue to its unreality."

"But then," I said slowly, "whatever projected those hypnotic attacks is inside this building."

"Yes, and so are the metals we want," Tharn said grimly. "We're going in."

The ceaseless waves of horror-charged thought beat upon us even more strongly as we went up the steps. Gibbering madness seemed to shriek in my brain as we opened the high doors.

And then, as we stepped into the vast, gleaming white nave of the building, all that oppressive mental assault suddenly ceased.

Our reeling minds were free of horror for the first time since we had entered this dead city. It was like bursting out of one of the great darkness clouds of the galaxy into clear space again.

"Listen!" said Tharn in a whisper. "I hear—"

I heard, too. We didn't really hear, of course. It was not sound, but mental waves that brought the sensation of sound to our brains.

It was music we heard. Faint and distant at first, but swelling in a great crescendo of singing instruments and voices.

The music was alien, like none we had ever heard before. But it gripped our minds as its triumphant strains rose and rose.

There were in those thunderous chords the titanic struggles and hopes and despairs of a race. It held us rigid and breathless as we listened to that supernal

The Dead Planet

symphony of glory and defeat.

"They are coming," said Tharn in a low voice, looking across the white immensity of the great nave.

I saw them. Yet oddly I was not afraid now, though this was by far the strangest thing that had yet befallen us.

Out into the nave toward us was filing a long procession of moving figures. They were the people of this long-dead world, the people of the past.

They were not like ourselves, though they were bipedal, erect figures with a general resemblance to us in bodily structure. I cannot particularize them, they were so alien to our eyes.

As the music swelled to its final crescendo and then died away, the marching figures stopped a little away from us and looked at us. The foremost, apparently their leader, spoke, and his voice reached our minds.

"Whoever you are, you have nothing more to fear," he said. "There is no life in this city. All the creatures you have seen, all the horror that has attacked you, yes, even we ourselves who speak to you, are but phantoms of the mind projected from telepathic records that are set to start functioning automatically when anyone enters this city."

"I thought so," whispered Tharn. "They could be nothing else."

The leader of the aliens spoke on.

"We are a people who perished long ago, by your reckoning. We originated on this planet"—he called it by an almost unpronounceable alien name—"far back in your past. We rose to power and wisdom and then to glory. Our science bore us out to other worlds, to other stars, finally to exploration and colonization of most of the galaxy.

"But finally came disaster. From the abyss of extra-galactic space came invaders so alien that they could never live in amity with us. It was inevitable war between us and them, we to hold our galaxy, they to conquer it.

"They were not creatures of matter. They were creatures made up of photons, particles of force—shifting clouds capable of unimaginable cooperation between themselves and of almost unlimited activities. They swept us from star after star, they destroyed us on a thousand worlds.

"We were finally hemmed in on this star system of our origin, our last citadel. Had there been hope for the future in the photon race, had they been creatures capable of creating a future civilization, we would have accepted defeat and destruction and would have abdicated thus in their favor. But their limitations of intelligence made that impossible. They would never rise to civilization themselves nor allow any other race in the galaxy to do so.

"So we determined that, before we perished, we would destroy them. They were creatures of force who could only be destroyed by force. We converted our sun into a gigantic generator, hurling some of our planets and moons into it to cause the cataclysm we desired. From our sun generator sprang a colossal wave of force that swept out and annihilated the photon race in one cosmic surge of energy.

"It annihilated the last of us also. But we had already prepared this buried city, and in it had gathered all that we knew of science and wisdom to be garnered by future ages. Some day new forms of life will rise to civilization in the galaxy, some day explorers from other stars will come here.

"If they are not intelligent enough to make benign use of the powers we have gathered here, our telepathic attacks should frighten them away. But if they are intelligent enough to discern the clues we leave for them, they will understand that all is but hypnotic illusion and will press forward into this tower of our secrets.

"You, who listen to me, have done this. To you, whoever and of whatever future race you may be, we bequeath our wisdom and our power. In this building, and in others throughout the city, you will find all that we have left. Use it wisely for the good of the galaxy and all of its races. And now, from us of the past to you of the future—farewell."

The figures that stood before us vanished. And we three remained standing alone in the silent, shimmering white building.

"Space, what a race they must have been!" breathed Tharn. "To do all that, to die destroying a menace that would have blighted the galaxy forever, and still to contrive to leave all that they had gained to the future!"

"Let's see if we can find the metals," begged Dril, his voice shaky. "All I want now is to get out of here and take a long drink of *sanqua*."

We found more than the metals we needed. In that wonderful storehouse of alien science, we found whole wave generators of a type far superior to ours, which could easily be installed in our crippled ship.

I shall not tell of all else we found. The Star Service is already carefully exploring that great treasury of ancient science, and in time its findings will be known to all the galaxy.

It took labor to get the generators back up to our

ship, but when that was done, it was not hard to install them. And when we had fused a patch on our punctured hull, we were ready to depart.

As our ship arrowed up through the eternal dusk of that ice-clad world and darted past its smoldering dying sun on our homeward voyage, Dril took down the bottle of *sanqua*.

"Let's get these cursed suits off, and then I'm going to have the longest drink I ever took!" he vowed.

We divested ourselves of the heavy suits at last. It was a wonderful relief to step out of them, to unfold our cramped wings and smooth our ruffled feathers.

We looked at each other, we three tall bird-men of Rigel, as Dril handed us the glasses of pink *sanqua*. On Tharn's beaked face, in his green eyes, was an expression that told me we all were thinking of the same thing.

He raised the glass that he held in his talons.

"To that great dead race to whom our galaxy owes all," he said. "We will drink to their world by their own name for it. We will drink to Earth."

383

Afterword:
What's Out There?

MIKE ASHLEY

It's hard to imagine the size of space. When you look at the stars on a clear night you're looking into distances of millions and millions and millions of miles. You're also looking back millions of years in time.

Our own sun is a star and is obviously the nearest one to us. It's about 93 million miles away (or 150 million kilometers) from the Earth. It's a fairly normal yellow star, about half-way through its expected life. On its surface the temperature is about 9,900°F, which is hot, though tungsten, which we use in the filaments of our light bulbs, is still liquid at that temperature on Earth. Of course, to use the word *surface* when talking about the sun is a bit misleading, because it doesn't have a hard surface like Earth. Like all stars, it's a ball of gas held together by immense gravitational forces. That pressure turns gas into a liquid, or plasma, state. There is no way humans could venture too close to the sun without considerable protection.

The nearest planet to the sun is called Mercury and it is about 35 million miles (or 57 million kilometers) distant. That's really too close for comfort. Because Mercury is quite small (a diameter of just over 3,000 miles or less than 5,000 kilometers, which isn't much larger than our moon) it can scarcely retain an atmosphere, though traces have been detected. The planet is open to the full force of the sun, without the protection of an atmosphere like we have. On Mercury, the sun would appear almost three times as large as it does from Earth. The result is that during the day temperatures can rise to over 800°F and at night plunge to around –279°F. Its surface looks like our moon's—that is, covered with craters—though it also has many long cliffs where the surface has split and dropped like a fault line. It was once believed that Mercury always presented the same face towards the sun so that it had a permanent night side and a permanent day side. That would have given it a twilight zone around the line called the terminator (where day becomes night), where science fiction writers once felt that temperatures might be sufficiently bearable for us to colonize Mercury. But we now know that Mercury does rotate, very slowly, so there's no escaping those extremes of temperature. Mercury would be a very uncomfortable place to live.

The next planet out from the sun is Venus, just over 67 million miles (or 108 million kilometers) distant. In size it's not much smaller than the Earth, but that's about all we have in common. Venus is covered by clouds, which has made observation of its surface impossible until recent years. These clouds, though, are highly reflective of sunlight, and as a result Venus is the brightest object in our sky (after the sun and the moon).

The atmosphere is almost entirely composed of carbon dioxide, which causes the greenhouse effect so often referred to on Earth, where the atmosphere traps the heat from the sun. The result is that the surface temperature on Venus is even hotter than on Mercury, upwards of 860°F, and this would be spread throughout the planet, even on its nightside. The presence of an atmosphere has not stopped Venus from being bombarded by space debris in the past, so that it still has craters, but not like the moon or Mercury. Its surface is more one of vast rolling plains dotted with mountains and volcanoes, many still active. It is probable that millions of years ago the surface of Venus was similar to Earth's, so it is possible that life might have started to form on Venus. Science fiction writers once pictured Venus as being similar to Earth back in the Jurassic Age, populated with dinosaurs and filled with tropical forests. Could this once have been the case? If so, we cannot know how far it evolved. As the sun became more powerful, the oceans evaporated, the carbonates leeched into the atmosphere, and the greenhouse effect would have taken over, destroying all life. Anyone seeking to explore Venus now would be crushed by its enormous atmospheric pressure, boiled by the suffocating temperature, and corroded by sulfuric acid rain.

Venus is an important planet for us to learn more about so that we can ensure the same fate does not befall Earth.

The moon is our nearest regular neighbor in space. It's only about 240,000 miles away (380,000 kilometers), which in astronomical distances is incredibly close. Also, the moon is quite large for a satellite (the usual name given to planets' moons). Its diameter is about a third that of Earth's, and it's larger than the planet Pluto, so you could state that Earth and moon form a double planetary system. The same thing can be said of Pluto and its satellite, Charon. The moon's not the friendliest of neighbors, though. Whereas once we dreamed it might contain life, and even today some science fiction writers keep coming up with ways in which microscopic life might have survived under the surface, I think we have to admit that the moon is a dead world. Interestingly, in 1995, the lunar probe *Clementine* reportedly detected traces of ice in the deep craters on the far side of the moon, but this remains unconfirmed. The moon has no atmosphere, leaving it open to radiation from the sun, and also extremes of temperature ranging from 260°F to −280°F. The moon was, of course, the first world to which humankind sent space probes. *Luna 2* landed on the moon as far back as September 1959. The first manned landing on the moon was in July 1969, with Neil Armstrong being the first man to step onto the surface of another world. The last man to stand on the moon was Eugene Cernan with *Apollo 17* in December 1972. Maybe we'll go back someday.

Mars is the next planet. It's about 142 million miles (or 228 million kilometers) distant from the sun, and at its closest is about 35 million miles (56 million kilometers) from the Earth. Mars is much smaller than the Earth, not quite half the diameter, and has always been our great hope for containing life. Back in 1877, the Italian astronomer Giovanni Schiaparelli claimed there were *canali*, or channels, on Mars, and this gave rise to intense speculation about life on the planet, especially by the American astronomer Perceval Lowell, who believed the "canals" were evidence of intelligent life. For many years science fiction writers wrote about Martians, and Earth was often subject to invasion from Mars, such as in H. G. Wells's *The War of the Worlds*. But the more we learn about Mars, the less likely that seems. It's a cold world. Its average surface temperature is about –9°F, though that doesn't make it totally inhospitable—not like Mercury and Venus. However, like Venus, most of the atmosphere is carbon dioxide, and it is only its distance from the sun that has kept Mars from also becoming overheated by the greenhouse effect. Although water exists on the surface, it is all trapped in the polar ice caps. The atmospheric pressure of the surface of Mars means that any liquid water would immediately boil away (in the same way that water on Earth will boil at lower temperatures the higher you climb up a mountain). All of this means that life as we know it on Earth would find it difficult to evolve on Mars, but it doesn't totally rule out all chance of some form of life. None has yet been detected, but I continue to live in hope. If you want to read some fascinating recent science fiction novels about Mars, then try *Mars* by Ben Bova, or the trilogy *Red Mars*, *Green Mars,* and *Blue Mars* by Kim Stanley Robinson.

Mars, by the way, has two mini-satellites, called Phobos and Deimos. They're tiny little things, really more like irregularly shaped lumps of rock, with Phobos about 11 miles long and Deimos 6 miles. They weren't discovered until 1877, when they were detected by the American astronomer Asaph Hall, but surprisingly they were predicted in fiction 150 years earlier by Jonathan Swift in *Gulliver's Travels*, simply by using the process of logic.

In all probability Phobos and Deimos are captured asteroids, though some science fiction writers have made them artificial worlds. The asteroids are the minor planets, the bulk of which orbit the sun in a belt between the orbits of Mars and Jupiter. They were once thought to be the remains of a planet that exploded, but they're more likely to be lumps of debris left over in space that never formed into a planet. There are probably in excess of 40,000 of these planetoids. The biggest of them is Ceres, which is about 250 million miles (or 400 million kilometers) from the sun. Its diameter is 600 miles (965 kilometers) which is almost a quarter the diameter of the moon, so it's a reasonable size, and is big enough to have a very thin atmosphere. Most of them are much smaller, and have been described as flying mountains! Science fiction writers have made great use of the asteroid belt for mining purposes, as it is suggested they are rich sources of various metals and ores. Indeed, most of the asteroids are carbonaceous and look darker than coal. Check out the Donald Wollheim story in this volume and you'll see what I mean.

Although most of these asteroids orbit between Mars and Jupiter, there are others scattered throughout the solar system. There are even some that orbit the sun closer than Mercury. The one with the closest orbit to the sun is named Ra-Shalom and was only discovered in 1978. Because the orbits of some of these planetoids are so eccentric, some come even closer to the sun, such as the aptly named Phaethon. (It's named after the son of Helios, the Greek sun god, who drove his father's chariot too near to the Earth and scorched it.) Phaethon gets as close as 13 million miles (21 million kilometers), when its surface temperature must exceed 932°F.

Some of these asteroids also pass fairly close to Earth. The closest are relatively small, only a matter of yards in diameter, though they would be fairly destructive if they collided with the Earth. It has been suggested that just such a collision caused the extinction of the dinosaurs. The largest asteroid to come near us regularly is Apollo, which approached to within 5.5 million miles (9 million kilometers) in 1982. It has a diameter of 4,600 feet.

Beyond the main asteroid belt we start to encounter the large planets, called the gas giants because, despite their size, they are composed almost entirely of gas with a much smaller solid core. Jupiter's diameter at the equator is about 89,000 miles (or 143,000 kilometers), eleven times that of the Earth, though its overall volume means you could fit over 1,300 Earths into Jupiter. But most of this is gas. There is only a small rocky core with a surface temperature of 43,000°F which is covered by a sea of liquid metallic hydrogen. Above this are turbulent clouds of ammonia and water. The pressures are enormous, with the "surface" of Jupiter having an atmospheric pressure three million times that of Earth. Little wonder that when the *Galileo* probe entered Jupiter's atmosphere in 1995, it could only survive for a short period before it was crushed. Jupiter's atmosphere is one of raging intense storms. As observers looking down upon the planet, we see one effect of this in the phenomenon called the Great Red Spot, which is a turbulence in the upper atmosphere, like a cyclone, which is the size of the Earth and has been raging for centuries. Although science fiction writers used to speculate about life on Jupiter, it is pretty remote, although Arthur C. Clarke, in his short story "A Meeting with Medusa," suggested that the upper atmosphere might have life drifting through it like giant jellyfish.

Jupiter has its own massive system of satellites—sixteen at last count. The outer ones of these are probably captured asteroids. They are all relatively small, only about twenty miles in diameter, and their orbits are all over the place. The interesting ones are the four giant satellites—Io, Europa, Ganymede, and Callisto. All, except Europa, are bigger than our moon, and Europa isn't that much smaller. But each is a totally different world. Io, the closest to Jupiter of the four, is highly volcanic and is probably covered with a sea of sulfur and sulfur dioxide. It doesn't have an atmosphere to speak of, but its gases are trapped by the gravitational pull of Jupiter, so that Io orbits in a haze of sulfur. Europa remains a complete mystery. The planet has virtually no surface features, and is probably covered by a thick layer of ice that hides any surface relief that there may be. If Europa has any impact craters, then these are below the ice, which must reform and freeze over anything that strikes the planet. Ganymede, the next satellite out, is also the largest and is bigger than the planet Mercury. It's also ice-covered, though this layer is probably thinner than on Europa, so that there is evidence of impact craters. There were probably volcanoes once, but these are all now inert, and Ganymede has no atmosphere.

Callisto is the most fascinating world. It is a bitterly cold world, around –248°F during its day, and is also covered in ice, but beneath the ice is probably a mantle of water, and it has been conjectured that conditions might be right for some forms of microscopic life to form in these deep oceans. Callisto is also far enough away from Jupiter to be beyond its radiation belt and thus would be less harmful to any human expedition that might one day venture there.

Only one other satellite of Jupiter is worth mentioning and that's Amalthea, which was the fifth to be discovered (back in 1892), though it is closer to Jupiter than Io. In fact the two *Voyager* space probes have since found two more moons closer to Jupiter, now called Metis and Adrastea, but for years Amalthea was thought to be Jupiter's innermost moon. Arthur C. Clarke wrote what is one of my favorite science-fiction stories about this planet, called "Jupiter V," which suggests it might have been hollowed out by the Jovians and converted into a home. The astronauts' exploration of Amalthea in that story reads like the discovery of the tombs of the pharaohs in Egypt.

The next planet is Saturn, which is about 888 million miles from the sun (or about 1,400 million kilometers). This planet is well-known because of its ring system, but attractive though this makes it look in paintings and photographs, it's just as inhospitable as Jupiter. Saturn is another gas giant, with a diameter only slightly less than Jupiter's and with a rocky core about the size of the Earth. The atmosphere is a turbulence of ammonia and hydrogen. It's still a hot planet, though not so hot as Jupiter, so the turbulence is less, but enough to give Saturn its own occasional giant Red Spot! Both planets have atmospheres of tremendous winds gusting at over 900 miles an hour.

The rings are rather like Saturn's own asteroid belt. They are millions of rocks from dust to sizable chunks that orbit the planet at different speeds, so it's a raging turmoil—a bit like a race track in space! The rings are thought to be the remains of a former satellite or perhaps a larger captured asteroid that was then pulled apart by Saturn's gravity. This space debris is circling the planet close to the uppermost clouds and stretches out for another 180,000 miles (300,000 kilometers,) which is about as far out as our moon. In fact within the ring systems are some more sizable chunks that are Saturn's innermost satellites, though only Mimas and Enceladus are of any significant size. Mimas is remarkable for having a crater that is about a third its size, and if this was caused by an impact from space, it's surprising the moon didn't break up. Saturn has around twenty satellites, and more may possibly be found. The biggest and most exciting is Titan. It is almost the same size as Jupiter's Ganymede, and is also bigger than Mercury. The surface is made up of rocks and ice and has a temperature of around –334°F. It has an atmosphere, mostly of methane and nitrogen, but the world is rich in hydrocarbons. It's another world that science fiction writers have high hopes of with regard to possible life forms.

After Saturn comes Uranus, which is almost 1.8 billion miles from the sun (2,900 million kilometers). This planet is not visible with the naked eye, so, was not known to the ancient astronomers. It was first discovered in 1781 by the famous astronomer of the day, Sir William Herschel, though it had been observed on several occasions since 1690 without anyone realizing it was a new planet. It's another gas giant, though its diameter is half that of Saturn's, at about 32,000 miles (51,000 kilometers). Its surface temperature is –357°F, and the atmosphere is a mixture of water, ammonia ,and methane ice crystals.

It was not until 1977 that we discovered Uranus also had rings, like Saturn, though not as impressive. Uranus has fifteen moons, although all but the four outermost ones are small and not much more than mini-asteroids. The four bigger ones are Ariel, Umbriel, Titania, and Oberon, the last two being about half the size of our moon.

We are now virtually on the edge of the solar system. The last large planet is Neptune, some 2.8 billion miles (4,500 million kilometers) from the sun. It's about the same size as Uranus, with an atmosphere of mostly hydrogen sulfide and methane. Its temperature is about the same as Uranus's despite its greater distance from the sun, because Neptune has a greater internal heat. It also has its own rings, but only one satellite of any size. Triton, with a diameter of 1,680 miles. Triton has an atmosphere composed mostly of nitrogen. It's an odd satellite because it orbits Neptune the wrong way around, compared to most other satellites.

Neptune has a cluster of six inner satellites, of which only Proteus is of a significant size, and a rather strange outer moon called Nereid, which has such an eccentric orbit that it is probably a captured piece of space flotsam.

The planet Pluto, which has an average distance from the sun of 3,600 million miles, also has an extremely eccentric orbit, so that at the moment it is closer to the sun than Neptune, and has been since 1979, but in 1999 will once again become our outermost planet. It isn't a gas giant, but is much more like the innermost planets or the satellites of the giant planets. Its diameter is only 1,730 miles, so it's not surprising it wasn't discovered until 1930. And it wasn't until 1978 that we discovered Pluto had a moon, Charon, which, at 762 miles in diameter, is half the size of Pluto, so the system is really a double planet. The Pluto-Charon system has all the hallmarks of being more space flotsam, but it is larger than the other rocks orbiting around the sun. Pluto has a surface temperature of –370°F and is covered in nitrogen ice.

All of these worlds seem so inhospitable that it is difficult to imagine any of them containing life, certainly not in the way we would normally imagine it, although when you consider some of the bizarre forms of life on the Earth, especially deep in the oceans, we cannot totally rule out the existence of life on some of the larger satellites.

Beyond Pluto there are probably more orbiting rocks. There is still talk of a larger outer planet that is needed to account for some of the oddities in Neptune's orbit, but this remains to be discovered. Even further out is something called the Oort Cloud, named after a Dutch astronomer who suggested that there might be a vast ring of small rocks and planetoids from which, in the past, some were dislodged by gravitational stresses and have become the comets. The most famous of these is Halley's Comet, which orbits every 76 years and will next be seen in the year 2061.

Then we are into the vastness of interstellar space until we reach the next sun. The nearest star to us is called Proxima Centauri. It's not like our sun. It's a red dwarf and is not only cooler than our sun, but is subject to periodic flares and bursts of energy, such that if there were planets circling it, they would experience sudden outbursts of radiation likely to make them inhospitable to the development of life.

Proxima Centauri is 4.25 light-years away. Now what does that mean? Well, a light-year is how far light travels in one year. Light travels at 186,000 miles a *second* (or about 300,000 kilometers a second), which means that the light from the sun has taken about eight minutes to reach us. In an hour, light will have traveled over 670 million miles, which is beyond the orbit of Jupiter. By the time a whole year's passed, it has traveled nearly six million million miles. So we can soon work out that the distance to our nearest star is about 25 million million miles.

And that's the *nearest!* If you traveled at a steady 24,000 miles an hour (which is the speed you need to escape the pull of the Earth's gravity) it would take you over 100,000 years to reach it! No wonder the starship *Enterprise* needs warp factor 5 to get anywhere. Fortunately, starships, once we've developed them, would travel at a steady acceleration, not a fixed speed, and the time taken to reach these stars would be much less, though still a long time. Science fiction writers long ago speculated on the idea of "generation" starships, meaning ships that housed whole families, who lived and died in space until later generations made it to the stars. Check out Peter Garratt's "No Home but the Stars" for an example of this.

Most of the bright stars that we see in the sky, like Sirius and Rigel and Betelgeuse, are much further away than Proxima Centauri, although Sirius is a rather reassuring 8.7 light-years. The nearest stars that are similar to our own sun are Epsilon Eridani and Tau Ceti, both about eleven light-years away. It is extremely difficult to detect from Earth whether any of these distant stars have planets of their own. After all, since we are still discovering minor planets and moons in our own solar system, what chance do we have to detect even a reasonable sized planet over such vast distances? Back in 1937 scientists believed that they had made measurements that suggested that Barnard's Star, which is a relatively minor star just over six light-years away, might have a planetary companion, but the measurements have never been wholly substantiated. More recently evidence has started to accumulate to prove the existence of planets around other stars. We will not be really sure until we travel to them, but there are millions and millions of stars and even if only a fraction of those have planets, it is still a large enough number for the law of averages to suggest that somewhere in the universe are other planets like Earth—and quite possibly thousands of them.

The problem is one of distance. After all, we are but a small planet on the edge of our galaxy and we are 28,000 light-years from the center of our galaxy. The nearest galaxy is 80,000 light-years from us.

And the farthest star? Back in 1988 astronomers observed a star that went supernova (that is, it exploded) that was over five billion light-years away.

These distances are just too huge to comprehend, but if you just look at a ruler for a moment that is about one foot long or thirty centimeters, and imagine the distance to the nearest star is the length of that ruler, then that farthest star is at about the same distance as our moon is from the Earth, that is 24,000 miles or about 380,000 kilometers. That's a lot of rulers.

So those stars are a long way away, and even once we perfect the technology, it'll take a long time to reach them. But we're on our way. Starting in 1973, there has been a series of deep-space probes launched by NASA. The earliest was *Pioneer 10*. That and its companion, *Pioneer 11*, and the later probes *Voyager 1* and *Voyager 2*, have each now made their way through our solar system, making spectacular discoveries and sending back remarkable pictures as they've gone, and they are all now leaving our solar system and traveling out into distant space. *Pioneer 10* is the farthest away but the *Voyager* probes are traveling faster. They are the first man-made objects to leave our solar system. They will go on forever and ever, unless some time in centuries to come they are captured by the gravitational field of a distant star and become its new satellite. Or maybe one day they will be encountered by a spaceship from another planet and contact between our civilization and another will at last have been made. In the hope of that possibility the probes have on board a gold-coated phonograph record (remember, they were launched before compact disks were invented). The record contains samples of our languages, the sounds of the Earth, a selection of music, and pictures of the planet and of human beings.

Of course if any other civilizations do find the probes, it would be a long time before we knew about it. But the great fun is that somewhere, sometime, some other civilization in space may also have launched exploratory probes, and they could be coming in this direction. It's just possible that one such probe could enter our solar system at any time. Who knows? It's what Arthur C. Clarke suggested in *Rendezvous with Rama* and there's something of the idea in the story "Derelict" in this volume.

So even if our solar system has no other life in it, there may well be life out there somewhere, and some of it may be heading our way. Just think what *that* encounter would be like . . .

Acknowledgments

Grateful acknowledgment is made for permission to reprint previously published material.

"In the Picture" copyright © 1996 by Stephen Baxter. Printed by permission of Stephen Baxter.

"The Space Butterflies" copyright © 1996 by Stephen Baxter. Revised from a version published in *Back Brain Recluse*, no. 13 (1989). Printed by permission of Stephen Baxter.

"The Lonely Alien" copyright © 1996 by Sydney J. Bounds. Printed by permission of Sydney J. Bounds.

"Intelligent Life Elsewhere" copyright © 1996 by Stephen Bowkett. Printed by permission of Stephen Bowkett.

"Status Extinct" copyright © 1996 by Eric Brown. Printed by permission of Eric Brown.

"The Cage" by A. Bertram Chandler from *The Magazine of Fantasy & Science Fiction* (June 1957). Copyright © 1957 by A. Bertram Chandler. Reprinted by permission of E. J. Carnell Literary Agency.

"The Long Night" by John Christopher from *Galaxy* (October 1974). Copyright © 1974 by John Christopher. Reprinted by permission of John Christopher and Watson Little Agency.

"City of Ancient Skulls" copyright © 1996 by Simon Clark. Printed by permission of Simon Clark and International Scripts Ltd.

"A Walk in the Dark" by Arthur C. Clarke from *Thrilling Wonder Stories* (August 1950). Copyright © 1950 by Arthur C. Clarke. Reprinted by permission of the author and the author's agents, Scovil Chichak Galen Literary Agency, Inc., New York.

"Thoughts That Kill" by John Russell Fearn from *Science Fiction* (October 1939). Copyright © 1939 by John Russell Fearn, renewed 1996 by Philip Harbottle. Reprinted by permission of Cosmos Literary Agency.

"Whooo-ooo Flupper!" from *Living Fire* by Nicholas Fisk (London: Corgi Books, 1986). Copyright © 1986 by Nicholas Fisk. Reprinted by permission of Laura Cecil Literary Agency.

"Protected Species" by H. B. Fyte from *Astounding SF* (March 1951). Copyright © 1951 by H. B. Fyte. Reprinted by arrangement with Forrest J. Ackerman.

"Derelict" by Raymond Z. Gallun from *Astounding Stories* (October 1935). Copyright © 1935 by Raymond Z. Gallun. Reprinted by permission of E. J. Carnell Literary Agency.

Acknowledgments

"No Home but the Stars" copyright © 1996 by Peter T. Garratt. Printed by permission of Peter T. Garratt.

"The Children" by Chester S. Geier from *Fantastic Adventures* (April 1951). Copyright © 1951 by Chester S. Geier.

"The Dead Planet" by Edmond Hamilton from *Startling Stories* (spring 1946). Copyright © 1946 by Edmond Hamilton. Reprinted by permission of Scott Meredith Literary Agency (New York) and A. M. Heath & Co. Ltd (London).

"Hally's Paradise" by Douglas Hill from *Out of Time*, edited by Aidan Chambers (London: The Bodley Head, 1984). Copyright © 1984 by Douglas Hill. Reprinted by permission of Douglas Hill and Watson Little Agency.

"Introduction: Space Explorers Start Here" copyright © 1996 by Douglas Hill. Printed by permission of Douglas Hill and Watson Little Agency.

"Quinquepedalian" by Piers Anthony Jacob from *Amazing Stories* (November 1963). Copyright © 1963 by Piers Anthony Jacob. Reprinted by permission of E. J. Carnell Literary Agency.

"The Chosen" by Samantha Lee from *Space 4*, edited by Richard Davis (London: Abelard-Schuman, 1977). Copyright © 1977 by Samantha Lee. Reprinted by permission of Samantha Lee and Dorian Literary Agency.

"To See the Stars" copyright © 1996 by Lawrence Schimel and Mark A. Garland. Printed by permission of Lawrence Schimel and Mark A. Garland.

"The Hunters" by Walt Sheldon from *Startling Stories* (March 1952). Copyright © 1952 by Walt Sheldon. Reprinted by arrangement with Forrest J. Ackerman.

"Scrutiny" copyright © 1996 by William F. Temple. An abridged version appeared under the title "The Unpicker" in *Androids, Time Machines and Blue Giraffes*, edited by Roger Elwood and Vic Ghidalia (New York: Follett, 1973). Printed by permission of Joan Temple.

"The Bells of Acheron" by E. C. Tubb from *Science Fantasy* (April 1957). Copyright © 1957 by E. C. Tubb. Reprinted by permission of E. C. Tubb.

"Jewels in an Angel's Wing" by Ian Watson from *Synergy #1*, edited by George Zebrowski (New York: Harcourt Brace Jovanovich, 1987). Copyright © 1987 by Ian Watson. Reprinted by permission of Ian Watson.

"Asteroid 745: Mauritia" by Donald A. Wollheim from *Orbit #1* (1953). Copyright © 1953 by Donald A. Wollheim. Reprinted by permission of E. J. Carnell Literary Agency.

400 PAGES OF FANTASTIC STORIES
BY SOME OF THE WORLD'S BEST WRITERS